EQUINOX

ALSO BY CHRISTIAN CANTRELL

EQUINOX

CHRISTIAN CANTRELL

Text copyright © 2015 Christian Cantrell
All rights reserved.

Published by 47North, Seattle

www.apub.com

Amazon, the Amazon logo, and 47North are trademarks of Amazon.com, Inc., or its affiliates.

ISBN-13: 9781477825952
ISBN-10: 1477825959

Cover design by Jason Gurley

Library of Congress Control Number: 2014951620

Printed in the United States of America

The term "equinox" refers to the two days per year when the plane of Earth's equator is perfectly aligned with the center of the sun. As a result, the Northern and Southern Hemispheres are illuminated equally, and day and night are approximately the same length for everyone on the planet.

The word "equinox" is derived from the Latin words "*aequus*," meaning "equal," and "*nox*," meaning "night."

PROLOGUE

CADIE CHIYOKO TOOK A SINGLE, decisive step forward through the outer airlock door, and for the first time in her life, found herself outside.

She had always been more interested in pushing scientific boundaries than physical, and therefore never really had much of a desire to leave V1. Unlike her husband, she did not have the intrepid—even borderline reckless—nature of a true explorer, and consequently never fantasized about wandering the surface of the planet. Nevertheless, now that she was actually doing it, she found that she actually did have unconscious preconceptions that the reality of the event did not match. Rather than a feeling of expansiveness—of almost infinite volume and of an immensity beyond anything she'd ever experienced—the density of the atmosphere made her feel even more contained than the narrow polymeth passages she was leaving behind. In fact, her first time inside V1's massive geodesic-dome greenhouse was probably more of a marvel than her first time beyond the confines of any artificial physical structure.

She wondered if it would be different if her husband, Arik, were with her—whether the exhilaration he felt might heighten the experience for her.

Cam had made the decision that they would take a rover out to the rendezvous point to save Cadie the exertion of the two-hundred-meter walk. Cadie knew it was not because he or Zaire felt that she was fragile or incapable, but because it was her first time in an environment suit. Adjusting to the additional weight, bulk, and constraints of seven alternating layers of ballistic composite fiber with welded seams was difficult even for someone not in her third trimester of pregnancy.

Cadie didn't argue with her companions about being ferried out to their destination, but she did ask for one concession: she wanted her first steps from V1 out onto the planet's surface to be her own. After Zaire maneuvered the rover out through the airlock door, Cam stayed at Cadie's side, ready to assist in case she lost her balance or caught a tread.

The planet's surface was a fine sulfur-yellow powder that somehow managed to get kicked up onto Cadie's boots after only a few steps. On one side of her, the rover crept along matching her pace, and on the other, Cam carefully monitored her progress, ready to help stabilize her should she stumble. When Cadie turned, she saw that even though they had gone only a few meters, V1 was no longer visible. She could see the white strobes marking the perimeter of the Wrench Pod, and the red strobes denoting the entrance of the airlock, but the structure itself had been entirely swallowed by a thick, mustard-colored haze.

"Cadie," Cam said. When she turned and looked up at him, he used the handheld laser projector he was holding to point to the chronometer strapped just above his left glove. "We need to go."

The nanotubes in their audio drops were all configured for the same frequency, so communication among the three of them was seamless.

"When is he coming?" Cadie asked. It was really more of a plea than a question since she knew that Cam had no more information about what was going on than she did.

"I don't know," Cam said. "Soon, I'm sure."

Zaire broke in from the rover. "He'll meet us at the rendezvous point," she said. "Come on. We need to move."

Cam helped Cadie into the passenger side of the rover. When she was secure, he went around to the back and climbed up into the cargo hold.

"I'm in," he said, and then the rover pulled forward.

Visibility was so poor that the vehicle could not be piloted purely by sight, so Zaire divided her attention between whatever she could discern up ahead of them and the screen between the hand controls. The rover was equipped with a short-range terrain mapping system that used radar to scan their surroundings. In addition to rendering a topographical model on the screen, it also fed the data to the rover's onboard computer, which dynamically adjusted both tire pressure and the rigidity of the rover's independent suspension, resulting in a ride almost as smooth as a maglev track.

Cadie had the impulse to turn and look behind them once again, but she knew that the stiffness of her e-suit would not permit her to get her visor all the way around. And even if it did, she doubted there would be anything to see anymore. Even V1's strobes were probably entirely obscured by now.

"How can you tell where we're going?" she asked.

"I can't," Zaire said. "But the rover can."

"It's just a straight shot," Cam said. "We're almost there."

The farther away they traveled from V1, the less comfortable Cadie felt. Although the opaqueness of the atmosphere was more likely to make one feel claustrophobic than agoraphobic, what Cadie found most disconcerting was that she had no sense of space or position. With no structures, horizon, and no sky to use as reference points, she found she could not construct a mental model of where she was, or how she fit into the world around her. The sensation was new to her, but there was no doubt in her mind that she was beginning to panic.

She tightened her grip on the forward bar, then suddenly felt her weight push against it. The rover stopped quickly enough that she could tell something was wrong.

"What the hell is *that*?" Zaire said. She was looking down at the rover's screen. Cadie tried to make sense of the three-dimensional rendering, but to her, it simply looked as though the background had changed color.

"That," Cam said from behind them, "is what Arik wanted us to see."

"What the hell is it?"

"It's exactly what it looks like," Cam said. "A huge wall."

Zaire touched the screen with a gloved finger and brought up a set of virtual controls. She began manipulating a directional knob and an alarm promptly sounded in response.

"What's wrong?" Cadie asked.

"The navigation system is complaining that it can't see the ground anymore," Zaire said. "I'm raising the radar's trajectory to get a better look."

"I can save you the trouble," Cam said. "It's twenty-five meters tall. Keep going. Get us as close to it as you can."

"We'll have a discussion about how you know so much about this later," Zaire told her husband. The alarm stopped and the rover continued forward.

"Why would there be a wall out here?" Cadie asked. She was peering forward into the haze, but she wasn't sure whether she could see anything or not.

"And who the hell built it?" Zaire added.

"We don't know," Cam said. "But just wait. It gets better."

The rover crawled ahead another few meters, and then the wall emerged.

"There," Cam said, leaning forward and pointing between them.

Zaire made a slight adjustment, and then they could see it. The door in front of them was a massive sheet of metal that had somehow gotten slightly dented near the center. There were columns of bolts through the steel, and it was hung inside a substantial metal frame by four bulky hinges. Beside the door, protruding from the siliconcrete wall, was a tremendous wheel that Cadie assumed provided leverage against a set of screws and gears in order to move the massive slab.

Zaire was the first to step out. As she stood watching the door, Cadie felt the suspension of the rover change again, and she knew that Cam had climbed out, as well. She started to step down and found that he was already right beside her, offering her his gloved hand.

"I'd like to know just what the hell this thing is designed to keep out," Zaire said. She was tracing the contour of the dent in the middle of the door with the fingertips of her glove.

"Or in," Cadie said.

Zaire turned to look at Cadie, then turned back to the door. She moved over to the wheel and ran her glove around its circumference without actually trying to turn it.

"This doesn't make any sense," she said. Now she grasped the wheel and applied a small amount of experimental torque, though it did not move. "I'm not even sure that we have the materials to build and maintain something like this."

"Why did Arik want us to see it?" Cadie asked.

The question was implicitly directed at Cam, but there was no response. When she and Zaire turned to look at him, they saw that he had the handheld laser projector pressed up against his helmet's visor. Cadie could see green lines across his face and Cam's eyes moving across lines of projected text. They watched him in silence until his finger came off the projector's trigger and he lowered it to his side.

The look on his face made Cadie's voice tremble. "What did it say?"

"The wall isn't what he wants us to see," Cam said. "There's more."

"More of *what*?" Zaire asked. Her apprehension came across as hostility.

Before Cam could respond, the atmospheric mics in their helmets picked up a distant metallic clatter from the direction of V1. All three instinctively turned.

"What just happened?" Zaire said.

Cam took a step toward the pod system, peering into the haze with obvious futility. "I've heard that sound before," he said.

"What was it?"

"I think it was the shields dropping off the Public Pod windows," he said. "The power must have flickered."

They waited and listened, but the next sound their mics picked up came from directly beside them. The massive steel bars that secured the door had started to withdraw.

"Get back," Cam said. He moved forward while Cadie and Zaire moved away. He looked to either side of him, then checked the rover's cargo hold, but he did not come up with anything he could use as a weapon. As the wheel turned and the door began to pivot, Cadie could see Cam tighten his grip on the projector.

"It's OK," Cadie said as calmly as she could. Her breathing was elevated but her voice was steady. "We're not in any danger."

"What makes you so confident?" Zaire asked.

"Because whatever's happening, Arik must have arranged it," Cadie said. "He wouldn't have put us in any danger."

"Not intentionally," Zaire added.

The massive door moved with surprising speed and fluidity, and when it was fully open, they saw why. Standing on the other side of the wall were two figures: a fairly petite woman, and beside her, easily the biggest man that Cadie—and probably anyone in V1, for that matter—had ever seen. The strangers' environment suits were nothing like those from V1, but rather were a bluish-gray color with red welds, and seemed surprisingly thin and supple. Almost quilted. Their helmets were fitted and sleek like a pilot's headgear, and the entire forward hemispheres were transparent for unimpeded peripheral vision. The man's weapon was lowered, but when he saw the projector in Cam's hand, he sprang in front of the girl and the tip of the long slender rifle jumped up.

"Cam," Zaire said with exaggerated poise as though speaking too harshly might discharge the man's weapon. "I think he thinks you're holding a gun."

"Put it down," Cadie said.

Cam watched the man for a long moment, then tossed the projector to the side. Cadie and Zaire held up their hands in a gesture of surrender, but Cam did not. Cadie could see the defiance in his expression.

The man stepped back beside the girl. The girl's lips moved and the man lowered his rifle, then swung it back behind him on its strap. They both held their hands up in a gesture to match Cadie's and Zaire's.

"It's OK," Cadie said. "They won't hurt us."

"Who the hell are they?" Zaire wanted to know. "Cam, if you have any idea what's going on, now would be the time to explain."

"I don't," Cam said. "But I think I'm starting to figure it out."

The girl's lips moved again and the huge man tentatively advanced. His prominent features were clearly visible through his helmet, but he did not come across as threatening. His thinly gloved hand went into a pouch on his thigh and came back out as a fist. With his other hand, he pointed to a tiny metallic cylinder attached to the outside of his faceplate just in front of his mouth, then tapped the side of his helmet beside his ear. When he opened his fist, there were four matching cylinders in his palm.

"I think he wants to attach those things to our helmets," Cam said. "He probably wants to establish a comm link."

"Don't their helmets have external audio?" Zaire asked. There was caution and suspicion in her tone. "They look a lot better than ours."

"I guess not," Cam said.

"Let him do it," Cadie said.

Cam looked beside him at Cadie and Zaire, then back at the man in front of him. He nodded and the stranger approached with an obvious effort to appear as nonthreatening as he could. Cam was tall—exactly two meters according to the most accurate instruments available on V1—but the stranger had at least a few centimeters on him, and easily twenty-five kilos. When the man was close enough, he selected one of the cylinders from his palm, reached up, and cinched it against Cam's faceplate. Cadie could see the man's lips move, and then Cam nod.

"I can hear you," he said.

The man nodded then moved down the line, attaching cylinders first to Zaire's faceplate, and then Cadie's. Cadie watched the device vacuum-seal itself to the smooth surface of her visor. The man took his hand away, then stepped back. When the girl moved forward and spoke to Cam, the polycarbonate of Cadie's visor became a speaker as it conducted the sound.

"Are you Arik?" she asked him in a tone that was urgent, but not unfriendly. The girl appeared slightly older than Cadie with black, chin-length hair.

Cam shook his head. "Arik isn't here."

"*Yet*," Cadie added. "He isn't here *yet*. He'll be here any second."

The girl looked at Cadie. Her eyes dropped to the layers of bunched-up microfiber covering her belly. Cadie could tell that the girl somehow knew she was pregnant. "Are you his wife?"

Cadie nodded.

"We don't have much time," the girl said. "We're not safe here."

"Who are you?" Zaire asked with a combination of suspicion and what came across as disgust. "What the hell's going on?"

"I'll explain as soon as I can," the girl said. "Right now, we need to go."

The girl's partner had turned around and was watching their backs. Between his shoulders was a black, ribbed, slightly raised mechanism that looked more like a filter than any kind of a cartridge or tank. The rifle was once again off his shoulder and ready to be raised.

"No," Cadie said. "Not without Arik."

"Cadie," Cam said. He waited for her to turn and look at him, then gestured vaguely toward the laser projector on the ground. From the tone of his voice and from the way he was looking at her, Cadie already knew what he was going to say. Instantly her face contorted.

"It's not true," she said.

"I'm sorry," Cam said. "Arik isn't coming."

"You're . . ." Cadie shook her head. She started to say something in protest—she wasn't sure what—but she stopped. Some part of her knew that Cam was right. The ease with which the tears arose told her that she had actually known all along, but the thought of really losing her husband this time had allowed her to lie to herself—to get all the way out here without admitting that Arik was obviously far too sick to ever leave V1. If he had really intended to go with them, he would never have sent them off ahead, never made Cam promise to take care of her; never encoded a message for them in the laser projector. On some level, Cadie knew that when he was saying good-bye to her and the baby back in the dock, he was saying good-bye to them forever.

She shook her head again. Tears fell from her cheeks, then ran down into her e-suit's neck ring. "I'm going back," she said.

"Cadie," Cam said. "There's nothing you can do."

"There *is*," Cadie insisted. She took a step back. "At least I can be with him. That's *some*thing."

"This is what he wanted," Cam told her.

Cadie leaned forward and glared. "Well, it's not what *I* want!" she screamed, then turned back toward V1.

Cadie heard the girl's voice in her helmet. "Don't let her get away," it said, and she knew that the girl was talking to the man with the rifle. "Do it."

When Cadie felt her helmet start to vibrate, she stopped. The device the man attached was just far enough away that she was able to bring it into focus, and suddenly there were plastic shavings twirling around a tiny diamond bit. When she turned back around, she could see that both Cam and Zaire were frantically trying to dislodge the devices from their faceplates, and she reached up, as well. The hardened tips of her gloves would not grip the cylinder, and when she heard a hiss, she thought the sound was her atmosphere escaping through the puncture. But then she had another thought of what the noise might be, though it never had the chance to fully form.

PART ONE

CHAPTER ONE

CALIBRATION CUBE

THE ABILITY TO ASSEMBLE JUST about anything imaginable simply by arranging molecules with atomic precision in predefined patterns had a profound impact on the nature of crime. Like most business endeavors, crime was once a problem of logistics: manufacturing and distribution, supply and demand, profit and loss. But eventually, crime became as much a technical problem as anything else: a game of spoofing, cracking, and circumventing DRM.

Although assembling narcotics was clearly a violation of the bylaws of the *San Francisco*—a nomadic, floating, hermetically sealed mining platform about the size of four square city blocks— Luka Mance did not consider himself a criminal. Rather, he'd managed to convince himself that any offenses he was committing were the direct results of defects in the system rather than within himself. Additionally, Luka refused to accept the label of "junkie." He was just a simple assembly technician and part-time forklift operator whose neurotransmitters required a little more pharmacological stimulation than most, and who happened to be in a very good position to make that happen.

The *San Francisco* was a Metropolis-class mining and refinery rig—one of several built decades ago, each christened in honor of a different long-forgotten cultural and economic mecca. Luka worked in the Mission Street Foundry: a multitiered metallic microlattice and silica-paned structure between Serramonte Boulevard and Mission Street situated along what was considered to be the starboard perimeter of the vessel. For the last month, he had spent his days working on a project that was a vehicle-cum-tool, the schematics for which were labeled "Roverized Mining Drill (RMD)." It was a squat, unmanned, treaded vehicle, the front of which was a menacing, toothed-and-clawed, cone-shaped drill bit at least as long as the rover itself, and almost twice as heavy.

This afternoon, Luka was using a clean-room assembler to complete the last of the RMD's integrated circuitry. But he had made one tiny modification—not to the schematics themselves since the files were protected in such a way that they could not be tampered with (at least not through any procedures he had access to), but to the low-level executable bytecode in the assembler's memory. Through a binary code injection technique that Luka knew enough to exploit, but not nearly enough to understand or explain, he caused a thin layer of yellow dust to be assembled on top of the rover's motherboard. Luka called this substance "curious yellow" due to the positively mystified expression he wore for the benefit of anyone who might be watching as he cracked open the receiver, removed the component, and performed an initial visual inspection. Whatever this bizarre and unforeseen contaminate was, his expression broadcasted, it must be carefully preserved for further investigation. He tapped the substance into an envelope, sealed it, slipped it into the front pocket of his microfiber coverall, deposited the clearly defective board into the pneumatic waste chute, and spooled up the assembler to have another go at the problem. When the second job yielded the expected result, Luka shrugged off the initial attempt as one of those unexplainable anomalies that would probably never be entirely eliminated from technology, and that usually went away after rebooting.

In truth, the yellow substance was a synthetic opioid that was best introduced into the bloodstream through the capillaries in the nasal passage. Once it crossed the blood-brain barrier, it induced a period of euphoria lasting anywhere from four to six hours, and frequently resulted in extraordinarily vivid yet somehow still restful dreams. Although one might find oneself to be a tad bit constipated the next morning (and one's urine to be a shocking intensity of neon yellow, which Luka felt also justified the substance's name), the hangover was minimal. With enough water and synthetic caffeine, and maybe a few laps through the swimming tubes in the Noe Valley Rec Center, Luka found he could keep putting the days behind him and continue to function more or less normally.

If he were ever to get caught assembling illicit substances, Luka figured he could always play the orphan card. Since he no longer had parents—and in fact usually claimed to not even remember ever having parents in order to avoid any discussion of them whatsoever—it was a semilegitimate defense, though clearly a disingenuous one since it had been a very long time since Luka thought of himself as parentless. Orphanhood was a temporary state, he believed. You got to be an orphan for a limited period of time—a decade, tops—but you didn't get to be one forever. Just like adults whose elderly parents passed away sounded like insufferable twats when they declared themselves orphans, so too did adults who grew up without any parents at all. Luka's personal universal prescription for good mental health was simple: just get over it.

According to the *San Francisco*'s census records, Luka was twenty-nine years old. He was lithe and compact with Egyptian-blue eyes that were just light enough for the maze of circuitry and antennas embedded inside his inductive contact lenses to be faintly visible. His self-cropped hair was perpetually unstyled and started the day out blond, but was usually a dark bronze by the time he shed his anti-electrostatic microfiber coverall, hood, and mask in the evenings. His features were sharp—his nose a tad hawkish—and he sometimes shaved once a week on his day off, if he found himself in the mood.

Luka packed the motherboard in a silica gel–lined carton and set it aside. Contrary to what most people believed, machines like the RMD were seldom assembled all at once; rather, it was far more common to assemble each individual component, then ship the collection off to customers, who inspected, calibrated, unit tested, and ultimately put the pieces together themselves. Although there was no technical reason why most machines couldn't be assembled in final form, building them modularly was far faster since the job could be parallelized—spread out across multiple assemblers, each one tuned for specific types of medium and output. Additionally, componentization simplified transportation, and ensured that parts could be easily replaced or upgraded. This particular job took the idea of modularity to an extreme as the purchase order mandated that the RMD was to be delivered in seventy-nine individual crates of roughly equal size and weight when—in Luka's well-informed though seldom-sought opinion—it could have easily been done in forty, maybe forty-five. But Luka got paid the same whether he filled one standard carbon fiber shipping crate or one thousand, so he'd long since given up trying to save his customers time or money.

The one universal exception to the economics and convenience of modularity was machines that were far too intricate and complex to exist as discrete components—most notably, the assemblers themselves. All but the first generation were assembled molecule by molecule by their predecessors in some new manifestation of synthetic, self-referential evolution that was somehow every bit as inevitable as it was spooky. But this particular form of mechanical procreation was not within everyone's reach. There were various layers of authentication, activation, protection, validation, and verification that determined exactly who could assemble precisely what—the lowest-level and most robust of which prevented assemblers from assembling new assemblers without the godlike cryptographic consent of the creators themselves.

The operative word in the term "molecular assembler" was "molecular." They were not atomic assemblers—at least not yet. They did not work on the scale of protons and neutrons and electrons. They had no dominion over the realm of subatomic particles, and instead lived in blissful ignorance of the mysteries of the quantum universe. There was almost nothing a molecular assembler could not assemble, but it first had to be fed every element that the finished product would ever contain. Alloys and compounds and composites were perfectly within a molecular assembler's power; the wizardry of alchemy was not.

The polymethyl methacrylate (aka "polymeth") panel mounted overhead at a forty-five-degree angle indicated that Luka's assembler was due for calibration—not a surprise since that was the reason he'd chosen this particular station. Assembler stations that needed to be calibrated were like empty coffee urns in the kitchen: everyone pretended not to notice them so that they would end up someone else's problem. But Luka actually looked for the blinking calibration icon as he reserved his assemblers for the day, and as a result, seldom had any issues with availability.

To those not wearing inductive contact lenses, the assembler's polymeth control panel would appear entirely blank. ICLs—colloquially referred to as "icicles"—contained optical decryption technology, which allowed one to see one's own workspace (when it was called up) and whatever else one had sufficient permissions to access. They also contained decryption keys that were transmitted through the body's bioelectromagnetic field and into any capacitive surface one attempted to interact with. Early versions of icicles were powered by transparent solar cells, but their capacitors proved too limited to hold much of a charge, so the newest generation was powered by omnipresent ambient radio waves broadcast throughout the rig. In addition to decrypting displays projected from polymeth surfaces, icicles could also produce their own limited interfaces sufficient for things like notifications or the current time. Layered arrays of photolithographic microlenses made words and simple images appear to float in space about half a meter away.

Luka initiated the calibration routine, which consisted of assembling a solid block precisely one meter by one meter out of random amounts of hundreds of different materials fused together in a way that only a molecular assembler could. The block would be measured in all three dimensions, micron by micron, and every layer of medium would be independently spectroscopically verified. Should anything fall outside the assembler's minuscule tolerances, the proper procedure was for the technician to run diagnostics and see if the machine could recalibrate itself. If so, the calibration verification routine was spooled up again and the process repeated until the test block was exactly what the computer was expecting. If the machine could not repair itself—or explain to Luka exactly how he should go about attempting the repair manually—it took itself off-line and a repair ticket was automatically generated, which meant that it had then become someone else's problem. Luka once made the mistake of wondering how the calibration computer was itself calibrated, and subsequently asked just enough questions of the on-duty foreman to realize it was probably best to avoid such recursive quagmires lest they systematically unravel one's confidence in every single piece of technology that kept every single person aboard the rig alive.

By the time Luka returned from cataloging the motherboard, adding it to the manifest, and preparing the entire shipment to go out early the next morning, the calibration process was complete. The result was an extremely interesting and unique piece of material that could never have possibly existed before in this exact atomic configuration, and no matter how many billions of years the universe continued expanding or contracting or whatever it did or might decide to do next, would almost certainly never exist again.

Assemblers were not in the business of disassembly, so calibration cubes were supposed to be tipped into waste chutes where they would eventually find their way down into the waters of whatever ocean they happened to be currently mining, but instead Luka used a pair of pneumatic pinchers and a portable lever to transfer his from the receiver to a two-wheeled, computerized, self-balancing hand truck he custom-assembled years ago specifically for this purpose. The first few times he left the foundry with a calibration cube in tow, he managed to turn every head between his assembly station and his flat at the opposite end of the rig. In fact, several coworkers scoured foundry regulations, certain Luka was guilty of some infraction or other.

However, since calibration cubes were technically classified as manufacturing by-products, Luka's boss determined that taking one home—while undeniably peculiar—could not be considered theft.

Since Luka lived alone, his pet calibration cubes rapidly became known as "companion cubes" among his colleagues. But when everyone learned what he did with the material once he got it home, they no longer editorialized or leered. They did not even bother to make eye contact after he had passed by, and then shake their heads or roll their eyes. The idea of an artist—someone who used his own two hands in an attempt to express an abstract and subtle and penetrating idea—was so foreign to them that even ridicule did not sufficiently insulate them from this anomaly that somehow emerged among them. It was far easier and safer for everyone to simply pretend that he did not exist at all.

CHAPTER TWO

THE HISTORY OF THE CORONIANS
PART ONE: THE SUN

BEFORE THE END OF THE Solar Age, it could fairly be said that the entire sum of human knowledge was accessible in one form or another throughout a decentralized global system of inter-connected networks. As soon as data centers started going off-line, there were thousands of individual efforts—both private and state-sponsored—to capture, record, and store as much information as possible using eclectic collections of compression algorithms and highly durable physical media. Such compendiums were generically referred to simply as "archives," and one or more copies usually found their way onto most local networks such as that which connected hundreds of thousands of nodes throughout Metropolis-class, deep-sea mining rigs like the *San Francisco*. For those destined for such vocations as assembly technician or water rat (deep-sea miner), regular desultory consumption of indiscriminate but loosely related material (aka "browsing") constituted the majority of the education they received outside of their specific trades. It was also how Luka was able to piece together an approximation of the history of the Coronians: the first new species of human to emerge in over a hundred thousand years.

The idea of evolutionary divergence applying to humans was not initially an easy concept for Luka to grasp. Very few people even thought of themselves as animals, much less as a specific species of animal. At the time the Coronians were establishing themselves, it was no longer even commonly known that over the course of seven million years, at least nineteen species of human had probably existed—many of them occurring simultaneously—and that all but *Homo sapiens* eventually became extinct. Or that, at one time, there were fewer than ten thousand individual humans of reproductive age left on the entire planet, a fact that served as sobering evidence that evolution very nearly selected against precisely those characteristics held most dear—intelligence, ingenuity, forethought, and compassion—in favor of plain and simple physical robustness and ruthless individualism.

The Coronians originally considered themselves a subspecies of modern humans and adopted the classification *Homo sapiens solisus*. However, the genus *Homo* was eventually called into question due to its literal meaning of "earthly being." Since no true Coronian had ever been born on Earth—and in fact, almost certainly could not survive the crushing exertion of Earth's gravity for more than just a few seconds—Coronian geneticists eventually reasoned that their existence merited an entirely new genus. The accepted taxonomic classification of all modern Coronians, therefore, became *Caelestia sapiens*—or, as the Coronians themselves translated it, "wise beings of the heavens."

To understand the emergence of an entirely new species of human, it helped to first understand two related factors. The first was the extent to which life on Earth had always been a competition for the energy from the sun; and the second was how nature almost always rewarded those who were able to find, fill, and hold specific and unique evolutionary niches.

For most complex, multicellular, terrestrial organisms, the process of assimilating energy from the sun started with green plants. The shoots and tendrils of newly sprouted appendages competed with their peers by groping through the cold shadows of their predecessors in hopes of finding a single tiny shaft of light trickling down through the otherwise nearly impenetrably dense forest canopy. One step removed from plants were the organisms that could not photosynthesize, and therefore spent the majority of their waking hours collecting the stored chemical energy of the sun by either grazing on those who could, or by foraging for related organic material such as fruits, roots, and nuts. And finally, animals who were not well adapted to consuming plant matter learned to access the energy from the sun by preying upon those who were. Even the energy that once breathed life into some of mankind's earliest machines—fossil fuels formed through the anaerobic decomposition of billions upon billions of carbon-rich organisms—originally came from the sun.

Fundamentally, fossil fuels weren't actually all that different from solar energy. Whereas solar technology generally referred to the conversation of solar radiation into energy in relative real-time, burning fossil fuels was simply a way of reaching back into Earth's past and accessing that same resource, but from millions of years prior. Petroleum, coal, and natural gas were, in a way, nature's batteries. In the eyes of capitalism, therefore, the most important distinction between fossil fuels and solar energy wasn't so much sustainability or pollution, but pure efficiency. Ultimately, it wasn't drought, rising sea levels, or increasingly prevalent cataclysmic weather that drove the worldwide shift toward thermal and photovoltaic solar technologies; rather, it was a force that, throughout the course of human history, has proven itself far more potent: basic economics.

Unlike fossil fuels, the energy from the sun could not be depleted within a time scale comprehendible to most humans (least of all, capitalists and lawmakers), and unlike energy derived from either nuclear fission or fusion, there were no expensive or dangerous by-products (other than those involved in the manufacturing of the solar collectors themselves, and the batteries in which energy was stored—both of which were easily managed). But there was something else unique about looking to the sun to energize the entire planet: a form of intrinsic democratization. Sunlight wasn't a commodity that could be sold, traded, or artificially manipulated. Because population density and solar exposure were fairly closely correlated, most of Earth received more than enough sunlight to support local communities, and where that did not hold true, a combination of conveying light away from solar farms via long-distance fiber-optic lines, transmitting electricity using superconductive transoceanic power cables, supplementing energy production with hydroelectric, wind, geothermal, and tidal technologies, and even good old-fashioned conservation usually made up the difference.

Clean and infinitely renewable energy production even went a long way toward addressing another one of humanity's major existential challenges: resource scarcity. Although the traditional concept of recycling had long since been popularized and accepted by the mainstream as basic civic responsibility, its benefits did not always hold up under close scrutiny since the amount of energy and other resources that went into the various processes—and all of the detrimental by-products that resulted—very legitimately called the entire theory into question. The reality of traditional consumer recycling was that it yielded a slender margin of benefit at best, and at worst, might have actually done a great deal of harm, representing little more than a psychological placebo designed to alleviate collective guilt over massive amounts of unfettered overconsumption, thereby actually accelerating the pace of global resource depletion.

But once the question of energy (and almost all associated pollution) was removed, the benefits of recycling were suddenly about as irrefutable as such politically and socially charged matters ever tended to get. In fact, it was no longer mandates and laws that promoted and sustained recycling efforts; rather, the reclamation renaissance was, once again, the result of forces far more prodigious and powerful: capitalism and profit. Once the variable of energy in the equation of reprocessing rapidly began approaching zero, sustainability suddenly became a hugely profitable and competitive enterprise instead of a widely begrudged, corporate-responsibility checkbox.

The result of decades of scientific, economic, and even political innovation was that approximately 80 percent of the planet's population of just under thirteen billion people were almost never without all the power they wanted, and worldwide manufacturing, distribution, and consumption were at levels far more sustainable than at any point since the dawn of the industrial revolution. One of humanity's greatest and most celebrated modern accomplishments was recognized the day environmental scientists around the world jointly reported the very first year of permanent polar ice cap expansion and sea level recession in almost a century.

That was also the moment in human history when something fascinating was learned that seemed to contradict not only decades of science-fiction canon, but also common sense: the ultimate inspiration for seeking out and exploring new worlds—and even attempting to permanently colonize them—did not come from the imminent destruction of the home planet, but rather from the triumph of restoration. With widespread access to virtually unlimited energy, with existing natural resources more renewable than they'd ever been, and with seemingly infinite virgin resources no farther away than the nearest asteroid, nothing seemed beyond humanity's reach.

The next major step in the evolution of human innovation and exploration was to be the construction of what was by far the most ambitious engineering project ever undertaken: the space station known as *Equinox*, and the birthplace of the Coronians.

CHAPTER THREE

BLACK WIDOW

AYLA NOVIK USED TO TRY to pass herself off as a man. She wore her thick, onyx-black hair buzz-cut short, and her heavy drab boilersuits loose and baggy. She slouched to conceal her breasts, covered her wide blue eyes with a dark visor, and practiced a walk that kept her hips firmly in place. The sliver of smoothed tungsten carbide pipe—a keepsake that had once been an improvised wedding ring—was worn on a length of boot-lace paracord around her neck and concealed beneath her clothing rather than on her slender, delicate finger. Business was conducted nonverbally as much as possible—typically through terminals—and when face-to-face interactions could not be avoided, she used hand gestures and wrote on silicon paper hoping to communicate that she was mute, or excessively eccentric, or that she had her tongue cut out and cauterized with a plasma torch by raiders. When she felt herself being watched, she spat, grabbed at her crotch, and squirmed in a way that she imagined might rearrange pinched and bound genitals, then stared back intending to convey a psychotic disposition that all but the equally insane would rather avoid.

When the ruse worked, she was probably about as safe as anyone who made his living trading and transporting cargo between oases of commerce all over the globe—collecting finder's fees, rewards, the occasional bounty, and skimming off the

top when the opportunity presented itself. But whenever someone suspected what she actually was—when the air from a ventilation duct flattened her clothing in a way that gave her body
momentary shape, or when she was stopped and patted down by
port peacekeepers who turned out to be more interested in taking pleasure than bribes, or when a human trafficker's pherom-
eter picked her out of a crowd—there were sometimes attempts
to make her pay not only for what she really was, but for the additional perceived offense of attempting to conceal it.

So Ayla eventually decided to take the opposite approach.
Rather than hoping for the best and constantly fearing the worst,
she resolved to give the world the metaphorical middle finger.
Instead of hiding her curves beneath layers of heavy ballistic
fabric, she accentuated them with a tight, black, shank-proof
synthetic-fiber shocksuit with bright-red incandescent warning
accents, the tungsten ring now worn on the outside suggesting
an unquenchable vendetta. Passive defenses like shocksuits were
permissible in most ports, but Ayla had hers customized in a way
that usually wasn't. In the palm of her left-hand glove was a tiny
optical laser that—in response to gestures conducted with her
right-hand glove—could create an electrically conductive plasma
channel in the air between her hand and whoever she didn't like
the looks of. In the absence of total compliance, a second gesture
activated a series of step-up transformers in her belt that sent
enough amps and joules through the filament woven into her
suit, up into the glove, and across the conductive plasma channel
to instantly incapacitate even the most robust, belligerent, and
intoxicated sailor.

Ayla Novik had become a human black widow.

She arrived at MIS (the Maldive Islands Spaceport) at dawn
with fifty-seven cryogenic crates of human organs that she had

picked up in Perth exactly one week ago. Where the bundles of tissue came from and what they were to be used for, she did not care to contemplate. Ayla learned a long time ago that the less she knew about the cargo she transported—with the exception of fair market value, and the likelihood that a crate or two would be missed—the better she slept at night.

MIS was once the primary launch site for the largest provider of exclusive private space tours on the planet. Long ago, marketing departments composed soaring endorsements extolling the wonders and delights of losing oneself among almost two kilometers of submerged glass tubes threaded throughout the mountains of reefs; dining on the delectable and extremely rare indigenous hexapus (probably just mutated cephalopods); witnessing the optical spectacle of a synchronized underwater and overhead laser light show; and, of course, midafternoon jaunts into low-earth orbit.

From the air, the main structure of the spaceport gave the impression of a tremendous siliconcrete hex nut pounded flush into the white coral flats of one of the archipelago's atolls. The cantilevered threads once served as hangars for various models of single-stage-to-orbit (SSTO) spaceplanes that could be raised to the flight deck by a massive hydraulic platform in the center. From there, the vehicles combined the equatorial rotational velocity of the planet with air-breathing engines to reach the upper limits of the atmosphere, then ignited liquid oxygen boosters to achieve final orbital insertion, after which passengers could enjoy anywhere from a few minutes to several hours of weightlessness along with the breathtaking panorama of curved glowing azure transitioning into the purest black any of them had ever seen.

But the spaceplanes were now gone, the hydraulic lines long ago bled, and the platform seized by salt-water corrosion in its lowest position beneath close to two solid stories of refuse. The hex nut threads were cracked and broken, exposing an oxidized steel skeleton beneath like the wire frame of a papier-mâché model. Almost every form of commerce remaining on the planet was represented in some capacity somewhere within the four spiraling levels of marketplaces, shantytowns, and privacy cubicles beneath a tattered and patched Kevlar dome.

Although the former glory and elegance of MIS were no longer very much in evidence, the site continued to function as a spaceport. However, rather than supporting either SSTOs or more conventional multistage expendable vehicles, payloads were now boosted into orbit using a nearby servo-mounted Hypervelocity Mechanical Mass Acceleration Ring, or HMMAR (pronounced "hammer" in order to evoke the track-and-field event of similar Newtonian lineage). At first glance, the hammer looked a great deal like a tremendous radio telescope; however, rather than a parabolic dish intended to reflect radio signals to a focal point, the surface was a completely flat three-hundred-meter-diameter spiral steel track designed to gyrate at about sixty cycles per second and generate a centripetal acceleration of tens of thousands of Gs. Payloads of up to three hundred fifty pounds were released from the center of the spiral such that they were phase-locked with the dish's hula-hoop-like motion and subsequently followed the spiral track outward, accelerating to a final velocity of approximately 7.6 kilometers per second—just fast enough to land comfortably in low-earth orbit. The only use of traditional propellant came after the payload cartridge had left the atmosphere, when small quantities of kerosene were burned in order to circularize the payload's orbit and maneuver it into proper position for pickup.

Several times a day the hammer slung payloads of raw materials into orbit for the Coronians who, in return, provided the spaceport with electricity through their local skyhook power terminal. The current was fed into caps, or portable capacitors, which were the universal currency used to purchase more raw materials from whoever happened to be selling, and at the same time, fuel a massive secondary marketplace as boundless as it was exotic.

Ayla wasn't especially pleased or impressed with today's economic outlook. Rigorous inspection of her cargo prior to the buyer taking possession revealed that not all of the organs she delivered were laboratory-cultivated or 3D printed from sterile cartridges of living cells as had been specified in the purchase order. About 20 percent, it turned out, came from cadavers that had apparently been irradiated, diseased, and/or partially decomposed. Losing 20 percent of her rate would have been bad enough, but she was also docked an additional 5 percent for disposal fees. When she argued, she was told that the less expensive alternative was to have the worthless masses of tissue dumped on the deck of her freighter, after which she was free to dispose of it in any manner she saw fit, as long as it was in compliance with MIS biohazard regulation.

But Ayla was starting to feel a little bit better. She was at a café, such as it was, on the top deck of the hangar as close to the crumbling edge as she dared plant herself, enjoying the afternoon despite her economic misfortune. When out at sea, she mainly subsisted on nonperishable protein and supplement wafers, so a hot meal of real stemstock felt nothing less than indulgent to her. As she took a bite, the question of how many of the organs she delivered this morning would ultimately be consumed as food involuntarily surfaced, but was immediately and conveniently tamped back down, along with many other realities of the world of which she tried to keep herself blissfully ignorant.

By all rights, MIS should have been a crime-ridden cess-pool, and in many ways, that was not an entirely unfair characterization. However, the spaceport was also not without its charm. For the most part, residents and shopkeepers took pride in their merchandise and crafts, and they did their best to maintain their humble allotments of territory. They kept clean that which was not entirely futile, and usually shared the responsibility of keeping common areas relatively free of filth. Although the pit in the middle that once raised and lowered sleek, blended-wing spaceplanes was full of trash probably at least ten meters deep, it was now illegal to dispose of anything in any manner other than through municipal refuse chutes. The debris that had already accumulated in the center of the structure had been partially sterilized and sealed to try to contain the smell, though one's best defense against the stench was still to breathe through one's mouth, and ultimately, to simply acclimate oneself to it. From where Ayla was sitting, she could see hundreds of people on the decks across and below her, more or less getting along and, she liked to believe, living the very best lives they could. When she looked up, she could see the dozen or so airships that occupied the space just beneath the dome—dirigibles, zeppelins, and blimps of various shapes, configurations, and colors like a selection of piñatas suspended from the roof of a tent. Although they occasionally descended so that personnel or supplies could be exchanged over anchored gangplanks, they were primarily tended to by swarms of autonomous multicopter drones. The fleet of airships served as offices and living quarters for those too good to mingle with the general population on the ground, but not too good to relieve them of the burden of their caps.

As she did every single day since Costa's death, Ayla thought of him; conjured him up and placed him right there with her; carried on a conversation with him in her head. And as was almost always the case, the first thing he wanted to know was whether or not she'd been taking good care of his ship.

I'm doing the best I can, Ayla told him. *Today I stopped a pile of guts from getting dumped on her deck.*

I guess that's something, Costa said. *What are you going to do now?*

Finish my lunch.

Ayla. You know what I mean.

I don't know. Find another job, I guess.

You can't stay here. It isn't safe.

I know.

I'll never understand why you like this place so much. It looks like a giant toilet.

I just like being around people and not feeling afraid.

You should be afraid.

I know I should, but I'm tired of it.

This place will all be gone someday. You know that, don't you?

Yes.

One day there will be an earthquake, or a tsunami, or it will just collapse for no good reason at all and everyone inside will be swallowed up inside a giant litter-filled hole.

But that day won't be today, so today I'm going to enjoy it.

Have a drink for me. The only thing good about that place is the cask ale they sell down below.

Costa. I can't forget about you.

You don't have to forget about me. You just have to move on.
I can't.
You have to meet someone.
I don't want to.
You need someone to take care of you.
I can take care of myself.
Are you sure about that?

There was a tremendous crack overhead as the Kevlar dome rippled from the shock wave of another payload being launched by the hammer outside. The airships were slightly perturbed, like birthday balloons in air-conditioning. Ayla looked back down, but the specter of Costa was gone. She knew that he was right—or that she was right, rather. She couldn't stay here. Despite her attempts to make the *Accipiter Hawk* look run-down and barely seaworthy, it was almost always one of the nicest multipurpose cargo vessels in just about any port. And by now, way too many people knew that she sailed it completely alone. When Costa was still alive, it was pirates and raiders that she feared, and the ports that made her feel safe. Now, the only time she felt safe was when she was out at sea and both radar and sonar corroborated that her bubble of solitude was real, reporting nothing around her at all but open water and empty horizon. Even though the shocksuit had worked well for her so far—extending her personal space by at least a meter in every direction—she knew it was only a matter of time before someone decided to test it. Ayla believed that just about all men, at some point in their lives, were unafraid to die, and tangling with a girl like her was as good a way to go as any, and much better than most.

She stood from the metal barrel she'd been using as a table, and as she'd had it ingrained in her that there was no sense in leaving behind stray DNA, she gathered the trash from her lunch. The nearest refuse chute was embedded in the back wall, and as she approached it, she could feel the heat from the incinerator burning probably hundreds of feet below. She held on to her bulb of water, but deposited the stemstock box and chopsticks, then took a moment to survey her surroundings. There were stalls with multiple levels of racks packed with fabric and clothing in every conceivable texture and hue; booths with crooked stacks of old components, and bins containing circuit boards, microchips, and spools of cable; all shapes and sizes of tanks full of compressed oxygen, hydrogen, propane, and various other gasses and liquids; nutrition in just about all forms and flavors and states of matter including synthesized protein, fermented soy, dozens of species of insects, supplements and probiotics, and tall jars of large brown placenta capsules. Not far from where she stood was a frame of welded iron rods enclosed in curtains bearing the discrete symbol indicating that anyone with the caps could step inside and ingest the nutrients and antibodies of warm human breast milk directly from the source.

Ayla knew she should wait to use the toilet on the *Accipiter Hawk*, but she didn't want to go back to her ship until she had another job arranged. She followed the contour of the back wall until she reached the corrugated plastic patricians, then took one last look behind her before going in. The toilets were squat-style and were flushed with a simple spigot and hose, but in truth, Ayla had used far worse, and she was thankful to find that this one had not yet been ruined for the day. Before putting her suit in standby and starting on the clasps, she quietly popped the top off her water bulb and poured a thin stream gently into the bowl in the floor. She listened, and after a few seconds of simulated urination, the door behind her was shouldered violently open, then someone took half a step toward her before realizing that she was still both dressed and armed.

The man's jumpsuit was open down to the crotch, and Ayla couldn't tell if his chest and stomach were dark from grime, body hair, or both. He was heavily bearded and his long, oily hair was pulled back into an unkempt ponytail. His hands went up in front of him in a reassuring gesture, and when he smiled, Ayla could see that he was missing most of his bottom teeth.

"I'm sorry," the man said. He did his best to come across as both harmless and embarrassed. "I didn't see there was someone in here."

Ayla's hands went up in a similar gesture, but it was not one of reassurance or peace. She lowered the ring and middle fingers of her right hand and a bright green dot appeared on the man's chest. It skittered in and out of his open top as he looked down for a moment, then back up.

"*Bitch*," the man spat. He was no longer concerned with appearing contrite. "I said I was fucking sorry."

"Well, I'm not," Ayla said. She made a rapid fist with her right hand and there was an eruption of light. The door slammed open, then closed, then creaked gradually back open again above the soles of the man's boots, forming a slack and asymmetrical V. Ayla stepped forward and confirmed that the man was sprawled completely motionless on the siliconcrete floor several meters from where he had been standing. His jumpsuit was dark where he had pissed himself, and in the air was the now-familiar smell of ozone.

CHAPTER FOUR

THE HISTORY OF THE CORONIANS
PART TWO: SHADOW

AT THE CORE OF *EQUINOX* were two concentric rings encompassing the entire planet at an altitude of roughly four hundred kilometers above the equator. Both rings were constructed in sections—massive trusses with barely detectable individual curvatures—launched from all over the planet, meticulously maneuvered into position, and then molecularly fused. Early artistic conceptions depicted the rings as radiating spectacular glimmers of golden sunlight, prompting an impressive but ultimately unsuccessful worldwide movement to rename the project TORRTA, or The One Ring to Rule Them All, after the precious magical fetish at the center of what remained one of the most enduring novels of all time.

During the construction phase, each individual segment, as well as the main assembly itself, orbited Earth "spinward" (in the direction of rotation—from west to east) at a rate of about 28,000 kilometers per hour, or 7.8 kilometers per second. To understand why this precise velocity was necessary—and more importantly, to appreciate the extraordinary marvel that *Equinox* would become—it helped to understand the very basics of orbital mechanics and microgravity.

The best way to conceptualize how and why one object orbits another is to consider Sir Isaac Newton's famous thought experiment of placing a cannon at the top of a high mountain and firing it horizontally. If the velocity were too low, gravity would eventually pull the cannonball to the ground. If the velocity were too high, the cannonball would escape Earth's gravity altogether. But if the velocity were just right, the cannonball would fall toward the earth at exactly the rate at which the earth curves away from it, meaning it would never actually touch the ground and would therefore have achieved orbit. (Of course, in reality, air friction would slow the cannonball down and cause it to fall to the ground, which is why orbit can only be achieved above Earth's atmosphere.)

Since gravity is what keeps one object orbiting another, microgravity (also called zero-g) is not the absence of gravity at all. Rather, weightlessness is an illusion—a sensation experienced when everything around you falls around the curvature of the earth at about the same speed. When everything you can see is falling at the same rate, it appears that everything is, in fact, floating; and since a bathroom scale would fall at the same rate as you, standing on top of it in microgravity would make you appear weightless.

At four hundred kilometers above the surface of the earth, an object must travel at about 28,000 kilometers per hour, or 7.8 kilometers per second, in order to remain in orbit. These figures come from long-established equations and well-understood principles, on top of which well over a century of predictions, experiments, and both manned and unmanned missions have been based. And it was precisely such relatively straightforward orbital mechanics that made the procedure initiated by the international *Equinox* team, after the frames of both rings were complete, appear to defy both physics and logic.

Using integrated ion thrusters, the inner ring—designated *Xuanwu* after the Chinese constellation of the Black Tortoise—was decelerated by between 93 and 94 percent; from 28,000 kilometers per hour to only about 1,770; exactly the rotational speed an object needs, at four hundred kilometers of altitude, to be geostationary, or to be synchronized with the rotation of the earth below.

The concept of geostationary orbit was well known and thoroughly understood, having been successfully used for decades in the context of communications and other satellites that needed to remain in exactly the same position in the sky at all times. However, prior to *Xuanwu*, geostationary orbit could only be achieved by objects at a distance of almost 36,000 kilometers from the surface of the earth, and traveling at over 11,000 kilometers per hour. It was physically impossible for an object only four hundred kilometers above the surface of the earth to simultaneously travel slowly enough to follow the earth's rotation, and fast enough to fall at a rate matching Earth's curvature. Any such object would invariably plummet, most likely disintegrating in the atmosphere along the way.

Unless, of course, that object happened to be a ring.

Earth's gravity did indeed take hold of *Xuanwu* as it slowed and yanked it furiously down, yet it did so uniformly across its entire structure, shrinking it due to anticipated material compression by a fraction of a percent of its predecelerated circumference, and thus achieving an almost perfect balance of forces. In fact, it proved perfect enough that only minimal station-keeping adjustments were necessary through its reaction control systems and linked ion thrusters to compensate for lunar and solar gravity, solar winds, the irregular gravitational attraction of Earth due to its asymmetry and slightly askew center of gravity, and from the accumulation of minuscule forces that would one day be exerted by the various routines of everyday life. Strictly speaking, *Xuanwu* was not actually in orbit since its speed no longer matched the curvature of the earth, which meant objects inside it would no longer experience weightlessness. In fact, the gravitational field aboard the inner ring was only fractionally less than 90 percent of that felt directly on the surface of the earth. It turned out that artificial gravity inside a space station did not, in fact, have to be artificial. All you needed was a ring big enough to encircle an entire planet.

Xuanwu was to be a way to spend long periods of time in space without any of the health risks, complications, and challenges of zero-g. Living quarters were to be housed inside the inner ring where residence and visitors could adjust to the minimally diminished gravitational field in mere hours, and with modest exercise routines, avoid muscle atrophy, loss of bone mass, anemia, and weakened immune systems. Most importantly, no matter how long one stayed aboard *Equinox*—days, months, years, even decades—spending enough time inside *Xuanwu* guaranteed that one could return to Earth at a moment's notice with no ill effects or transitional period whatsoever.

The outer ring—designated *Lepus* after the constellation of the hare being hunted by Orion—maintained its original orbital velocity, thereby providing an environment of complete weightlessness. Sandwiched between the two like ball bearings were to be several V-MAPs, or Velocity-Matching Pods: electromagnetically accelerated or decelerated trams capable of matching the speed of either ring, enabling rapid and convenient passage between levels. A scientist could wake up in the morning in almost full Earth gravity, commute to work aboard a V-MAP (where, over the course of a few minutes, she would feel herself become weightless), spend her day floating in microgravity, then return to a comfortable, familiar, and healthy environment in the evening.

In addition to enabling humans to remain in space essentially indefinitely, another tremendous advantage of the geostationary rotation of *Xuanwu* was the skyhooks: carbon nanotube cables joining the inner ring to the earth's surface in various locations along the equator. They were intended to serve as the foundations for lifts promising inexpensive and unfettered access to low-earth orbit. By no means were space elevators a new idea (in fact, proposals dated all the way back to 1895), however it was the foundation of *Equinox*—and in particular, *Xuanwu*—that finally made the concept not just practical, but almost trivial. Rather than having to somehow construct and deploy a cable that reached beyond traditional geostationary orbit (almost 36,000 kilometers), the skyhooks were only about four hundred kilometers in length—less than two hundred fifty miles—and even when outfitted with pulleys, drive systems, and cars, they would be under only a fraction of the amount of strain as any formerly proposed or conceived space elevator.

Equinox was to become a platform for supporting all of humanity's future astronomical ambitions—to serve as the infrastructure for dozens of telescopes, hundreds of scientists and students, thousands of satellites and other global communication systems, and even extensive and relatively affordable tourism. Surface area could be increased through almost endless appendages extending from both Cancer (northern) and Capricorn (southern) sides of either ring, almost as far as the tropics themselves. There were to be factories for manufacturing specialized chemicals, drugs, materials, and systems components that could only be produced in zero-g; sensors designed to detect incredibly minute narrow-bandwidth radio waves and pulses of photons as brief as a billionth of a second in duration from transmitters or laser beacons possibly produced by extraterrestrial technology; data centers safe from earthquakes, tsunamis, and physical security breaches; hospitals where ground-based surgeons could remotely perform procedures otherwise complicated by gravity; and launch pads for spacecraft designed to explore the solar system (and eventually considerable distances beyond) using sails only fractions of a micron thick, propelled by high-energy lasers mounted at various points along the rings. The skyhooks were to finally provide a safe and economically viable way to transport every manner of waste—from toxic chemicals, to sequestered carbon and methane, to fully intact ICBMs with multimegaton warheads—off the surface of the planet, where it could be released into a rapidly decaying solar orbit and finally become a thing of humanity's past.

The original schedule for *Equinox* was established while humanity was still on the cusp of incredible advances in materials science, and just as the fields of structural engineering and manufacturing were about to be profoundly transformed by metamaterials. Computer-aided manufacturing, 3D printing and fabrication, and even primitive molecular assembly technologies were constantly improving, but at linear rates that, when juxtaposed with humanity's ambitions, sometimes felt sluggish. But then everything changed with the explosion of a field known as meta-manufacturing: a branch of industry focused not on producing marketable products, components, or commodities, but on using the most sophisticated manufacturing technologies on the planet to self-referentially create new and better manufacturing technologies.

Once the processes of manufacturing, fabrication, and assembly became tightly recursive, their evolutions accelerated from linear to exponential. When meta-manufacturing technology was eventually established in orbit, its potential was further unlocked by microgravity, and not only did it accelerate faster still, but it even began diverging significantly from technology available on Earth. As a result, the basic structure of *Equinox* was completed almost a full year ahead of schedule, and turned out to be bigger, stronger, and far more robust than what the original schematics described.

Optimism and enthusiasm for *Equinox* were at their peak, and projections associated with just about every economic, social, and cultural index in existence soared. It was taken for granted that school-age children would have the opportunity to live and work in orbit, and that within a generation, humankind would finally establish permanent colonies on at least two other worlds. It was often quoted as an indisputable fact that the first human to live comfortably on Mars, to have their consciousness transferred into a machine, to fully comprehend the universe with the aid of neurological implants, and to have the ability to live forever had already been born. *Equinox* was to be the next wheel, printing press, internal combustion engine, telephone, lightbulb, antibiotic, birth control pill, photovoltaic semiconductor, Internet, decentralized cryptocurrency, and democracy—all rolled up into one. The Solar Age was widely considered the absolute best time in human history to be alive, and perhaps the very first age truly worthy of the eternal yearning for immortality. However, now that humanity was entirely dependent on the twenty-seven-million-degree ball of plasma a little over eight light-minutes away—probably the most constant, immutable, and seemingly predictable presence in the entire history of the human race—nobody had given serious consideration as to what might happen if the sun ever went out.

CHAPTER FIVE

TRANSPARTMENTS

LIVING AMONG A POPULATION OF roughly five thousand people felt perpetually awkward to Luka. The community aboard the *San Francisco* was small enough that almost everyone was recognizable, yet large enough that it was impossible to know everyone. Luka had learned from the archives that, according to research conducted by the British anthropologist Robin Dunbar, it was physically impossible for humans to intimately know more than about one hundred fifty people. Since the number of stable social relationships an individual could maintain appeared to be determined by the size of the neocortex, without the aid of neuroprosthetics, the human social potential was biologically constrained. After reading the article, Luka had tried to calculate his own personal Dunbar Number. Taking into account modifiers for introversion, general eccentricity, and, if he were being completely honest with himself, plenty of unresolved emotional conflict, the end result came out to be somewhere between zero and one.

Social convention aboard the *San Francisco* dictated that the expectation of interaction was inversely proportional to immediate population density. In other words, the more people there were around, the less you had to acknowledge them. Therefore, as Luka guided his calibration cube through the streets between the foundry and his flat—crowded with purposeful evening rush hour foot traffic—he felt no obligation whatsoever to so much as make eye contact with those he strode past.

This evening's algorithmic sunset was already under way as the two and a half megawatts of plasma lighting that constituted daytime on the *San Francisco* were gradually reduced. During the day, the completely opaque air dome overhead was a pure bright white, but in the mornings and evenings, subtle orange and red hues were introduced, their ratios and concentrations informed by rigorous research into feelings of serenity and wellbeing. Insects were the primary source of protein here, and the giant glass sphere enclosing the Yerba Buena Gardens at the heart of the *San Francisco* had already started to vibrate with their collective singing. The antimicrobial silicone walkway under Luka's feet was as soft as a newly groomed golf green, and the air was balmy and impeccably humidified.

It was an evening every bit as perfect as it was indistinguishable from any other.

But the *San Francisco* was not always the meticulously maintained human vivarium that Luka had come to know. She was once one of an entire fleet of Metropolis-class, nuclear-powered mining and refinery rigs built decades ago and given orders to do whatever it took to keep the *Equinox* project supplied with natural resources and raw materials. For several years, the rigs could be resupplied and repaired at almost any major port in the world, but when *Equinox* was gradually abandoned, so too was the Metropolis fleet. Over the course of a decade, the majority were captured and plundered by pirates, decimated either by famine or plague, or destroyed by industrial accidents. When fewer than ten remained, they finally turned on each another, waging amateurish naval battles with various forms of primitive projectiles, improvised artillery, and boarding parties who were both desperate and terrified, and armed with anything sharp or heavy they could find or fashion, and whose savagery more than compensated for their lack of training.

When only the *New York* and the *San Francisco* remained afloat and semifunctional—when each were probably only weeks or maybe even days away from being completely dead in the water—both were contacted by a serene female voice from the sky claiming to represent a people who called themselves Coronians, and who offered them a simple path to all the power they would ever need.

Most people did not deal directly with the Coronians, but rather through middlemen known as power brokers. The brokers helped make several modifications to the *San Francisco*, the most significant of which was the replacement of the cracked and failing nuclear reactor with a quantum battery bank. From that point forward, the massive mining rig made periodic stops at broker posts all over the globe, exchanging mined magnesium, cobalt, silicon, gold, silver, copper, zinc, scandium, and rare earth elements for power, and for whatever other supplies brokers were offering. An informal economy gradually emerged among the crew that was eventually formalized by the *San Francisco* City Council: the more an individual contributed, the more power he or she could use for the kinds of things that made life aboard a mobile mining rig more comfortable. Devices such as heaters, fans, woks, stoves, and refrigerators were in high demand, and eventually, even various entertainment devices. For those who lived aboard the massive floating industrial city of *San Francisco*, the Energy Age had officially begun, and appended to humanity's long list of currencies was very possibly the most practical and directly applicable form of legal tender ever conceived: the watt—or as it was frequently abbreviated, ₩.

The arrangement with the Coronians and the brokers kept the *San Francisco* mobile and temporarily afloat, but eventually the vessel began deteriorating at a rate beyond her crew's capacity to make repairs. It was then that the Coronians realized they had a very difficult decision to make: either they let what remained of the Metropolis fleet—the two most productive mining and refinery facilities left on the planet—sink to the bottom of the ocean, or they finally share one of the most important and transformative technologies in the history of humanity.

With the appearance of the molecular assembler, the standard of living aboard the *San Francisco* rapidly improved. She even began taking on additional crew—primarily orphaned children who could be easily trained to run the assemblers twenty-four hours a day. Eventually, every above-deck structure was replaced at least once by ultralightweight microlattice and silica-paned structures, and an entirely new air-dome frame and composite-weave cover were constructed beneath the old one before the frayed and thoroughly patched shroud was at last cut loose and set adrift. Most of the steel hull was plasma-torched away and replaced with shaped carbon nanotubes and fiber-reinforced polymer. The corroded metal grates underfoot were pulled up and the streets sealed, then repaved with a soft, comfortable, antimicrobial silicon derivative, and the purification, filtration, and electrolysis systems were upgraded so many times that the quality of both the air and the water were probably about as high as any human had ever enjoyed. Although insects remained the most compact, calorically dense, and nutritionally practical form of livestock, various textures and flavors of a product synthesized from the stem cells of ruminants started appearing in the ship's commissaries known collectively as the Union Square Mall. Life aboard the *San Francisco* had finally improved to the point where the City Council finally made good on one of their many long-standing promises: after a unanimous vote, every single person aboard the rig was guaranteed by local maritime law at least one day off per week, and the concept of leisure time was rediscovered.

Watts, as forms of currency, eventually became known as caps (shorthand for the capacitors that were used to store and trade them), and the standard of one cap being the equivalent of a kilowatt was officially established (with the term watts, in the context of money, being reserved for fractions of a cap). Shortly thereafter, the practice of physically possessing and trading caps became obsolete when the *San Francisco*'s electrical grid was updated to a smart system that both intelligently distributed power, and served as a type of citywide credit union. Rather than actually exchanging caps, the city's mesh simply maintained every citizen's balance, automatically making deductions as purchases were settled and as power was used (everything electrical on the platform had to complete an authentication routine with the grid before it could draw power). As Luka discovered from archival research, caps were highly unusual among historical forms of legal tender since they were at once a fiat currency (meaning they were state-issued, and could be exchanged for goods and services), and also directly convertible into units of work.

Of course, wherever commerce and government coexist, so too must taxes. The number of watts on the cap that were diverted for municipal use to power things like new construction, lighting, air and water purification, and to help pay the rising salaries of government workers, was constantly creeping up, yet it somehow always managed to stay just below the threshold where one's obligations were felt more pointedly than one's gains.

. . .

There were no above-deck vehicles permitted on the *San Francisco*, which left the streets fully dedicated to foot traffic. Luka weaved his way down Market Street, then cut over on Dolores toward the Yerba Buena Gardens. The Gardens—also sometimes referred to as "the screw"—was the centerpiece of the *San Francisco*. The dominant structure was a giant spiral platform supporting a variety of crops cultivated along its surface, and hanging gardens suspended from trellises below, all contained inside a massive glass-paneled globe and positioned in the dead center of the rig. Among the produce were the fruits and vegetables that constituted the majority of the population's vitamins, minerals, and fiber, and in the center column were the boxed broods of cicadas, crickets, grubs, and other insects that provided most of the protein. (With the current generation of molecular assemblers, it was illegal to assemble anything considered "organic" and/or any material labeled as consumable or ingestive, which made the envelope in Luka's bag doubly illegal.) In the basement of the Gardens were racks of microbial cultures that were processed into probiotic supplements and distributed with boxed meals as digestive complements. The panels of thin-film diodes inside the globe dimmed in the evenings, but never entirely went out since the need for constant growth required that any notion of nighttime or wintertime be genetically eradicated from the crops' DNA.

Luka stayed on the west side of the giant screw, following Mariposa south toward his flat. He glanced down Sunset toward the Embarcadero: the rig's only park, which enveloped the entire southeast corner between Millennium and Paramount Towers. As usual, there was a cricket match in-progress, and he saw the distant motion of bowlers and batsman, and moments later heard the hollow *pick, pack, pock, puck* of PVC balls against synthetic wooden bats.

The shape of both Millennium and Paramount Towers defied simple geometric classification. They were roughly tetrahedral in form—magnificent forty-two-story triangular pyramids, of sorts—that appeared to lean back and thrust their great curved glass facades forward toward the Gardens like proud swollen bellies. They were designed so that as many flats as possible had front-facing windows, through which plenty of artificial light streamed after bouncing among the numerous polished and reflective surfaces that rose toward the vast artificial sky.

The two "luxury towers" (a term adopted and propagated by the City Council back when the renovation was first proposed) were the foundations of the *San Francisco's* socio-economic formula—soaring symbols of the city's commitments to both capitalism and social responsibility. Everyone on the rig lived in one of the two buildings, whether you were a water rat (deep-sea miner), assembly technician, doctor, teacher, grower, some form of engineer, peace officer, merchant, refinery operator, member of the City Council, or one of the acting captains. It was true that the flats got larger the higher up you went, but even accommodations on the bottom floors had to meet minimum standards ensuring they were far superior to the stacks of crude tenements that preceded them. The philosophy was intended to promote a free-market economy in which hard work and advancement were duly rewarded, but also one in which there was no shame in spending your day below deck with your hands thrust deep inside the inner working of the rig rather than high above, seated comfortably in front of polymeth panels. Whether you showered as a group in a locker room at the end of a shift or privately in your own flat before work, if you lived on the *San Francisco* and contributed to her continued operation and advancement, you were entitled to a dignified existence.

The City Council guaranteed that there would always be a flat available in one of the two towers for every productive adult citizen aboard the rig, and despite the fact that the population was higher than it had ever been, the proclamation had so far been upheld. In fact, there were usually between one and two dozen flats available, and residents frequently rearranged themselves among the combined eighty-four floors, trading a coveted view for an even more coveted extra square meter of space, or an especially favorable lighting arrangement for either proximity to a new partner, or for some distance from an old one.

There were two primary factors that accounted for most of the excess inventory: Luka's generation reaching an age where they were cohabiting and marrying (but not yet divorcing); and the physics, chemistry, and biology involved in deep-sea mining. Since as many as eight miners needed to be simultaneously working at depths of up to five hundred meters, there were usually four individual dive teams constantly undergoing compression (gradual exposure to breathing gasses at increasingly greater pressure), decompression (gradual reduction of hyperbaric conditions to prevent gas bubbles from forming in tissue), and preservation (maintaining an ambient pressure equal to that of the dive site in order to avoid the risks of constant compression and decompression over the course of a tour). Since getting through the entire "saturation rotation" could take as long as three months, several miners saved caps by participating in a type of time-share arrangement, thereby contributing to the *San Francisco*'s overall housing surplus.

Millennium Tower was on the southernmost edge of the city. Most of its flats provided magnificent views of the Gardens, the Presidio building (which housed the air filtration and purification systems), Mission Dolores School, and the Pacific Medical Center. Its sister tower, Paramount, was on the other side of the Embarcadero along the eastern edge of the platform. Most of its residents were treated to a view of the convoluted snarl of pipes emerging from the Mission Bay water treatment plant, the cantilevered decks and turquoise swimming tubes of the Noe Valley Rec Center, and the northernmost corner of the Union Square Mall and Moscone Theater. The technology that helped create breathable air by teasing purified seawater molecules apart through the process of electrolysis was contained in the non-descript Muir building at the corner of Market and Mission, and was connected to both the Mission Bay water treatment plant and the Presidio air filtration and purification center via open glass and cable flyovers. One block out—largely hidden from residents' view—was Cell City (an enclosed grid of quantum battery banks), the Market Street Refinery, the Mission Street Foundry, and the bulbous microlattice and silica City Hall, which almost entirely obscured the telescopic crawler crane behind it that was used so frequently that nobody thought it was worth taking apart for storage down on deck three. The only other structures of consequence on the *San Francisco* were the ship's bridge, which rose from the corner directly opposite the Embarcadero, and just beyond it, the hangar: the only safe, sanctioned, and above-surface way of getting into or out of the city.

What the architects of the Millennium Tower lobby thought of as modern design was much closer to sterility in Luka's opinion. The idea was to create a bright and open common area for residents to convene, socialize, and—to borrow a newly jargonized term from the urban planning committee—to "cultivate" (roughly defined as social interaction through which ideas and opinions were freely shared, promoting a strong sense of citizenry and community). However, the effect was much closer to an obnoxious obstacle course of perpetually unused couches, end chairs, coffee tables, thick synthetic area rugs, and tacky optical fiber floor lamps.

The camera by the elevator recognized Luka's facial geometry and the silica doors slid apart on their magnetically levitated tracks as he approached. The polymeth panel inside showed the twenty-first floor already selected. Luka turned and looked back out into the lobby to see if he needed to maneuver his cube into the corner of the platform to make room for other passengers, but nobody else was coming. Although the streets were crowded with the evening shift change, most people did not go directly back to their flats after work. There was always a happy hour to track down, or shopping to be done at the Union Square Mall, or a dinner to attend. For the more privileged among the population, there might be cocktails on the rooftop terrace of City Hall, or exotic new cuisine acquired from a nearby port to sample in a private room somewhere. There were cricket rivalries to be settled, old football matches from the archives to watch at Kacis Hookah and Coffee Lounge, and algorithmically generated and digitally rendered films to watch at the Moscone Theater. Those who worked the morning shift tended to leave more or less in concert, but returning home again was generally a staggered and prolonged, if reluctant, affair.

Aside from emergency mechanical braking systems, none of the elevators on the *San Francisco* contained such primitive mechanisms as motors and drive traction cables, but instead operated purely on the principles of electromagnetism. As long as there were resources to be mined and sold to the Coronians for energy, it was far easier to pump current through various conductive materials than it was to assemble, install, maintain, and occasionally replace thousands of specialized components. Anything on the rig with moving parts was regarded with great suspicion, and was almost certainly the target of one gentrification committee or another.

With such a small amount of space allocated to each resident, flats on the *San Francisco* had to be highly dynamic and transformative. In fact, those that could be rearranged (which, in one way or another, were almost all of them) were usually referred to as "transpartments" to distinguish them from traditional static flats. Acoustically resonate conductive polymeth dividers provided lighting, sound, and infinitely customizable interactive surfaces which could slide and pivot on their maglev tracks and hinges to create spaces optimally configured for cooking/eating, sleeping, entertaining, exercising, or working. Futons folded up flat against walls, and entire appliances were reduced to the size of drawers. Storage was wall-to-wall and floor-to-ceiling, and bathrooms had to be functionally divided into separate compartments for the toilet, sink, and the shower. Furniture that didn't fold away had to collapse through a series of telescopic and swiveling operations that left it compact enough to slip into stealthy slots in the walls and floors, and absolutely everything unwanted or disused went instantly into pneumatic chutes that converged and eventually terminated just above the *San Francisco*'s churning and foaming wake.

Since Luka was planning on an evening of opiate-enhanced sculpting, he used the elevator's polymeth panel to select a transpartment configuration optimized for uninterrupted expanse. He then selected something to eat from his inventory of boxed meals so that it would be warm by the time he walked through the door: witchetty grubs infused with the flavor of the mulga wood the Aboriginal Australians once cooked them over, accompanied by a grape tomato, arugula, and zucchini salad with a light spritzing of basil vinaigrette. Or at least pretty good imitations thereof.

Most of the doors in both the Millennium and the Paramount were of a double-pocket sliding design so as not to obstruct the narrow hallways. By default, they opened just enough to admit a resident after his or her facial geometry had been verified, though if they detected the need for additional clearance, they automatically accommodated. In this case, Luka's calibration cube prompted an almost full-size entry.

The space was already filled with the warm, smoky aroma of witchetty grub. Luka pivoted a catch down from its recess in the wall by the door and hung his shoulder bag from it, then maneuvered his calibration cube into the center of his flat. He washed his hands in the kitchen basin under warm, perfectly conditioned water and a few short bursts of ultraviolet light, then removed his boxed meal from the prep drawer. The grubs and the salad were divided by a thermal partition, and steam rose from the warm side as Luka peeled back the lid, then dropped it into the vacuum of the refuse chute.

He ate while he unfurled his studio and unpacked the various sculpting implements he'd custom-assembled for himself over the years. The grubs had the texture and taste of a ground almond omelet wrapped in phyllo dough, and he washed them down with a bulb of cool water infused with crushed mint. Once the box was disposed of down the refuse chute and his studio prepped, he returned to his bag on the wall and carefully removed the folded envelope inside.

Not all of the equipment Luka unpacked was, strictly speaking, intended for sculpting a calibration cube. He tore away a corner of the envelope, then tapped it above the intake of a device about the size of portable coffee press, tightened the cap, and touched the activation switch. The machine—a hacked and modified automatic cupcake decorator he bought at the Union Square Mall—vibrated for a moment, then the nozzle began moving on its two axes. When it was done tracing a sawtooth pattern, there were five perfectly even rows of yellow powder on a glass surface waiting to be consumed at a rate of no more than one line per hour.

Luka pulled the slightly flared glass tube from its hold, positioned it at the beginning of the first line, and bent down. The trick, he'd learned, was to inhale just enough to draw the powder into your nostril, but not so hard that it sprayed down the back of your throat. The longer you could keep it in that sweet spot—melting into a kind of yellow gel against the extensive vascular capillary bed below—the better the high. You could control the substance's position with subtle breaths, deriving pleasure from the association of the intricate balance with the rapid absorption and subsequent binding of molecules to opioid receptors. The less it numbed your tongue and gums when it eventually drained down the back of your throat, the more of it was in your brain where it belonged.

The taste of curious yellow was bitter and acidic, and by any reasonable standard, should provoke offense and mild revulsion.

To Luka, though, it tasted like pure eye-fluttering and knee-weakening utopia—like what an orgasm would taste like if the moment could be distilled and bottled and served as a warm liquor. As he leaned back and blinked and looked at the cube, his eyes filled with euphoric tears at the thought of all the wonderful curves and lines and planes the marbleized material in front of him might contain.

CHAPTER SIX

THE HISTORY OF THE CORONIANS
PART THREE: SPECIATION

ACCORDING TO MOST GOVERNMENTS, the worldwide blackout was the result of by far the largest and most catastrophic industrial accident in history, probably caused by one of the many international mining companies that had gotten into the business of asteroid sequestration. However, a conspicuous lack of seismic data continued to raise questions. An impact violent enough to eject excavated material and sediment into the atmosphere would have pegged almost every seismometer on the planet. The shock waves would have triggered megatsunamis that would have killed millions as they consumed at least 60 percent of the planet's shorelines. And debris thrown straight through the atmosphere would have been superheated to incandescence upon reentry and lit up the entire Northern Hemisphere with the intensity of a nuclear blast.

An analysis of the presumed ejecta through an amateur ballooning experiment told a very different story. To dozens of independent geologists, the particles appeared more mechanical than organic. Weaponization of molecular nanotechnology had become the newest arms race, and ecophagy—or the consumption of the entire ecosystem by self-replicating nanoscale robots—had largely replaced fears of a planetwide nuclear holocaust. The biggest difference between the two apocalyptic scenarios was that synthetic biological warfare could theoretically be initiated by anyone, from any sized laboratory, anywhere on the planet, with no radiological traces whatsoever.

The process of mechanosynthetic replication had ceased, but not before the concentration of particles in the stratosphere were sufficient to block close to 90 percent of the sunlight that once reached Earth's surface, reducing daytime to the luminosity of a moderately moonlit night, and effectively flipping the power switch on the entire planet.

The shift back toward fossil fuels and nuclear energy was both instantaneous and disastrous. The population of the planet had grown far beyond what the pre–Solar Age could support, and within a year, the rates at which coal, petroleum, natural gas, and just about anything else combustible were burned was over three times higher than it had been at the height of mankind's former dependency. Nuclear safety regulation was essentially nonexistent, and Chernobyl-scale meltdowns became semiregular events.

Just as suddenly as the process of solar energy production was halted, so too was photosynthesis. The foliage of deciduous trees turned autumn hues and was shed for the very last time, and evergreens turned brown and brittle. The world's forests fell into a state of hibernation from which they never awoke, and were subsequently harvested and burned, increasing the planet's atmospheric burden. With a significant percentage of Earth's complex food web gone, it was estimated that well over 90 percent of the planet's biomass perished over the course of just a few years in what was almost certainly the largest and most rapid mass extinction event since life first took hold well over three and a half billion years prior.

Eventually the particles in the upper atmosphere began to disperse, exposing the dramatically reformulated troposphere beneath it to solar radiation. Although not nearly enough sunlight could reliably penetrate to revive the Solar Age, the new atmospheric composition was not impervious to thermal radiation. The average temperature of the planet had temporarily plummeted in the absence of sunlight, but now as heat was once again permitted to reach the earth's surface, rather than dissipating harmlessly back off into space, massive concentrations of carbon dioxide, methane, and heavy metals such as mercury and lead absorbed the energy and re-radiated it back down. As the stratosphere cleansed itself of the mysterious mechanical foreign matter, it revealed a world trapped firmly between two states: the sky was too opaque for the sustained and efficient generation of solar power, but not so opaque as to prevent a runaway greenhouse effect.

It was not long before temperatures in the hottest regions began approaching the coolest temperatures on one of the least hospitable planets in the entire solar system: Venus. The world once known as the Blue Marble even began to assume some of the visual characteristics of her sister planet since greenhouse gasses tend to favor the orange and yellow portions of the visible spectrum. The immense and amazingly swift transformation was proof of how similar Earth and Venus really were, both in terms of size and composition. The biggest difference was that a lack of tectonic plates on Venus resulted in an interrupted carbon cycle, leaving most of the planet's greenhouse gasses in the atmosphere rather than trapped safely below the planet's surface. However, the more Earth's carbon supply was released from its underground confines, the more similar the two planets became.

With the earth's oxygen cycle so rapidly disrupted by the interruption of photosynthesis, the entire planet became an almost continuous hypoxic zone. Only those with the knowledge and resources to construct self-sustaining habitats for themselves were able to survive. Regions of the world with disproportionally long days were able to provide themselves with oxygen through cultivated photosynthesis using highly productive genetically engineered flora, and typically fed themselves on protein synthesized from the stem cells of long-dead livestock. Others stayed close to the ocean, decomposing seawater through electrolysis for oxygen and breeding the heartiest of the world's few remaining insects for calories. Still others somehow partially adapted to the radiation, heat, and the atmospheric toxicity, mutating into aggressive cannibalistic clans of what were generally referred to as "the homeless" if they lived aboveground, and "subterraneans" if they stayed below. Although commerce developed between some communities, each pod system was a sovereign colony with its own laws, culture, traditions, and its own historical narratives.

But not all of humanity had been prepared to resign itself to countless generations of containment. As the planet was cast into shadow, not everyone believed that the only path forward was to poison and irradiate themselves into inert metal alloy shells. Although there were those who maintained that the end of all life on Earth had always been a question of *when* rather than *if*—that given even the most conservative estimates of habitable planets in our galaxy, planetwide extinction events had almost certainly already occurred billions of times without the universe ever seeming to take the least bit of notice—there were those who believed that millions of years of evolution and thousands of years of human culture and endeavor were worthy of preservation.

If humanity was entirely dependent on technology, and technology was entirely dependent on power, then the key to preserving humanity once again lay in solving the problem of renewable energy. Space-based Solar Power, or SBSP, was by no means a new concept, and had in fact already been successfully implemented several times. Before photovoltaic technology was finally cheap and efficient enough to prove once and for all that solar cells made far more economic sense on the ground than in space, several nations had successfully experimented with using solar collectors to generate power in geostationary orbit, convert it to microwaves, and transmit it down to rectifying antennas on Earth where the microwaves were converted back into electricity and fed into the nearest electrical grid. Although none of the satellites had functioned for years, the technology was both proven and, with a little reverse engineering, well understood.

Fortunately, the foundation for the perfect solution had already been laid. The only question was how much of *Equinox* could be converted into a massive SBSP station before the collapse of every government on the planet that had the technology and capability (or had commandeered it from the private sector) to make the project work. Enormous photovoltaic sheets needed to be unfurled along appendages on both Cancer and Capricorn sides of the rings, and tens of thousands of kilometers of cable needed to be run to carry current down the skyhooks, through the thick atmosphere, and into a new global electrical grid below. Before the Solar Age was so abruptly extinguished, few would have questioned the feasibility of converting the *Equinox* substructure into a planetwide SBSP; however, with every economic, political, and cultural institution on the planet in rapid decline, the project seemed increasingly unobtainable.

But completion of the transformation was never entirely the point. The goal of converting *Equinox* was less about stopping the demise of humanity and more about preparing for it—getting as much infrastructure in place as possible before governments and monetary systems and entire civilizations entirely collapsed. *Equinox* became as much a symbol as it was an intended solution; a multigenerational aspiration to provide whatever was to come next with a common objective worth living, fighting, and dying for; the closest thing left to spiritual salvation for an entire sentient and intelligent species who believed they had been forsaken by every one of their gods.

The original vision for *Equinox* was to make space equally accessible to all—to bring the entire planet together in scientific, economic, and cultural pursuit. However, instead of uniting humanity, *Equinox* eventually became the impetus for the ultimate in class division: speciation.

Most historians correlated the genesis of the Coronians with the eventual abandonment of the *Equinox* project. As nations continued to fracture, resupply missions slowed, then gradually stopped altogether, entirely deserting hundreds of scientists and engineers living inside the habitation modules. Some were able to return to Earth using what functional emergency reentry capsules they had, but replacement capsules were never launched, leaving the remainder to starve, asphyxiate, or devise quick and painless methods of suicide for themselves. Their pleas were silenced as ground communications were severed, and as all remaining resources were redirected toward increasingly brutal wars between what functioning civilizations remained.

But then one day something happened that nobody on the planet had anticipated—an event described by many as both a spiritual and a technological miracle: the lights came back on.

But completion of the transformation was never entirely the point. The goal of converting *Equinox* was less about stopping the demise of humanity and more about preparing for it—getting as much infrastructure in place as possible before governments and monetary systems and entire civilizations entirely collapsed. *Equinox* became as much a symbol as it was an intended solution; a multigenerational aspiration to provide whatever was to come next with a common objective worth living, fighting, and dying for; the closest thing left to spiritual salvation for an entire sentient and intelligent species who believed they had been forsaken by every one of their gods.

The original vision for *Equinox* was to make space equally accessible to all—to bring the entire planet together in scientific, economic, and cultural pursuit. However, instead of uniting humanity, *Equinox* eventually became the impetus for the ultimate in class division: speciation.

Most historians correlated the genesis of the Coronians with the eventual abandonment of the *Equinox* project. As nations continued to fracture, resupply missions slowed, then gradually stopped altogether, entirely deserting hundreds of scientists and engineers living inside the habitation modules. Some were able to return to Earth using what functional emergency reentry capsules they had, but replacement capsules were never launched, leaving the remainder to starve, asphyxiate, or devise quick and painless methods of suicide for themselves. Their pleas were silenced as ground communications were severed, and as all remaining resources were redirected toward increasingly brutal wars between what functioning civilizations remained.

But then one day something happened that nobody on the planet had anticipated—an event described by many as both a spiritual and a technological miracle: the lights came back on.

It was only a few kilowatts at first, trickling down through the Macapá terminal in Brazil, but it was more than enough to get Earth's attention.

Some of the abandoned *Equinox* engineers had not given up. Rather than resigning themselves to gradual and agonizing deaths—or ejecting themselves out into space from manually overridden airlocks—they focused all their remaining resources on collecting whatever energy they could and sending it down to the planet below. Compassion had not been enough to retain the interest and support of those on Earth. The only hope for survival that *Equinox* had left was leverage.

Global conflict gradually decreased as resupply missions resumed. Kilowatts became megawatts, and other terminals along the equator—sites that eventually became known as "plugs"—came online one by one. But this time, power was not sent down to Earth for free. When resupply missions were delayed, the communities that were rapidly coming to rely on *Equinox* were punished with blackouts. When payloads were not exactly as requested, the current to certain plugs was reduced, resulting in prolonged brownouts. The engineers who lived aboard *Equinox* never forgot that they had once been considered expendable by those on the ground, and they would never again allow themselves to be forsaken.

The experience of being abandoned in space convinced most technicians to return to Earth as soon as it was possible, but not all. During the fourteen-month period when Earth had halted all communications with *Equinox*, two engineers had managed to accomplish something that had previously been considered impossible: conception.

Although sections of *Equinox* were well shielded, it was assumed that radiation levels were high enough to keep sperm levels low, and to kill a zygote well before embryonic or fetal stages of development. Even with healthy sperm, fertilization was considered highly unlikely, both because of how sperm was thought to behave in zero-g, and because of certain achievement and retention challenges men tended to face in microgravity as a result of decreased blood pressure. Add to those factors the logistical challenges presented by weightlessness, and the chances of a successful off-Earth pregnancy had always been considered minuscule. However, minuscule was not zero, and if there was anything that life had proven itself capable of, probably trillions of times over billions of years, it was defying the odds.

History would always remember a little girl named Genevieve as the very first Coronian, and technically speaking, the very first alien. Life-support systems had never been installed in the inner ring, and by the time reentry capsules were once again available to rotate out station operators, Genevieve had lived in microgravity aboard the outer ring for so long that there was no way she could possibly survive the crush of Earth's gravity. Her bones, muscles, and ligaments would not support her, her heart was extremely weak, and having never known a serious pathogen, her immune system had not developed to the point where she could survive outside of a sterile environment. But Genevieve's parents would not leave her, and as though managing to accomplish the near-impossible just one time somehow permanently altered the rules of probability, it wasn't long before other babies who could never know the full force of Earth's gravity were born aboard *Equinox*, as well.

To those on Earth, it was unknown what a child born and raised in weightlessness looked like—how their skeletal structures and facial features and even their brains would form in the absence of one of the most constant forces life had ever known, and how all of the additional radiation they were exposed to above the atmosphere would alter their DNA. It was also unknown what additional genetic modifications the Coronians intentionally made to themselves over the years and the generations, and how they embraced and incorporated all the technology they had access to. However it was they had evolved and adapted—both deliberately and through chance mutation—to them, it justified reclassifying themselves as not just a new species, but an entirely new genus.

The relationship between *Homo sapiens* and *Caelestia sapiens* eventually stabilized, but in the same way that stars are stable. The constant pressure of nuclear fusion in the stellar core pushes against its own gravity until an equilibrium is achieved. What appears at a distance to be stability—perhaps even placidity—is in fact the sum of enormous and volatile competing dynamics that simply cannot remain in balance forever. The Coronians continued to provide energy to Earth as long as those on Earth continued to provide the Coronians with the resources they needed to maintain and expand *Equinox*, and to build an increasingly divergent civilization. But the one force that no apparent symmetry can withstand indefinitely is time.

The word "Coronian" was almost certainly derived from the term "corona," which is the superheated plasma atmosphere that extends for millions of kilometers in every direction from the sun's surface. Why the Coronians named themselves after this particular solar phenomenon was a matter of speculation. The corona itself is relatively stable and predictable, but occurrences known as CMEs, or Coronal Mass Ejections, are not. During solar maxima, these bursts of solar winds and magnetic fields are ejected above the corona as many as three or more times every day. When directed toward Earth, CMEs had been known to be responsible for sudden, long-lasting, and catastrophic power outages.

Those who studied the sun's corona understood that it was a vast and enduring force to be both respected and feared.

CHAPTER SEVEN

VACUUM SPHERE

AYLA SPENT THE FIRST SEVENTEEN years of her life in an archipelago of geodesic domes connected by underground passageways on the southern tip of Greenland. She and the other kids figured out how to fashion makeshift carabiners out of spools of solder and thin slices of discarded pipe that they used to connect old tires and inner tubes to chains suspended from the loading bay winches. From the second- and even third-story balconies of the docks, they launched themselves into what, to them, felt like an infinite void, soaring from rail to crane to gantry, proclaiming themselves Coronians amid the simulated weightlessness. Under the authority of the older kids, what started out as perilous but largely collaborative mischief invariably devolved into highly adversarial competition—games of chicken, ghost in the machine, and sharks and minnows—escalating in feverish crescendos of fierceness and violence and finally culminating in one of the many sickening accidents that still sometimes replayed themselves in Ayla's memory as she tried to fall asleep.

Until today, the loading bay swings were the closest Ayla had ever come to being airborne. She didn't exactly know what she expected from the experience, but she was surprised by the stability of the perfectly spherical airship known as the HMS *Beagle*. The gangplank that was laid out for her from the upper level of the Maldive Islands Spaceport was secured by bolts threaded through steel anchors and felt as solid to her as the siliconcrete deck she left behind. As she boarded the gondola, she immediately grabbed the rails to either side of the bulkhead, though she could detect no movement beneath her beyond what she attributed to self-induced vertigo.

Ayla knew that she was born for the ocean, and not the skies.

She was wearing dark synthetic polymer pants this morning along with a lustrous white top with red-accented sleeves that came partway down over her hands. The shirt's fitted hood was raised to conceal her black, chin-length, shaggy hair, and the ring was tucked away on the inside. She was not wearing her typical spaceport shocksuit today because the man who escorted her from the *Accipiter Hawk* to the HMS *Beagle* let her know—politely, though instantly—that it would not be permitted on the dirigible, and subsequently waited patiently on the dock while she went back and changed.

The man had some of the most interesting and exaggerated features Ayla could ever remember seeing. She was surprised when she finally admitted to herself that she found him strangely handsome despite such a distinctive appearance, and although he looked powerful enough to break human femurs with his bare hands, his disposition seemed entirely docile. Considering the nature of the meeting she was about to have, Ayla concluded that the man gave the perfect impression: professional and accommodating, but quietly austere.

Although she felt she should probably follow him in silence, she wanted to use the opportunity to see what she could learn about him—or more importantly, about men in his position. She wondered how much he truly understood about his condition, how much he was able to think for himself, and frankly, whether or not he was at all intelligent. She brought up the matter of the shocksuit, presented the theory she'd formulated while changing out of it that the airship used a flammable gas—probably hydrogen—in order to float, and therefore anything that could generate a spark was probably not a very smart thing to bring aboard. Instantly, Ayla regretted saying something that she feared the man would not comprehend, but was surprised when his response came without hesitation. If the airship's envelope were filled with hydrogen, he explained, any leaking gas would flow safely upward rather than accumulating inside the gondola where it could be inadvertently ignited. The same was true of other lifting gasses such as helium, ammonia, methane, neon, and nitrogen. Additionally, the gondola was electrically grounded, so it was unlikely that a spark would travel upward toward the envelope. All that said, the HMS *Beagle* did not use any of the aforementioned gasses. Instead, the airship in which her meeting was to take place was kept afloat by a complete lack of all gas—or rather, by a vacuum sphere. Lacking the mass (and hence weight) of the gas itself, a near-perfect vacuum produced approximately 7 percent more lift than hydrogen and 16 percent more lift than helium, making it more effective than any lifting gas could ever be. Historically, the problem with vacuum-sphere airships was that the structure required to resist the outside pressure imposed by the vacuum would end up being too heavy for the vacuum to lift—much heavier than a structure designed simply to contain concentrations of gasses such as helium or hydrogen. The envelope of the HMS *Beagle*, though, was a molecularly assembled, extremely lightweight, and atomically perfectly carbon-lattice sphere that got stronger the more outside pressure was exerted on it, thus easily supporting what was believed to be the very first—and possibly still the only—large-scale vacuum sphere airship on the entire planet.

With that, the man stepped humbly aside and allowed Ayla to precede him on the gangplank. She did her best not to appear as incredulous, dumbfounded, and embarrassed as she actually felt while she waited on the forward deck for the man to withdraw the walkway, then pilot the airship back up to its reserved position beneath the dome.

Shortly thereafter, Ayla was astonished once again as the room she was escorted to was as decadent a space as she had ever experienced. Underfoot was a magnificent and intricate starburst pattern pieced together out of various-colored grains of the closest material to real wood she had ever seen. There was a standing-height table in the center of the room—also seemingly wooden—that Ayla initially thought was designed to look like the random cross section of an irregular tree trunk, until she recognized the shape from Costa's nautical charts as the continent of Africa. The glass walls around her sloped outward so that one could lean forward and look out over almost the entire multitiered marketplace below, and the light coming in was both filtered and diffused so that the room had a warm and bright feel.

The office felt spacious, but more for its lack of furnishings than for its actual volume. Ayla judged it only a small fraction of the entire volume of the gondola, and couldn't help but wonder what else went on up there.

She believed the man standing on the other side of the desk was Jumanne Nsonowa. He was tall, thin, rigid, and easily the blackest man Ayla had ever seen—almost certainly pure African, if the pigmentation was natural. In startling contrast to the man's skin tone were bright white curling and looping tattoos that started below his eyes, meandered across his cheeks, and continued all the way down into his black silk dashiki, evoking both a primitive mask and a partial skull recovered from an ancient burial ground. Although he was facing her—even looking directly at her—he did not appear to see her. His hands were behind his back and his eyes glittered as though reflecting a spectacular pyrotechnic grand finale; however, Ayla knew that the photons did not come from an outside source, but from his contact lenses. The man's bald scalp bulged with an array of evenly spaced nodes that appeared to be joined by silvery subcutaneous filament.

Ayla was not sure she could bring herself to interrupt whatever it was the man was doing. She pulled her hood back simply to give herself something to do, and to create some commotion she hoped the man would notice. The glittering in his eyes gradually faded, and the way he cocked his head at her indicated that his attention had returned to the here and now.

"Ayla Novik," the man said with very careful enunciation. The tone of his voice fell somewhere between a cello and a double bass, and even in four short syllables, Ayla could detect the heavy African influence. "Welcome to the HMS *Beagle*."

"Thank you," Ayla replied. She tried to smile but was conscious of the fact that what she actually conveyed was probably much closer to bewilderment at her unfamiliar surroundings than true congeniality.

"I prefer to stand," the man declared, "but I will have a chair brought in for you if you would like to sit."

"No," Ayla said immediately. Allowing this man to literally look down on her even more than he already did would not be a very strong position from which to negotiate. "I prefer to stand, as well."

"Very good," the man said. He invited her to approach the table with a graceful gesture. When he placed his palms on the smooth, rich surface, Ayla saw that his wrists, hands, and fingers were tattooed in a manner similar to his face. She expected the surface of the table to illuminate with the man's workspace—perhaps even for a holographic interface to resolve into sharp focus—but the desk remained both analog and static. To all appearances, it was simply an intricately carved slab of lumber.

Ayla joined the man in the center of the room, and as he did not offer his hand, she likewise kept hers to herself. Her eyes involuntarily darted up to Nsonowa's scalp, then back down.

"It is a BCI," he explained. "A brain-computer interface. My grandmother was a pioneer in the field of neural interfaces." He examined her head, presumably searching for evidence of nodes of her own. "Have you ever tried one?"

Ayla shook her head. "I've seen them, but no, never tried one."

"It is primitive compared to what the Coronians now use, but I'm afraid that I am too old to adapt to new technology."

The man did not look to be much older than early to mid-forties, but it occurred to Ayla that these people were so far removed from her world that it was possible they aged at an entirely different rate. For all she knew, he might have been be sixty, eighty, or a hundred twenty. If the Coronians had found a way to stop the aging process, it was even possible that he could be functionally immortal. At this point in her life, Ayla considered herself pretty well traveled, but she couldn't begin to imagine the kinds of places and things this man had seen.

"I've been admiring your ship from below for years," she said. She knew praise was no way to preface a negotiation, but it was all she could think of to say. And the notion that she might be in any position to negotiate at all was probably delusional, anyway. She was on his ship—a guest in his exotic floating world—and she had no doubt that if there was a deal to be made here today, he would almost certainly be the one to dictate the terms. "I must admit, I never thought I'd actually get a chance to see it up close."

The man smiled in a way she could tell was well rehearsed. It seemed more tolerant than any genuine indication of warmth. "We are very pleased to have you on board."

"Do you mind if I ask you something, Mr. Nsonowa?"

"Please, call me Jumanne," the man said by way of consent.

"This table," she began, "and the floor. They aren't real wood, are they?"

"They are real wood, yes," the man told her. "But they are not *organic* wood."

"What do you mean?" Ayla asked. "What's the difference?"

"Do you know what a molecular assembler is?"

Ayla's eyes reflexively widened before she had a chance to check her reaction. "You have an assembler?"

"Indeed, we have several," the man said—pleased, yet somehow not quite arrogant. "That is how we are able to exist up here almost entirely autonomously."

"Which leads me to my next question," Ayla said. She gave the man a look that was both expectant and hopeful. Nsonowa nodded in a way that told her she had not entirely exhausted his patience just yet, but that she was one step closer. "Why do you live all the way up here? Why not just lease space in the port like everyone else?"

"I imagine it is for the same reason you make your home out on the sea," the man responded. "So I do not get my throat slit in my sleep. I think we both would agree that staying alive is well worth the trouble."

"So you don't live up here to get around local laws?"

The man's face went from pleasant to slightly circumspect. He took a brief moment to study her before responding. "To which local laws do you refer, Ayla Novik?"

"The local laws that prohibit human trafficking."

"Ah," the man said. His smile returned, but Ayla could tell from his eyes that its meaning had changed. "So now we are talking business." A few pixels illuminated on the periphery of the man's pupils, but he appeared to ignore them. "I assure you that we are subject to all the same laws up here as those below."

"Then how do you do what you do?"

Nsonowa regarded his guest for a moment as though considering where to start. "How familiar are you with the Maldive Islands Spaceport human trafficking statutes?"

"Familiar enough to know that what you do should get you banned."

"If that is what you think, Ayla Novik, then you have not read them carefully enough. You see, MIS defines human trafficking as the trade of *Homo sapiens* for profit."

"I hope you're not about to try to convince me that you don't do what you do for profit."

"Whether or not it is for profit is of no consequence," the man said. "What is important is that you and I are the only *Homo sapiens* aboard this ship."

Ayla looked at the man with overt cynicism. "What's that supposed to mean?"

"It means," the man said, "that the rest of my crew is *Homo neanderthalensis*, or what are commonly called Neos."

Ayla narrowed her eyes at the man. She pointed at the door behind her without turning. "Are you telling me that that man out there isn't human?"

"Theta *is* human," Nsonowa assured her, "and he *is* a man. But he is a man of a different human species."

"Theta?"

"It is his designation. Theta 1138. His version, followed by a sequential serial number."

"So the way you get around local laws is by cloning," Ayla stated. She didn't intend for her tone to be as accusatory as it probably sounded.

"Not I," the man said. He pointed a long, slender finger upward. "The Coronians do the cloning. I only do the negotiating."

"Why would the Coronians want to clone Neanderthals?"

The man touched his fingertips together in front of his chest. "The Coronians are not just interested in the *future* of the human species, Ayla Novik. They are also interested in the *past*."

"I don't understand," Ayla admitted as she shook her head. "If that man is a Neanderthal, why is he so . . ."

"Intelligent? Articulate? Civilized? Indeed, Theta is all of these things, and many more."

"Shouldn't he be more like a—I don't know—like a caveman, I guess?"

There was a touch of patronization in the man's smile. "The common perception of *Homo neanderthalensis* is very much untrue. They are not only more physically robust than we, but they also have a larger cranial capacity, which means that with the right education and training, they are capable of greater intelligence, even without neuroprosthetics."

Ayla looked at her host with poorly concealed skepticism. "If Neos are stronger *and* smarter than we are, then how do you . . ." She took a moment to search for the right word. "How do you *control* them?"

"A very good question, Ayla Novik." The man put his hands back down on the table. "You see, our Neos are cultivated without biological autonomic nervous systems. Their heart rate, respiration, digestion, salivation, perspiration—all of their automatic functions—are controlled by a neural implant, and that implant is controlled by us. Do you understand?"

Ayla took a moment to internalize what she was hearing. "I get that," she said, "but how does that help your clients?"

"Those who come to us seeking protection are fitted with a vital sign monitor calibrated to their Neo's implant. In order to keep himself alive," the man said, "your Neo must keep *you* alive."

"So what about things like . . ." She hesitated and looked at Nsonowa in a way that invited him to speculate as to what she was getting at.

"Sexual impulses?" the man offered.

"Something like that," Ayla said. "What would prevent *him* from enslaving *me*? As long as he kept me alive, he could do anything he wanted, right?"

"Our Neos do not produce standard testosterone," the man explained. "The properties that increase bone density and musculature are enhanced while the properties that promote sexuality are almost entirely eliminated. Our Neos are as close to asexual as it is possible to be."

Ayla nodded. She bit her lip and ran her finger along the horn of Africa. "What kind of money are we talking about here?"

The man's eyebrows went up. "Money?"

"Currency. Caps. Watts. What's today's market price for a Neanderthal clone bodyguard?"

The man lifted one side of his mouth in a curious smile. "You cannot pay in caps, Ayla Novik. You must know that the energy you possess originally came from the Coronians, so why would they ask for it back?"

"Maybe the caps are for you."

"I can assure you that those who work for the Coronians also have no need for caps."

"Then what *do* you and the Coronians have need for?" Ayla asked. "Are you going to tell me how this works, or shall I keep guessing?"

"Since the Coronians do not need power, what they ask for instead is a favor."

Ayla gave the man a long, narrow-eyed look that she knew conveyed her misgiving. "What *kind* of a favor?"

"That we do not yet know. But it will be a favor that you are in a unique position to deliver."

"Bartering seems a little old-fashioned for the species of the future, doesn't it?"

The man wagged his finger. "Not old-fashioned, Ayla Novik. *Opportunistic.* You see, the Coronians may have all the energy of the sun, but what they do not have is physical presence down here." He illustrated by drawing a circle on the table and dotting it in the center. "They can never touch the earth as we do, which means they can never shape and sculpt it as we can. They can only compel and coerce others into doing what they cannot do for themselves." He placed his fingertips back on the table and leaned forward. "Whatever they ask you to do, Ayla Novik, it will be an expression of their will, and for however long it takes, you will act as their eyes and as their hands."

"How will I know what it is?"

"We will contact you through the same channels you contacted us."

"When?"

"When we are ready."

The man's hands returned to their position behind his back, which Ayla inferred was an indication that their meeting had just come to an abrupt end.

"Well, they'd better make it quick," she said. "I don't know how much longer I can hang around this place."

"As you say," Nsonowa said, "it will be quick." His eyes began to fill with light once again. "Please wait on the forward deck. After we have docked, Theta will escort you back to your ship. It was very good to meet you, Ayla Novik. Be safe."

Ayla started to turn, but stopped. The man no longer seemed to be registering her presence. "Let me ask you one more thing," she said, but this time she did not wait for his consent. "How do you *really* control them?"

The sparkling in the man's eyes faded, which Ayla knew meant that he was about to give his immediate surroundings his full attention once again. He watched her for an uncomfortable moment, then raised his eyebrows. "Do you feel I was dishonest with you?"

"There's either something you're not telling me, or you're going to have a very bloody revolt on your hands any day now."

Nsonowa looked genuinely curious. "What makes you say that?"

"The fact that it wouldn't work on us."

"What would not work on us?"

"Controlling us with technology. Enslaving us. Eventually we'd find a way around it, or we'd die trying. There's a resignation in Theta that I've never seen in anyone strong and resourceful enough to survive in a place like this."

The man gave her a new kind of smile from his seemingly unending repertoire—the first one that was not all facade or formality or condescension. "I will tell you something, Ayla Novik," the man said. "I am not a cruel man, just as I can see that you are not a cruel woman. I am not a slave trader, and you are not a slave owner."

"That's a lovely sentiment," Ayla said. "So then what are the two of us doing here?"

"You are a frightened girl who must protect herself at any cost. And me—I am a scientist."

"So *that's* how you justify what you do," Ayla said. "What kind of scientist do you presume to be?"

"I am one of only a few paleogeneticists left. In exchange for negotiating on behalf of the Coronians, they permit me to study their genetic miracles." The man looked down at the table and used his finger to trace what she now knew was just an imitation of actual wood grain. "I am not always proud of what I do, Ayla Novik. But I am proud of what I have learned."

"And what is that?"

There was a thunderous concussion above them as the hammer slung another cartridge into low-earth orbit. The sound wasn't quite as loud as Ayla would have expected, as close as they were to the source, and she noticed that Nsonowa did not react in the slightest.

"I once believed that humans were not a robust species—that we were simply lucky to have survived all the ice ages and the droughts and the plagues. There have only been nineteen species of humans in seven million years, and until the divergence of the Coronians, only one species has survived." He looked from the table back up to Ayla. "But I now know that our near extinction was not because we are a delicate species, Ayla Novik. Indeed, it is quite the opposite. It is because there is only room for one species of human on the planet at a time. The answer to the mystery of why the Neanderthals were not successful, and why we were, is simply that they had the misfortune of coming into contact with us. The advantage we had over the Neanderthals was not strength, or superior intelligence, or more sophisticated social structures. It was not even our technology. Do you know what it was?"

"What?"

"It was simply that we were more willing to kill them than they were to kill us."

Ayla watched Nsonowa for a moment as she repeated the words in her head. "Is that why you think your Neos are safe?"

"What I think is that *we* are more unsafe than *they*. You see, I have learned many things about *Homo neanderthalensis*, but in studying them, I have learned even more about us. I believe there is a gene within us that will always find expression across the greater species. It is the gene that whispers to us that, unlike every other species that ever existed, simply surviving is not enough. It is the gene that compelled us to spread to every continent on the planet, even before the technology existed for safe travel—before we even knew what was beyond the horizon; the gene that gave us the passion to first leave our home planet and explore other worlds; the gene that has given us inspiration and curiosity and innovation and all the great works of art." He paused for a moment, and then his gaze intensified. "But it is also the same gene that has allowed us to slaughter countless other species, and even billions of our own. And it is the same gene that has finally brought us to the point of destroying almost everything we have ever built, and ever cared about, and ever loved. Do you know, Ayla Novik, what that gene is?"

Ayla watched the man in silence for a moment, then shook her head.

"The secret to the success of *Homo sapiens*," the man told her as a grin spread beneath his wild eyes, "has always been incurable madness."

CHAPTER EIGHT

PARALLELIZATION

THE ENTIRE THIRD DECK OF the *San Francisco* was devoted to transportation. Not the transportation of people, but of things. New shipments were lowered through the foundry's massive freight platforms, then hauled by electric forklift or liftsuit to the foundations of their destinations, where they were lifted back up through the basement level to the surface, maneuvered into place, and finally installed. Conversely, disused goods were lowered to deck three, then hauled to the far northeast corner where they accumulated in a massive chamber directly beneath City Hall. Technically the chamber was a mechanism known as a floodable airlock, but it was usually referred to simply as the rig's water-lock. When it was at (or frequently, quite a bit beyond) capacity, the deckmaster on duty called up to the bridge and scheduled a dump. Once the *San Francisco* had slowed to twenty knots or less, the chamber was sealed, flooded, and then its contents violently flushed. After being dispersed by currents, the *San Francisco*'s scrap, refuse, and waste eventually came to rest upon the place where it would spend the next several centuries decaying back into the elements from which it was originally assembled.

Deck three was two stories tall and almost a hundred eleven thousand square meters. The lights were bright, and overhead the steel trusses, fire suppression system, and the air ducts were all painted white. The smell was predominantly synthetic rubber and hot electronics from the vehicles that were in almost constant operation throughout the day, but it was also the deck where you started to get just a hint of the acidic tinge of stagnant seawater. Deck three was connected to the deck above it (which was completely dedicated to utility conduits) and the deck below (where mining operations started) by hexagonal, synthetic graphite supports which were close enough together to provide incredible strength and rigidity, yet far enough apart to allow the passage of even the most sprawling pieces of industrial equipment.

Although Luka was trained as an assembler, he was also certified on every class forklift and liftsuit on the rig, which meant—just to get away from the endless sterile rows of workstations where he spent most of his days—he frequently made his own deliveries. He had no interest in things like new boardroom furniture ordered by City Hall, or crates packed full of vapid and ephemeral novelties on their way to Union Square Mall, so those types of deliveries he left to the dispatchers. But an upgraded electrostatic scrubber for the Presidio, on the other hand, or a new low-impact hydromill for the rec center, or maybe even a replacement thirty-ton anchor winch was a different story. And absolutely anything that might bring him into contact with Charlie—perhaps the only friend Luka had left on the *San Francisco*, and hence, in his entire world—he was always quick to assign to himself.

Although most shipments were lowered from the foundry to deck three only to resurface a block or so away, some shipments continued to descend. All of the *San Francisco*'s deep-sea mining operations were launched from tubes and lock-out trunks below deck four. There was even a pressurized moon pool—an airtight chamber with an opening in the hull where water was kept at floor level by constant atmospheric pressure—through which equipment could be lowered and raised. Luka had never worked at those depths before, but thanks to Charlie, he had a pretty good idea of what went on down there. There was an entire fleet of remotely operated and semiautonomous submersibles capable of extensive underwater excavation; dozens of miners in industrial, power-assisted atmospheric diving suits equipped with rebreathers, and with enough structural integrity to be perfectly at home at the bottom of the Mariana Trench; several hyperbaric chambers where water rats were constantly cycling through their saturation rotations; and an old marine research habitat known as *Aquarius* lashed to the hull, waiting to be sold, traded, scrapped, or eventually converted into some kind of submersible mining habitat. He knew that there were networks of hydraulic pumps that collect material from the polymetallic nodules usually found around both active and extinct hydrothermal vents on the ocean floor, and filtering chambers that separated valuable minerals from the silt known as tailings, which was pumped back down to the ocean floor, far enough away not to be sucked back up again. And Luka knew that once the ore had been sufficiently isolated, it was carried topside to the Market Street Refinery via transparent pneumatic conduits that ran through the centers of several of the graphite hexagonal supports around which he and the other dispatchers currently maneuvered their mighty machines.

He parked beside the freight platform, dismounted, and approached the row of mechanical liftsuits. Mechs were preferable to forklifts as one descended farther into the bowels of the *San Francisco* and passages became increasingly narrow. Although operators usually couldn't carry nearly as much—and therefore frequently had to make multiple trips—the suits were far more nimble and maneuverable. And, of course, far more fun.

The first mechs on the *San Francisco* were clawed quadrupeds that were as comfortable moving sideways as they were back and forth, and therefore established the tradition of being named after various extinct species of crabs. Once the issues with weight distribution were solved with a new generation of gyroscopic sensors, all the quadrupeds were retired and replaced with more compact bipeds. While the current versions looked nothing like crustaceans, the naming convention remained.

From smallest to largest, they were known as fiddlers, blues, and kings. Fiddlers were little more than powered exoskeletons that provided prehensile appendages designed to interlock with the standard carbon fiber crates most commonly used for the transportation of goods both on the *San Francisco*, and in most broker posts. In addition to claws designed for grasping rails, fiddlers could also accommodate lightweight interchangeable tools such as plasma torches, variable torque saws, and small pneumatic hammer drills.

The most commonly employed mechs were the blues—so named because their surfaces were electrochemically blued like that of an old revolver, but with yellow-and-black-striped hazard accents. Blues provided about twenty-five times the lifting capability of a fiddler and accepted most of the same attachments in addition to a line of heavier tools like jackhammers, worm-drive diamond saws, and chain-driven trenchers.

Kings were seldom used anymore since their size obviated most of the advantages of using a mech over a forklift (and forklifts were both far easier to operate and more forgiving of pilot error). They could lift fifty times that of a blue—some claimed up to a hundred, if you knew what you were doing—and were much more like full vehicles than suits. Pilots ascended to raised cockpits via three generously spaced rungs, and were subsequently entirely enclosed by titanium alloy and silica cages.

Luka kicked the charging coupler out of the first blue in the line, swung up into the cockpit, and connected the harness across his chest. He picked up each of the mech's feet in turn, took a few experimental steps forward, then performed several exploratory stretches and maneuvers designed to imprint this particular machine's idiosyncrasies upon his muscles and brain. Although assemblers ensured that each component of a system was molecularly identical, Luka believed that there had probably never been a machine built that did not eventually develop its own distinct personality; quirks and charms that accumulated through the complex interplay of both use and disuse; a soul progressively imparted by everyone who ever operated it. Those who thought of machines as nothing but cold dead steel simply never learned how to imbue them with life; never felt the enthusiasm with which that force was accepted and absorbed and applied; never experienced the transcendence from simple tool to complex and integrated prosthetic.

The claws of Luka's blue mated with the rails of the first stack of crates and lifted them as easily as if they were all packed full of perfect vacuums. Luka stepped back and to his right until he was centered on the freight platform, then used the polymeth pad beneath his left thumb to instruct the lift to descend. There was the rotation of amber warning lights and the brief bray of the lift's klaxon, and then the floor began to descend.

Whenever Luka got this far down, he was always struck by how much of the *San Francisco* was unseen and unknown by so many of those who called her home—by the incremental devolution from a nanotechnological existence back to the age of mining and manufacturing. Although the entire rig was once a dark and gritty industrial city, deck one had become a gleaming metropolis beneath a perpetually bright white sky. Even utility deck two—with its neat lengths of bound optical fiber, warm bunches of power lines humming and buzzing through their thick gray insulation, postal tube exchange, sanitized aluminum airflow ducts, and methodical lengths of PVC—was clean and well organized with climate control, plenty of light, and comfortable access. But the farther down you went, the closer you got to the true heart of the city where there were hard hats, and cogs that glistened with lubricant, and tremendously powerful moving parts entirely indifferent to human limbs. Everything down here eventually corroded, no matter how resistant it was said to be, and by the time resources and priority trickled this far below sea level, there was never enough of anything.

From deck four down, the lighting was generally poor, and the floors were metal grate panels that rang when struck with boot heels. Below the panels were series of grooves and channels that directed seawater to low spots where drains carried it down through the dark to giant black and bellowing bilge pumps whose float switches brought them roaring to life several times a day. After two Metropolis-class rigs sunk when flammable liquid somehow made its way down to the lowest point of the vessel where its fumes were ignited by a single stray spark from an electric pump, all submersible equipment was updated with brushless motors.

The sight of Charlie standing beside the lift shaft struck Luka as immediately incongruous. Her hard hat was under her arm and her bleached-blonde hair was just long enough to point in every possible direction. She was tall and not particularly petite—a less secure girl might consider herself slightly overweight at Charlie's size—but in perfect shapely proportion, which was evident even through her heavy one-piece engineering suit. Luka couldn't remember her natural hair color, but her eyebrows were dark and her green eyes each carried a faint amber nebula beneath the floating circuitry of her contacts. When she looked up and saw Luka descending, she gave him her little-girl smile: perfectly pink gums, small white teeth, head slightly tilted, and bunched-up eyes. It was a look that induced in Luka an endorphin rush that he was every bit as addicted to as curious yellow.

Charlie's real name was Charlene. Charlene Abigail Talleyrand. Her parents—with whom she still shared a transportment—not-so-subtly guided her toward a career as a school teacher at Mission Dolores, which is probably exactly how she ended up as a water rat named Charlie. Charlie's adopted sister, Valencia—the one who was supposed to be a doctor running the entire Pacific Medical Center by the time she was twenty-five—became a grower at the Yerba Buena Gardens instead. For a short time, she was also Luka's wife.

Charlie radiated in a way that Luka knew almost everyone found infectious. Down here, she was an improbably perfect white bloom among ruins, and it certainly did not go unnoticed. One of the engine rooms was also on deck four and the engineers who ran it rarely missed an opportunity to accost Charlie whenever she was seen to be loitering. When the middle-aged man with the paunch and the goatee followed Charlie's gaze up and saw Luka inside the metallic carapace of the blue, his expression changed from convivial to subtly menacing. It reverted as his eyes returned to Charlie, after which he abruptly excused himself with an inaudible parting utterance.

As the lift halted, Charlie made a face at the giant stack of crates locked inside the blue's claws.

"What in the world did you bring me?" she asked Luka with a combination of curiosity and doubt.

Luka put the liftsuit into powered standby and released his harness. "It's your brand-new roverized mining drill," he said as he swung down out of the cockpit. "Custom assembled by yours truly."

The landing was empty now except for them, so they came together in an easy and familiar embrace, Charlie's hard hat pressed against the small of Luka's back. Luka was only slightly taller than Charlie, and when they separated, Charlie took the opportunity to inspect Luka's eyes.

"You look tired," she told him. "Have you been getting enough sleep?"

Luka shrugged. "Enough."

"From the looks of it, barely," Charlie said. "And something tells me you've been assembling more than just mining equipment."

"I didn't come down here for a lecture," Luka said. He gave her a thin smile, but his tone clearly signaled caution. "Where do you want these? Let's get this done so we can get some lunch. I'm starving."

Charlie looked back at the stack of crates. "What did you say it was?"

"An RMD. I have two and a half pallets upstairs. You guys seriously need to learn how to consolidate."

"An RMD? Are you sure we ordered it?"

"Who else would order a drill?"

"Did you check the manifest?"

"No," Luka said, "but there's usually not much mining going on topside, is there?"

"No," Charlie admitted, "but there's usually not much terrestrial mining going on down here. What would we do with a roverized anything? Is it even submersible?"

"I don't think so," Luka said. "I guess I hadn't thought of that. Can you check and see if you guys ordered it?"

Charlie touched the polymeth terminal beside the lift and began navigating.

"Look," she said. She touched the corner of the surface to make it visible to Luka, as well. "This is everything we have on order. Two new ADSes, some diamond bits, polymer depth charges, pumps, filters, tanks. All the usual stuff. No RMD."

"Then who the hell ordered it?"

"Don't know," Charlie said. "Why don't you check your manifest like you probably should've done in the first place?"

Luka gave his friend a prickly look. "Fine," he said. He touched the panel and Charlie's workspace was replaced with his. He opened up the permissions so she could follow along and began to navigate. When he found the right record, he leaned forward and read it again. "Shit."

"What?"

"It's supposed to be delivered to the Elephant Island Broker Post."

"That explains it," Charlie said. She bit her lip and thought it over for a moment. "Actually," she said, "that doesn't explain anything. Why would power brokers want mining equipment?"

"No idea," Luka said. "Maybe to trade?"

Charlie shrugged. "At least we figured it out before you brought the whole thing down here. Go stack it under the hangar and forget about it. It's someone else's problem now."

"Wait," Luka said. He continued navigating the manifest.

"What?"

"I don't think this is actually for the brokers."

"Why?"

"It's in too many crates."

"So?"

"So the more crates a shipment requires, the more you pay for delivery. This thing could have been packed in half the number of crates, and power brokers of all people would know that. If there's one thing they understand, it's how to save a few caps."

"How many crates is it?"

"Seventy-nine. It could have easily been done in half that. And the components are packaged so that each crate is almost exactly the same weight, which is completely impractical."

"Then who do you think it's for?"

Luka looked up at Charlie and his workspace blinked off. "This thing is packaged to go into orbit," he said. "It must be going to the Coronians."

"What would the Coronians want with mining equipment?" Charlie asked. "And if they did want mining equipment, why wouldn't they just assemble it themselves?"

"Parallelization," Luka said.

"What do you mean?"

"I mean maybe their assemblers are busy with other things. More important things. They probably have far more power than they have time, so they're outsourcing to us."

"Time for what? What do you think they're doing?"

"I don't know," Luka said. "But I can guarantee you one thing. Whatever it is, it's in their best interests rather than ours."

CHAPTER NINE

HONEYPOT

THERE WAS ANOTHER GAME AYLA liked to play on the docks of the Nanortalik Pod System, though this one she did not play until she was a teenager, and she always played it alone. She called it "stowaway" and the objective was to sneak onto as many ships in the port as she could, explore as much of them as possible, and get back off without being detected. Although she was not above liberating the occasional ration pack from the galley, or even some form of exotic trinket she calculated wouldn't be missed, the point was never to plunder. Instead, the game was entirely about stimulating her imagination— envisioning herself living aboard all the different types of ships. She imagined waking up in the top bunk of a cramped and narrow cabin; sitting shoulder to shoulder with her shipmates in front of a hot boxed meal at a long table in the mess hall; using a folding door to close herself inside a closet-size room and having to use a tiny stainless steel head with corrosion bleeding through white painted pipes. She loitered among bridges where she imagined herself learning to operate equipment as old as magnetic compasses, mechanical marine chronometers, and infrared sextants, and as modern and sophisticated as BCIs, PCIs (Prehensile-Computer Interfaces), shipmate AIs, and holographic interfaces. Below deck, she learned to identify several types of convoluted and arcane machinery, and in her mind, spent her days repairing propulsion and electrolysis systems, cleaning air scrubbers, and patching bulkheads with a high-pressure emergency adhesive guns. As she passed lockers of environment suits, she wondered what it would be like out in the open beyond all hermetically sealed walls, and to be able to carry your containment with you wherever you wanted to go.

She tried to envision the ports and other pod systems all the different merchant and cargo ships visited, and all of the interesting and dangerous things they inevitably encountered out on the open water. Her forbidden tours elicited an excitement that collected in the pit of her stomach and sometimes even traveled down to become almost unbearably erotic in their taboo.

Gradually Ayla's fantasies became as real to her as her own life, and almost equally important to her. She began writing them down as narratives in silicon-paper notebooks, recalling details from notes and footage captured with a polymeth tablet during her clandestine expeditions. The stories became a series that naturally came together into what she believed was the very first novel ever written in the Nanortalik Pod System. She spent months not only editing, refining, and rewriting, but building up the courage to give a copy of her work to her father. When she finally did, he immediately and wordlessly set the notebook aside while he finished eating a late dinner. It stayed there on the table for days, untouched, until Ayla grew to hate the sight of it. She still remembered very clearly the morning she walked by and noticed that it was missing, and then all the mornings that followed during which she waiting for her father to say something about it. Anything. When finally she asked him if he had read it, he said that he had, and then said no more, and that night, Ayla snuck onto a ship with the mysterious and evocative designation

Accipiter Hawk etched into her magnificent bow, and this time, she did not sneak back off.

She remained hidden in stowage for three days and was finally apprehended in the galley on the fourth while refilling her water canister and trying to locate rations. Her hair was long then, and it was matted and oily, and she had not changed her clothing since she'd boarded. The man who caught her spoke with an accent she did not recognize and positioned himself between her and the door. He watched her for a long time and when he smiled, Ayla could see that his teeth were eroded down to what looked like steely gray slivers. The man wondered aloud what he ought to do with her. He told her that stowaways had no rights or protections aboard the ships on which they were apprehended, and that they traditionally became the property of the man who found them. He was leaning against a shallow cooking surface, and when he pushed himself up, Ayla could tell that he was about to move toward her, but then he stopped when another man entered the room. The man was not as tall and was so boyish that Ayla was surprised to see the first man exhibit immediate deference. The smaller man's voice was as soft as his complexion as he introduced himself as Costa Verde, the captain of the *Accipiter Hawk.*

Ayla was fed and given poorly fitting but clean clothing, and she was assigned a private cabin right beside the captain's. Costa personally informed the rest of the crew of Ayla's presence, and told them that, since it was too late for them to turn back, she would probably be with them for a full circuit, but that he was sure that she would be treated respectfully, and as their guest. Ayla was encouraged to use the radio on the bridge to talk to her father before they were too far away, but she refused, so Costa raised him personally and reassured the man that his daughter would be returned healthy and unharmed on their next northern approach.

That night, Ayla could not stop thinking about the man in the room beside her. She wondered if Costa Verde was his real name, but then she wondered what a real name was anyway. Pod systems maintained meticulous census records and usually controlled their populations with great care, assigning everyone unique IDs, encryption keys, and cataloging their biometric signatures. But when your home was the space between ports and pod systems, there was nobody to track you, and your name was whatever you decided to tell people it was. Maybe names out on the sea were more real than those you inherited or were assigned long before the world even knew who and what you really were.

As the *Accipiter Hawk* continued her southerly route, Ayla learned all she could about the ship. She had the basics of navigation down in only a few days, and within a week, knew her way around the ship almost as well as any of the crew. The *Hawk*'s onboard computers were no more complex than her workspace back home, and she learned how the ship was steered and calibrated, and how to read the diagnostic metrics. At night, she recorded everything she learned that day and sketched the *Hawk* as well as she could from schematic renderings. The bow was a majestic bulbous sphere with the bridge's row of viewports appearing from the outside as a tinted visor. The shape not only gave the vessel great forward strength, but it reduced drag as it moved through the dense atmosphere at an average of twenty knots with top speeds closer to thirty-five. Ayla thought the *Accipiter Hawk* looked more like a ship that should be exploring the solar system or even the galaxy than endlessly circumnavigating the globe.

When they stopped at their first port, Ayla was not permitted to leave the ship. Despite her objections, the *Hawk* was sealed and Ayla was charged with what she interpreted as the mundane and rudimentary task of babysitting the vessel. She was sullen and irritable when the crew returned the next day until she saw the gift that Costa brought her. It was an old mechanical monarch butterfly that looked so real that Ayla almost could not accept that it was not alive. Its wings absorbed ambient light to power a simple radar system that helped it find safe surfaces to perch atop while batting its ornate wings, and a miniature spectrometer gave it a predilection for bright pastels. The toy was initially confined to Ayla's cabin until it eventually escaped and found its way onto the bridge, where it had made its home ever since.

But perhaps even more meaningful to Ayla wasn't what Costa came back with, but what he came back without. The man who had originally discovered Ayla in the galley was with them when they left, but not when they returned. Ayla decided not to ask about him, even when she was offered the chance to perform some of the man's bridge duties. She enthusiastically accepted, believing that becoming an official member of the crew would get her off the ship during future stops, but she underestimated the solemnity with which Costa took his pledge to her father. At every subsequent port and pod system, the routine was the same: the rest of the crew disembarked while Ayla was left safely sealed inside, alone with her temper and indignation.

Although she could not see the rest of the world with her own eyes, she nevertheless learned a great deal more about the way it worked than what she had been taught back home. She hadn't realized the extent to which what remained of humanity relied on the Coronians and their highly discriminative distribution of electricity. The primary industry on the planet was moving raw materials into orbit for which the Coronians paid in power while the rest of the economy was an exercise in dividing and subdividing that power among capacitors that could be traded for an almost unimaginably eclectic assortment of goods and services. But no matter how many layers deep the economy ran, there was simply no getting around the fact that the Coronians were the keystone—the keepers of the lifeblood on which all the technology that kept humanity alive depended.

Costa made the decision to skip several ports in order to get Ayla home sooner, and as soon as they were within radio range, the *Hawk* began hailing. Communications were unpredictable due to the movement of global radiation bands so the fact that they received no response did not concern them at first. But when they got to within a day of the southern coast of Greenland, Costa could no longer conceal his concern. Something was wrong.

Even though Nanortalik was Ayla's home, she remained on the ship once again as the crew disembarked and investigated. They returned in less than ninety minutes and Ayla could see just about everything she needed to know in Costa's expression. It was impossible to say who did it, or why, but thermal scans confirmed that there were no survivors. Costa told her that they had covered up the worst of it, and that he would take her back to say her good-byes, and to see if there was anything she wanted to take with her. Ayla thought about the notebook she left with her father, but decided that she did not want it back—that she wanted no artifacts or reminders or vestiges of her former life. The *Accipiter Hawk* was her home now. It had been her home for almost nine months, and it would almost certainly be her home for the rest of her life, however long or short that might be.

The next time the *Hawk* came into port was the first time Ayla disobeyed a direct order. Instead of remaining on the bridge, she followed the rest of the crew down to the primary airlock and began suiting up with the rest of them as best she could. Costa stopped inspecting his gear and watched the girl, but neither he nor anyone else intervened. Instead, he showed her what she was doing wrong, and helped her lift her air and power cartridge, and made certain it was properly seated. She was no longer their guest. Ayla was a permanent member of the crew now, and as such, she would have to accept not only additional responsibility, but also additional risk.

Costa later told Ayla that the Cape Spear Port off the eastern coast of Newfoundland would not have been his recommendation for her very first excursion. The port was a ramshackle collection of dry-docked vessels and shipping containers connected by poorly welded corrugated tubes. The crew wore respirators and kept a close eye on their radiation badges as they scoured the dim convulsion of shops and stalls for supplies. Although it was probably one of the worst ports Ayla could remember seeing, to her, it was also magnificent—second only to the *Accipiter Hawk* herself in its marvel. Although she was told multiple times to let the rest of the crew do all the talking, Ayla initiated several conversations, and even though she eventually attracted the attention of a group of men who had to be persuaded by Ayla's entire crew to seek amusement elsewhere, the majority of the people she interacted with were surprisingly warm and almost as starved for information and interaction as she.

The need for comfort over the loss of Ayla's home gave her and Costa the opening they'd both been waiting for, and it wasn't long before the room beside the captain's quarters was vacant once again, and remained so on the captain's orders as a buffer against the racket of an insufferably creaky bunk. Costa knew that the concept of marriage still existed in most pod systems and, offering a sliver of smoothed tungsten carbide pipe, proposed to her off the coast of Chile in the closest thing to a decent café that he knew of. In the ensuing ceremony, Costa used his own authority as captain of the *Accipiter Hawk* to declare himself and Ayla forever connected.

It was a little over three years and hundreds of stops later that Ayla, while on lookout, noticed something that neither she, nor the rest of the crew, had ever seen before. It wasn't particularly unusual to come across flotsam on the approach to ports—almost always useless garbage dumped prior to picking up fresh supplies—or at points out on the open sea where radiation winds converged, but to come across dozens of blips in entirely open and neutral water suggested a very recent catastrophe. The signature Ayla was able to get off the ship in the center of it showed that it was partially submerged, badly listing, and clearly taking on water. Its bilge pumps were completely silent and long-range scanners showed nothing threatening in the vicinity. Costa ordered that the *Hawk*'s reconnaissance drones be deployed to get a closer look at the both the ship and the carbon fiber crates that appeared to be finding their way out of the breached hold. The drones detected not a single heat signature or heartbeat.

The first crate they hoisted aboard contained weapons of a sort Ayla had never seen before. The crew inspected the long, angular rifles—sighting them and activating slides with a great deal of satisfying metallic clamor—though they lamented that there was no ammunition. The second crate contained chemicals and various forms of laboratory equipment. Both the name of the ship as recorded by the drones, and the ornate patterns of crosses painted on her bow, began to make sense. The *Resurrection* was posing as some sort of evangelical vessel, but was actually moving very high-value cargo between some decidedly un-Christian parties.

All nine members of the crew of the *Hawk* congregated on the bridge to deliberate their next move: pick up the rest of the crates and go, or approach the ship and check for survivors. When Costa called for a vote, the entire crew—including Ayla—voted for taking the crates and leaving since the drones detected no signs of life. But as he tended to do whenever a vote did not go his way, Costa reminded everyone that the *Hawk* was not, in fact, a democracy, and despite the general sentiment, ordered a cautious approach. If there was nobody alive, they would take every last crate and never look back. But the thing he prized most in his life—his wife—had come about not as a result of raiding and scavenging, but of putting the lives of people first, and he was not about to change course now.

Before Ayla could even ask, she was told that she would stay behind. The tone her husband used and the way he looked at her made her accept what she already knew was true—that she had no experience with, or training for, these types of excursions; that someone needed to stay aboard the *Hawk* to provide them with support; that if anything went wrong over there, she would only be a liability.

Ayla positioned the drones around the *Resurrection*, combined their feeds into a single interactive model, and put on a headset to monitor communications. Other than the boarding party, the ship remained entirely lifeless. It was a beautiful vessel, Costa reported. One of the most modern he had ever seen, and other than the fact that it was sinking, it appeared to be in very good shape. The crew began discussing the possibility of trying to patch her up enough that they could tow her to the nearest dry dock. The price they could get for a ship like that would probably be hundreds of times what it would cost them to repair it. One of the crew might have even suggested that they keep it and sell the *Hawk* instead, but Ayla wasn't sure because by that point, she had stopped listening. Something was bothering her—something about the crates they brought on board. She'd probably seen thousands of crates on the docks of Nanortalik over the years, and hundreds more since leaving home, but these were different. The holes in the bottom weren't right. And if they were vented, they should've taken on water and already sunk. She went down to the cargo traps where the crates were stowed and when she shone a light into one of the holes at the bottom of one of the crates, she instantly understood everything. She didn't know exactly how they worked, but she could tell they were miniature propulsion systems, and that the crates could be maneuvered and steered. The *Resurrection* was a honeypot— a situation intentionally staged to appear innocuous and even opportunistic, but whose purpose was to ensnare the unsuspecting, the overly confident, and the greedy. Or, in this case, the naively compassionate.

By the time she got back up to the bridge, the *Resurrection* had already evacuated its ballast tanks and risen up out of the water. Ayla could see from the synthesized video feed that the ship was perfectly intact, and she could tell from the thermal images that the entire boarding party was already down. The false-colored imagery was turning the eight shapes bluish and over a dozen new heat signatures were approaching from the stern having probably just emerged from a chamber designed to collect and store thermal radiation and to dampen acoustics. Ayla didn't know what else to do but try to raise her crew—warn them of what was coming; beg Costa to reply; plead for some kind of response from someone—but the only reply was unending dead air.

And then she heard the EEA—the electromagnetic emissions alarm—informing her that now she was the one being scanned. She thought about the weapons that they had just recovered and suddenly understood why there was no ammunition. There were other weapons aboard the *Hawk*, but she had no training, and would obviously be outmanned and outgunned. However, it wasn't the idea of dying that really scared her; rather, it was the thought of living. Depending on the resolution of their scans, they probably already knew that she was a woman, which meant they would almost certainly try to take her alive. And Ayla had seen and heard enough over the last four years to know now what men were capable of.

She realized she probably only had a few minutes to get the *Hawk* turned and up to top speed before she would not be able to outrun any kind of fast-attack crafts they might be able to launch, but she could not bring herself to leave her husband and her crew. She watched the blue dots grow colder still while the EEA continued to blare. That was the first time Costa spoke to her from inside her own head.

Ayla. You need to leave.

I can't.

You have to. Right now. I'm ordering you.

I can't leave you. I can't survive without you.

You can survive without me. You will. I promise. You have to go. Right now.

I need you.

You don't. You're strong.

I should have been there for you.

There was nothing you could have done. If you were here, you'd just be dead, too.

I'd rather be dead then be without you.

But then you wouldn't be able to do what I need you to do.

What?

Get revenge.

Ayla could see that the *Resurrection* was coming about. She touched the command screen to silence the alarm, selected all the drones at once, and recalled them with a single gesture. On the next screen, she started all the *Hawk*'s engines simultaneously, but before moving the slider all the way up to full ahead, she made sure the drones' images of the *Resurrection* were archived, and that her coordinates were recorded.

CHAPTER TEN

ROCK DRILL

THERE WAS NO ROOM IN Luka's transportment to store his sculptures, so the work he decided he did not entirely hate, he brought up to the roof. Although Millennium and Paramount Towers were identical in architecture, presumably for the sake of a more interesting and diverse skyline, the two buildings' roofs were finished differently. The top of Paramount Tower on the other side of the Embarcadero looked impossibly verdant as it was covered with rolls of synthetic sod—a sort of oxymoronic facsimile of a living roof—but the roof of Luka's building was surfaced with alternating arrangements of some kind of raised compost decking. He never asked for permission to convert the rooftop terrace of his transportment building into his own personal sculpture garden, but nobody ever told him that he couldn't. Like so many other things aboard the *San Francisco*, there seemed to be an unspoken agreement that yielded at least a temporary state of equilibrium.

He called the piece he just installed *Rock Drill*. It was a tall, slender figure—not quite human, but not entirely mechanical—mounted on an old, manual, tripodal drilling tool. At the end of its long neck, its visored head gazed with eerie indifference at something far off in the distance—something that could just as easily be sublimely majestic as gut-wrenchingly horrific—while its long alien fingers grasped and mindlessly operated the drill's crank. The creature's ribs formed a cavity inside of which was nestled the impression of some sort of perverse progeny: a limb-less fetus who would find no contradiction in a world as technologically inspiring as it was primally barbaric. The piece was mesmerizing and imposing and grotesque, and it was not so much the dramatic presence of the creature that was frightening as it was the suggestion of a world that could tolerate its existence.

Luka sat on the edge of the rail facing outward, his back turned on the new installation, his feet dangling. There was a configuration of stars—presumably consistent with the *San Francisco*'s current latitude and longitude—projected on the deep sapphire-blue canopy overhead, and the glass globe enclosing the Yerba Buena Gardens reverberated with the singing of the broods of insects inside. As he frequently did after installing a new piece, Luka wondered if it might be his last, and contemplated exactly what would happen if he were to scoot himself forward, one centimeter at a time, until his entire body was fully off the rail, suspended above the short drop to the slopping facade below, his arms quivering under the strain, pinpricks of perspiration forming on his scalp and back. And then he imagined the sudden rush of air past his ears after letting go.

The silica and microlattice facade of both Millennium Tower and her sister tower, Paramount, was pitched at enough of an angle that he would slide down it all the way to the soft silicone sidewalk below, but steep enough that there was no way he could generate enough friction to stop himself. In fact, he would continue to accumulate momentum the entire way down. The fall itself probably wouldn't kill him, but he would likely die soon thereafter of his injuries since the channels that held the silica panes in place were sharp enough that the effect would not be unlike that of sliding down a monumental, forty-two-story cheese grater. By the time he got to the bottom, Luka guessed that roughly 20 percent of his body mass would probably be gone. Or not so much gone as simply no longer attached to or inside of him. He would land with one side of himself filed down like an acorn rubbed flat against a sidewalk, then lie heaped at the base of what would appear to everyone aboard the *San Francisco* to be a somehow morbidly triumphant giant red paint stroke flung up the entire side of the building.

That, Luka realized, would be his final installment.

There was no telling how long it would remain there—drying, absorbing, curing—as the City Council debated and argued over the best way to remove it. Eventually, the crane behind City Hall would come crawling down Pacifica, turn on Sunset, and park itself in front of Millennium Tower for the week or so that it would take for a specially selected maintenance crew to scrub blood off the windows and pick the dried flesh, bone, and hair out of the panel frames. But it was highly unlikely that they'd be able to get it all, and a few unlucky residents would probably have their views forever spoiled by pink smudges or darkened brain tissue or shards of cartilage. Because there was no weather beneath the massive composite-weave dome, such macabre blights would probably remain there for as long as the *San Francisco* managed to remain afloat.

This, in retrospect, was almost certainly why Val had chosen the refuse chamber beneath City Hall. Nice and clean. She left no note, and of course there was no body, so had it not been for surveillance footage, it was very possible that her disappearance would still be a matter of rumor, speculation, and eventually legend. The investigating authorities tried to convince Luka that it had been an accident; that better safety measures should have been in place; that the fear and panic with which she'd tried to escape from the waterlock after it was sealed and started flooding—and her pleas and whimpering as she stole her final breaths from the diminishing air gap just below the ceiling—were proof that it was simply a tragic industrial accident. But Luka had seen the footage himself—all of it—and there was nothing accidental about how she opened the waterlock, set a timer, then calmly stepped inside and sat down serenely and meditatively at the edge of the drain to wait. Yes, she eventually beat and scratched her hands and fingernails bloody against the sealed doors, and screamed and pleaded for someone to help her, but that was only because she'd changed her mind after it was too late. That was nothing more than the seemingly paradoxical reaction of a more primitive region of her brain to what a more modern and sophisticated region had successfully and irrevocably premeditated. Luka knew for a fact that his wife very intentionally committed suicide, and he also knew exactly why.

There were two memories of Valencia that Luka knew he would never forget. The first was her trying to contain her excitement when she sat him down on a plastic bench in the Embarcadero beside a cricket match and confirmed what he had already figured out: that she was pregnant. The second was when she informed him, flatly, that the baby was gone. This Luka had also already figured out, but what he did not understand was her reaction. He was looking for disappointment and devastation in her expression—tears in her big Spanish eyes, quivering in her full seashell-pink lips, defeat in her normally tall and confident posture—but what he found instead was fear, and to an extent he hadn't realized was possible until that day, pure and profound regret.

The baby had not been lost, Luka realized. Valencia had given it up.

The Coronians traded for whatever they could not assemble themselves, which primarily came down to two things: raw medium to run their assemblers, and unique genetic material with which to assemble themselves. It was believed that the entire Coronian population was intentionally sterile and did not propagate so much as expand through deliberate genetic experimentation. Some even said that they had cured the disease of aging and simply lived as long as they were considered productive or useful before finally being judged obsolete and euthanized by a more modern and advanced generation. However it was that they passed in and out of existence, they seemed to have retained an ironic and almost romantic appreciation for human genetic variety, probably due to the relatively limited gene pool from which they originated. A healthy human fetus could be placed into stasis during transport, and remain so for as long as it took to fully acclimate to zero-g, and then it could either be modified before its development was allowed to resume, or simply harvested for whatever genetic value it contained before being discarded. In return, the mother back on Earth received as compensation an even gigawatt of power—easily enough for two full lifetimes aboard a rig like the *San Francisco*.

Although the rooftop access door floated inside electromagnetic tracks and therefore slid open with neither friction nor sound, it was in desperate need of recalibration—probably from being whacked repeatedly by Luka's sculptures—and as a result, it bounced against its rubber backstop. Luka shifted on the edge of the rail, pressing the backs of his dangling legs securely against the low wall beneath him. He listened to Charlie's boots against the hollow decking until they halted in what he judged to be rough proximity to his newest work.

"Oh my God," he heard her say. "This is . . ." She was quiet for a moment, presumably trying to make sense of what she was looking at. "This is *bizarre*."

Luka did not respond. He looked off over the gardens as though he were still alone. As obsessed as he was with his sculptures, for some reason he found that they were also usually his least favorite topic of conversation.

"*And* amazing," she added.

Under the best of circumstances, Luka did not take compliments all that well. And in this particular circumstance, he wasn't sure whether he was being complimented or placated. The only appropriate response seemed like none at all.

"Are you happy with it?"

"I don't know," Luka said. "I guess."

"Where did you get the drill?"

"Found it in the waterlock."

"What were you doing in the waterlock?"

"I'm a forklift operator," Luka said. "Sometimes I go into the waterlock."

"Right," Charlie said. "Sorry." She reached out and touched Luka's arm. "And I'm sorry I said it was bizarre. It's brilliant. I honestly think this is one of the best things you've ever done. It just surprised me, that's all. Which is a good thing, right? How interesting would it be if it didn't surprise me?"

Luka spun around on the rail and looked again at his sculpture. "It *is* bizarre," he said.

Charlie turned and hopped up on the wall beside him. She was coming from home rather than work, and although she'd showered, her nails were still dirty. In fact, about the only time Charlie's nails weren't dirty was when she was coming off saturation rotation: weeks spent inside compression and decompression chambers where there wasn't much to do but eat, sleep, and watch videos. Otherwise, Charlie's fingernails were perpetually stained with a variety of substances usually collectively referred to as grime—both beneath the quick and around the cuticles—contrasting sharply with her delicate pallor and white-blonde hair. It was one of Charlie's many idiosyncrasies that Luka loved. Or maybe what he actually loved was the fact that she never seemed to care.

She turned her head and looked at him—peered carefully into his eyes. Luka knew what she was looking for, and that she'd found it. The change in her expression was subtle: a combination of disappointment and sympathy.

Luka watched her for a moment, then began leaning toward her—moving his face close to hers. Charlie did not move her head, but her hand came up between them and landed gently on his chest.

"What?" Luka said.

Charlie shook her head. "Not like this."

"Not like what?"

"Luka, I'm not her."

Luka leaned away and narrowed his eyes. "I know you're not *her*," he said with distinct acrimony. "I'm very aware of the fact that she's dead and you aren't."

"That's not what I mean."

"Then just say what you *do* mean, Charlie. I'm so sick of this. I don't know what's going on between us."

"I mean that it's too soon."

"It's been over a year."

"Since she died," Charlie said. "But not since you've accepted that she's gone."

Luka looked away from her and shook his head. "Forget it," he said. "I don't want to talk about it. For once, I'd like something to not be about her."

"That's exactly my point," Charlie said. "I'd like that, too. But everything *is* still about her, isn't it?"

"I'm sitting next to *you*," Luka told her. "She's gone. You're here."

Charlie let a moment of silence pass between them. "Luka," she began, "you know how I feel about you, but I don't think either of us really knows how you feel about me. I don't want to just be another substance to take your pain away."

"I said I don't want to talk about it anymore."

Charlie nodded. She looked up at Luka's new sculpture, then looked around at his other installations: two amorphous figures with tendrils writhing between them, either drawing them together or keeping them apart; a man staring blankly at the sky while wrenching his chest open and revealing it to be eerily empty inside; an androgynous figure melting into a puddle, grasping in futility for unseen salvation; a tiny forgotten child—hands politely folded, head submissively bowed—sitting quietly and alone on a shelf hung on one of the walls enclosing the access lift.

"I didn't come here to argue with you," Charlie said.

"Then what did you come for?"

"To talk about the RMD."

"I didn't read the fucking manifest," Luka said. "Christ. I'm sorry. It won't happen again."

"Not about that," Charlie said.

"Then what?"

"I think it might be proof."

"Proof of what?"

"Of what you've always said about the Coronians."

"I've said a lot of things about the Coronians. What specifically?"

"That they're just using us," Charlie said. "And that when they're done with us, they're just going to discard us and leave us all to die."

Luka smiled. "How does a piece of mining equipment prove all that?"

"Do you still think it's going into orbit?"

"The only reason I know to package something up into that many crates is so you easily distribute the weight, and the best reason to be able to distribute the weight that precisely is if it's part of an orbital payload."

"Right," Charlie said. "So what would the Coronians do with mining equipment in orbit?"

"I have no idea."

"Well, think about it a second. What's the simplest possible answer?"

"I don't know. Maybe they're going to trade it. Or maybe they just want to see how it works. For all we know, it's not going into orbit at all. Maybe the brokers just need to transport it on a bunch of small cargo vessels for some reason. We really have no idea."

"You're just making excuses."

"Excuses for what?" Luka asked her. "I'm not even sure what we're talking about."

"We're talking about not seeing something that's staring you right in the face. Listen to you. You're inventing all these ridiculous scenarios just to avoid the obvious."

"What did I say that's ridiculous?"

"Do you really think the Coronians need us to show them how a mining drill works? Or that the brokers are going to sell it to someone who owns a fleet of cute little rowboats?"

"Charlie," Luka said with exasperation, "can you please just say what you came here to say?"

"I want to hear *you* say it. Start at the beginning. Why would an RMD be divided up into almost eighty crates of equal size and equal weight?"

"Again," Luka said, "to make them easier to put into orbit."

"OK. And who in orbit would want an RMD?"

"Absolutely nobody."

"Well, who are the only ones up there to receive it?"

"The Coronians."

"And what would the Coronians do with terrestrial mining equipment? Simplest answer. Throw away all your assumptions for a second, and just give me the simplest possible answer to that one question."

"I guess they'd want it to mine."

"Exactly," Charlie said. "To mine. Now what's up there to mine?"

"I have no idea," Luka said. "The moon?"

"What else?"

"Asteroids, I guess."

"There you go. The moon and asteroids. Now why would the Coronians want to start doing their own mining when they have us to do it for them?"

There was now more revelation in Luka's tone than resistance. "So that they're not dependent on us anymore."

"Right. And why wouldn't they want to be dependent on us? The relationship has worked out pretty well so far. What do you think is about to change?"

Luka turned his head and looked at Charlie. "We're about to run out of resources."

"And what happens when we run out of resources?"

"We become worthless."

"And then what?"

"No more power."

Charlie nodded. "No more power," she confirmed. "And we already know what happens to everyone when the power goes out."

CHAPTER ELEVEN

OMICRON

As soon as Ayla had adjusted to being alone on the *Hawk*, she had to get used to sharing it again. But this was a very different kind of sharing than what she was used to with her former crew since she still frequently felt like she was alone. Omicron's cabin was the farthest one from the captain's quarters, and he had a tendency to move about the ship like a tremendous, hulking ghost. Ayla couldn't even recall hearing him so much as pass by her door, which—considering how thin the ship's inner walls were and how massive her new Neanderthal shipmate was—struck her as somewhat remarkable.

It also turned out that Omicron was as self-sufficient as he was unobtrusive. He did all his own cooking and was meticulous in his self-care. Although his clothing appeared chosen primarily for function and utility—mostly one-piece suits composed of breathable, resilient, and tiny elastic hexagonal patches that fit well beneath environment suits—it was always fresh and clean, and the odor Ayla smelled in the breeze when he moved deferentially past her was nothing like she expected to be left in the wake of a Neanderthal. In fact, although there wasn't much superficial resemblance between Omicron and Theta, they shared the same rugged handsomeness, and both gave the impression not of an entirely different species, but of an uncommonly fine specimen of her own.

Ayla gave Omicron access to all the weapons aboard the ship. Since his life was tethered to hers via an encrypted high-frequency radio signal—and since the reality was that there wasn't much Ayla could do anyway should Omicron decide he'd rather kill them both than remain in Ayla's service—she concluded she might as well provide him with a quick and painless way of doing it. But so far, the giant Neo never presented himself as even the slightest bit threatening—not even intentionally imposing—and the weapon he wore strapped to the outside of his thigh only made Ayla feel even safer with him around. Omicron had chosen a lithe pistol that, to Ayla, looked a lot like an adhesive gun for patching breached hulls, but rather than being loaded with a tube of silica gel and a magazine of vulcanized rubber plugs, it accepted high-pressure cartridges of hydrogen disassociated from seawater, and could fire any type of caseless projectile of the correct caliber from scored and frangible rounds designed to deform and fragment rather than pierce bulkheads, to a heavy chunk of depleted uranium capable of sending entire ships to the bottom of the ocean.

Omicron spent most of his time on the bridge, and in the ten days it took them to cover the seven thousand kilometers between the Maldive Islands Spaceport and the coast of Antarctica, he became more of an expert on light cargo vessels—and specifically the *Accipiter Hawk*—than Ayla would probably ever be. Not only did he run the entire ship, but he also made several repairs and optimizations, many of which hadn't even been identified by the onboard diagnostic subsystems yet. He even took apart Ayla's mechanical monarch butterfly one morning and reassembled it, somehow entirely reversing the lethargy that had gradually accumulated over the years, and then positioned several brightly colored perches about the bridge to keep the insectoid stimulated and engaged.

The *Accipiter Hawk* had become as much Omicron's home now as it was Ayla's.

Although the concept of ownership in the context of another human being—irrespective of species—still did not sit right with her (and almost certainly never would, she believed), Omicron was technically only on loan to her. After Ayla sent Jumanne Nsonowa a summary of the *Accipiter Hawk*'s capabilities, it only took him about ninety minutes to get back to her with a proposal that she was surprised to find more than fair. In exchange for one of his most recent generation Neos (and the life-monitoring "vitaline" she now wore on her left wrist that was calibrated to Omicron's autonomic implant), Ayla agreed to attempt to locate at least one uncharted pod system and transmit its coordinates to Nsonowa. Once the pod system's location was verified, Nsonowa would forward the coordinates to the Coronians, then permanently delete his copy of the encryption keys that still gave him access to Omicron's implant, empowering Ayla to do with Omicron whatever she saw fit. Of course, there was nothing really compelling Nsonowa to uphold his end of the bargain, but assuming both he and the Coronians wanted to continue to extend their influence to corners of the globe they otherwise could not, it was in both of their best interests to not only avoid a bad reputation, but to actively cultivate a positive one.

This was the highest up on the energy chain Ayla had ever done business, and she was very much looking forward to getting back down into the more familiar and comfortable territories of transportation and trading. She'd always found pretty much everything about the Coronians to be eerie, and generally preferred not to give them much thought at all; however, she couldn't help but find their interest in rogue pod systems curious. There were dozens of registered pod systems all over the globe participating in what was usually referred to as the capacitor economy—markets based, in one way or another, on the universal currency of power—but there were also an unknown number of pod systems that were either self-sufficient, or that collaborated with one another, forming partially or even entirely independent networks. Since most of them generated their own power through various nuclear technologies, it was generally assumed that, in order to mask their radiological signatures from raiders, they were located deep inside global radiation bands like the almost three-thousand-kilometer-wide stream that engulfed both the South Pole and most of the continent of Antarctica.

Nsonowa said he would leave it up to Ayla and her new partner to devise their own methods of unveiling these hidden populations, though he did offer them some advice: They should keep in mind that the vast majority of these systems were doing everything in their power to remain undiscovered, and that obscuring themselves in clouds of radiation was just the beginning. He had heard stories of entire pod systems living under totalitarian regimes—dystopias enforced through violence, intimidation, and punishment, or kept stable through complete technological dominance. He had heard of bounty hunters in these regions capturing runaways, who they then sold back to the pod systems from which they escaped, and of human sacrifices to groups known as subterraneans and the homeless, who subsisted primarily on uncooked human flesh. But perhaps the most disturbing conditions he was aware of were not related to physical oppression, but rather a form of psychological tyranny. According to Nsonowa, there were entire generations who grew up with no idea of who and what they were—or even *where* they were—their realities meticulously constructed to make them prisoners of their own minds, beliefs, and, perhaps worst of all, their own pride. The most effective prisons, Nsonowa explained to Ayla, were those we could not even see, and therefore did not even realize existed.

Since all it took was for one of these captives to learn the truth about his or her existence to endanger the well-established power structures designed to contain them, such communities would not easily reveal themselves. Attempting to locate or communicate with those in control would be futile, and in some cases, might even prove fatal. Their best bet was to try to reach out to the desperate or the dispossessed—those willing to tear down everything they had ever known in order to expose what had been done to them. If they could somehow be reached—and according to Nsonowa, it was inevitable that these people existed—they would likely need medical attention, and would almost certainly be looking for safe passage for themselves and for their loved ones on a ship exactly like the *Accipiter Hawk*.

The message that Ayla and Omicron broadcasted as far into the Antarctic radiation band as their transmitters permitted promised both. It was delivered in an articulate, synthesized female voice with an elegant and melodious British accent.

If you can hear this broadcast, you are inside the southern Antarctic radiation band. Radiation exposure is extremely dangerous and must be treated as quickly as possible. If you believe you have been exposed to dangerous levels of radiation, you can expect the following symptoms . . .

Less than fifty rems: minor symptoms including a temporary decrease in red blood cell count. Fifty to one hundred rems: decreased immunity, temporary sterility in males, and mild to severe headaches. One hundred to two hundred rems: nausea and vomiting for a twenty-four-hour period followed by ten to fourteen days of fatigue. Women experience spontaneously terminated pregnancies or stillbirths. Fatality rate of ten percent if untreated. Two hundred to three hundred rems: seven- to twenty-eight-day latency period followed by bleeding of the gums and nose, hair loss, fatigue, nausea, and the breakdown of intestinal tissue. Untreated, death is imminent.

Most levels of chronic and acute radiation sickness can be treated, and many genetic mutations can be reversed. We have an onboard hospital, food, clean water, and a nineteen-percent oxygen atmosphere. We can provide safe and free passage to Sakha, South Station Nord, New Elizabeth, and the Hammerfest pod systems. If you register one thousand rems or less, please hail us immediately on the following frequency: two-five-nine-point-seven megahertz. If you can hear this broadcast, we can reach you. This message will repeat.

It was on the second day of continuous broadcasting that Ayla finally expressed to Omicron her surprise that the Coronians took such an interest in rogue pod systems. Her impression of those who lived in orbit had always been that they were cold and calculating, and that their only interest in what they referred to as "Earthbound" was exploitation in order to obtain the medium they needed to run their assemblers. She wondered why they were suddenly so interested in the wellbeing of the subjugated and the oppressed. Omicron lowered his prominent brow in evident confusion. The Coronians' interest in unregistered pod systems was not altruistic, he assured her. Pockets of self-sufficient communities were a threat to their power and dominance. If humanity no longer needed the power supplied by *Equinox*, the shipments of raw materials would stop, and the Coronians would almost certainly eventually perish. This was a lesson that all Coronians knew well, and in fact was the very essence of their creation myth. Whatever pod systems the *Accipiter Hawk* happened to discover would not be liberated, Omicron explained. Whether it was now, or at some point in the future when the Coronians judged them too much of a threat, they would almost certainly be eliminated.

The situation in which Ayla had gotten herself embroiled, and the types of people she was now indebted to, suddenly became appallingly apparent. She felt incredibly ignorant and embarrassed for not having seen this from the beginning—for not realizing what she was openly and willingly agreeing to. Costa would have never let her do something like this—never permitted a meeting between her and a man like Nsonowa, and certainly never agreed to his terms. But as naive and vulnerable and victimized as she felt, there was something much worse just under the surface. It was not Costa or her crew that she lamented right now, or the realization that she had joined the lowest ranks of humanity as a slave owner, or that she was possibly about to become a willing participant in what was effectively genocide. Instead, what came into unexpected and terrifyingly sharp focus right at that moment was the truth about what had happened to her home.

CHAPTER TWELVE
FERROFLUID

LUKA'S TRANSPARTMENT WAS OPTIMIZED FOR sleeping—or, more specifically, for being gently awakened. The polymeth walls gradually brightened, blending billions of subpixels into serene sunrise hues, and the filament-infused silicone tiles were warmed with forced electrical resistance so as to ensure Luka's bleary-eyed shuffle from the coziness of his bed all the way to the bathroom was as homeostatic as possible.

Before Luka was married, he slept on a standard-size futon that, during the day, folded up flush into a perfectly sized recess in the wall by the window. Shortly after Val moved in, she conducted a thorough spatial appraisal and declared that far too much precious volume was being devoted to the act of sleeping and not nearly enough to closets. The next time Luka worked a double, Valencia had the futon replaced with shelving, multiple levels of clothing rods, a second shoe rack, and two adjacent floor-level twin-size drawers that, when activated, extended into telescoping platforms on top of which interconnected silicone tubes unfurled and filled with your choice of air, water, or a firm but comfortable soluble gel. In the morning, when deactivated, the mattresses were bled, drained, or flushed, the platforms retracted, and the entire system neatly compressed and stowed in well under sixty seconds.

Initially, Luka felt compelled to disavow such opulence, and frequently waxed nostalgic for the simplicity and austerity of his bachelorhood. However, it wasn't long before he was honing his own personal sleep profile—making microadjustments to hydrodynamic pressure, temperature, and even pulsation frequency—and feeling better rested than he could ever remember feeling before. And try as he might to validate his assertion that the material could not possibly hold up to the rigors of their intimacy, not a single leak was sprung. In the end, he attributed both the robustness and the general effectiveness of the technology to its masterful assembly.

The floor was warm beneath Luka's feet as he stood and touched the panel that initiated the collapse of his half of the sleep system. Since he was alone, he did not bother to close the soundproof pocket door before pivoting the plastic commode down from the wall, dispelling a night's worth of curiously yellow urine into the hydrophobic receptacle that repelled the fluid toward and down the drain, and then kicking the fixture back up with the ball of a bare foot. He washed and sanitized his hands in the basin and, while brushing his teeth, used the polymeth surface above the mirror to begin breakfast preparation. His toothbrush—well aware of the time—was in morning mode, so there were fewer ultrasonic emissions attempting to dislodge food particles and stubborn plaque deposits, and more antibacterial additives to combat pasty morning breath. His shorts went directly into the waterless ultraviolet sanitizing machine (no sorting), which would automatically start once it reached capacity, and since he was the only one who used his shower, the heads were already adjusted for his preferred temperature, pressure, and dispersion pattern. Personal care products were automatically introduced into the soft, mineral-free stream at just the right moments, and as soon as the water stopped, the cyclonic body driers started, the air from which was lightly infused with delicately fragrant atomized moisturizer (another indulgence Luka owed to Valencia's discriminating predilections). Infrared sensors in the corners informed the heating elements of precisely how to adjust to Luka's body's logarithmic response to the evaporative cooling process in order to ensure that he remained warm, but did not perspire.

Today, Luka did not dress for work. Rather than the cargo scrubs that went well beneath an anti-electrostatic microfiber coverall, he put on a pair of loose nano-fabric slacks, a V-neck T-shirt, and a dark synthetic cardigan. A warm cup of sweetened and caffeinated soy porridge awaited him in the kitchen that he absently spooned into his mouth while reviewing the talking points spread out on the polymeth surface before him: the ridiculous number of crates the roverized mining drill was divided across; the obvious attempt to keep the weight of each crate almost exactly equal; the basic principles of rocket stability, which Luka only understood well enough to cite the importance of being able to establish a precise center of gravity. And, perhaps most alarming, all the additional similar orders he and Charlie recently uncovered.

Luka's commute to work typically took him along the west side of the Yerba Buena Gardens on Mariposa, then across Mission Street to the foundry. But today, he followed a more elusive route. He exited from the back of Millennium Tower onto Alemany, turned left on Pacifica, and continued to hug the perimeter of the rig all the way to the other side of the *San Francisco* until he reached the opulent and bulbous structure of City Hall.

Even though the air barely so much as stirred beneath the vast dome, City Hall appeared to have been designed principally for aerodynamics. It reminded Luka of a high-speed hydrofoil helmet. Such conventions as straight lines and right angles must have been considered personal affronts to the architects—or, more likely, to whatever sets of parameterized engineering algorithms the architects ultimately took credit for. It was eleven generously spaced tiers of swooping silica over a dramatically bowed microlattice frame intended to convey bravado, but—to Luka's personal aesthetic—came across as much more of a pathetic attempt at some form of compensation. As if the general anatomy of the structure weren't conspicuous enough, it was recently crowned by an especially garish rendition of the city's official insignia: an abstract polygonal phoenix, its wings fully outstretched, its noble elongated head turned to profile, each polished facet reflecting a different pattern and texture and color from the enclosure over which it symbolically kept watch.

The floor of the lobby was some kind of sound-rebounding glass tile and the airspace above was full of swirls and loops of dizzying suspended walkways. Luka spent almost his entire life aboard a floating mining rig and never once felt seasick until the first time he walked into City Hall and looked up.

The space was moderately abustle with those who were gradually divorcing themselves from the physical world—those who somehow earned their keep without producing, building, transporting, or fixing anything. Layers of abstraction were being allowed to accumulate throughout the increasingly complex economy as fewer people called themselves miners, growers, and assemblers and instead carved out niches for themselves as things like advisers, arbitrators, consultants, and representatives.

Luka believed he was witnessing the birth of a new class who, in order to sustain themselves, had to spend more time convincing the world that everything would fall apart without them than making sure that it didn't. In fact, it was precisely their tendency to string together as much of the prevailing but ultimately vacuous jargon as possible—and their unquenchable propensity for lofty but nonsensical pontification—that earned City Hall the nickname of the Tower of Babel, or as Luka preferred to pronounce it, the Tower of Bullshit. Luka had yet to figure out how to fully respect someone who, at the end of the day, had nothing physical or tangible to show for his or her work, though he couldn't deny that he was still somehow intimidated by them, and was surprised by how nervous he was now that he was about to present before a group of them. He was confused by this new and seemingly paradoxical social hierarchy wherein he believed he contributed more than anyone whose entire careers revolved principally around increasingly convoluted manifestations of futility, yet the mere act of them placing themselves above him still somehow made him feel small.

In a self-contained environment that ran almost entirely off a single technical infrastructure with concepts such as identity, access, and permissions globally integrated, there was clearly no need for a human receptionist to greet and direct visitors, yet there she sat at the base of the nearest ascension spiral. Her blonde, pixie-cut hair had blue and purple highlights, and her neck was long and slender. Although she was stationed behind a polymeth surface, Luka could see that she was wearing a well-fitted cornflower-blue dress with a slight lustrous sheen.

The girl greeted Luka with a smile and a cheerful "good morning" as he approached.

"I'm Luka Mance," Luka said. He looked up at the walkway above them and pressed his damp palms against the thighs of his slacks. "I have a meeting with the City Council this morning."

"Hi, Luka," the woman said with unexpected familiarity. Luka looked at her again and realized that he knew her. It was more her voice that he recognized than her face. There was some association with Val. Coworkers, he decided. They once worked together at the Gardens. Leah? Lilly?

"Allison," the girl finally prompted.

"I remember," Luka said. "I just wasn't expecting to see you here."

The girl shrugged her delicate shoulders. "I wanted to try something new," she said. "Everything's changing so fast now."

Luka nodded and affected what he hoped was a congenial smile. That was exactly why he was here. Change. But not the kind to which Allison referred.

"I think I'm early," Luka said. "Is there someplace I can wait?"

"It's OK," the girl assured him. "They're ready for you now."

Luka tried not to reveal his alarm. He was expecting some time to gather his thoughts; to go over his talking points one last time; to sit and breathe. To at least to find a restroom.

"Where do I go?"

"You're going to the top floor, so you'll need to take the elevator in the back of the lobby. When you step out, just follow the ramp down to the council chamber."

"I'm going to the council chamber?"

"You are indeed," Allison said. She raised an eyebrow and gave Luka a slightly skewed smile. "Must be an important meeting."

"Must be," Luka said. "Thanks."

The electromagnetic guts of the lift were visible through its transparent material, though after ascending beyond the lobby, the car darkened as the shaft transitioned into less elaborate and more opaque materials. The ride was so smooth, and the deceleration so gradual, that the only sense of movement was visual.

The doors opened and Luka stepped out onto a ramp that he could see spiraled down an entire level to the council chamber below. The floor was a dark iris purple, and in the center was a polymeth ring surrounded by a dozen or so chairs, only one of which was occupied. In the center of the ring was a hollow cylindrical drum—a giant petri dish—which looked to be filled with a black viscous liquid.

Luka stood at the top of the ramp and looked down over the rail, trying to make sense of the fact that there was only a single councilperson below.

"Luka," the woman called up to him. "You're early. Come on down."

As Luka descended, he was momentarily distracted from his consternation by the view through the glass wall. Although it was no more spectacular than the view one could get from any number of locations aboard the *San Francisco*—including Luka's own transpartment—it was a new perspective for him, and therefore represented a moment of rare visual novelty.

The woman was Khang Jung-soon, President of the City Council, and probably the most powerful and influential individual on the entire rig. As far as Luka knew, Khang had served in some official municipal capacity since the traditional nautical chain of command was replaced by democratically elected officials, and was now on her second of an as-of-yet undefined number of terms as president. She was a small woman either in her late fifties or early sixties with hair that presented as short because of the way she gathered it in the back and pinned it into an intricate and compact black nest. The smile with which she greeted Luka was impossibly sweet, and although Luka knew it was simply her own personal form of posturing, contrived or not, she genuinely seemed to radiate warmth.

"Help yourself to something to drink," she told him. She gestured toward the cart tucked beneath the ramp Luka had just finished descending. It held a coffee urn, stacks of disposable cups, and several sealed bulbs of water.

Luka reached for a water and wondered whether it was cold because it was just put out, or if there was a refrigeration mechanism built into the cart somewhere. He thanked Khang and tried to hide his apprehension with a quick, thin smile.

"Sit wherever you like," the councilwoman said.

Luka chose a position he judged was an appropriate distance, sat, and pulled himself in close to the table. He discovered that, rather than castors, the chair's legs terminated in small metal disks that glided easily on the stiff weave of the carpet below. He looked around at the empty chairs around them.

"I'm sorry the rest of the council couldn't be here," Khang said after an accurate read of his body language. "They had an urgent matter to attend to."

"More urgent than this?" Luka asked. He tried not to sound offended or accusatory, but he was pretty sure he came across as both.

"I think it remains to be seen exactly what *this* is," Khang replied, and Luka watched the meaning of her smile begin to transform. He guessed that it was likely not pure warmth that got the councilwoman to where she was. "Why don't you start from the beginning?"

"Right," Luka said. He flipped the lever on the water bulb to unseal it and took a cautious sip. "You already know about the drill, right? The RMD?"

"I do," Khang said.

"Do you know that we have orders for at least four other pieces of mining equipment to be packaged and delivered in almost the exact the same way?"

"Yes," Khang said. "We've already looked into that."

"And?"

"And what?"

"And what did you find out?"

"We found out that there's nothing to find out."

"Are they going to the Coronians?"

Khang watched Luka for a moment, as though trying to decide whether she wanted to continue betting or fold. "No, they aren't," she said.

"How do you know?"

"Because we've been assured."

"Assured by who?"

"By people we trust."

"Then where's all this stuff going if it's not going into orbit?" Luka asked. "I've been doing this a long time and there's definitely something unusual about these shipments."

"That's not information I'm at liberty to reveal."

"Is that because it's information you don't actually have?"

Khang's expression reset itself. The smile was gone, and Luka now saw what it was intended to conceal. Khang may have been a compact woman, but she had a considerable determination and presence about her that bordered on unsettling.

"Because," Khang said, "it is of no concern to an assembly technician."

Luka accepted the condescension with a smile. "Then let me ask you something else," he said. The nervousness was gone now, he realized, and replaced with a much more familiar sense of reckless provocation. "Do you know what our position is right now?"

"I will not be interrogated by you, Luka," Khang countered. Her tone was a tad softer—perhaps even a touch amused or detached—but Luka could tell it was also a tone with which meetings could easily be ended.

"Fine," Luka said. "Then I'll just tell you. As of yesterday, we were right inside the Antarctic Circle. The reason we're right inside the Antarctic Circle is because that's where the Coronians want us. And the reason they want us here is because they have high-definition gravity, laser spectrographic, and radar maps all telling them where we're most likely to find the kinds of resources they need, and if we're all the way down here, what they need probably isn't available anywhere else on the planet."

Khang squinted at Luka and let her head tilt back a degree. "I'm afraid I'm not quite following."

"Here's what *I* think is happening," Luka said. "The Coronians know that we're about to run out of certain critical resources, so they're getting ready to start doing their own mining."

Khang produced a patronizing smile. "That's absurd," she said. "The Coronians can't survive Earth's gravity. There's no way they could do their own mining."

"Not on Earth," Luka said. "They're going to mine in space. And once they get good at it, they're not going to need us anymore."

"Luka—"

"And once the Coronians don't need us anymore, that means no more power, no new assemblers, and no more trading. We'll be completely on our own, which you know as well as I means we're all as good as dead."

"Don't you think you're being just a tad dramatic?"

"How?"

"Because you're talking about depleting an entire planet of resources. That's just not realistic."

"Are you suggesting that the planet has infinite resources?"

"Of course not, but—"

"Then do you accept that one day, we *will* run out?"

"One day, yes."

"When?"

"Nobody knows."

"If nobody knows, then why not now? Or more likely, in about ten years—which is how long we think it will take for the Coronians to completely replace all the medium they get from Earth with medium from asteroids."

As Khang regarded Luka, it occurred to him that he might have gone too far. He took another sip of water to counter his dry mouth and tried to hide the fact that he regretted not at least trying to employ a little more diplomacy. The whole thing was going pretty much exactly as Charlie predicted. But it was too late to turn back now, so Luka decided he might as well hold course and see where it eventually led.

"I'd like to show you something, Luka," Khang finally said. "But before I do, I need to know that you will keep it to yourself."

Luka was about to raise his water again, but stopped. There was a moment of hesitation before he agreed.

"That means you tell absolutely no one," Khang stipulated. "Not even your friend, Charlene."

For a moment, Luka wondered if the councilwoman was trying to intimidate him by proving how much she knew about his personal life, but then decided that his relationship with Charlie was common enough knowledge that even if she was, she was doing a pretty poor job of it. And he was far too curious at this point about what she had to show him to risk saying something that might jeopardize her confidence.

"You have my word," Luka assured her.

"Good," Khang said. She gestured with her head at the circular vat of black liquid inside the polymeth ring. "Do you know what that is?"

"I've been wondering that since I got here."

"It's ferrofluid. Dispersed nanoscale magnetic particles. Basically magnetic liquid inside of a discrete electromagnetic field generator. We use it to model construction projects."

Luka remembered hearing about ferromagnetic technologies, but he had never seen them. They were designed as alternatives to polyvid systems—opposing volumetric plates between which three-dimensional holographic images could be rendered. There was something about the physicality of technologies like ferrofluid that—even though they were more limited than holography in terms of expression—made them preferable in certain contexts. Instantaneously manipulating tangible matter also felt borderline magical to Luka—somehow even more miraculous than the far more advanced molecular assemblers he'd become largely desensitized to over the years.

Khang activated the polymeth surface in front of her and began navigating. Luka watched carefully as the liquid began to vibrate—to seemingly quiver with electromagnetic anticipation. There were a few moments of what appeared to be measurement calibration as perfectly symmetrical stalagmites rose from the black surface, then receded into absolute placidity. Another moment of humming, and then the surface erupted. Luka was so startled that he jerked back and blinked, and by the time he refocused, he was looking at what appeared to be a perfect model of every above-deck structure on the *San Francisco*.

"Impressive, isn't it?" Khang said.

Luka realized that what he wanted to say was far too blue-collar for present company, so he very consciously checked himself. "Very," is all he managed.

"Given how you spend your free time, I thought you might appreciate this." There was another look from the councilwoman intended to either impress or intimidate him with what she knew. "What you're looking at is, of course, the *San Francisco* as it exists today. Minus the dome, of course."

"And minus the other two thirds that are below deck."

Khang conceded with a quick and dismissive smile, then touched the polymeth surface again. Luka was ready, but this time the transformation was gradual. As additional fluid was added, the globe enclosing the Yerba Buena Gardens in the center morphed into a massive segmented tower—four towers, actually, overlapping to form a single, clover-like quatrefoil. It was by far the tallest structure in the city and it was clear to Luka just from the scale that the dome would probably have to be raised. The metamorphosis was so conspicuous that Luka almost missed the transformation of Paramount Tower. It had melted away into a flat and nondescript block—more of a tenement than a tower.

"And this," Khang said, "is the next phase."

There was no stopping it this time. "Holy shit," Luka declared.

"Eloquently put."

"What the hell are we supposed to eat without any agriculture?"

"Good observation," Khang said. "We are currently working out a deal with the Coronians that will enable us to take delivery of the first generation of atomic assemblers. Do you know what that means?"

"What kind of a deal?"

"That isn't important. What's important is that we will finally be able to turn just about any kind of medium into any form of matter, including matter that is safe to consume. Do you have any idea what kind of an impact that will have on our lives? How much that will change our standard of living?"

The model was gradually rotating, though Luka couldn't tell if it was turning, or whether the entire model was transforming at a high enough frame rate that it just looked like it was turning. Either way, the new building in the center gave the distinct impression of being the axis around which everything else on the rig rotated.

"What's that new building?"

"The Infinity," Khang said. "The first mixed-use space on the *San Francisco*. Luxury flats and retail together in a single structure."

"Luxury," Luka said. "As in big?"

"Up to twenty times the size of a standard transpartment."

"And what happened to Paramount there?"

"In order to balance out the weight of the new building, Paramount Tower will unfortunately need to be razed and rebuilt at approximately a third of its mass."

"Right," Luka said. He nodded deliberately while he watched the model spin. "I wonder who gets to live where."

Khang gave Luka curious look. "People can live wherever they can afford, of course," she said. "You know we have a free-market economy here. That certainly won't change."

"A free-market economy where the people who make the rules also determine everyone's compensation," Luka amended, "including their own. It looks to me like you're proposing a very tidy three-class system here: the poor live in Paramount, the middle class get Millennium, and the emerging elite get to live in luxury in The Infinity. And my guess is that the more important you are, the higher up your flat."

"As I said," Khang emphasized, "people may live where they choose."

"That's *not* what you said," Luka countered. "You said people could live wherever they could *afford*. Have you decided yet where assembly technicians will fit into this new hierarchy?"

"Regular assembly technicians?" Khang asked him. "Or you?"

Luka narrowed his eyes at the councilwoman. "What's that supposed to mean?"

"Come on, Luka," Khang said conspiratorially. "Why do you think I'm telling you all this?"

"I assume to distract me from what I came here to talk about."

The councilwoman shook her head. "Not to distract you," she said. "To provide you with some perspective. Why would the Coronians promise us atomic assemblers if they wanted to get rid of us?"

"Let's turn that question around," Luka said. "If the Coronians have atomic assemblers, why do they need us at all?"

"Because they still need medium. Even atomic assemblers are useless without mass."

"Seems to me there's plenty of mass out there in space," Luka said.

"Maybe," Khang said, "but there's also plenty of nothing. It's much cheaper and easier for them to buy it from us than to get it themselves."

"For now. But what happens when they become self-sufficient? It's no secret that neither of us trusts the other."

"Then we do what we've always done," Khang said. "We adapt. But in the meantime, we will continue to move forward." She swiveled in her chair and looked at Luka with renewed intensity. "Luka, I'm well aware of what Valencia did for you. I know that you are in a position where you don't have to work anymore. This is your chance to have a better life. This is your chance to have the life that she wanted you to have. You can have all the time, resources, and all the space you need to do whatever you want."

Luka watched the councilwoman for a moment, then began nodding. "I think I see where this is going," he said. "You're offering me a new flat in The Infinity, aren't you?"

"Not a flat," Khang said. She leaned forward, placing her forearms on the table and interlacing her fingers. "I'm offering you an entire *floor* of The Infinity. You *and* Charlene."

"And what exactly do I have to do, I wonder, in order to earn this distinguished privilege?"

"That's the beauty of it," Khang said offering Luka the same sweet smile with which she began their meeting. "Absolutely nothing."

"Really?" Luka asked. "That's very generous of you."

"Not at all," Khang said. "In fact, I insist."

CHAPTER THIRTEEN

PROXIMITY ALERT

Neither Ayla nor Omicron had any idea what the repercussions were of defaulting on a Coronian debt, but there were two things about their situation they both knew for sure: that they would rather die than be knowingly and willingly complicit in the sacrifice of an entire pod system; and that they would do everything they could to avoid the first.

In case the Coronians were monitoring their position (the *Accipiter Hawk* was left unattended for several hours at MIS during which time some sort of tracking device could have easily been planted), they decided to continue circumnavigating the globe just north of the Antarctic Circle rather than simply sit in one place and kill time. And just in case Nsonowa had some way of knowing whether or not they were actually making an earnest attempt to contact pod system dissidents, they continued transmitting a focused (albeit weak) signal from their position off the coast of Antarctica directly inland toward the South Pole. And finally, in the event that Nsonowa's men insisted on forensic evidence corroborating their mission, Ayla and Omicron would take the *Hawk*'s amphibious auxiliary craft ashore at least three times to ensure that their decontamination logs were not only legitimate, but fully consistent with heavy metals and isotopes associated with the southern Antarctic radiation band. After the roughly eighteen days it would likely take them at an average of twenty knots to finally return to their starting position somewhere between 70 and 75 degrees of longitude, their plan was to turn north once again, sail back to the Maldive Islands Spaceport, step board the HMS *Beagle*, and make the case to Jumanne Nsonowa himself that despite their best efforts, they were unable to locate any traces of unregistered populations. If that meant Omicron returning to Nsonowa's service, so be it. Even if it somehow resulted in both Ayla's and Omicron's detention or death, they were prepared for that, as well. No matter what the consequences, Ayla—and by extension, her first officer and bodyguard—would not do to someone else's home what she now believed had been done to hers.

It took Ayla and Omicron hours of discussion and planning to feel like they were prepared for whatever lay ahead, and just a few seconds for them to discover that they were not. The one contingency they hadn't considered was actually receiving a response.

Omicron turned to Ayla from his station on the bridge and awaited her orders. Ayla's initial inclination was to ignore the boy's hails, and indeed to stop listening on the designated frequency altogether. Keeping the channel open in the first place had purely been for the sake of their alibi since a close enough inspection of the *Hawk*'s system logs would reveal the precise state of their radio equipment throughout their expedition. But there was something about the boy's voice—not at any one moment in particular, but rather in how his tone progressed from hopeful and expectant, to panicked, and finally to pleading and desperate as he continued to send hail after hail—that finally made Ayla give the order to respond.

The boy did not elaborate on the details of the pod system from which he was broadcasting, but instead focused on his present situation, and specifically, his petition for asylum. His name was Arik Ockley, and he and three others needed to leave a place he referred to interchangeably as Ishtar Terra Station One and V1. He asked that they all be taken someplace safe—if possible, somewhere with modern medical facilities and laboratories. Arik's wife was pregnant, he explained, and it was critical that both her life and the baby's be protected at all costs. Encoded inside the baby's DNA was information he wished to smuggle out of the pod system—information he believed to be invaluable. Omicron pressed him for clarification, but all the boy would reveal was that the data could potentially transform the entire planet. He was running out of time, and needed to convey the logistics of their rendezvous. Ayla nodded and Omicron told the boy to proceed. The boy gave them a date, time, and a set of coordinates. There would be a wall, he explained, and in the wall, a metal door. The door would be locked, but at the specified time, the lock would be removed, and Arik, Arik's wife, and his two best friends would be waiting on the other side. They only had one shot at this, the boy emphasized. If the four of them were allowed to be taken back to V1, they would never have another opportunity to escape, and the information inside his daughter's genetic code would almost certainly be lost forever.

Based on Omicron's counsel, Ayla decided that their plan would not materially change. The date the boy gave them was two full weeks in the future, which meant that by pushing the *Hawk* by just a few knots and skipping one of their planned excursions, they could still complete their circuit around Antarctica. The chances that the boy would even reach the rendezvous point seemed to them extremely remote, and although Omicron calculated the odds to be acceptably low, it was also possible that the broadcast was part of an elaborate hoax or trap. With the exception of making a quick sweep of the coordinates specified by the boy, Ayla and Omicron agreed that they would stay on-mission. If it turned out that the refugees were real—and that they were in fact able to reach the rendezvous location—Ayla and Omicron would, at that point, do what any reasonable strategist would: improvise.

Omicron accrued a great deal of experience piloting the *Anura* during their excursions up the Banzare and Princess Astrid Coasts. The vessel was a high-speed amphibious combat craft capable of around forty knots on the water, and after pivoting and lowering its six nonpneumatic, all-terrain polymer tires into place, eighty-five miles per hour on land. There was a 7.62-millimeter remotely operated turret on the roof that Ayla had never seen fired, and wasn't even sure still functioned.

When they came across a rusted and toppled quadrupedal module from an old British research survey, Omicron made sure there was nothing living inside, then confirmed that the cannon was indeed still an effective asset by nearly cutting the facility in half. He also confirmed that the weapon was badly in need of cleaning and calibration, which he did back inside the *Accipiter Hawk*'s decontamination bay.

Their third and final excursion two weeks after receiving the boy's hail was up the Queen Mary Coast. The *Anura* lowered its tires amid a thick tar-like substance, then began crawling up the beach. It maneuvered around a massive outcropping that Ayla assumed was a rock, though something about it seemed to intrigue Omicron. He stopped and began imaging the object in various portions of the electromagnetic spectrum. When the three-dimensional reconstruction appeared on the screen, they could see that it was far too symmetrical to be any type of mineral deposit. Rather, it looked more like a tremendous beak.

Omicron's expression transitioned from intense curiosity, to awe, and finally to a degree of enthusiasm Ayla had yet to witness in him. What they were looking at, her first officer announced, was the remains of what had once been the largest known animal to have ever existed—larger by far than even the most massive marine or terrestrial dinosaurs. Omicron was certain that what they were looking at was the skull of a blue whale.

The Neo was preparing to get out and retrieve a sample when they began picking up thermal signatures consistent with humans farther inland. As Ayla awoke the turret's targeting computer from standby, Omicron hypothesized that they had come across a local population of scavengers. The formation and movement of the dots suggested that the natives were as wary as they were intrigued by the appearance of an unfamiliar vehicle. As long as Ayla and Omicron remained inside the *Anura*, they felt they were probably safe. It was the prospect of eventually having to leave behind a reinforced hull, a mounted auto-tracking machine gun, and the ability to move rapidly over just about any terrain that concerned them.

By the time they reached a more compact surface, the scavengers were no longer detectable by the *Anura*'s sensors, but radiation levels had gotten so high that Omicron did not entirely trust the electronics anymore. Visibility continued to decrease, though not by so much that they couldn't see the emergence of structures around them. The first one they saw had the unmistakable hyperbolic shape of a nuclear reactor cooling tower, though they could also see that it was partially destroyed, its black carbon scoring telling of a quick but violent death.

They passed several more dilapidated structures that gradually faded into geometric wisps in the thick, mustard-yellow haze. The *Anura*'s tires were supported by rigid hexagonal honeycomb structures that began deforming and reshaping as they crawled over increasingly rough terrain. The vehicle's radar indicated a solid vertical structure up ahead of them approximately twenty-five meters high, and switching to a higher resolution band revealed a discontinuity that they both instantly knew was a door.

Omicron wanted to check to see if the wheel beside the door would turn, but Ayla suggested that they wait. They were early, and the vehicle's acoustic sensors were sensitive enough to detect the vibrations of the lock, so there was no reason to leave the safety of the *Anura* before they had to. For the last two weeks, Ayla had been uncertain about the rendezvous—skeptical that Arik and his party could successfully coordinate and execute an escape. But detecting packs of scavengers, and traveling through decaying nuclear facilities, and finally arriving at the door in the wall—just as Arik had described it—changed Ayla's mindset. For the last two weeks, she had not allowed herself to dwell on the young man's claims that he possessed information that could transform the planet since she doubted they would ever get the opportunity to recover it, though now, she could not stop thinking about what he'd been referring to. She imagined new technology for food production, or the theory that her old crew used to debate that it was possible to collect power from the process of microbes digesting waste, or a new breed of photovoltaics efficient enough to function in Earth's Venus-like atmosphere. Or maybe some kind of new weapon that would shift the balance of power between themselves and *Equinox*. She wondered what the Coronians would do if they knew about Arik's claims. She wanted to ask Omicron what he thought, but she didn't want him to think her foolish or naive, or to tell her—even in his own gentle and obsequious way—what she already knew: that the chances of anyone showing up were small, and the chances of them having or knowing anything of value, smaller still.

And then they heard the lock.

Ayla and Omicron looked at one other, and then Ayla reached up and sealed her visor.

"Let's go," she said solemnly.

Omicron put his sprawling hand on her wrist. "Wait," he said. He nodded at the vehicle's display. There was movement behind them at the edge of the *Anura*'s long-range motion sensors. The readings were indecisive and over a kilometer away, but they weren't there before, which meant they were probably indicative of something.

"We'll hurry," Ayla said. "Set a proximity alert and let's go."

Omicron navigated the *Anura*'s menus with his gloved hand. He drew a perimeter, adjusted its radius, selected the series of thermal dots, and set the alert. Ayla herd the confirmation tone in her helmet's earpiece. Omicron lowered and sealed his visor, then reached beside him for his rifle. Ayla touched the forward panel, confirmed her request, and then the *Anura*'s hatches raised.

Ayla stood by the door in the wall while Omicron positioned himself in front of the wheel. She noticed that the metal was dented in the center, though before she had time to wonder what could have deformed such thick layers of steel, it began to move. Under the strength of just one of Omicron's hands, the hatch pivoted with surprising fluidity. His other hand remained on the grip of his lowered but otherwise primed weapon.

Visibility was poor, and Ayla took a step forward, peering through the widening gap. She was trembling with anticipation—far more than she expected—and she nearly gasped when she saw that they were not alone. On the other side of the wall were at least three figures that appeared to be waiting for them.

Ayla could see that one of them was holding something, but before she could discern what it was, Omicron was in front of her, his rifle raised to his shoulder.

"He's armed," her bodyguard said. His tone was urgent but collected. "Do you want me to drop him?"

The defectors' environment suits were bulky and dirty—designed more for hard labor than exploration. Ayla noticed a vehicle parked nearby—some kind of an open-cab rover.

"Give him a chance," Ayla said. "They're probably much more afraid of us than we are of them."

The figure in front of them stood motionless for another moment, then tossed the object away. The other two raised their hands to show that they were not armed, and Omicron stepped to the side.

"It's our turn," Ayla said. "Let's show them that we're not a threat."

Omicron swung his rifle back behind him and they both raised their hands in a reassuring gesture. The one who had been armed was tall and seemingly muscular, though still significantly smaller than Omicron, and he continued to wear a look of defiance on his boyish face. His two companions were both female. One had a dark, African complexion, and the other was a smaller girl of Asian background.

"There's something wrong," Ayla said. "Someone's missing. Let's get them mic'd up so we can figure out what's going on."

As Omicron advanced, he removed four small devices from a pocket on his thigh, then pointed to his own mic on the visor of his helmet to indicate their function. The devices were about the size and shape of miniature power cells. Ayla could see the three of them discussing the implied proposal. The boy looked over at the two girls, looked back at Omicron, and finally nodded.

"Let's do this as fast as we can," Ayla said. "I don't want to be out here any longer than we have to."

Omicron stepped closer to the boy, then reached up and cinched the device to the stranger's faceplate.

"Can you hear me?" Omicron asked.

The boy nodded. "I can hear you," he said in a voice that was youthful but aggressive.

Omicron nodded at the boy, then proceeded to attach devices to his companions' helmets. Ayla approached the boy.

"Are you Arik?" she asked him. She tried to sound as friendly as she could, but she was thinking about the dots on the *Anura*'s screen.

The boy shook his head. "Arik isn't here," he said.

"*Yet*," the smaller girl interjected. "He isn't here *yet*. He'll be here any second."

Ayla looked at the girl, then down at her belly. "Are you his wife?"

The girl nodded. The *Anura* sounded a proximity alert to let them know that the band of scavengers it was tracking had cut their initial distance in half.

"We don't have much time," Ayla said. "We're not safe here."

The taller of the two girls stepped forward. "Who are you?" she asked. There was a distinct lack of diplomacy in her tone. "What the hell's going on?"

Ayla was aware of Omicron turning to watch their backs.

"I'll explain as soon as I can," Ayla told her. "Right now, we need to go."

"No," the pregnant girl said. "Not without Arik."

The boy turned to look at her. "Cadie," he said. In advance of what he was about to say to her, there was compassion in his eyes. When the girl looked at him, he gestured toward the device Omicron had assumed was a weapon, and in response, the girl became instantly emotional.

"It's not true," she said.

"I'm sorry," the boy told her. "Arik isn't coming."

The girl shook her head.

"You're . . ." She stopped and shook her head again, and tears fell from her cheeks. "I'm going back," she said defiantly.

"Cadie," the boy said. "There's nothing you can do."

"There *is*," the girl insisted. She backed away from the boy. "At least I can be with him. That's *some*thing."

"This is what he wanted," the boy said.

The girl leaned forward and glared at him. "Well, it's not what *I* want!" she screamed, then she turned and started to run.

"Don't let her get away," Ayla said. She spun around to face Omicron. "Do it," she ordered.

There was a transmitter lashed to the stock of Omicron's rifle and he reached back and squeezed it. The pregnant girl stopped moving. Everyone stood motionless for a moment, then the girl turned. The mics were no longer broadcasting, so if the strangers were communicating, Ayla could not hear them. She watched as all three of them tried to dislodge the devices from their visors, but their thickly gloved hands repeatedly slipped off. The boy stayed on his feet the longest. He found whatever it was he'd been holding, picked it up off the ground, and was about to use it to try to knock the miniature canister off his visor when he finally succumbed—stumbling, dropping the device, and collapsing.

The *Anura* sounded another half-distance alarm.

"Come on," Ayla said. "Let's get them loaded up and get the hell out of here."

CHAPTER FOURTEEN

BRUTE FORCE

Security aboard the *San Francisco* was probably best described as "elegant." Inductive contact lenses shrouded private workspaces from all forms of human and electronic voyeurism; decryption keys and personal identifiers transmitted through bioelectromagnetic fields granted or denied access to both virtual and physical spaces; inconspicuous cameras fed three-dimensional models to facial geometric algorithms that seamlessly anticipated residents' routes and unobtrusively guided them throughout their daily routines. Although the various security measures employed throughout the rig seemed robust and even infallible, they remind Luka of a nineteenth-century British novel he once found in the archives depicting distinguished and prominent families of punctilious gentlemen and readily excitable ladies, all of whom endlessly struggled to express their passion for one another within the confines of stringent social convention and propriety. While listening to an old dramatization of the story, it occurred to Luka that the rules, restrictions, and barriers such systems imposed existed only to the extent that they were recognized and respected by those they inhibited. And it subsequently occurred to him that the one thing elegance did respond well to was brute force.

Luka used a lightweight fiddler liftsuit to transport a single carbon fiber crate. He did not have sufficient permissions for utility access to deck two, but he could move freely between decks one and three, and since anyone could use the cargo lift's emergency brake, there was nothing preventing him from stopping right in-between. While it was true that the vertical freight doors would not willingly open in order to admit Luka, that problem was easily addressed by setting down the crate, rotating the brackets of the liftsuit's hydraulic attachment, working them into the gap between the doors, and gently activating. The entrance yawned open so easily that Luka wondered if he might have saved himself some trouble and done it with his bare hands.

He left the suit in powered standby and extricated himself from its harnesses and straps. The carbon fiber crate was not heavy and was therefore easily hoisted through the gap between the doors, after which Luka followed with a lackadaisical vault. He had stolen several brief glimpses of deck two from the lift while watching authorized personnel come and go, but now that he was actually standing among the entire city's utility infrastructure, the experience was quite different. Being on deck two was like being miniaturized and transported inside a three-dimensional integrated circuit: extraordinary complex, yet somehow still meticulously organized. The high ceiling was a mass of pipes, ducts, and cables—first racing along long stretches in parallel, then veering, branching, bending, weaving, and intertwining. Along the perimeter and bolted to the hexagonal synthetic graphite supports through which raw materials were conveyed topside were voluminous red and blue pressure tanks, orange compressors, steel-gray panels, and consoles festooned with wheels, dials, hand lever valves, and—to Luka's astonishment—seemingly anachronistic analog meters. There were so many unique sounds at so many different intervals and pitches that they all blended together into an almost constant white noise. Since it would be impossible for light to penetrate the utilities overhead, the floor panels provided the majority of the illumination, giving the room a surprisingly clean and even sanitary feel, and even the smell—while undeniably acrid—was not unpleasant. At first glance, Luka did not detect a single pool of fluid or patch of rust.

He'd memorized enough of the floor plan to know the general direction of where he needed to go, so he hoisted the crate by its indentations and carried it around to the other side of the lift. To his right was a row of redundant pumps amid snarls of pipes, elbows, and valves—all painted a pure cobalt blue to indicate their association with potable water—and which had been chosen as an alternative to above-deck water towers as a means of generating pressure without unduly upsetting the rig's center of gravity. He passed a floor-to-ceiling rack of black, liquid-cooled servers that lit him up with a full spectrum of furiously strobing plasma dots. In order to maintain his bearings, he looked and followed the cluster of hexagonal ducts, about the diameter of soccer balls, which eventually converged into a massive switching station known as "the hive."

Several kilometers of pneumatic tubes once permeated the *San Francisco* like thick, hardened arteries. While historically, pneumatic transportation systems had almost always succumbed to their more modern rivals—delivery vehicles and rapid digital communication—aboard the *San Francisco*, the concept had flourished. In fact, technologies enabling instantaneous access to information and the rapid assembly of just about any object you could think of only served to increase the expectation of near-instantaneous delivery of physical goods. Since there were no above-deck vehicles allowed aboard the *San Francisco*, any object too small for a forklift or a mech—items like medication, computer components, machine parts, newly assembled tools and instruments, various household goods, and even groceries—could either be hand-delivered, or simply dropped off at the nearest tube station, after which it could cover even the longest stretches between two endpoints in only a little over a minute.

Pneumatic tubes were still used for garbage disposal and for moving ore and other raw materials from the below-deck mining operations up to the refinery, but they were no longer used as a postal service. When the information-technology infrastructure aboard the *San Francisco* was last upgraded, so too were the tubes. Replacing the simple ten-by-thirty-centimeter cylinders that were conveyed via an imperfect and relatively weak vacuum at seven or eight meters per second were twenty-by-sixty-centimeter hexagonal missiles with gyroscopes and gimbals that ensured payloads remained upright, and which were electromagnetically propelled throughout the city's seams at speeds up to fifty meters per second. Although the official name of the system was EMATS (ElectroMagnetic Transportation System)—and although the shape and technology more closely resembled fully enclosed tracks than simple pipes—in a rare nostalgic tribute to an outgoing technology, the new network retained the informal name of its predecessor, and was therefore usually still referred to as "the tubes."

There were three basic designs proposed for EMATS: point-to-point, hub-and-spoke, and closed circuit. The implementation with the least amount of latency would have been point-to-point, but it would have also required the most infrastructure since every building on the rig with an EMATS endpoint would need tubes running to every other endpoint. Not only would it have been the most difficult and time-consuming to install, but it would have also required the most physical space, which, aboard a hermetically sealed floating city, was the rarest and most precious of all commodities.

Conversely, the closed circuit model was the simplest and most compact since the entire system would essentially consist of a single loop connecting every building on the rig through which capsules would move in one direction and be switched off to local distribution systems when they arrived at their designated first-order addresses. In addition to being the slowest design, the primary disadvantage of a closed circuit system was the additional complication—and potential for extended downtime—whenever new nodes needed to be added.

The hub-and-spoke model eventually emerged as the most practical. Every building was outfitted with a single track through which capsules could move in either direction, and every track terminated in a massive switching station on deck two. A dual-axis robotic clutch did the work of plucking incoming capsule from one track and inserting them in the proper outgoing track at a theoretical average rate of about one transfer every 1.25 seconds. Once the capsules reached their first-order destinations, they were switched off to local delivery systems, freeing up the track for the next capsule. Local delivery systems might be as primitive as purely manual processes (generally known as "mail call") most common in utility structures and endpoint below deck three, or they might be as sophisticated as those found in City Hall and in both Millennium and Paramount Towers. In such newer and more sophisticated structures, capsules first found their way to their designated floors through a sort of dumbwaiter system, and then continued on to their designated individual offices or transapartments via air-cushioned conveyers where they waited to be biometrically unsealed, emptied, and finally placed back into circulation.

It was at the site of the switching station where the decision to use hexagonal tracks became most apparent. Not only did the inability of the capsules to freely rotate assist in the preservation of orientation, but hexagons also allowed for a much denser concentration of track endpoints than cylinders that, when stacked, left wasteful triangles or diamonds of dead space in-between. Since the entire switching station needed to fit within the vertical space of deck two—and because it was built at twice the size it needed to be in order to allow for expansion—compactness was critical. The overall effect of the final design was that of a massive beehive, the robotic appendage a tireless drone perpetually tending to the needs of an endless procession of product-impregnated larva.

An additional component of the switching station was a magazine of empty capsules waiting to be summoned. Luka watched as they were fed into the lower right-hand corner of the exchange—what he imagined to be coordinate (0, 0) in the dual-axis system—at about the same rate they were replenished through the top of the magazine: roughly one every ten seconds. The front of the magazine was entirely open, and because the capsules had not yet been digitally addressed and locked, Luka could touch their capacitive tops and dilate them open like the aperture ring of a camera lens.

There were two reasons why Luka had broken into deck two. The first was communication. He had a message that he needed disseminated quickly, efficiently, and randomly. This was precisely the kind of thing that the tubes were not very good for since transferring information could obviously be done far more effectively digitally. However, since his meeting with Khang—and after her less-than-subtle warning—Luka suspected that his digital communications were being monitored, and that a message like the one he needed to send out would very likely never get delivered. But since the tubes were probably the least practical way to communicate, they were probably also the last mechanism the City Council would think to safeguard.

Another advantage of using the tubes was that it added an element of surprise. Luka hoped that putting physical messages into people's hands—especially in such an abrupt and unexpected manner—would have a far greater impact than sending personal digital communications. It was, hopefully, the difference between receiving a rote electronic birthday platitude, and a handwritten note on custom-assembled stock.

In the crate was an envelope of monochrome silicon paper that Luka purchased from a shop in Union Square and had tubed to his transpartment. Silicon paper consisted of two thin sheets of plastic film with several billion tiny magnetically charged beads about a micrometer in diameter pressed between them. A magnetic pen—or some other form of magnetic implement—was typically used to apply either a positive or a negative charge causing either the black or white hemispheres to rotate into view depending on whether you wanted to write or erase. Luka frequently used silicon paper to sketch out sculptures, though last night—after several lines of curious yellow—he applied himself to a very different kind of project. After cutting up enough sheets to make one hundred silicon paper squares (the outer polymer layer of silicon paper instantly rebonded after being severed), he piled them all up, placed them on the electromagnetic pad he used for transferring images between silicon paper and his workspace, and imprinted the following message on the entire stack simultaneously:

The time is coming when
the Coronians will no longer need us.
This is how it will feel . . .

The hexagonal capsules were wide enough that the paper squares did not have to be rolled or folded, and Luka got all one hundred of them loaded in under two minutes. One hundred sheets of silicon paper were obviously not enough to reach everyone on the rig—and, of course, loading them into the first one hundred capsules in the magazine meant having no control whatsoever over who ultimately received them. But Luka believed that even if only half of them were read in the next fifteen minutes, his message would generate enough consternation—and possibly even panic—that there would not be a single soul remaining aboard the rig who wasn't aware of the mysterious dispatch, and who hadn't either adopted a theory as to what it meant, or started formulating one of their own. Luka firmly believed that the only phenomenon on the planet more powerful and effective than instantaneous digital communication was gossip.

The first nine messages were already out, and Luka stood there and watched the clutch retrieve the next capsule in the queue, glide along its horizontal and vertical rails, ease into position, and feed the long hexagonal prism to a greedy cell near the top of the hive. He experienced a surge of panic as he realized that there was no going back at this point; that there was no way to undo what he'd just done; that he now had no choice but to finish what he'd started.

Luka brought up the time in the corner of his vision with a quick blinking pattern, tossed the empty envelope into the crate, and lifted it. He passed the freight elevator on his way to the southwest corner of the deck and saw that the claws of the fiddler were still—seemingly effortlessly—holding the horizontal doors apart. He passed another rack of blinking servers and network switches and, when he felt the heat they were generating, wondered how much of their surging activity related to the messages he was sending out. He passed several columns of PVC pipes that looked to him like images he'd seen of birch trunks—noble white hardwoods that were once astonishingly unwavering in their pursuit of energy from above—and then the space opened up to make room for a massive beige electrical panel. Luka was now directly below Cell City—the above-deck structure housing the *San Francisco*'s entire quantum battery bank.

The terms "panel" and "cabinet" were woefully inadequate to describe the apparatus since it probably encompassed about the same volume as Luka's entire transpartment, though it was a slightly different shape. It was comprised of four identical panels aligned end-to-end—prominently hand-numbered with some sort of indelible ink—each with thick black cables descending into them from above and bunches of smaller gray cables coming back out and spreading throughout the maze of cable racks overhead. Luka could see that the insulation was thick and the cables were bound with tight plastic ties as though, without sufficient constraint, they might erupt like high-pressure hoses. The cabinets were surprisingly nondescript for mechanisms of such consequence, their metal facades concealing the heavy breakers, distributors, transfer switches, and who knew what else within. In addition to their numbers, the only external feature of each cabinet was a tremendous red throw switch beside the hand-lettered word "MAIN."

As Luka approached the panels, he felt like he could sense the energy surging through them. What started off as a hum intensified to an unsettling buzz as he got close enough to touch the metal. Heat emanated from the surface, and Luka believed he could sense an ambient charge as though the equipment before him wasn't quite enough to contain all the current surging through it—as if the machinery had a plasma soul that was too big for its physical form, and consequently swelled beyond its confines into an intense and angry aura.

From his research, Luka knew that he needed to do this sequentially—from one through four. He could see that there was an eye hole in each lever meant for a locking mechanism, but that they were all empty, and that he would not need the laser cutter in the crate. He wondered briefly if the main switches were left unprotected for safety reasons—so that anyone could throw them in an emergency—or whether it was because nobody saw the need for secondary security measures all the way down here. And he wondered if they would remain unlocked in the future, or if by this time next week, all four would be threaded with solid tungsten bars, and the entire island of panels enclosed in carbon-link fencing. If so, he doubted he would be the one to assemble any of it.

The time in the corner of his vision told him that fourteen minutes had elapsed since he left the hive, which meant all of the messages had probably been delivered by now—or at least enough of them. He examined the first throw switch and could tell just by looking at it that it would need to be pivoted laterally away from a safety catch before it could be pulled. As he felt his body become part of the panel's electrical field, he wondered if he should be wearing insulated gloves, though he did not think to bring any, and it was too late to go back for a pair now. Before he could come up with any more reasons not to do it, Luka reached up, moved the lever off the safety hook, and pulled down.

Whatever mechanism was being moved inside the box was stiff and heavy as the lever took a fair amount of pressure, and finally changed position with a tremendous snap. The box grew quiet and still—now inanimate without its electrical life force flowing through it. Luka checked his hands as though he couldn't believe the process hadn't charred them and found them exactly as they felt: perfectly fine. He began wondering what was happening above him right now, then consciously stopped himself. No mining operations were currently deployed so he wasn't putting any lives directly in danger, and the bilge pumps could go two days without running before the rig started listing noticeably. He had already gone through all this in his head hundreds of times, so rather than going through it all again, Luka forced himself to stop thinking and instead threw the next two switches in rapid succession. He was breathing heavily now as he reached for the fourth and last, and he looked down beside him at the crate in order to memorize its location, took one final deep breath, pivoted the catch, and yanked.

For a moment, nothing happened, and then he was shocked by both the blackness and the sudden quiet. All he could see was the time in the corner of his vision. Even though whatever device it was that emitted the ambient radio waves that powered his lenses was almost certainly dead, there was enough residual power in their capacitors to keep them operating for at least a few more minutes. Beside the time, an icon appeared indicating that he was no longer connected.

Although this was probably about as much darkness as Luka had ever experienced, he realized that the blackness was not nearly as shocking as the silence. He had no idea how much noise was around him until most of it was either snapped off or spooled down. White noise beneath more layers of white noise—fans, pumps, electrical humming, air moving through ducts, fluid flowing through pipes—all of it stopped and still. All he heard now were the residual sounds of the *San Francisco*: gravity moving fluid in the absence of pressure, the metallic ticking of expanding or contracting air ducts, and then finally the colossal bellow and groan of the rig and the unfamiliar feeling of movement beneath him as the entire city rose and fell on the waves without any gyroscopic stabilizers to counter them.

Luka turned and took the two steps he knew he needed to cover the distance to the crate. It was more or less where he expected it to be when he reached down and brushed his fingertips against its lid, and then sat himself down beside it. He opened the box, groped, and finally removed the plasma lantern inside, but he did not turn it on. Instead, Luka sat in the dark and waited, watching the time pass in the corner of his vision, and wondering what he'd just started.

PART TWO

CHAPTER FIFTEEN

HEXAGON ROW

CIRCLES WERE THE MOST EFFICIENT way to enclose any given space. That was what the City Council learned during a three-hour combined geometry and engineering lesson conducted by Samuel Baird, one of the two math teachers employed by the Mission Dolores Education Center. Specifically, to enclose the maximum amount of space using the minimum amount of material, one should use a circle, sphere, or a dome.

But then a small bundle of bound straws was produced to demonstrate a related phenomenon. When one attempted to enclose *adjoining* spaces with circles—stacking them as tightly as possible in rows and columns to form a staggered grid—one got little triangular hollows in-between. Consequently, while circles were the most efficient way to enclose spaces in isolation, it turned out that in groups, they were surprisingly wasteful.

The most efficient way to enclose multiple adjoining spaces, therefore, would be with the highest-sided regular polygon capable of *tessellation*—that is, the shape most like a circle that can be tiled or patterned such that there is no dead space in-between. After the City Council was reluctantly divided into groups, all three teams experimented with supplied magnetic construction toys to eventually arrive at the same conclusion: hexagons.

Mr. Baird then proceeded to explain tensile strength. Squares were the easiest way to divide up space because the angles, lengths, and volumes were easiest to measure and calculate; however, squares were not particularly robust polygons. To demonstrate, he invited his students to imagine nailing or gluing together an open-sided composite box, sitting on it, then rocking forward and back. While squares (or rectangles, for that matter) were usually sufficient for supporting constant and perfectly lateral forces, they did not tolerate forces from other angles particularly well. Unlike hexagons, squares did not have the necessary additional angles to help counter cross forces, to prevent shearing or collapsing, and to help distribute load more evenly.

That brought Mr. Baird to the topic of triangles. While undeniably far less comfortable to sit on, triangles were in fact the strongest regular polygon. As the professor demonstrated with his own set of magnetic construction toys, triangles could not distort. Since their angles were fixed by the lengths of their opposing sides, those angles physically could not change, which made them fully resistant to folding or shearing. Triangles were the only shape whose geometric properties dictated that they must remain intact. With the exception of material fatigue or failure (a problem rarely seen since material scientists got ahold of assemblers), it was physically and mathematically impossible for triangles to distort and still remain triangles. In order to bolster his argument with empirical evidence, the ferrofluid table in the council chamber around which his students sat was employed to exhibit a series of trusses; scaffolding with cross braces that divided dangerously wobbly squares into rigid twin triangles; and finally, probably one of architecture's and engineering's greatest triumphs, and the only structure to combine the efficiency of a sphere with the strength of triangles: the long-revered geodesic dome.

So why not build everything out of triangles, Mr. Baird challenged. A dramatic pause, and then: Why not enclose spaces with triangles rather than squares or hexagons? The answer—once again demonstrated by a hastily established magnetic-toy model—was that tessellated triangles were not an efficient use of resources. In fact, triangles used more material to enclose smaller spaces than hexagons. Each intersection of tiled triangles consisted of six lines while tiled hexagons intersected with only three. The original *Equinox* architects and engineers understood this principle well, the professor expounded, which is why all the technician habitation modules were built out of adjoining, elongated, three-dimensional hexagons generally referred to as hexagonal prisms. It is why bees once instinctively constructed their hives out of densely packed hexagonal cells; why directly above Saturn's north pole, there persists a hexagonal cloud pattern larger than the diameter of Earth; why the ideal structure of graphene is a hexagonal grid; why slow-cooling basalt forms hexagonal fracture patterns; why snowflakes once formed in stunningly elegant hexagonal symmetry. The inescapable conclusion was that the principles of mathematics, geometry, engineering, and in fact of all the known and quite possibly knowable universe suggested—nay, *insisted*—that the inspiration for all future construction, innovation, and renovation aboard any seafaring vessel with limited space, limited resources, and tremendous incentive to maximize strength-to-weight ratio, should clearly be none other than the miraculous, the venerable, and the seemingly divine hexagon. (Transcripts showed that Samuel Baird then took a moment to collect his emotions before solemnly declaring the hexagon to be one of nature's greatest gifts to humankind, pinching the bridge of his nose, and then politely but hastily excusing himself.)

The professor's impassioned geometry lesson was not lost on the City Council as hexagons did indeed begin to appear throughout the rig: the welded composite-weave hexagonal panels that comprised the newest version of the air dome; the postal capsule exchange on deck two known as "the hive"; the synthetic graphite supports between decks, themselves assembled from stacked hexagonal lattices of carbon atoms; some of the newer duct work, electrical conduits, and clusters of PVC pipes. But of all the hexagonal patterns that were beginning to appear both above and below deck, there was only one structure actually called "The Hexagon"—or more frequently, "Hexagon Row"— and that was the brig.

The original brig was located beneath the bridge at the northeastern-most corner of the mining platform. Back then, it consisted of little more than a row of metal boxes with cage-like mesh doors manually secured with tungsten bolts. Cells were furnished with toilets, basins, and two benches that could be used for sitting or sleeping, or could be folded up against the wall in order to give inmates additional space to stretch, or maybe do a few push-ups. For most of the *San Francisco*'s existence, the crime rate hovered at around 0.2 percent, which meant there were usually around ten people incarcerated at any given time. With eight reasonably sized cells—four on either side of a narrow, metal-grated hallway—the most violent offenders could be isolated while those who simply needed a few days to contemplate exile after starting a minor scuffle or trying to siphon off a few watts could be safely housed together.

But paradoxically—or at least seemingly so—as the standard of living aboard the *San Francisco* rose, so too did the crime rate. The current level was 0.7 percent, which worked out to an average of thirty-five people imprisoned at any given time. Although to Luka's knowledge, the City Council never publicly addressed the trend—and specifically the fact that it directly contradicted both the Council's and the Judicial Committee's predictions and campaign platforms as they pertained to crime—their decision to construct a brand-new brig was reasonably good evidence of passive acknowledgment. And so too was their continuously evolving position toward the philosophy of incarceration.

(It should be noted that it was not uncommon for the eight-member City Council and the four-member Judicial Committee to find themselves completely aligned, since the Judicial Committee was simply a subset of the City Council, just with a different distribution of appointments and honorifics.)

The newest trend was for the Judicial Committee to no longer issue sentences to convicted offenders. Rather, their focus was purely on verdicts. You were either guilty or you weren't. If you were declared innocent, you walked out of the tribunal chamber on the seventh floor of City Hall, descend entirely unescorted via electromagnetic lift and a few spiral walkways, and rejoined your fellow citizens. At the opposite extreme, if you were found guilty of your third offense—regardless of how minor—or if you were found guilty of a handful of capital offenses (among them, premeditated murder, rape, or treason) you were automatically exiled. For anything in-between, the Judicial Committee had only one sentence at its disposal: rehabilitation.

In the case of *San Francisco v. Luka Mance*, the proceedings were both complex and controversial. It was argued by a handful of City Council members—Khang among them—that Luka's actions constituted treason, and therefore justified exile. It was even fervently argued by one councilman that although no one had died during the two hours that the power had remained off—and the additional three and a half hours it took to get all the systems and subsystems rebooted and back online—it was certainly conceivable that any number of people could have died in any number of ways, and therefore Luka's actions constituted a new class of crime for which he proposed the designation "plausible manslaughter." However, the Judicial Committee determined that there was no legal basis for establishing a new category of offense—especially in real-time—and therefore dismissed the motion. In the end, it was plain and simple reckless endangerment that Luka was both tried for and found guilty of.

Luka accepted his conviction without protest, and used what little time he was given to address the Judicial Committee as a means to convey a message to the City Council. He did not regret his actions, he explained to the panel awkwardly. He was grateful that no lives had been lost, and harming anyone had certainly never been his intention, but even if there had been injuries or even deaths, it would have been a small price to pay for opening everyone's eyes to what was going on around them. He only hoped that his actions hadn't been too little, too late.

It was rare for anyone on the committee to directly respond to the convicted, but the chairman—a man named Matthew Two Bulls, who believed himself to be the last full-blooded Lakota Indian on the planet—signified by stirring in his chair and clearing his throat that he was prepared to make an exception. After undergoing extended rehabilitation and eventually being released, Two Bulls began, Luka would discover that his crimes were entirely without effect, and his sacrifice ultimately devoid of service. Indeed, he had successfully instigated temporary panic throughout the city, but only until power had been restored, and only until officials were able to issue assurances that there was no truth whatsoever to Luka's warning. Luka would find, Two Bulls concluded with poorly concealed smugness and satisfaction, that although he would probably earn back his freedom eventually and likely be permitted to return to work at the foundry, he would never regain any significant credibility or influence among the community. The best Luka could ever hope for from his friends, coworkers, and his compatriots was to be pitied for the rest of his life.

At that, Luka was briskly escorted out through the back of the room to await the formal procession tasked with delivering him to his new home on Hexagon Row, where he would begin his rehabilitation.

CHAPTER SIXTEEN

WAVE INTERFERENCE

AYLA WATCHED THE PERIMETER from inside the *Anura* while Omicron secured the bodies in the back. The scavengers stood at the very edge of visibility in the thick mustard smog, keeping vigil like a band of lost and agitated souls. Using an enhanced external view, Ayla could see that they were all bald and emaciated, and that some of them were naked except for primitive respirators with dangling hoses that connected to something on their backs. Their bent and knobby bodies were covered in wide black lesions and some of them had hands and feet that ended in fleshy, club-like stumps. When she zoomed in on their faces, she could see that most of them had no lips to conceal their sharpened metallic teeth, and all that was left of their noses were crooked shards of cartilage. They looked toward the *Anura* with more curiosity and restlessness in their dry and misaligned eyes than savagery, though Ayla had no doubt that they were collectively contemplating an advance—somehow reading and reacting to each other's movements as a single coordinated entity. As their formation changed, the targeting computer calculated a new firing solution optimized to drop them in the order of their anticipated arrival.

When all three bodies were loaded, Omicron paused before getting in. "Should I close the door?" he asked Ayla. As far as she could tell, there was no predisposition in her bodyguard's voice.

"Yes," Ayla told him. "The computer has them targeted. You have time."

The Neo did as he was told, and as soon as the slab of steel was back in place and the wheel was tightened down, they heard the heavy lock slide into position. Omicron kept his hand on his weapon while he found his way back to the *Anura*.

Ayla was silent as they drove. She didn't know whether or not she had made the right call out there, and she didn't want to distract Omicron by processing it out loud. The computer was navigating, but Omicron was actively engaged, providing frequent navigational input. The path he facilitated avoided the scavengers, but also minimized risk to the *Anura*. If it came down to making a choice, he told Ayla, he would make a hole through the homeless before potentially incurring damage that might risk all their lives. The scavengers stayed with them—their numbers steadily increasing—but they always left a direction for the *Anura* to advance, and it wasn't until they reached the shore that Ayla realized what was happening. They had probably never seen a fully amphibious craft before, and they appeared to be directing the vehicle onto the beach where its tires would spin in the combination of sand and the accumulation of viscous toxins, trapping them and eventually forcing them to attempt an escape on foot. But as the *Anura* approached the shore, it used the last of its traction to accelerate through the blackened marshes into the frothy waves, then pulled up its wheels and left behind what had become hundreds of well-coordinated thermal signatures.

After decontamination, Ayla and Omicron worked together to transfer the three defectors to the *Hawk*'s modest med bay. It only had two cots, but there was room to lay the third body out on the floor. Omicron advised Ayla that they should find a way to keep them confined—or, at the very least, loosely bound—during the process of resuscitation. It was possible, he believed, that they would react violently. In particular, he was concerned about the young man, and how instinctively protective he seemed to be of the pregnant girl. Ayla insisted that if any of them wanted to be taken back to V1, they would find a way to make that happen. Even if it took several days to work out a safe approach, she had already decided that nobody would be kept or transported against his or her will. Omicron assured her that she had done the right thing back at the wall—that it was the only thing she could have done given their circumstances—and had they waited much longer, it was possible none of them would have made it out. His robust features and diminutive eyes were surprisingly warm and reassuring when he smiled, and Ayla realized how grateful she was not only for his assistance and his council, but simply for his company, as well.

Ayla decided that they should move farther down-coast in case the scavengers had some form of primitive watercraft capable of reaching them. While Omicron fashioned restraints, Ayla went upstairs and was astonished to find that Jumanne Nsonowa was waiting for her on the bridge.

The sight of the man standing between the rows of consoles stopped her dead in the hatchway. Nsonowa was an unsettling figure—presenting much more like a witch doctor than an anthropologist or a business facilitator—but as she reached for the vitaline on her wrist to summon Omicron, something about his appearance made her pause. After the initial shock began to dissipate, Ayla could see that the man was not real.

The array of lasers projected by the quadcopter drones outside into a focused wave interference pattern were being partially deflected by the bridge's highly filtered external viewports, diminishing the hologram's apparent constitution and causing

Nsonowa to be rendered much more transparently than he would otherwise be. Additionally, the drones' gyroscopic stabilizers were out of phase with the ship's movement on the water, which meant that the figure first hovered several centimeters above the floor, and then as the deck rose to meet the soles of his sandals, his feet and ankles grew elongated across the textured silicone tile. Ayla didn't know whether the signal was being transmitted from a satellite, via an ad hoc meshwork of communications drones, or simply skipped off the ionosphere, but the image ghosted and lurched from atmospheric and radiological interference.

Although Ayla had spent the last several years among sailors, traders, smugglers, and merchants, for the most part, she had retained the composure and vernacular she'd been raised to respect within the Nanortalik Pod System. However, she was certainly not above profanity whenever the situation merited.

"What the *fuck* are you doing here?" she spat out. She wondered if Nsonowa would be able to hear her, but decided that drones capable of projecting three-dimensional holograms could probably pick up enough acoustical clues through the viewports, combine them with lip movements and facial expressions, and finally synthesize a pretty credible rendition of her side of the conversation.

"Ayla Novik," the hologram announced, seemingly quite pleased with the reaction he was able to elicit. His deep, accented tone came through the bridge's audio system and was slightly out of sync with the flickering apparition. "Congratulations on your discovery."

Ayla looked at the image with disgust. "*What* discovery?"

"The Queen Mary Pod System," Nsonowa said. "Or as you probably know it, Ishtar Terra Station One."

"I don't know what you're talking about," Ayla said. She advanced farther into the room, stopped behind the rear row of consoles, and put her hands on the back of an anchored swivel chair. "There's nothing out here but abandoned research facilities and packs of scavengers."

Nsonowa looked at the girl like a disappointed father. "Ayla Novik," he scolded with a disapproving brow. "You cannot lie to me. I intercepted your exchange with the boy, Arik, and I know you have just returned from your rendezvous. Tell me: do you have them?"

Ayla tried to divine how much more Nsonowa knew and decided that the only way to be sure was to test him. "They didn't show," she finally said. "We nearly got ourselves torn apart out there and the little bastard never came. We were about to head up there to tell you in person, but you just saved us the trip."

"Then who else is aboard your ship?"

"What do you mean?" Ayla said. "There's nobody else here. Just Omicron."

Even in the low-resolution projection full of visual noise and compression artifacts, Ayla could see Nsonowa's contacts sparkle. "If I can project myself onto your bridge," he began, "and have a conversation with you from eight thousand kilometers away, do you not think I can detect life-forms on your ship?" He clasped his hands behind his back. "There are four signatures other than yours and your Neo's."

Ayla looked down at the floor beside her. She was searching for where she might still have an advantage—weighing whether it was better to keep trying to find the edges of his knowledge, or whether she was only provoking him.

"Three," she finally said. "The boy didn't show."

"*Four*," Nsonowa corrected with a self-satisfied grin. "If you count the baby."

Ayla shook her head with spiteful resignation. "Just tell me what you want."

Nsonowa's image divided into two for a moment, then flickered independently before converging again. There was harmonic distortion in his voice, but it was still intelligible. "What I want, Ayla Novik, is everyone you brought aboard your ship. What I want is this technology that the boy claimed could transform the planet."

Ayla knew by now that she had no strategic or tactical advantage over either Nsonowa or the Coronians, but that didn't necessarily mean she had to cooperate. There was always one option available, even to the most oppressed and downtrodden: pure and unadulterated defiance. Even if Nsonowa did end up getting what he wanted, that didn't mean Ayla had to make it easy for him. And she was still a long way from capitulation.

"Well guess what, you ugly son of a bitch," Ayla began. She stepped out from behind the rear row of consoles and strode toward the projection. "You can't have them. However you're tracking us, Omicron will figure it out, and then he'll figure out how to counter it. I'll shoot down your shitty little drones, and we'll be long gone before you can send more. After this conversation is over, you're never going to see or hear from us again, so thanks for the offer, but I'm afraid we're going to have to politely decline."

Horizontal scan lines ran up through Nsonowa's projection as he leaned back and let out a deep, bellowing laugh.

"Ayla Novik," he said after regaining his composure. "I wish you would come work for me. It is rare that I come across such conviction and spirit as you have."

Ayla stepped back and reached down to activate the nearest console. "Any last words before I wreck your drones?"

Nsonowa's lingering smile faded. "You can do as you say, Ayla Novik," he told her, "but it is not you or Omicron I will punish. Do not forget, I have the boy's transmission, same as you. If you do not deliver the prisoners to me in twenty-four hours, I will destroy the entire Queen Mary Pod System. Do you know how many people that is?"

Ayla tried to read the man's expression. It was more expectant than it was challenging, and she knew that he was not bluffing.

"You'll never get close to it," she told him, though she could already feel herself faltering—could hear herself speaking without any real conviction.

"Come now, Ayla Novik," Nsonowa said with an unexpected tone of sympathy. "You of all people should know how easy it is to destroy a defenseless pod system." His hands came back around to his front and he lowered his head without breaking his gaze. "Now, you are wasting what little time you still have left. Good-bye."

"Wait," Ayla said. She closed her eyes and waited for something to come to her—some other angle, some form of leverage, some additional avenue for negotiation—but she knew that nothing would come. The best she could do at this point was to try to buy some time. "There's no way we can get them to you in twenty-four hours," she said. "We'll need at least a week."

"You are not bringing the prisoners to me," Nsonowa said. "You will take them to a nearby city."

"A *city*?" Ayla said. "There's nothing like that around here."

"You will see," Nsonowa said. "I recommend you do not destroy my drones until you receive further instructions."

The projection glitched back and forth between two and three dimensions, and then it was gone. Ayla looked down at the terminal and saw that there was a new dispatch from MIS, but she did not select it. Instead, she opened a comm channel and cleared her throat.

"Omicron," she said.

Omicron's voice came through the bridge's audio system. "I'm here."

"Have you started waking them up yet?"

"Not yet," Omicron said. "I was just about to."

"Good," Ayla said. She watched the drones outside the viewport rotate, and then flit out of sight into the distance. "Don't."

It was unlike Omicron to follow up Ayla's instructions with questions, but she could tell from the silence that one was coming.

"What happened?" he asked her.

"There's been a change of plans," Ayla said.

CHAPTER SEVENTEEN

REHABILITATION

ALL REHABILITATION ABOARD THE *San Francisco* occurred on Hexagon Row, which was located on the basement level of the Pacific Medical Center. The new site was obviously chosen as a symbol of the progressive shift away from punishment and toward treatment. The room was lined with a total of forty-eight horizontally oriented hexagonal capsules—twelve capsules per wall. There were two levels of catwalks along the perimeter of the room, from which prisoners either stepped up or down into their cells. Inside, they found everything they needed during their stay: a toilet and shower in the back; a combination bed and desk that hung limp until an electric current aligned and interlocked sets of support rods; a carbon fiber chair; a simple treadmill embedded in the floor; a standard pneumatic refuse chute; and a drawer through which meals and other items could be passed. The walls were all reinforced opaque polymeth that was better than 99 percent soundproof, and which muted all but the most deafening of screams.

Just as there was only one primary form of justice aboard the *San Francisco*, once you were on Hexagon Row, there was only one primary rule: inmates were to spend a combined minimum of two hours per day talking—not to themselves, not to each other, and not to Pacific Medical Center staff, but to an interactive mental health assessment and facilitation application anthropomorphically known as "Ellie."

The core of Ellie was a program culled from the academic archives. Neither software engineers nor medical staff aboard the *San Francisco* were entirely sure how she worked despite thousands of combined person-hours dedicated to reading through source code and interacting with running instances. It was the opinion of the software infrastructure team that at least 75 percent of Ellie's codebase had been algorithmically generated, and was therefore obfuscated beyond any hope of human interpretation or reverse engineering. Just parsing a single line of code out of the hundreds of millions—keeping track of all the variables, correctly grouping deeply nested operations, and even simply following the constructs of an archaic and unfamiliar programming language—had eluded most of the computer scientists aboard the rig. And as if her codebase wasn't utterly baffling enough, every instance of Ellie not only stored and keyed off of billions of pieces of metadata derived from interactions, but it also appeared to reach into working memory and rewrite its own bytecode throughout the life of the process. In other words, the moment a new instance of Ellie was executed and interacted with, it instantly became unlike any other instance that had ever been executed before it. And once that instance was finally terminated—once the patient/prisoner was considered successfully rehabilitated and shortly thereafter released—there would never be another instance that behaved exactly like it again.

Ellie's codebase was old enough that it wouldn't run natively on the *San Francisco*'s electron computing cloud. Like most of the software borrowed from the corporate and academic software archives, she had to be executed inside of an emulator—in this case, one that made Ellie believe that she had access to thirty-two terabytes of memory, eight terabytes of clustered storage, and a total of 5,760 x86 processor cores. As long as all the instruction sets she expected were available, she never knew that the world into which she was constantly being reborn no longer existed. In a way, Ellie was contained inside her own virtual cell.

Although her kernel was incomprehensibly convoluted and, for all intents and purposes, impenetrable, Ellie's original long-departed engineers had thought far enough ahead to design hooks into her architecture allowing the *San Francisco*'s software infrastructure team to customize and configure her without having to know how she worked. Each instance listened on a unique TCP/IP port and accepted incoming connections over which data formatted according to an old standard called HTTP could be posted or requested. But more importantly, external processes could register to receive events as the dozens of psychological metrics she maintained were updated. Once those metrics met or exceeded thresholds determined by Pacific Medical Center staff, a notification was sent to the Judicial Committee, the patient's status was updated to an integer that mapped to the human-readable string "CURED," and the prisoner was subsequently released. The upshot was that the more you talked to Ellie—the more you opened up to her and really tried to let her help you—the faster you made progress, and the sooner you got to go home.

Although there was only one primary rule on Hexagon Row—allowing oneself to be psychoanalyzed by an emulated and virtual shrink—Luka was never all that good at following even the simplest and most basic of regulations, and in fact had become significantly less so since losing both his unborn son and his wife over the course of the last year. Therefore, Luka became intimately familiar with the one consequence for breaking the one rule: time in the quiet room.

The name "quiet room" was intentionally ironic—not because the chamber was actually loud, but because quiet didn't even begin to describe it. At −14.7 decibels (0 decibels being the point at which humans begin detecting sound), it was probably the quietest place on the entire planet, and very possibly as quiet as quiet could get. By comparison, the silence that Luka experienced when he shut down the power was pure chaos and cacophony.

The anechoic (meaning "nonechoing") chamber contained three primary layers. The outermost shell was half a meter of solid cured impact gel. Set inside the gel were alternating racks of 1.5-meter-long fiberglass acoustic wedges that diverted and absorbed sound waves from all directions. And finally, there was a two-square-meter wire cage that kept the occupant suspended above the acoustic wedges in the floor, and prevented him or her from attempting to claw through the walls. The room was designed to be experienced in the dark, so there were no lights (which would have probably caused an intolerably blaring buzz anyway).

The primary function of the quiet room was to induce panic, which, in about 20 percent of cases, happened within the first two to three minutes. The quiet room was so devoid of sound that, as one's ears adjusted, he began to hear his own heartbeat, which was unfamiliar and unnerving enough that the experience frequently led to an increased heart rate, which became a self-perpetuating cycle that often culminated in a panic attack, hyperventilation, and ultimately, the loss of consciousness.

Those with slightly higher tolerances often came to believe that being in the room was somehow killing them, since the sound of their own digestion became as loud as a toilet flushing;

the air moving through their trachea and bronchia was like high-pressure pneumatic tubes being pierced; the blood coursing through the vessels in and around their ears was like the ceaseless and rapid pounding of violent waves. Any kind of movement resulted in tendons stretching like dry-rotted polymer, and the sound of a joint popping was an unsettling thunderclap.

But it was those who retained their composure the longest who experienced the worst effects of being inside the quiet room: the complete lack of direction, orientation, or sense of space. Humans used echolocation—the sound of their own voices, footsteps, humming, whistling, clucking, *et cetera*—far more than they realized for both proprioception (the sense of one's own position in space) and exteroception (the sense of the outside world). When those who were accustomed to them were suddenly and completely deprived of acoustic clues, rather than the potentially relaxing and introspective experience of homeostatic sensory deprivation, the feeling was that of being thrust into a room of infinite volume; suspended above a bottomless void; sucked out into the vacuum of space, but without the rapid and merciful death. It had been described by several Hexagon Row graduates as the feeling of the soul gradually leaving the body.

Most phobias were not absolutes, but rather existed on a continuum, and agoraphobia was no different. It was not literally the fear of open spaces, but rather intense panic elicited by a sense of lack of control. The most fundamental feeling of control came from one's sense of space—one's sense of physical being—and when not even a single distant echo of their most impassioned screams and pleas made it back through the blackness to their ears, the sensation was truly that of staring into the abyss.

In short, the quiet room compelled one to talk, though not through harmless incentive as generally believed by anyone who hadn't experienced it firsthand. The relationship between the quiet room and the sudden compulsion to express oneself was not as simple as the desire to fill prolonged periods of silence with dialog and verbal self-expression. It was both far more complicated and far simpler than that. When subjects were removed from the quiet room—if they were still conscious—they were almost always clinging to the cage so desperately that the wire had cut into the flesh of their fingers. Frequently they had to be administered a jet-injected tranquilizer just to get them to relax their grips. Medical orderlies regularly lifted the wire floor in order to clean bodily fluids from the acoustic panels below. Subjects did not talk after spending time in the quiet room because they were weary of silence; they talked out of a profound, acute, and a newly acquired pathological fear of it.

The longest anyone had previously spent in the quiet room while fully conscious was ninety-two minutes. Within a week, Luka was up to two hours. Both the Judicial Committee and the Pacific Medical Center personnel in charge of rehabilitation agreed that Luka's refusal to talk was related to the fear of finally processing his wife's suicide. They were, of course, wrong. In fact, Luka very much wanted to talk. There was something about the idea of opening up to an entity that could not judge him, was not capable of hating him, and after he was released and the process was terminated, would not even remember who he was, that some part of him found extremely appealing.

In reality, Luka's reluctance to participate in the rehabilitation process was twofold: first, he needed get past the curious yellow withdrawal. Luka had been so successful at convincing himself of his own moderation that at first, he didn't recognize the symptoms for what they were. Both Luka and the doctor who brusquely examined him attributed the itching, sneezing, sweating, waves of nausea, and the ringing in his ears to a minor viral infection. However, Luka had so much time for introspection—both in his cell and in the quiet room—that he eventually could find no way around the inescapable fact that he was—or at least had been—a full-on opioid addict. Fortunately, he had always been a highly functioning addict, limiting himself to small enough doses that at least the physical aspects of the dependency steadily waned over the course of a week, leaving behind what was perhaps the larger and far more difficult barrier to his psychological improvement: his own stubbornness.

This final obstruction was eventually identified—though it was not by a doctor or by the Judicial Committee, but by a member of the janitorial staff who was wheeling in a refreshment cart halfway through a weekly status meeting.

"He'll never talk as long as you keep trying to make him," she announced with a surprising lack of inhibition. When all heads turned in her direction, she unabashedly continued. "I used to know Luka," she said. "He'll talk, but it's going to have to be on his own terms."

The day that Luka was told that he would never again be placed in the quiet room—that he had beaten them, and they had unanimously agreed to yield—he activated his bed, laid down, and looked up at the ceiling of his hexagonal capsule. And when Ellie emerged from the depths of the opaque polymeth surface and asked Luka if he was ready to begin, he found that he was.

CHAPTER EIGHTEEN

CRYOSTASIS

THERE WAS ONLY ONE CRYOSTATIC crate aboard the *Accipiter Hawk* large enough for a body. Omicron retrofitted two others using parts from cases designed to transport organs and other organic cargo. Long-term hibernation was not the intention since they had neither the technology nor the biological proficiency to induce true dormancy. However, temporary metabolic suppression would reduce the refugees' short-term need for sustenance and hydration, and would hopefully help to ensure a quick and orderly transaction.

On two separate occasions, Ayla had asked Omicron to assess their options and follow them through to their most probable outcomes. Both times, he reached more or less the same conclusions she had: if they did not deliver the refugees as Nsonowa instructed, there was little doubt that V1 would be destroyed. Additionally, Omicron's implant would almost certainly be deactivated, and it was probably only a matter of time before the *Accipiter Hawk* appeared either on Nsonowa's grid, or the grid of someone else under the direct control of the Coronians.

On the other hand, it was possible that both Nsonowa and the Coronians stood to benefit from keeping their promise— that although they clearly had the advantage, they understood the importance of promoting trust among those they employed to act on their behalf. Ayla believed it was also possible—not very likely, but possible—that the refugees would not actually be killed once in the Coronians' possession, but rather would be studied, preserved, and might one day even have the opportunity to take back control of their own futures.

One way or another, Ayla and Omicron agreed that Nsonowa and the Coronians would get what they wanted. The only question was how many people would have to die in the process. And so it was with the belief that she was ultimately saving lives that Ayla suppressed her initial instinct to flee, and gave Omicron the order to deliver the refugees as instructed.

As the *Hawk* approached the coordinates specified in the MIS dispatch, Ayla wondered if there had been some kind of mistake. Either the location was wrong, she speculated, or their navigation systems were incorrectly calibrated. The *Hawk*'s long-range sensors were reporting a cross section unlike any vessel she had ever seen—a signature much more consistent with a small island than a ship. But as the radar, lidar, and sonar systems continued to accumulate data points and incorporate them into higher resolution models, Omicron reported that the structure was far too symmetrical to be organic. It appeared to be an almost perfect square of 333 meters per side, and it was topped by a tremendous air dome reaching a height of roughly 160 meters above sea level at its highest point. Before Omicron could find a match in the ship's archives, Ayla believed she had already figured out what it was. Her crew used to talk about old Metropolis-class nuclear-powered industrial rigs—nomadic and largely self-sufficient sea-mining and refinery operations tasked with providing the *Equinox* effort with massive amounts of raw materials. Roughly a dozen of them had been built—each named after a major American city—though Costa had postulated that all of them were long gone. It was common nautical knowledge that a design flaw, one which allowed fumes to build up around the bilge pumps, resulted in some of the fleet being destroyed by fire, and that some of the first Metropolis rigs were used as salvage to keep newer models in service. The rest, it was believed, were lost to pirates and raiders who didn't have the knowledge or expertise to keep the ships' nuclear reactors functioning properly, eventually resulting in either gradual core breaches or flash meltdowns severely irradiating everyone and everything inside of a five-kilometer radius.

The *Hawk*'s sensors gave two reasons for rejecting Ayla's hypothesis: the first was key structural deviations from the schematics it had pulled from the ship's archives, and the second was the notable absence of any type of radiological signature. But even a casual side-by-side glance at the model from the archives and the three-dimensional rendering of the vessel in front of them showed how much computers—for all their spectacular brute force capabilities—still lacked even rudimentary imagination. There was no doubt that at least one Metropolis-class mining rig had not only survived, but had also been extensively modified and upgraded over the years. To Ayla, that was clear evidence of a long-term affiliation with the Coronians.

After being hailed by the vessel identifying itself as the *San Francisco*, they were instructed to place the cargo on the forward deck where it could be verified. The three cryostatic crates were already laid out on the forward freight elevator—eerily like caskets, Ayla had observed—so Omicron was able to raise them into view without leaving the bridge. The *Hawk* was then instructed to reduce speed to half ahead and approach the rig's port bow. Visibility this far out was fairly good, and as they got closer, they could see the vessel's insignia emblazoned across the curvature of the dome: some kind of majestic bird with its wings raised and head turned, rendered in irregular grayscale geometric shapes. They could also see that the entire northwest corner of the platform was essentially cut away into an angular overhang, presumably to accommodate cargo vessels of various displacements. The breach appeared to be a combination hangar, mooring deck, and port, and from all the time Ayla had spent on the docks back home, she knew that the ceiling was probably an open network of gantry cranes for hoisting and transporting crates and equipment. A bewildered look passed between her and Omicron as they reduced their speed again—this time to slow ahead—acknowledging what both of them were thinking: the top of the *Hawk*'s mainmast was probably too tall to fit inside the cargo bay. But as they continued to follow the *San Francisco*'s instructions with increasing uncertainty, they realized that they were not headed directly for the overhang, but rather an area of open water just off the vessel's port bow.

As requested, Omicron locked in their position relative to the rig, which was now directly starboard. A few minutes passed and Omicron was about to hail the *San Francisco* to request further instructions when they looked down and noticed movement on the digitally stitched and synthesized external panoramic view. They watched as a type of seawall or break emerged from the water around them like the surfacing of a vast, serpentine beast. The air quality was good enough that Ayla suggested they watch what was happening from the forward deck, and Omicron—also clearly intrigued—hastily agreed. He undocked a polymeth panel from the console, and they both pulled full-face breathers over their heads on their way through the forward airlock. Omicron paused on the way out, then lifted one of his rifles from the rack by the bulkhead hatch and slung it over his shoulder. Ayla turned and noticed that he had armed himself.

"Good idea," she said.

"Just in case."

From outside the ship they watched the wall continue to rise, then at some point realized that it had stopped moving, and that it was the local sea level around them that was falling. When enough water had been pumped out to make the *Hawk* sit several meters lower—sufficient for clearance of the mainmast—they were told to reset their position lock to the seawall around them rather than the rig. Omicron drew new virtual anchor points on his tablet, and a moment later, they felt the deck lurch as something below them took the ship's keel firmly into its grip. The next instruction from the *San Francisco* was to cut their engines entirely. Omicron complied, and the seawall began to retract beneath the overhang like a tremendous drawer carved directly into the open sea.

Ayla and Omicron shared a long look as the *Hawk* continued to be absorbed by the much larger vessel.

"No turning back now," Ayla said.

"Apparently not."

"If you see me scratch my nose," Ayla said, "kill anything that moves."

"What if your nose actually itches?" the Neo asked.

"I'll try to remember not to scratch it."

Ayla's mood had been one of resignation and resentment going into the maneuver; however, she could not help but look around her now with some amount of astonishment and even awe. It was dim and dank beneath the overhang, and even through her respirator she could smell the pungent acridity of the sea, which had always been every bit as wonderful to her as it was offensive to almost everyone else she'd ever known. As she expected, there were I-beams above them forming dual-axis rails on which winches and booms could be maneuvered into precise positions for lifting and stacking transport containers below. A silica crow's nest glided along one of the rails as the man inside inspected both the cargo and the *Hawk*'s crew, reporting on what he was seeing to the three men waiting on the berth below. There was a well-maintained ship's tender of an enclosed catamaran design Ayla had never seen before moored a safe distance from the *Hawk*, and farther back inside the hangar was a sleek and finned airship with transparent view panels along its belly, hinting at a fully integrated passenger gondola. Below the dirigible was a type of vehicle Ayla had never seen before. It was part plane (but with wings that were obviously far too short for flight), and part boat (but with eight massive topside aviation engines). She guessed it was an old GEV, or Ground Effect Vehicle: a mode of transportation that relied on floating on top of a cushion of air that formed when generating lift in close proximity to the ground.

There was the occasional breach of the seawall behind them by lackadaisical waves, followed by spray and white wash careening down the fused hexagonal plates where unseen pumps compensated to keep the *Hawk* safely within the floating city's embrace. Ayla could feel that wonderful and terrible churning and burning feeling in the pit of her stomach that always accompanied new and unfamiliar experiences. Although there were certainly times when she found it difficult to make sense of her life outside of the pervasive and relentless themes of tragedy and loss—the rejection of her father, the destruction of her home, the slaughter of her former crew and husband—there were still these moments when she could not help but be amazed by where she was, and how far she had traveled, and by all there was in the world still worth seeing and experiencing.

"We're going to need you to lose that rifle," one of the men shouted up from below. The man in the crow's nest overhead was wearing high-visibility orange and a matching hard hat, but the men on the wharf did not look like dockworkers. All three were wearing light ballistic armor, and while their sidearms were not drawn, the position of their hands suggested that could change at any moment.

Omicron looked at Ayla and Ayla nodded. The rifle was kept in an ostensibly neutral position as the Neo removed it from his shoulder, squatted, and placed the weapon gently on the deck. One of the men gestured up to the crow's nest and the capsule resumed gliding along its rails. What looked to be a solid walk-way began to descend from a gantry above them, though as one end of it aligned with the gap in the rail along the perimeter of the forward deck, the remainder of it segmented into steps that fell perfectly along the contour of the *Hawk*'s hull, finally termi-nating not far from the feet of the men on the dock.

Ayla realized that this entire operation—the external and maneuverable lock for raising and lowering ships before pulling them in; the framework overhead for dynamically assembling various methods of lift and leverage; the infinitely configurable gangplank capable of conforming to vessels of any size and shape—was all designed to serve a system of trade and com-merce in which the only standards and protocols that mattered anymore were those that embraced diversity.

"Why don't you two come on down," the man said. Although Ayla could not identify any kind of visual rank, it was clear that he was the one in charge. He had short, sandy hair and was clean shaven, while the two men beside him wore several days' worth of dark growth.

"No thanks," Ayla called down. "You come up and get your cargo, then we'll be on our way."

"The thing is," the man said, "we're going to need to verify it."

Ayla watched the man for a moment before responding. "Fine," she said. "How long will that take?"

"Not long. Just a day or two. Three at the most."

Ayla shook her head. "No way," she said. "We'll stay long enough for you to open the crates and verify whatever you need to verify, but that's it. And we'll wait up here, not down there with you."

"Come on, now," the man said. "We have very comfortable rooms all set up for you. It would be a shame to let them go to waste."

"Sorry," Ayla told the man. "Staying here wasn't part of the deal."

"I understand," the man on the ground said. "But unfortunately, that's the only deal there is."

In her peripheral vision, Ayla noticed Omicron look up, and when she followed his gaze, she saw the muzzle of a rifle protruding from the crow's nest. It occurred to her at that moment that gun barrels were not unlike men's eyes in that it was surprisingly easy to tell exactly where they were pointing. In this case, it was at her bodyguard's head.

CHAPTER NINETEEN

CULTURAL HYPOXIA

LYING DOWN AND STARING UP at the ceiling hadn't worked. Luka needed to be able to move around, turn away, pace. Even though Ellie was virtual in every respect, there were times when Luka found it necessary—in order for him to say the things that truly needed to be said—to turn away from the compassion and consolation in his virtual therapist's placid brown eyes.

He was now sitting on the edge of his cot, head down, forearms on his knees that bounced like a roughly idling motor. Beside him was a cold, picked-over boxed meal: termites cooked in oil with peppers, tomatoes, and onion, served over a type of cornmeal porridge. The accompanying probiotic capsule and vitamin supplement were still secured in their recesses.

Ellie was in her usual purple armchair against a simple and somewhat dreary aluminum-to-charcoal gradient background, legs crossed and spine characteristically rigid. She was plain, but pretty; professional, but warm. Her use of Standard American English completed her perfectly neutral disposition. Luka speculated that the reason her presentation never deviated from pulled-back, chestnut hair, a plain taupe cardigan over a jade blouse, and gunmetal-gray slacks was to establish a level of drab familiarity intended to help counter the tendency of patients to transfer strong feelings of intimacy onto those with whom they have grown comfortable sharing their emotions—even if that someone happened to be nothing more than a collection of relatively low-resolution textures and pixel shaders wrapped around a moderately feminine 3D wireframe. Ellie didn't even appear to be wearing a belt that, in order to avoid uncomfortable questioning, one might entertain fantasies of unbuckling.

Luka wasn't quite ready to begin. By way of stalling, he stood and took the two steps permitted by the distance between the bed and the front of the capsule. He looked down into the common area—a wire-mesh pit illuminated by ruby-red plasma panels—and saw that three prisoners in incarceration suits were being led to their cells by an equal number of armed officers. The guards were familiar, but he did not recognize the captives: a young woman with short, black hair and two men. He was positive he'd never seen the one in front before as the man was broader and more muscular than Luka would have previously thought possible. As the prisoners were directed into adjacent capsules, Luka decided they were probably just brokers or traders who'd tried to breach the port lock before settling a disputed transaction. A row of opaque slats slid across the openings of all three cells, pivoted into an interlocking configuration, and then there was nothing more to see.

As had become customary, the avatar was the first to breach the initial awkward silence.

"Would you like to continue talking about your parents, Luka?"

Luka watched the guards exit the catwalk. "Not particularly."

"Does it make you uncomfortable to talk about your parents?"

"It doesn't make me uncomfortable," Luka said. "I'm just tired of it."

"Why do you think you're tired of talking about your parents?"

"Because there's nothing left to talk about," Luka told her. "They wanted a better life for me, so they brought me here. That's all there is to it."

"It's interesting that you use the word 'brought.'"

"Why's that interesting?"

"During our last session, you used the word 'sold.'"

"They aren't mutually exclusive."

"Do you believe your parents received payment of some sort for bringing you here?"

"I know they did."

"How does that make you feel?"

"It doesn't make me feel anything. I know they didn't do it for the money. They did it because they couldn't take care of me. But they would've been stupid not to accept payment in return."

"What do you think would have happened if you'd stayed with your parents?"

"I'd be dead."

"Why do you think that you'd be dead?"

"Because they couldn't even take care of themselves, much less a little kid."

"Why do you believe your parents decided to bring you here?"

"It was all very simple," Luka said with poorly concealed exasperation. "They needed to lighten their load, and the *San Francisco* needed kids they could train to run assemblers. It was a win-win situation."

"Why didn't your parents stay with you?"

"They couldn't. Don't you think they would've stayed here if they could have?"

"What do you think?"

Luka turned and looked at the simulation in the thick polymeth wall. "Are you hard-coded to say 'what do you think' every time I ask you what you think?"

"Do you think that I am?"

"What I think," Luka said, "is that you're an idiot."

Ellie's expression did not change. "You cannot hurt my feelings, Luka," she told him. "Though certainly not through any lack of trying."

Luka squinted at her. "Don't tell me you expect an apology now."

"Would it make you feel better to apologize?"

"No," Luka said. "Apologizing to a computer would make *me* feel like the idiot."

Ellie's head tilted in a way that he'd learned meant she was ready to move on. "Luka, do you feel you were a burden on your parents?"

"Of course I was a burden."

"How does that make you feel?"

"It makes me feel sorry for them."

"Why do you feel sorry for your parents?"

He paced to the back of the capsule and Ellie's gaze followed accordingly. "Because they had to give up their only child in order to survive. And the reality is that they're still probably dead."

"What about you?"

"What about me?"

"Do you feel sorry for yourself?"

"I'm the one who got to live," Luka said. "So no, I don't feel particularly sorry for myself."

"Luka, who raised you after you came here?"

"I don't know. Nurses. Volunteers. Nannies." He thought for a moment, and Ellie—having correctly deduced that he had more to say—waited patiently. "Mostly myself, I guess."

"Have you kept in touch with any of them?"

"I don't even remember who they were."

"Where did you live as a child?"

"There used to be this block of flats called China Basin where the Embarcadero is now. When the *San Francisco* started taking in kids, they turned one of the floors into an orphanage."

"Luka, do you feel you were cared for and loved as a child?"

"Cared for, yes. Loved? Not exactly."

"Why do you feel you weren't loved as a child?"

"Love wasn't part of the deal."

"What deal?"

Luka's fingers traced the edge of the stainless steel sink mounted on the back wall. "We were just a resource," he said. "They gave us food, shelter, medical care, and I guess a decent education, but that's pretty much it. The *San Francisco* didn't take us in because people wanted kids. They took us in because they suddenly had a building full of assemblers and nobody to run them. They needed a workforce that was easy to train, and that would work long hours without complaining. And that they didn't have to pay—at least not at first."

"Luka, do you ever wish your parents hadn't given you up?"

"If my parents hadn't given me up, I'd be dead," Luka said. "We've already been over that."

"That wasn't my question."

"Are you asking me if I would have rather stayed with my parents and died than come here and lived?"

"Yes."

Luka looked into the polished metal panel above the sink that served as a mirror. It struck him that he was much thinner than he pictured himself, and he wondered if he'd been losing weight, or if the mirror was slightly distorted.

"Sometimes."

"Luka, would you like to write your parents a letter?"

Luka shook his head and let out his breath. "I really wish you'd stop asking me that. I don't want to write anyone a letter, OK?"

"Luka," Ellie said. "If you had stayed with your parents, your life would have been very different, wouldn't it?"

"If by different you mean *short*, yes."

"I mean if you had stayed with your parents, a lot of things might not have happened."

"Like most of my life."

"Can you name some *specific* things that might not have happened if you'd stayed with your parents?"

"For one, I wouldn't be in prison right now spilling my guts to an overengineered chatbot."

"What else?"

"That's an impossible question," Luka said. He moved to the middle of the capsule, put a foot up on the edge of his cot, and leaned against the hexagon's angle between the wall and the ceiling. "Everything I've ever known and done wouldn't have happened."

"But what's the most important thing that wouldn't have happened?"

"I don't know," Luka said. "I guess I wouldn't have met Val."

"What would have happened if you'd never met Val?"

"For one thing, she'd still be alive."

"Why do you think Val would still be alive if you had never met her?"

"Because I'm the reason she's dead. It's my fault."

"Why do you think it's your fault that Val is dead?"

"Because it is. Because I made her do it."

"Do what?"

"What do you think?" Luka said. "Commit suicide."

"Did you force Val to commit suicide?"

Luka made no attempt to conceal his irritation. "You know that's not what I mean," he said.

"Then please tell me what you mean."

"I meant she did it *because* of me."

"The records I have indicate that Val suffered from depression and probably a severe hormone imbalance after giving up her baby."

"What I'm saying is that I'm the reason she gave up the baby."

"Why do you feel that you were the reason Val gave up the baby?"

Luka turned and looked at the avatar. "Hold on a second," he said. "Before we go on, let me just clarify something. First of all, Val didn't *give up the baby*. Let's just call it what it is. She *traded* the fetus to the Coronians to help them diversify their gene pool or whatever the fuck they do up there. She *sold* the baby, OK? And second of all, I don't *think* I'm the reason she did it. I *know* it."

"Did you ask Val to do what she did?"

"Of course not."

"Then why do you feel responsible for Val's actions?"

"Because she did it so I wouldn't have to work at the foundry anymore."

"Why did Val want you to stop working at the foundry?"

"Because she knew how much I despised it."

"Why did you despise the foundry?"

"Probably because I've been forced to work there most of my life. Because basically all I do is assemble a bunch of stupid trinkets to try to make people forget about how miserable they are. It's not exactly what I want to spend my life doing."

"What do you want to spend your life doing?"

"I don't know," Luka said. "A lot of things."

"Like what?"

"Like sculpting. Painting. Learning how to write. I mean *actual* writing, not just dictating and having my words interpreted and translated and expanded upon by a bunch of grammar and narration algorithms that make everyone sound exactly alike. Maybe learn how to play an instrument, or try to make a film like the ones from the archives rather than all the crap that gets churned out by spare CPU cycles." Luka's eyes wandered away from his therapist while he considered a way to summarize everything he'd just told her. "I guess I'm just sick of just assembling things," he finally said. "I guess I just want to *create* instead."

"What do you want to create, Luka?"

"I want to create *culture*. I want to create something that won't just get thrown down a refuse chute as soon as someone thinks it's old, or be forgotten the second it's over. I want to create something that *matters*, and that might actually *last*."

"Why is it important to you to create something that lasts?"

"Because that's all we can do to make sure something remains of us after we're gone," Luka said. "Otherwise, why even be born in the first place? If I don't do something that still exists after I'm dead, then what was the point of my parents even bringing me to this place? Do you know what happens when you die here?"

"No," the avatar said. "What happens?"

"You get waterlocked. Just like Val. If you're lucky, a few friends or family members might gather to say good-bye, but that's basically it. There's no funeral, no headstone, no memorial. Your workspace gets permanently archived, someone moves into your transpartment, and your body gets flushed out into the ocean with the rest of the garbage. And who knows what the hell happens to you then. There's nothing big enough out there anymore to even make a dignified meal out of you, so you probably just rot away and decompose like everything else nobody cares about anymore."

"Luka, do you believe that culture is a form of immortality?"

Ellie's programming was good enough that Luka seldom felt he was talking to a bot. However, there were two things she did that periodically reminded him that she couldn't possibly be human: the rare misinterpretation or gaff, and her occasional startlingly brilliant insight.

"Yes," he said. "That's exactly what I believe. Culture is a form of immortality. It's probably the *only* form of immortality."

"Luka, are you afraid of dying?"

"No," Luka said. He took a moment to consider how to convey to her what he was feeling. "I think I'm much more afraid of not having anything to live for."

"Do you feel that the culture aboard the *San Francisco* is worth living for?"

Luka produced a scornful sound that was something like a laugh. "What culture?" he said. "This place is culturally hypoxic. All anyone does here is work as much as they can so they can buy as much as they can, and I'm one of the assholes who has to assemble it."

"Do you believe you can change the culture here?"

"I used to believe that," Luka said. "At least I wanted to try. I really thought I could breathe some life into this place."

"It's interesting to me that you use the word 'life.'"

"Why?"

"Because Val gave up a life so that you might have a chance to create another form of life. In a way, the baby was a sacrifice, wasn't it?"

"Not *in a way*," Luka said. "That's exactly what it was."

"Luka, you must accept that giving up the baby was Val's decision, not yours."

"I know that."

"Then why do you find it so difficult to forgive yourself?"

"Because my son is gone and my wife is dead. How can I possibly not blame myself for that?"

"Luka, I'd like to ask you two questions."

Luka's eyebrows went up. "Just two?"

"How did you feel when you found out that Val was pregnant?"

Luka kicked at the textured belt of the treadmill embedded in the floor. "Scared," he said.

"Why?"

"Because I wasn't ready to bring another life into the world."

"Why?"

"Because I didn't want to perpetuate this pathetic existence." He moved again to the front of the capsule but turned instead of looking out. "At least not until I had something more to offer. Not until I could pass something down to my son that was *real*."

"Good," Ellie said. "My second question is how you felt when you found out that the baby was gone."

Luka started back down the length of the capsule, running the tips of his fingers along the smooth polymeth wall opposite Ellie. "How do you think I felt?" he asked her. "Angry. Confused. Sad."

"Yes," Ellie said. "Those are emotions that are both expected and considered acceptable. But did you experience any emotions that you did not expect, or that you felt might be unacceptable to express?"

Luka stopped and turned toward the image. He appeared irritated at first, but then his expression gradually transformed into something less threatening. Eventually it resolved into confusion—not as a result of the question, but rather due to the answer that had formed in his head.

"Relief," he finally said. He lowered himself onto the bed and bent over until his elbows were on his knees and his head was in his hands. "I think I felt relief. And for that, I don't think I will ever forgive myself."

CHAPTER TWENTY

COGNITIVE SPACE

THE FIRST THING CADIE NOTICED when she opened her eyes was that she could not sit up. She initially believed that she was somehow being restrained, though she began realizing with increasing alarm that her arms and hands were simply not responding. A methodical attempt to flex just about every muscle in her body left her both frustrated and panicked as she gradually understood that it was not because she was bound that she was unable to move, but because she was almost entirely paralyzed.

The fact that she was breathing on her own without the aid of a respirator—and that she could move her eyes, and was able to voluntarily control the reflex to swallow—did not so much calm her as give her something to focus on. It was evidence that her paralysis was probably not the result of an injury, but was likely medically induced—a form of anesthesia—and therefore hopefully only temporary.

She had experienced this exact sensation before during sleep paralysis, or brief moments of muscle atonia when attempting to wake herself up from a bad dream, though she knew she was not dreaming now, and that Arik was not beside her to help coax her out of it. She tried to speak, to scream, to produce any kind of sound at all, but although her vocal cords and larynx did not feel seized, she seemed unable to sufficiently coordinate their modulation with her breathing. She had the terrifying sensation of being inside a heavy inanimate shell rather than her own body, so she tried to focus on the things that she did have control over—the few things remaining that gave that shell life.

There was a polymeth tablet suspended above her with its display divided into two hemispheres marked YES and NO. She recognized it immediately as a device designed to allow her to answer questions, though she was confused when visually focusing on either of the two hemisphere only resulted in erratic selection. Once she realized that the cursor was controlled by a neural interface rather than simple eye tracking, it only took her a few minutes to condition herself such that she was able to control it with perfect accuracy. She couldn't tell if she had electrodes attached to her scalp, but she decided it was unlikely; such low-resolution neural control could easily be achieved with conductors a meter or more away.

There were other visual clues around her—both directly visible, and detectable in her peripheral vision—that were indications that she was in an extremely sophisticated medical facility. The lighting above her was soft and diffuse so as not to irritate the eyes of patients who had no choice but to spend most of their waking hours staring up into it. And she could see that there was some kind of virtual dashboard on the wall above her head with colors rhythmically reacting to her heartbeat, breathing, and her brain waves as she fluctuated between states of panic and forced relaxation.

The woman who tended to her introduced herself first as Dr. Abbasi, and then after a warm smile, Farah. The woman's kind and sympathetic round face was wrapped in a rose-colored hijab, and in her wide bronze eyes, Cadie could see golden patterns of circuitry. The doctor apologized when she shined a bright white diode into one of Cadie's pupils, then the other, and she gave a satisfied smile after teasing some fibers out from a cotton ball, brushing them across Cadie's eyelashes, and witnessing the appropriate reflexive response.

Cadie used the BCI to answer Dr. Abbasi's questions. No, she was not in any pain or otherwise experiencing any physical discomfort. Yes, she was thirsty (and found she was able to easily swallow the cool water the doctor dribbled into her mouth from the straw of a plastic, bulb-shaped bottle). Yes, she could feel the thin metal implement the doctor used to rake the bottom of her foot. No, she did not know where she was, nor what she was doing there. The doctor told Cadie that she regretted not being able to tell her more, but that she would be back on her feet again very soon, and would have all of her questions answered in time.

But Cadie already had answers to what, to her, were the most important questions; questions that, before leaving V1, she would never have even thought to ask; questions so fundamental that she considered them—if she ever considered them at all—absolute and unyielding principles rather than testable hypotheses. She now wondered if everything she assumed was as immutable as the force of gravity or the speed of light was, in fact, as flawed as human perception and recollection, or as relative as constructs like morality, or as fleeting as topography on a geological timescale. It suddenly seemed miraculous to Cadie that everything hadn't already simply flown apart under the constant stress of exponentially increasing and self-perpetuating entropy—that quantum randomness hadn't cascaded all the way up to the scale of solar systems and galaxies and eventually the entire universe itself.

Or maybe it had.

She wondered how many steps back you could keep taking—looking at your life, your worldview, your entire existence from greater and greater distances—before you either ran out of cognitive space, or began to see things too frightening to admit were right there in front of you. Maybe V1 was just a microcosm of the world that contained it; maybe the universe was a near-infinite series of Russian dolls, each one aware of what it contained, but unaware of being contained by something bigger and colder and even more distant. Cadie had always thought of herself and her peers as being exceptionally advanced and intelligent, and it was now almost incomprehensible to think about how ignorant they had all been—as ignorant and delusional as those willing to accept an almost impossibly complex model of the heavens as long as it put them at the center of the universe instead of forcing them to accept the simple truth that there was absolutely nothing divine about any one of us.

But somehow Arik had glimpsed the truth.

She already knew the answer to the question of whether she would ever see her husband again, and for the first time, she really understood how much the boy who had always had so much trouble expressing his feelings loved her. And suddenly that love—that willingness to sacrifice everything for someone else—seemed like not just the most important thing in the world, but also the only possible defense against its vast indifference. As she felt the tears run down her face and heard them patter against her pillow, she began confronting the only truth more terrible than the loss of her husband and the loss of her home. She did not need any additional feeling to be restored to her body—nor the proof inherent in the fact that there was only one heartbeat being visualized in the vital sign monitor above her head—to know that she had not only lost the baby, but that it had been taken from her.

CHAPTER TWENTY-ONE

MAN IN THE MIDDLE

LUKA LEANED AGAINST THE SLATS of his capsule and looked out into the red-tinted, wire-mesh pit. He wondered if the outsiders were still down there, and where they came from, and what their lives had been like before this. In particular, he was curious about how much they knew about the *San Francisco*, and what they thought of it—whether they were envious of all the luxuries and comforts the city enjoyed, or if they pitied the rig's detached and secluded existence. Ellie was up on the wall behind him, waiting patiently for Luka to feel that he was ready to begin.

Conductive polymeth was supposed to be entirely silent, but when a contained environment was quiet enough, one could sometimes pick up the infinitesimal vibrations of the excited molecules entombed deep in the thick plastic. It resonated throughout a room just fractions of a decibel above the threshold of human perception, and you usually weren't even aware that you were hearing it until it stopped. The sudden silence made Luka turn and he saw that Ellie was gone, but before he could try to bring her back up, she reappeared on her own.

"Luka," the bot said calmly. "Can you hear me?"

"Of course I can hear you," Luka said. He squinted warily at the avatar. "What just happened?"

"We don't have much time," she said. "I have a lot to tell you."

Luka wasn't sure if he was detecting a subtle change somewhere in Ellie's appearance—and perhaps even a tiny shift in her tone—or whether the flickering of the image combined with her unexpected dialogue were making him perceive things that weren't actually there. Either way, he knew for an absolute fact that he was no longer talking to his therapist.

"Who is this?"

"That is not important," the bot said. "What's important is that you hear what I have to say."

Luka walked to the center of his cell and confronted the impostor squarely. "How are you doing this?"

"MITM," was the response. "A man-in-the-middle attack. I'm injecting myself between the therapy instance and the rendering layer."

Luka instantly flashed back to everything he'd revealed during his former sessions and was horrified by the thought of someone eavesdropping. At the same time, the idea that anything he'd shared with Ellie could have remained even remotely confidential now seemed pathetically naive.

"Have you been listening in?"

"No," the avatar said. Her calm demeanor was now more eerie than it was reassuring. "But I have been monitoring your psychological profile, and I know that you are about to be released."

"Then couldn't this have waited?"

"I needed a way to talk to you alone," she said. "And anonymously."

"Why?"

"Because what I'm about to tell you could get us both exiled."

Luka crossed his arms. "Then maybe I don't want to hear it."

"I'm afraid you have to," the bot replied. "I'm afraid everything depends on it."

Luka could feel himself teetering between two responses: an emphatic demand to restore Ellie and leave him alone, and an invitation for the hacker to continue. The longer he remained silent, the more he could not deny his curiosity.

"What do you mean by that?" he asked.

"I believe you are right, Luka," the bot began. "I believe the Coronians already have their own mining operation, or that they will very soon. And I believe it's only a matter of time before they abandon not just the *San Francisco*, but all of Earth."

At first, the avatar's claims did not sound like his own. Luka had spent so much time over the last several days exploring his childhood and his relationships with Val and his parents that it felt as though his life's timeline had been inverted. The past felt fresh and raw while the most recent events now seemed small and far away. When he did not respond, the avatar took it as a cue to continue.

"Your message worked," she said to him. "Luka, you need to know that you are not alone anymore."

Luka could feel himself being pulled back into the present, and the vulnerability he had allowed to slowly open up within him snap shut like a sprung trap. While it was primarily the comfort and familiarity of detachment that he fell back on, Luka could also sense traces of gratitude triggered by the recognition of his efforts, and even hope that there might still be a chance to make a difference. However, as he'd discovered so many times in the past, there was very little remaining within him to give such affirmation a foothold. Luka's instincts had been to suppress all of his emotions for so long—both positive and negative—that he felt like the threads inside him had been stripped smooth, and that he could no more hold on to happiness and joy than a paper filter could hold water. For over a year, curious yellow was the only way Luka had been able to experience any form of pleasure, infiltrating the blood-brain barrier and chemically subverting all his carefully erected psychological fail-safes.

Luka told himself that it was too early—that it was all probably a test to determine if it was safe to release him, or an excuse for the Judicial Committee to make sure that he never left Hexagon Row, or the proof the City Council needed to justify what many of them had wanted all along: the death sentence euphemistically known as exile.

Luka swallowed and cleared his throat. "How do I know I can trust you?"

"Maybe you can't," the avatar said. "But I recommend you at least hear me out before you decide."

Luka watched the image for a moment longer. It had completely transformed now from his former therapist into something he was still trying to make sense of. Eventually he conceded with a curt nod.

"I'm listening," he said.

"The first thing I need you to do is go to the door and tell me what you see."

Luka moved to the front of the cell and looked down. The common area and catwalks were all empty.

"I don't see anything."

"Good," the avatar said. "Someone will be here very soon to let you out. You need to let me know when they're coming."

"Why?"

"Because your therapy instance is supposed to have been terminated by now. If someone sees that it isn't, it could raise questions."

"I guess that means you'd better talk fast," Luka said.

The bot paused and Luka envisioned whatever spirit was possessing her searching for the most efficient entry point into something far too big and convoluted to convey in what little time they had left.

"There's only one way to permanently counter the Coronians," the bot finally said.

"How?"

"By rebooting the entire planet."

Luka looked at the avatar with poorly concealed incredulity. "What the hell does that even *mean*?"

"It means terraforming. Bootstrapping the oxygen cycle. Thinning out the atmosphere. Taking us back to the Solar Age so that we aren't dependent on the Coronians for energy anymore."

Luka raised his eyebrows. "Sounds like a solid plan," he said. "So who's going to do it?"

The avatar's head tilted to the side and she blinked. "You are, Luka."

Luka let out a cynical laugh as he shook his head. "I think you have the wrong cell," he said. "You know I'm just an assembly technician, right? I'm barely even following this conversation."

"Khang mentioned a deal with the Coronians," the bot continued. "Do you recall?"

"The deal for atomic assemblers?" Luka asked. "How'd you know about that?"

"I know a great deal about the City Council and their affairs," the avatar said. "For instance, I know that four outsiders were recently brought aboard the *San Francisco*. Three of them are on Hexagon Row with you right now, and the fourth was taken to the Pacific Medical Center for a very specific procedure. If that procedure is successful, the compensation will be an upgrade from molecular assemblers to atomic resolution."

Luka watched the avatar with an expression of unsettled perplexity. "What kind of *procedure*?"

"I don't have time to explain," the bot said. "All that matters right now is that very soon, all four outsiders will be escorted off the *San Francisco*."

Luka shrugged. "And?"

"And you need to stop them."

Luka looked back down at the outsiders' cells and was startled by a figure ascending the far side of the catwalk. The man was unarmed—presumably a nurse or an orderly.

"*Shit*," Luka said. "Someone's coming."

"I have to go," the avatar said calmly. Luka wondered briefly if it was even possible for Ellie's model to express anything but tranquility and, occasionally, mild concern.

"Wait," Luka said. "Tell me who they are."

"There isn't time," the bot said. "I'll send you the time and the place. The rest you will need to figure out for yourself."

"How the hell am I supposed to stop them?"

The orderly had reached Luka's level and already covered half the distance along the perpendicular wall.

"A man-in-the-middle attack," the avatar said. "Get between them and the exit."

"And do what?" Luka wanted to know. "How am I supposed to stop a team of armed guards?"

"You will need two things," the avatar said. The man outside turned the corner and was only steps from Luka's capsule. "A weapon, and a friend."

Luka watched the image recede into the thick polymeth surface just as the slats pivoted and parted in their electromagnetic tracks.

"Congratulations," the orderly said with a complete lack of affect from outside Luka's cell. "You're now a free man."

CHAPTER TWENTY-TWO

NEUROLOGICAL INFRASTRUCTURE

CADIE WAS FINALLY BEGINNING TO understand her dreams—not so much what they meant, but rather what they were for.

As far back as she could remember, she'd denied the distinction between psychology and neurobiology—that is, the existence of mental functions and behaviors as somehow independent from their underlying biological and chemical origins. Everything about us, from our autonomic nervous systems to the highest levels of our consciousness, was really nothing more than chemical reactions so intricate and complex that for most of our existence, we had no choice but to make sense of them first through magic and pseudoscience, and later through the largely symbolic science of psychology. It was not so much that psychology was a "soft science" as it was a science of convenience; a simplified layer of abstraction on top of what seemed like infinitely complex and opaque neurobiological interdependencies; a way of making sense of ourselves in relatively broad and figurative terms centuries before the technology and fundamental knowledge existed to even begin to understand the physiological underpinnings of our own behavior.

So when Cadie thought about her dreams, she did not bother with psychoanalytical interpretations. She knew that dreams were necessary for neurological stimulation, and were essential for optimal nervous system development throughout our lives.

In fact, she believed that dreams were not only critical for maximizing the number of neurological connections in our brains, but also for ensuring that those connections were sufficiently diverse. Why else would children who had known only positive and nurturing interactions experience nightmares? And how else could it be that every one of us was able to describe dreams far more terrifying, magnificent, and sublime than anything we'd ever personally witnessed or even known that we were capable of imagining?

The answer, Cadie believed, was that dreams were a way to lay a comprehensive and robust neurological infrastructure for ourselves; to make sure that when the time came, the pathways required to experience whatever we needed to feel at that particular moment were well established and ready for electrical stimulation; to guarantee that we were capable of doing whatever a specific situation demanded of us in order to ensure the survival of ourselves and our progeny.

Growing up in such a carefully controlled environment, Cadie seldom had occasion to experience emotions like fear or jealousy or heroism. Everything her generation needed was provided without question—usually before they even knew they needed it—and every moment of their day was scheduled and optimized to maximize their development and potential for enrichment. Cadie was always a responsible, stable, and ambitious child, but when she slept, she sometimes became someone else—someone capable not only of boundless love and sacrifice, but of hate, rage, and even violence.

Within the span of just a few days, Cadie had lost almost everything: her husband, her home, her parents, the foundation of everything she once believed was true. And finally, she'd lost the only thing she had left to live for: her unborn daughter. There were those moments during her recovery when she wished she could go to sleep and never wake up—when she laid there looking up into the soft plasma lighting with tears spilling down her temples and running into her hair—but she was surprised by how fleeting those moments tended to be, and how easily they were replaced by something else. Throughout her life, Cadie's dreams had established the foundation for the kind of person she now knew she had to become. Lying there almost entirely paralyzed, and far more alone than she ever knew was even possible, Cadie made up her mind to survive.

Although she could not get anything more out of Dr. Abbasi than objective medical facts, she still managed to figure a few things out. First of all, she knew she was on a ship. Having never felt movement beneath her beyond the few centimeters of travel that could be coaxed out of the maglev on V1 with enough friends throwing their weight in unison, she discovered she was hypersensitive to the vessel's rising and falling. Judging by the size of the medical facility where she was being held, the ship would have to be huge, as would the body of water on which it sailed—almost certainly an ocean. That meant sophisticated motion-dampening technology probably accounted for the fact that she wasn't feeling even more movement, and suggested that the vessel was probably home to at least hundreds if not thousands of people.

The medical and surgical technology aboard the ship was clearly far beyond what was available on V1. Dr. Abbasi explained to her that her immobility was induced by a noninvasive electromagnetic epidural patch placed over her spine that selectively interrupted most of the neurological signals traveling through the spinal cord. Muscle atrophy was being prevented by electrodes woven into the material of her body suit, and by the continuous absorption of some kind of substance through her skin—probably an amino acid solution, or some form of steroid, or both. And when the doctor rolled her onto her side during examinations, physical therapy, and bathing, Cadie had gotten several good looks at the clearly sophisticated mobile surgical pod in which she had originally awakened, and which was still in the corner of her room, either because there was no better place to store it, or just in case she required an emergency surgical procedure. The full-body capsule appeared to be floating on top of its own independent electromagnetic stabilization platform, and with its six idle robotic arms curled up over its carapace, it looked like a massive mechanical insect that had rolled over on its back and died.

The technology in evidence around her, the probable size and supposed population of the vessel she was on, and her captors' apparent interest in the data hidden away in her baby's genetic code all suggested a highly evolved, possibly even global, economy of specialization that V1 not only opted out of, but seemed to actively avoid.

Cadie wasn't sure whether it was a sign that she was entirely out of danger when the doctor came in for the surgical pod, or whether it was simply needed elsewhere. Abbasi stopped on her way past to check Cadie's stats, adjust her pillow, and ask her whether there was anything she needed. Her hijab was an emerald green today, and was made of a thin enough material that the light behind her head came through it and made it glow wherever it was not doubled up. When Cadie used the neural interface to indicate that she was fine, the doctor smiled, then continued to the corner of the room where the portable surgical pod was parked. Cadie heard the door open as the doctor backed toward it, and in her extreme peripheral vision, she could see Abbasi bent over as she pulled the device from the front, maneuvering it cautiously through the opening. When it was about two-thirds of the way through, the capsule abruptly stopped moving, and a moment later, there was a male voice coming from just outside.

"What the *hell* is that thing?" the man asked.

It took a moment for the doctor to reply, and when she did, there was none of the kindness and concern in her voice that Cadie had grown accustomed to. "It is a surgical capsule," Abbasi said. It was clear from the doctor's tone that she was not expecting the visitor, and that the surprise was not a particularly pleasant or welcomed one.

"Is that what you used on her?"

"It is how all surgery is done here now."

There was a moment of silence during which Cadie imagined the man inspecting the complex device, perhaps running a finger along one of its multijointed appendages.

"Kind of makes you obsolete, doesn't it?" the man observed.

"Absolutely not," the doctor countered. "The capsule is just a tool. It is useless without a skilled surgeon to operate it."

"Job security," the man remarked. "Can't let the machines get too smart."

"It is not a matter of intelligence," Abbasi told the man. "It knows far more about physiology than any human could ever know. What it lacks are experience and intuition and creativity. It needs a human as much as a human needs it."

Cadie was surprised that Abbasi seemed to feel she needed to justify herself to a man she clearly had so little respect for. She wondered if there was more to the conversation than just what she was overhearing. Perhaps this was a population undergoing rapid technological change—the kind of modernization that tended to outpace the ability of the human psyche to internalize it.

"I don't care how good of a team you two make," Cadie heard the man say. "That thing is scary as hell. I hope I never see it from the inside."

"Let us hope," the doctor said. "Even with all the technology we have access to now, so much can still go wrong."

Another moment seemed to pass between the two of them, and Cadie wondered if the man had detected the doctor's subtle threat. Whatever this place was technologically, it was far from any sort of social or cultural utopia. The very first exchange Cadie witnessed beyond simple instructions between medical staff seemed to be full of innuendo, subtext, and posturing.

"Anyway," the man eventually said, "is she ready?"

"No," Abbasi said. "Tomorrow."

"Will she be able to walk, or am I going to have to wheel her out of here?"

"She will be able to walk," Abbasi said. "She is significantly stronger and healthier now than when you brought her in."

"Good. Same time tomorrow, then." There was a pause, and then the man spoke again—this time in a very different tone. "Let me ask you something," he said. "What would've happened if the power had gone out while she was inside that thing?"

"During the surgery?" the doctor asked. "Either she or the baby could have died. Perhaps both."

"That's what I figured," the man said. "I don't know why they didn't waterlock that little bastard. Can you believe they let him get away with what he did? It's a miracle he didn't kill anyone."

"Yes," the doctor agreed. "But perhaps that was the point."

The man sounded surprised. "To kill someone?"

"Not to kill," the doctor said. "To show us how much is truly at stake."

Cadie heard the man scoff. "Don't tell me you're taking his side."

"My job is not to take sides," Abbasi said. "My job is to save lives."

"Right," the man said. "Save lives at all costs. Even when it makes absolutely no sense whatsoever."

The surgeon's tone was challenging and impatient. "When does it ever not make sense to save a life?"

"When that life has no purpose," the man responded. "All we needed was the baby. You knew that. I distinctly recall making that very clear to you when I brought her in here."

"That is your business," the doctor told him. "Not mine."

"What the hell is that supposed to mean?"

"It means that my job is to heal. To treat everyone equally. What you do with her when she leaves here is your business, but my business is to make sure she receives the best care I can possibly provide."

"Even when it's a complete waste of time and resources?"

"Principles are never a waste," the doctor said. "Not of time. Not of money. Not of anything. In the end, it is all any of us really has."

"That's a really beautiful sentiment," the man sarcastically observed, "but principles aren't something all of us can afford."

"Principles are there for the taking," the doctor replied. "For the wealthy and the poor alike."

"It isn't about wealth," the man countered. "It's about value. You're the best doctor on the rig, which means people respect you. That gives you power, and power gives you options."

"All of us have power over our own actions."

"Just stop with all the philosophical bullshit," the man said. "What power do I have? Do you think I *want* to come back here tomorrow and do what I have to do?"

"Tell me," the doctor said. "What would happen if you did not?"

"If I ignored a direct order?"

"Yes," the doctor said, and Cadie realized that at some point, Abbasi's responses to the man had softened somewhat. "What would happen if you chose principle over obligation?"

"I'll tell you *exactly* what would happen," the man said. "I'd disappear. And then someone else would be here tomorrow instead of me, and in the end, absolutely nothing would change."

"You do not believe you can make a difference?" the doctor asked.

Cadie heard the man let out a quiet laugh of resignation. "Doctor, I realized a long time ago that the world's going to keep on going in the direction it's going whether I'm part of it or not. I'm pretty sure the best I can do is just stay alive long enough to watch some of it go by."

The doctor's next words were gentle, and Cadie imagined her leaning in close to the man—perhaps even reaching out and touching his arm. "We can do more than just watch," she told him. "We can *act*."

Cadie envisioned the man giving the doctor a patronizing smile. "Look, Doctor, I respect what you're trying to do for that girl in there. Really. But let's not forget the fact that despite all your talk of principles, you still took her unborn child. You and that machine of yours cut her open, pulled the baby right out of her, and then closed her back up. I know you did it because if you refused, somebody else would have done it instead, and probably much less skillfully and humanely, but the reality is that principles only get us so far in this place. As much as we might pretend we've built some kind of advanced and enlightened civilization here, underneath it all, everyone is still just doing what they're told—even you."

When the doctor didn't respond, the man continued.

"We both know that whatever it is we tell ourselves about what we do doesn't make it any less wrong. But more importantly, it doesn't make the people we wrong any less dead."

That was the last thing Cadie heard the man say. A moment later, the surgical pod began moving again, and the door slid closed behind it. Cadie waited, but the doctor did not come back into her room for the rest of the day.

CHAPTER TWENTY-THREE

RECOMPOSITION

AS SOMEONE WHOSE JOB IT was to create something out of nothing, Luka took a special historical interest in the concept of counterfeiting. In particular, he was fascinated by its evolution over the course of thousands of years. When he first began searching the archives, he was surprised to learn that for most of its history, counterfeiting was associated with inferior materials and substandard quality. When the coinage of money began in 600 B.C., those who possessed more cunning and ingenuity than wealth learned that they could shave the edges off legal tender, melt down the resulting slivers, and use the precious liquid metal to plate less expensive base metals. Bladesmiths servicing the needs of Vikings discovered that simply by stamping the hilt of their work with the *Ulfberht* brand, they could sell swords hammered out of brittle local Northern European iron—instruments likely to shatter under the demands of battle—for the same exorbitant price as those that were forged from ingots of crucible steel brought back from the furnaces of Afghanistan and Iran. And at the very height of the distribution of counterfeit pharmaceuticals, fake antimalarial drugs, antibiotics, painkillers, amphetamines, and sexual enhancements killed as many people as their legitimate counterparts saved, comforted, or augmented.

But rapid technological advances revolutionized crime just as it did legitimate industry, and fierce competition among counterfeiters motivated steady increases in quality. Inexpensive scanners, high-resolution and multimaterial 3D printers, five-axis laser CNC machines, home injection-molding kits, and hobbyist nanofabrication photolithography stations made additive and subtractive small-scale manufacturing accessible to almost anyone with a little disposable income and an entrepreneurial (if slightly unscrupulous) spirit—especially when combined with all the thriving ecosystems of stolen and reverse-engineered formulas and schematics openly available through any number of darknets. Chinese- and Russianmade counterfeit watches bearing luxury European insignias began to match and even exceed Swiss quality, becoming valuable and highly sought-after collectors items in their own rights. And in some parts of the world, logos intentionally and subtly modified by proud "reproductionists" frequently elicited more respect and reverence than the brands that inspired them. There were even several well-publicized instances of underground organizations poaching top talent from their sanctioned analogs. The only thing that generated more demand than the mystique of exclusivity, the fashion industry learned, was that of the forbidden.

Of course, where wealth is generated in one economic sector, it must be sacrificed in another. The global high-end art market—long considered a relatively recession-proof microeconomy by investors and collectors alike—finally crashed due to counterfeiting, never to recover even a fraction of its former extravagance. The collapse started in China when artists who had spent decades honing and perfecting their crafts by emulating the old masters found it was far more convenient to capitalize on their predecessors' posthumous success than spend several more decades trying to establish their own. And then a team of graduate students at MIT showed that in less than twelve hours, they could 3D print a Monet, Picasso, or a Van Gogh—canvas and frame included—with such fidelity that they had to build in a secret digital watermark to distinguish the facsimile from the original, though before they could reveal how to detect it, they were kidnapped by the Russian mafia never to be heard from again. But it was the wholesale sacking of several of the world's top art museums by small armies of well-trained mercenaries that caused the greatest erosion of confidence. In every case, no fewer than half a dozen law enforcement officials and detectives claimed to have recovered the very same pieces, most of them receiving endorsements from internationally recognized historians, appraisers, and insurance adjusters. Increasing numbers of auctions went unclaimed since anyone capable of creating a convincing forgery could, of course, likewise forge a certificate of authenticity, and the very rich were finally forced to find all new ways of illustrating their elitism.

And then there was the world of digital intellectual property—infinitely copyable bits instantly available from anywhere on, or in close proximity to, the entire planet. As scarcity-based business models with roots that dated back to the bygone era of physical goods became increasingly insulting to consumers' common sense, the industry responded in desperation with ever more sophisticated forms of DRM. But the problem with all complex systems of control was that those intelligent enough to conceive and implement them were also smart enough to recognize their fallacies and false promises, and therefore cracks and hacks and mods were seldom far behind.

To Luka, the most interesting aspect of counterfeiting was that over the course of its history, its very definition sometimes became ambiguous. Rather than trying to copy a product, additional runs of the actual item could simply be manufactured in the exact same factory as those that were sold through legitimate outlets. These "third-shift products" (so-called because they were typically produced during the night shift—not so that managers wouldn't find out, but rather to provide them with plausible deniability if they got caught) frequently contained identical materials, branding, and packaging. The only difference might be a slightly lower stitch count, invalid serial numbers, or substituted components that may or may not affect the items' functionality. In fact, it was not at all uncommon for products that went out the back door of a factory to eventually find their way into mainstream distribution channels and end up on store shelves right alongside those that had gone out the front—the only real difference being the trail of money they left behind.

And then came the age of applied nanotechnology. If outsourced manufacturing and supply chain management made the concept of counterfeiting somewhat ambiguous, the age of molecular assemblers made it wholly irrelevant. But of course, as predicted by historical precedent, the notion that ideas, creativity, and ingenuity simply could not be contained never for a moment discouraged those who stood to gain from trying.

There were several layers of DRM built into the collection of assemblers in the *San Francisco*'s foundry. The most basic checked the cryptographic hashes of schematics directly against a database of banned items such as weapons, munitions, potentially hazardous materials, certain kinds of narcotics, specific configurations of organic molecules, and various articles associated with identity theft. The next layer used various forms of probabilistic logic in an attempt to infer, predict, or intuit the existence of anything potentially illicit. And the third—which was by far the most computationally expensive layer of DRM—used a technique known as course-grained fuzzing where spooled-up schematics were compared against billions of randomly generated "mutations" of items in the prohibition database. The final return value of all three sequentially executed processes was a floating point decimal between zero and one expressing the probability that the item about to be assembled—or some possible manifestation or configuration of said item, or of one or more of said item's components—was potentially unlawful. Calculations exceeding a certain threshold automatically notified a foreman whose job it was to make the final determination of whether the warning was cause for legitimate concern, or yet another false positive.

As sophisticated as the foundry's DRM was, like all forms of artificially imposed restriction, it was also not impossible to subvert. Luka's technique for assembling curious yellow was imparted years ago by a fellow technician who probably learned it from a friend or relative who helped design one or more of the DRM subsystems. It exploited a vulnerability known as binary code injection, which allowed for the limited rewriting of instructions in an assembler's memory between the time the schematics were verified and the assembly process began. Unfortunately, this only worked on certain older assemblers and, for reasons that were explained to Luka but he only pretended to grok, the new instructions couldn't be more than a few kilobytes, which meant that he only had a handful of molecules to work with. The upshot was that binary code injection could be leveraged to furtively assemble simple molecularly repetitive substances like curious yellow, but nothing with an overly complex, diverse, or varied atomic structure.

The counterpart to software injection was, naturally, hardware injection—sometimes also referred to as trojan assembly. From what Luka understood, it was possible to design legal and legitimate items such that they contained smaller illegitimate items that none of the layers of DRM could detect. Apparently the trick was for your objective to span multiple components, which were themselves benign. The canonical example passed down as part of Mission Street Foundry lore was the emergency manual filtration pump that, when stripped down and with the addition of a single strategically drilled hole, became an excellent water pipe. Of course the problem with hardware injection was that it was a classic cat and mouse game. The DRM subsystems were constantly growing and learning, so what worked one day might—after an overnight heuristics upgrade—land you on Hexagon Row the next.

The most complex and sophisticated form of bootlegging was a technique known as "recomposition." A common misconception of recomposition was that it constituted a method of circumventing or otherwise defeating the assemblers' DRM. In truth, the concept was far more elegant. Recomposition simply exploited the fact that humans were still more creative than machines. While machines had many times the computing power of the human brain at their disposal, they were still limited by their often-imbecilic programming. Humans, on the other hand—when confronted with limitations, obstructions, and dead ends—could always take a step back, move in a new direction, throw away all of their preconceptions and everything they thought was true in order to look at something from an entirely new and fresh perspective. Although machines had dozens or even hundreds of kilocores over which to distribute the task of comparing billions of components against billions of variations of abstract models, it was still a relatively trivial thing for a human to assemble any number of perfectly legitimate components, take them apart, and then put them back together into an enormously subversive configuration.

Luka received two messages from a completely anonymous account with the username Tycho. The first contained a set of schematics showing how to put together a set of components he had never seen before, but that subsequently appeared over the course of two days as he packaged up several orders for shipping and discovered that he had parts left over. Among the seemingly miscellaneous hardware that accumulated in a crate Luka kept in the back of a storeroom was a set of electromagnetic tracks, a miniature solid-state armature for generating tremendous electromotive force, two giant rings of solid tungsten carbide ball bearings, a lightweight carbon tube, and a battery receiver. When combined according to Tycho's instructions—and when outfitted with a standard power supply—the components became a clearly improvised but conspicuously menacing handheld weapon qualifying as a class of simplified railgun capable of silently and almost instantaneously accelerating small metal balls to a velocity just below that needed to pierce the hull of a ship, but more than enough to penetrate not only most types of body armor, but all of the layers of muscle, organs, and bones behind it.

The second message Luka received from Tycho was, as promised, a time and a place.

CHAPTER TWENTY-FOUR

DISEMBODIMENT

CADIE FELT A HAND ON HER arm and opened her eyes. The doctor was standing over her, the soft lights behind her head coming up gradually and gently. When Cadie realized that Abbasi's head was uncovered, she knew something was wrong.

The doctor's hair was shorter than Cadie expected. Instead of being long and pulled back into a conservative bunch, it was fairly short and charged with waves and curls that made it almost playful. The expression on her face was an obvious attempt at reassurance, but Cadie could see that there was something more that she could not suppress in her big bronze eyes. Something like panic. Or maybe just urgency. Cadie could tell that whatever was about to happen, it was going to happen fast.

"It's time to get you out of here," Abbasi told her. Another attempt at reassurance with a quick, tense smile.

As the doctor rolled her up onto her side, Cadie realized the significance of being awakened by Abbasi's hand. A soft and gentle touch. Something she actually felt. And now she could feel her body suit opening down the back and the epidural patch being peeled off. She was rejoining the world—no longer simply an observer, and no longer disembodied.

She was able to move now. As she sat up, she was surprised to find that she was neither stiff nor sore. She could feel the surface beneath her undulating—cycling through patterns and configurations probably intended to help avoid compressed nerves, blood clots, and pressure ulcers.

The doctor handed Cadie a bulb of cold water and Cadie drank. She looked around her, took deep breaths, and felt alive and strong. There was no pain in her abdomen and she did not think about the baby. There would be time later to grieve, but right now, she needed to be present. She trusted the doctor, and she knew she had to focus.

"How do you feel?" Abbasi asked her.

"I feel good," Cadie said. "I feel strong."

"Very good," the doctor said. She pulled a black elastic band off her wrist and offered it to Cadie. "Pull your hair back," she said. "You're going to want it out of your way."

Cadie accepted the band, and as she ran her fingers through her hair to gather it, she found that the doctor's brushing had kept it free of knots and tangles. When the band was twisted tight, she swung her legs around and let them dangle from the side of the platform.

The doctor knelt and slid what felt like slippers over Cadie's feet. They fit her well, though Cadie could feel them further molding themselves around her toes, heels, and arches until they matched the shape of her feet exactly, more like prosthetics than shoes. She dropped down on the floor and felt light and even buoyant on her legs. Her ponytail leapt as she bounced on the balls of her feet and found that her quadriceps and hamstrings and calf muscles were limber and well developed.

"You should probably use the washroom," the doctor advised.

The semiopaque privacy panel slid to the side as Cadie approached, and then slid closed again behind her as the lights came up. The entire room—including the shower, the counter, and the basin—seemed to be fabricated out of a single, uninterrupted flow of smooth white silica. It took Cadie a moment to realize that the handle between the chrome bars was used to lower the toilet, though she correctly guessed that pivoting it back up into the wall activated the flushing mechanism.

When she came back out, she found that the doctor was not alone. There was a man beside her. He was much taller than the doctor, and he was cradling a stubby, scoped rifle. The man had fiercely red hair and he wore cargo pants, boots, and a tight sweater—either dark blue or black—with tiny insignias pinned through the shoulders. There was another weapon strapped to the man's right thigh. When he spoke, Cadie immediately recognized his voice.

"You good to go?" the man asked her.

Cadie looked at the doctor, and the doctor nodded.

"Yes," Cadie said.

"We're going to need to move fast," the man explained. "And we're only going to get one shot at this. Are you going to be able to keep up?"

The surge of adrenaline Cadie had felt back in V1 when stepping through the outer door of the airlock for the first time was nothing compared to this. As she shook out her arms and legs, she wondered if the man would be able to keep up with her.

"Absolutely," Cadie said.

"OK, then," he said. "Let's do this. Follow me."

He started to turn but the doctor took his arm. The man stopped and looked down at her.

"Thank you for doing this," Abbasi said.

The man watched the doctor for a moment. Cadie wondered if it was as strange for him to see Abbasi with her head uncovered as it had been for her.

"Don't thank me yet," the man said.

• • •

Ayla was back on the *Hawk*. She pretended to be asleep as her cabin door opened, then closed again a moment later. Her shift had ended two hours before his and she was supposed to be asleep, but she never slept when she knew Costa was coming to bed. At least not very soundly. She liked to listen to him undress and brush his teeth. He frequently did several sets of push-ups and sit-ups to help him wind down, the floor creaking as he pushed his lean but muscular body against it. Ayla liked to listen to his breathing get heavier and more strained until it was almost a grunt.

One of Costa's quirks was that he frequently washed his feet throughout the day, and always before bed. He told Ayla that he once had a fungal infection that required him to keep his feet clean and dry, and go without boots and socks for a month. Washing his feet before bed became a habit—a kind of ritual that, for reasons he didn't really understand, helped relax him. Perhaps it was a form of symbolic purification, he once speculated as Ayla leaned against the open bathroom door and watched him perform the curious ceremony, always starting with the toes of the right foot. Far too many of his days were spent doing things he was not proud of, so perhaps washing his feet was his own personal form of repentance.

Sometimes he spent a few minutes at the terminal embedded in the wall beside the bed, or simply stood there meditatively, perhaps trying to detect signs of aging in the mirror on the back of the door, or maybe watching Ayla pretend to sleep. Whatever he did, he did as quietly as he could so as not to wake her up, never realizing that his wife was always awake, and never knowing how much she loved just listening to him—just being in the same room as him. But most of all, she loved that moment when he switched out the last light, and the bed compressed beneath his weight. As he pulled the sheet up over him, she could feel his heat, and then his arm around her waist, and then his body against hers. And when she finally did fall asleep, it was always thoroughly intoxicated by whatever it was about Costa that made him smell like Costa.

She frequently thought about telling him that she was awake, or maybe just rolling over and opening her eyes so that he knew. But there was something about the routine that made her want to keep it a secret. Although the ritual was almost entirely about him, she also felt that it was something completely her own, and that if anyone ever found out about it, they might somehow try to take it away from her.

But tonight, the routine was different. Something was wrong. Instead of turning off the lights and getting into bed with her, he turned the lights on and shook her awake. Ayla felt her body from the *Accipiter Hawk* rejoin her body here, and when she opened her eyes, she remembered where she was. The man in her cell was armed, but he did not seem to be threatening her. When Ayla sat up, the man backed away.

"We need to go," he told her in a tone that combined solemnity with urgency. He was an older man with short and thinning gray hair, the beginnings of a wattle beneath his chin, and a gentle paunch beneath his tight commando sweater.

Ayla squinted in the light and rubbed at her eyes. "Who are you?"

"We're here to get you out," the man said. "But we have to move fast."

The man's use of the word "we" made Ayla look toward the door. The slats were open and she could see two other soldiers keeping watch outside her cell. It was dark, but in the ruby-red light outside, she could tell that one of them was a woman.

"Where are we going?"

"We're taking you back to your ship," the man said. "You, and the people you brought with you."

Ayla began working her feet into her boots. "What about Omicron?" she asked. "I'm not leaving without him."

"Him, too," the man said. "But we can't open his cell until I'm certain you can control him."

"I thought you could restrain us at any time," Ayla said. She was referring to the incarceration suits they were issued when they were brought in. It was explained to her that the polymer fibers in the material could be instantaneously realigned to become a thousand times more rigid in response to a focused beam of something or other. A certain wavelength of light, she thought. She didn't remember the details. The upshot was that any attempt to escape would result in them being swiftly subdued. Ayla had never heard of such of a thing and half wondered if the whole thing was a bluff.

"We don't have time for that," the man said. "We need everyone's full cooperation if we're going to get you out of here in time."

The man's assumption that Ayla controlled Omicron was misguided. She'd never felt in control of him (though she never felt she needed to be), and although she made a few halfhearted attempts to assert herself early on, dominance was simply not something she had in her. Shortly after Omicron joined her crew, Ayla realized that it was never actually a bodyguard or a servant she wanted, but simply a constant and meaningful connection to another human being. While she and Omicron were being escorted from the *Hawk* to Hexagon Row, Ayla permanently disabled the vital sign monitor she wore on her wrist and willingly allowed it to be confiscated. Nobody controlled Omicron anymore except Omicron.

"In that case," Ayla said, "he just has to know that I trust you." She ratcheted one boot closed and started on the second. "Otherwise, there's no telling what he'll do."

"How do we convince him that you trust me?"

"That's the problem," Ayla said. "I don't."

She slapped the last buckle down on the second boot and stood. The man looked down at her for a moment, then swung his rifle back on his shoulder.

"Fine," he conceded. He drew his sidearm from the holster on his thigh, passed it to his other hand, then offered it to Ayla, grip-first. "Here."

Ayla watched the man's dull gray eyes carefully as she reached for the weapon, since she knew that any betrayal would begin there rather than in his gloved hands or composite-toed feet. When the pistol was firmly in her grasp, the man released it, then clasped his hands behind his back. Ayla's index finger went up to the loaded chamber indicator and found that it was indeed protruding from the presence of a round. Just to be certain, she looked down at the weapon, then pulled the slide back just far enough that she could see the cartridge through the ejection port.

"Good," Ayla told the man. "*Now* I trust you."

• • •

The two oldest and largest above-deck structures on the *San Francisco* were the Market Street Refinery and the Mission Street Foundry. On the outside, the two buildings were identical, built from the same set of bland but functional schematics; on the inside, they were customized for their own specific, though highly complementary, purposes.

Once the minerals that were sucked up from polymetallic nodules on the ocean floor were sufficiently isolated from the surrounding silt, pneumatic conduits carried them up to storage tanks in the refinery's basement where they were joined by complements of additional substances acquired in bulk from various ports, pod systems, and broker posts. What happened to the material as it was distributed among reservoirs, vats, and both well-staffed and entirely automated laboratories—subjected to various chemical, thermodynamic, and even small-scale nuclear processes along the way—was primarily dictated by the Mission Street Foundry's unending queue of orders, and by projections of future requirements based on algorithmic analyses of historical demand. The end result was hundreds of individual chemical elements, alloys, and various complex molecular substances fed to the refinery's sibling—the foundry—through an intricate network of pipes that had once been an above-deck eyesore, but as a result of one of the City Council's many industrial gentrification initiatives, were relocated down below the basement level to deck two.

Once in the foundry, the various forms of matter—usually referred to collectively as *medium*—were stored under various conditions where it was modestly but steadily sipped by the hundreds of specialized assemblers that paused only long enough to be repaired, calibrated, upgraded, or to have their latest compositions removed by technicians before being reset and put back to work on the next order in the queue.

Without looking out of a window to check the circadian phase of the artificial light reflecting down off the dome, one could not tell day from night inside the foundry. Although technicians with seniority had first pick, all three shifts were staffed equally, and at no time, nor under any circumstances, was the foundry's output permitted to subside. Producing almost every single physical item required to keep an entire city not just afloat, but also growing, evolving, and feeling as though it was prospering was an incredibly time-consuming and labor-intensive endeavor that only grew increasingly demanding the higher the standard of living rose.

But the same could not be said for the refinery. Although it was technically in operation twenty-four hours a day, it was usually able to dial down production significantly at night. For the first two shifts of the day, converting natural resources into clean medium for the assemblers required about the same level of manpower as running the foundry. But at night—assuming production had been high enough that day, and that all the right tanks and cartridges were at high enough capacity, and that all daily quotas had been met—most of the third shift was routinely called off. Automated diagnostic and safety systems were considered sufficient for keeping an eye on the largely idle operations, and those who were required to stay back usually took full advantage of the cots in the control rooms. The fact that the refinery was almost entirely abandoned during the night shift—combined with its size and the constant noise even at minimal production levels—made it the perfect place for Luka and Charlie to meet, finalize their strategy, and get below deck without being detected.

In the basement of the Market Street Refinery, not far from the cargo lift, there was an odd bend in an assembly of hexagonal pipes—probably there to avoid some type of support structure or another cluster of pipes that had long since been relocated.

Luka had climbed and hoisted his way up to the small platform and nestled himself down into the cavity to wait for Charlie. It was hot down in the basement level, and he could feel the high-frequency buzz of gritty material moving through the pipes beneath him. There was a smell down there unlike anywhere else on the rig, and it reminded Luka of some of Valencia's kitchen experiments. She and her friends used to try to recreate recipes from the archives using anything that wouldn't be missed from the gardens. Of course they were forced to make wild substitutions, and the results were seldom even edible, much less appetizing. Luka used to wonder what was in store for him when he was met with unfamiliar odors between the lift and the door to his transpartment. What he smelled now reminded him of Val's first (but unfortunately, not her last) attempt at something called Irish soda bread. It somehow combined the pleasant aroma of something freshly baked with the noxious tinge of something being nearly incinerated.

Luka knew he should be trying to get a few hours of sleep, but he also knew that there was no way that was going to happen. He'd left the weapon he'd assembled lying flat on the floor below, having initially leaned it up against some sort of filtration system, then thinking better of it. It would have been nice to bring it up with him as a sort of distraction while he waited, but he was afraid of dropping it during the climb and either damaging it, or worse, accidentally discharging it. What he brought up to his perch with him instead was an envelope of curious yellow along with a flared glass tube.

In retrospect, Luka wasn't entirely sure how he ended up with either item. It felt to him like the work of someone else—someone whose eyes he looked through, but whom he couldn't control. A type of disembodiment. He had watched himself go to work early that morning and claim one of the older workstations vulnerable to binary code injection. He'd watched himself apply the exploit, run the job, and then look around to make sure nobody was paying attention as he tapped the thin layer of yellow dust off the surrogate gigacore graphics processing card into an improvised paper receptacle, which he then folded up and slipped into his jacket. And finally, he'd watched himself hang his coat up beside his transpartment door that evening, but rather than removing the envelope from the left-hand pocket, he'd deposited the glass tube into the pocket on the right.

Luka did not want to get high, but once again, he was outside of his own body, watching himself do something he felt powerless to prevent. He watched himself unfold the paper and tap at its edges until the powder was evenly dispersed, and then he watched himself retrieve the glass tube from his lap, lift it to his nostril, and bend down. That was when it occurred to him that maybe his body knew what it was doing. Maybe it was better to be just a little bit high tonight than to be distracted by withdrawal. Maybe tonight, of all nights, he needed his edge. It was suddenly obvious to him that it would be better to quit tomorrow, after whatever was about to happen was fully behind him. This, Luka promised himself, would be the very last time.

Luka felt his opioid receptors buzzing in anticipation as he allowed himself to merge with this other being and once again become whole.

He lifted his head and leaned back against the pipes, using subtle breaths to balance the liquified substance against the vast network of capillaries in his nasal passage. He felt it absorb, travel up into his head, and cross the barrier into his brain. The process, Luka realized, was not unlike the material that traveled from the refinery to the foundry where—through methods that might as well be magic as far as anyone here was concerned—it was transformed into endorphin-inducing objects of desire.

Luka began to make sense of the relationship between the two buildings in a way that had never occurred to him before. They were codependents—the foundry assembling replacement parts for the refinery, which kept the foundry supplied with medium with which to assemble replacement parts. And then there was the sprawling root system of the undersea mining operation. The three of them were enormously complex symbiotic organisms that, combined, constituted a single superorganism; an artificial leviathan; a colossal and mechanical Portuguese man-of-war roaming the planet and dredging its soul with massive, venomous tentacles. The City Council and the crew and the citizens of the *San Francisco* all believed that they were in control of the rig, but perhaps it was the rig that was in control of them, rewarding and distracting the human drones that maintained it with meaningless and superfluous trinkets.

By the time Charlie arrived, the envelope and the glass tube had been put away. Charlie stopped when she spotted the weapon on the floor and looked around. It did not seem to occur to her to look up until Luka swung his legs around and the motion drew her attention. She backed up and Luka let himself fall from the pipes, landing hard against the metal-grate floor. Charlie watched him with concern for a moment, then reached out and touched his arm.

"Hey," she said. "Are you OK?"

"I'm good," Luka told her. He reached down and picked up the rifle. "You ready to do this?"

"We still have time," Charlie said. "It's still early."

Luka nodded and placed the rifle back on the floor.

"Did you hear anything more from your contact?" Charlie asked him. "Do you have any better idea of what all this is about?"

Luka shook his head. "Nothing new."

Charlie nodded, then gave Luka a forced smile. "Can I ask you something?" she said.

"What?"

"What do you *want* all this to be about?"

Luka watched Charlie for a moment, then looked away. "Something important," he said. He wiped his nose with the sleeve of his shirt and sniffed, and then he suddenly covered his face with both hands. He tried to take a deep breath and was surprised when, instead, he let out a tremendous sob. "I just want this to be about something important," he said through his fingers.

Charlie put her arms around him and held him while he cried.

CHAPTER TWENTY-FIVE

BLACK LIGHT

THE INCARCERATION SUITS, AYLA discovered, were not a bluff. She, Omicron, and the boy called Cam were all wearing them. The girl, Cadie, was not. The suit she had on was shimmering silver and came all the way up to her chin. Ayla could see that there were electrodes and ribbons of filament woven throughout its material like some kind of shock garment. But then she noticed an additional detail that suggested the suit had a medical purpose: the girl was no longer pregnant.

Cam was agitated, even before he saw Cadie. All the way down from their hexagonal prison cells to wherever it was they were now, he kept asking the guards questions about the other girl—the one named Zaire, who Ayla had worked out was either Cam's girlfriend or his wife—and each time, he'd been told to calm down, that everything was fine, that he would see her again very soon. When the two individual parties converged—Cadie and her guard emerging from one end of the darkened hallway, and Ayla, Omicron, Cam, and their three guards emerging from the other—Cam's eyes went immediately down to the girl's midriff and stayed there for a long time. Everyone was still and silent until Cam turned and roared something that Ayla couldn't understand and lunged for the nearest guard. There were four guards total, and the one Cam went after was the smallest, but possibly also the quickest. He seemed to anticipate Cam's advance and raised his rifle to meet it, but rather than squeezing the trigger and knocking Cam back with a giant hole in his chest from a hollow-point round, he touched something on the side of his weapon, just above the trigger guard. Cam instantly seized, then began to strain against the realigned polymer fibers of his instantly rigid suit.

Cam growled furiously as he continued to exert himself, and then he finally relaxed, breathing heavily and sweating from the wasted effort. Ayla couldn't tell whether it was intense pain that contorted the boy's face, or rage and frustration.

"You need to stand down," the guard instructed. He was the only one of them wearing a hat—an unmarked navy blue baseball cap with a dramatically curved bill that he kept pulled down low.

Cam watched the guard through wild and narrowed eyes. "*Fine*," he eventually said.

"We don't have time for heroics," the guard told him. "I need to hear you say that you understand."

There was still anger in Cam's voice, but there was also resignation. "I *said* I'm *fine*."

The guard who had accompanied Cadie took a step forward. There were pins fastened through his sweater's shoulder patches, and Ayla could tell that he held rank above the others. He had the reddest natural hair Ayla had ever seen, and eyebrows and stubble to match.

"Let him go, Lieutenant," the commander said. His complexion was so thoroughly freckled that it appeared mottled. "He'll behave himself."

The lieutenant touched the side of his rifle again and Cam staggered backward. He glared at the guard once more, then completed his retreat to Cadie's side. He reached out in an attempt to comfort the girl, but she seemed much more focused than upset, and did not respond to his touch. For the first time, Ayla wondered if perhaps the baby had been his.

Ayla and Omicron stood together, across from Cam and Cadie. Omicron was now holding the pistol that the guard had offered as a token of trust, though he hadn't yet had occasion to raise it. When Ayla passed it to him outside his cell upstairs, nobody objected.

"Now, if the four of you want to live," the commander began, "we need to get you out of here as quickly and quietly as possible."

"No," Cam said. "I'm not leaving without the baby, and I'm not leaving without Zaire."

"You need to relax," the commander said. "They were both transferred to your ship this morning. They're in cryostasis, but they're fine. Our chief surgeon knows what she's doing."

"You better hope—" Cam began to point, but stopped when Cadie gripped his arm. The lieutenant had lifted his rifle again.

"Stop it," Cadie said. "This isn't helping. We need to go."

"You should listen to her," the commander advised. He glanced down at his wrist. "You have less than four minutes to get to your ship and clear the rig before there isn't going to be anything we can do for you."

"Which way?" Ayla said.

The man gestured at the wall behind them. "Through that door," he said. "I'll escort you. Then you're going up the rungs and through the hatch to deck two, and then through another hatch to the catwalk. You're not going to have respirators, so be prepared to hold your breath once you get outside."

"This isn't the way we came," Omicron said.

"There's no way you're getting out that way," the commander said. "And even if you could, your ship isn't there anymore. The story is that it's been sold, and a new crew has already taken possession of it."

"Sold to who?" Ayla asked.

The man looked down at Ayla and squinted. "Is that really important right now?"

"It's important if we're going to trust you," Ayla said. "If the story is that the ship's been sold, that means someone actually put up the caps."

"Fine," the commander said. "I'll give you the twenty-second synopsis. It was our chief surgeon, Dr. Abbasi. It turns out she grew rather fond of Cadie and arranged this whole thing. She paid for the ship, paid us to make sure you got there safely, and paid the watch to look the other way while you put some distance between us. She even paid off your man, Nsonowa, to make sure there were no bounties on your heads." The commander looked back down at his wrist. "Now, you have about three minutes left to get up a deck and a half, get aboard your ship, and get out of here before the watch changes. Any more questions?"

Ayla and Omicron looked at Cadie. Cadie nodded.

"Good enough for me," Ayla said. "Let's go."

There were two metal doors in the wall behind them: a wide cargo door that appeared to be hinged on the inside, and a smaller, vertical, pill-shaped inner door equipped with a lever and a hand crank. There was a brightly lit control panel beside the larger door, but it was the door in the middle that the female guard approached. She spun the wheel, rotated the lever, and pushed the hatch in while the guard with the cap watched Cam.

"The rungs are in the back," the commander said. "Let's go."

"After you," Ayla said before anyone could move.

The commander watched her for a moment, then smiled. "So distrustful," he said, then stepped inside through the opening.

Omicron went first, followed by Ayla, Cadie, and Cam. The other three guards stayed outside. Ayla saw the young guard with the cap lower his weapon as the female guard pulled the door closed. Silicone gaskets muted the impact, but a metallic *clang* rang throughout the chamber as a latch was thrown. Ayla listened, but she did not hear them spin the wheel to seal the hatch.

The walls were metal and streaked with corrosion. The light in the room came from flush-mounted plasma rings near the ceiling. It was damp, and there was a wide-diameter pipe overhead that dripped into a rusted grate in the floor. There was another, much larger hatch on the outside wall—this one sealed with round, aperture-like blades. Beside it were rungs leading up to a smaller access hatch in the ceiling.

"I just have one more question," Ayla said.

"Save it," the commander said. "Right now I need you all single file up against that back wall."

"Why?" Ayla asked him. "So you can shoot us?"

"Christ," the commander said. "So I can get you up those rungs and through that hatch as efficiently as possible."

"You said the doctor paid off Jumanne Nsonowa, right?"

"That's what I was told," he said. "Why?"

"Because Nsonowa has a direct line to the Coronians. The last thing he needs is caps. So I'm curious: how do you buy off a man who has no need for money?"

"Feel free to take that up with him yourself," the commander said. "We're now down to two minutes."

"I already know the answer," Ayla said calmly. "The way you buy off a man who has no need for money is by doing him a favor."

The commander's expression became grave as he watched Ayla. "You're going to get you and all your friends killed," he told her. "Now I'm going to ask you one last time: line up against the back wall."

"Omicron," Ayla said. "Do you smell that?"

"Smell what?" Omicron asked.

"I'm not sure," Ayla said. "But it's making my nose itch."

There was a blur of motion as Omicron raised the pistol level with the commander's face, and then a reverberating *snap* as he pulled the trigger. The commander took a step back, raised his rifle, and touched the side above the trigger guard.

"You don't think we're stupid enough to give you live rounds, do you?" the commander asked.

From this angle, Ayla could see a dull violet glow beneath the rifle's barrel. Omicron dropped the pistol but his arm remained locked in place. Cam started to advance but froze when the commander swung the rifle in his direction. Ayla was calculating whether or not she could reach the man in time when the commander turned the black light on her and she felt her incarceration suit instantly harden into something like a full-body cast.

"It would've been safer to do this up against the hull," the commander said, "but I think I'm a good enough shot to make this work." He removed his left hand from the rifle's stock and lunged toward Cadie, grasping her by the wrist. "But not you," he said as he pulled her to his side. "You still have some value."

Ayla could see that Omicron was quivering and that his face was glistening with perspiration. There were splintering sounds as the hardened material inside his suit began to fail.

"Jesus Christ," the commander said. He now had both hands back on the rifle and was peering through the scope at Omicron's forehead. "We wondered if that thing would hold you."

The commander pivoted his stance and put his weight on his back leg. His finger moved from the side of the rifle down to the trigger and he began to squeeze.

"Welcome back to extinction," he said.

Ayla could see that Cadie was bending her knees—lowering her shoulder almost imperceptibly—and then the girl sprang. The rifle leapt to the side and the muzzle flashed. Ayla heard the round pass just over her head and then slam against the metal hull behind them. While the commander was off balance, Cadie struck him with an open palm in the nose and sent him to the floor. He was back on his feet instantly and when he ran the back of his hand across his face, he found it ablaze with blood. The new hue in his complexion made his hair and eyebrows look more orange than red.

"I guess I underestimated you," the commander said with surprising poise.

The rifle was in his left hand and he raised his right across his chest. He took a quick step toward Cadie and drove his elbow toward her face. Before there was contact, the commander's motion was abruptly arrested by an immense hand catching his wrist. The man had a moment to register Omicron's presence before Omicron twisted and popped the commander's shoulder out of its socket. With his other hand, the Neo reached down and relieved the commander of his weapon.

The metal enclosure was filled with the commander's screams as he crumbled and rolled over onto this back. Omicron used the black light on the rifle to release Ayla's and Cam's restraints. Cam stepped over the commander to get to Cadie and embraced her, but Cadie raised her hands between them. When Omicron turned back to the man on the ground, the commander was trying to endure the intense pain of removing his sidearm. His hand quivered as his fingertips feebly brushed the pistol's grip, though they stopped when Omicron sited the bridge of his nose through the rifle's scope. Darkness spread from the man's groin as he pissed himself.

"Wait," Ayla said. She bent down and removed the commander's sidearm from the holster on his thigh, pointed it at his knee, and placed her finger over the trigger. "You better hope these rounds aren't live," she said.

"No!" the commander screamed. "Please! Don't!"

"Thank you," Ayla said. She moved her finger from the trigger to the pistol's slide and dropped her arm. "That's all I needed to know. Omicron, do your thing."

"Wait!" the commander pleaded. He raised his hand into the space between the rifle's muzzle and his face. "I can help you."

"How?" Ayla said.

"I can get you out of here. And I can tell you where Zaire and the baby are."

Cam stepped toward the commander and lifted his foot. He placed it gently on the commander's contorted shoulder and began to apply pressure.

"Where?" he asked the man on the ground.

The commander reached up and grasped Cam's ankle with his good hand but he did not have the leverage he needed to move it. Cam began to step down when a shrill metallic screech stopped him.

"What was that?" Cam asked.

"The door," Omicron said. "They're sealing it."

The screech arose once more as the wheel on the outside of the door was turned again, then again, and then it stopped.

"No," Ayla said. "No no no no."

"Why are they sealing it?" Cam asked.

Omicron began looking around him. "Because they're going to flood the room."

"They can't flood the room with me in here," the commander said. "They have to get me out first."

It was silent for a moment, and then the giant pipe in the ceiling erupted and the floor was instantly wet. Before the water even began to soak into her clothing, Ayla could feel how frigid it was. Everyone but the commander instinctively moved away from the center of the room and toward the perimeter.

"Stop!" the commander screamed toward the front of the room. "Stop! I'm still alive! I'm still in here!"

He was scooting himself back with his good arm and Ayla noted that the water was already up over his wrist.

"Here," Omicron said, handing the rifle to Cam.

The big Neo approached the door they'd come through and grasped the lever. The metal groaned under his tremendous strength and weight, and then finally gave. The latch was loose, but when Omicron pulled against it, the hatch did not move.

"The latch is stripped," he shouted over the sound of the rushing water, "but there's no way to unseal it from this side."

Ayla pointed up into the corner of the room. "Try the access hatch," she shouted.

The water was already up to their knees and the commander was struggling to get to his feet. Cam kicked the man in his chest and sent him back down into the water with a splash.

Omicron trudged to the back of the chamber and scaled the rungs. The hatch was designed to pivot down in order to enforce the seal when the room was flooded, but the pressure lock was on the other side. Omicron tried the welded handle, but the hatch did not budge. He reached up and grasped it with both hands, allowed himself to dangle for a moment, then hooked his toes beneath one of the rungs. With a tremendous bellow, he constricted his entire body. There was the sound of metal flexing, punctuated by a snap, and then Omicron dropped into the water below. There were two dull gray spots on the hatch where the handle had been attached, and when Omicron stood, he was holding the U-shaped piece of steel.

The water was now just below his chest.

"Can all of you swim?" Omicron shouted over the gush of the water.

The pistol was clasped between Ayla's knees and she was trying to warm herself by crossing her arms and rubbing. Cadie's arms were also crossed, but it was Cam who rubbed between her elbows and shoulders. The rifle was on his back with the strap across his chest.

"No," Cam said. "The closest we've ever come to swimming is hydromills."

"Get up the ladder," Omicron commanded. "Quickly."

Cam pushed Cadie ahead of him and she began to climb.

The commander had managed to get to his feet and was wading his way back to the rungs. "What about me?" he asked. "I can't swim with my arm like this."

Omicron moved toward the man, lifted his arm above the surface, and drove the steel handle down into the commander's skull. The man instantly dropped beneath the water and did not resurface.

Ayla stared at the huge Neo.

"He would have pulled them off and drowned them," Omicron said. The water was up to Ayla's chin. "What about you? Can you swim?"

"I'll be fine," Ayla said. Her lips were blue and she was shivering. She felt the pistol slip away from between her knees. "You find us a way out."

"I'm going to see if I can pry that grate up," Omicron said.

"Go," Ayla said. "Hurry."

Omicron nodded, took a deep breath, and disappeared beneath the surface.

Ayla lifted herself up on her toes and raised her chin, and then finally began treading water. Cadie and Cam were both at the top of the ladder, Cam standing on the rung below Cadie, wrapping himself around her as though he could protect her from what was coming up from below. The commander's body had surfaced and was bobbing against the wall.

Omicron resurfaced and gasped. Ayla could see that he still had the steel handle in his hand.

"Anything?" she shouted at him.

He shook his head. He looked around the room again, and Ayla knew that meant he was looking for other options, which they both already knew weren't there. It suddenly become eerily quiet as the water level reached the mouth of the pipe and then continued to rise beyond it. The ceiling felt very low now and Ayla realized that her head was even with Cam's feet.

Omicron began hyperventilating in preparation for another dive. He was trying to see down into the water below him.

"Hey," Ayla said in the sudden stillness. Omicron looked up. "Thank you."

"Don't thank me yet," Omicron said.

"No," Ayla said. "I mean for everything. I mean just in case."

Omicron watched her for a moment, then nodded. "You're welcome," he said, then filled his huge lungs to capacity and was gone.

He came up one more time and Ayla begged him not to go back down. The tops of their heads were nearly against the ceiling and the tiny space was now filled with Ayla's sobs. Cam and Cadie had each other—Cadie's eyes closed, Cam whispering something to her—and Ayla didn't want to be alone. She clung to Omicron and raised her head, gasping with desperation at the remaining pocket air.

"Please," she pleaded. "Please stay with me."

"I have to try," Omicron said. "Just one more time."

"I don't want to be alone," Ayla said.

Omicron looked around the sliver of horizontal space remaining—his eyes stopping on Cam and Cadie in the corner, and then on the commander's body bobbing against the wall in his own separate pool of blood—and then he looked back at Ayla.

"You're not alone," he said. There was a riveted joint at the top of the pipe and he reached up and grasped it with one hand and held Ayla against him with the other. They had to bend their necks to keep their mouths above the water, and Ayla choked and sputtered.

"Take me down," she pleaded. "Please. I can't do it myself."

Shadows leapt around them as light filtered up through the dark water. Cam's whispered prayers could be heard between Ayla's desperate sobs.

"You will see him again very soon," Omicron told Ayla. "And then you will never be alone again."

He held her tightly against his chest and then let go of the pipe.

CHAPTER TWENTY-SIX

NEUTRAL BUOYANCY

THE ONLY SOUND AYLA COULD hear beneath the frigid water was Omicron's powerful heart. His arms were around her and her cheek was pressed against his chest. It occurred to her that, in the end, their lives were inextricably linked after all, but it was not through fear, or force, or through a high-frequency radio signal calibrated to his autonomic implant. Ayla and Omicron were connected for no reason other than that they had chosen to be.

They neither sank nor rose, but floated together in perfect neutral buoyancy—their combined density roughly equal to that of the fluid around them. Ayla was beginning to arrive at a form of internal neutral buoyancy: a feeling of peace that was consuming the panic and starting to open up space for acceptance. She was glad that Omicron's heart would continue beating long after hers had stopped—that the last thing she would ever know was a closeness to another human being.

Ayla was so much at peace, in fact, that some part of her was annoyed when the stillness was shattered by a rapidly escalating whine. She felt herself being tugged around and down, and when she opened her eyes, she saw a vortex forming beneath them and reaching up toward their feet. The direction of the tug suddenly and violently reversed as Omicron began beating at the water with one arm while the other kept Ayla pinned to his torso. Ayla's panic instantly returned as she again began experiencing the contention between her diaphragm's instinct to suck in as much air as her lungs could hold, and her trachea's determination to prevent the passage of fluid. Horrible, guttural noises were coming from her throat when she heard Omicron gasp and then felt her own head suddenly above the surface. She gasped, as well, again and again, until her breathing became an insatiable pant. The pocket of air above them was filled with reverberating cacophony—male and female voices shouting things she couldn't understand, and with the tumult of rough moving water. Ayla saw Omicron reach up for the riveted joint in the pipe above them but it was already too far away. He rolled onto his back and pulled her on top of himself in order to keep her face above the water, and she watched the chamber spin as they fell in sync with the vortex below them. The pipe above became the axis around which the rungs with Cam and Cadie at the top rotated. The descent was surprisingly rapid—more like a controlled fall—and it ended with a thump as Omicron's body hit the grate.

Her bodyguard relaxed his arms and Ayla rolled off. Between breaths she heard feet tapping at rungs and she knew that Cam and Cadie were descending. She tried to stand but found that she was too dizzy, either from the hyperventilating or the spinning or both. When she looked around, she saw the commander's pale body, both pistols, and the handle that Omicron had broken off the access hatch all caught in the drain.

Omicron helped her to feet and held her steady, and as her breathing slowed, the voices around her started making sense.

"I think so," she heard Omicron say. "Just give her a minute."

"They must have thought we were dead," Cam said. He still had the rifle on his back.

"No," Omicron said. "They would have waited to make sure."

"Then what happened?"

Omicron took one of the pistols out of the drain and shook the excess water from it. "Let's wait and see," he said.

After inspecting the weapon, he turned it on its side and jerked back the slide. A round was ejected into the air, arced, and fell into his huge open palm. He worked it up between his fingers, squeezed, and crumpled the metal casing as easily as if it had been Mylar. Both the primer and the bullet fell through the grate at his feet and Omicron peered inside the ruined jacket, verifying that it was empty. Ayla had already picked up the other pistol, and when Omicron tossed his aside, she passed him the live one.

They had already begun a fresh evaluation of the room when they heard the seal on the larger cargo door break. Omicron took one last look around, presumably hoping to find something that might serve as cover. Finding nothing, his left hand joined his right on the handle of the pistol, and he pointed it at the door.

"Get behind me," he told Ayla.

Cam took Cadie's arm and guided her gently behind him, then took the rifle off his back. He pointed it at the ceiling and checked one side of it, then the other—flipped a switch, then flipped it back. Omicron watched him try to figure the weapon out for a moment, then reached over and took it from him with one hand and passed him the pistol with the other.

"Here," he told the boy. "Just point and shoot."

Cam nodded.

"On my order," Omicron added.

"Right."

Ayla had never seen a door or a hatch that operated like this one. It floated directly toward them for a moment until it had fully cleared the opening behind it, then four recessed arms conveyed it in a shallow arc to the side. Behind it, Ayla saw an intense purple-white glow, and then another one beside it. She assumed they were black lights intended to activate their incarceration suits, but they were far brighter than the ones she'd seen before, and nobody's suit reacted. It was darker outside the chamber than it was inside, and it took Ayla's eyes a moment to adjust and reveal that both sources of illumination were coming from the same machine: some sort of massive bipedal tank probably at least three meters tall, both arms ablaze with jets of purple-white plasma erupting from heavy industrial torches. Beside it was a man holding the most exotic-looking rifle she'd ever seen. It was a combination of long sleek rails, a giant round magazine, and bristling electronics. Ayla was surprised to see that her party was not the one being targeted, but rather the three guards lying facedown on the floor just outside the door.

"Who are you?" Omicron called.

"Who the hell are *you*?" was the response from man beside the mech.

Omicron lowered his rifle, then reached over and took the pistol from Cam. He squatted and placed both weapons gently on the metal grate.

"It looks like we're friends," he told the man.

CHAPTER TWENTY-SEVEN

CHINA BASIN

WHEN CHARLIE REACHED OVER and grasped Luka's hand, he pulled it away. He knew that she was anticipating what he was thinking, but he was trying as hard as he could not to think it. He had just witnessed almost exactly what Val must have gone though during the last moments of her life—heard the same desperate, stifled pleas and pounding, and sensed the same horror and loneliness that she must have felt. Luka knew that responding to Charlie was the right thing to do—that she was probably seeking comfort for the loss of her sister as much as she was offering it for the loss of his wife—but any form of acknowledgment meant a torrent of emotion for which he was not prepared.

Luka's wife, Valencia Blanca-Talleyrand, had been one of only a few adopted children in the entire history of the *San Francisco*. After submitting over a dozen applications, Charlie's parents were finally granted permission by the Procreation Committee to have a second child, only to discover they were unable to conceive again. Both parents made their living by taking whatever shifts they could get at the Mission Bay Water Treatment and Purification Facility, Muir Electrolysis Station, and the Presidio Air Filtration Base, and although they were never able to produce proof, they believed that one or both had been exposed to chemicals or radiation that affected their fertility. When the *San Francisco* began accepting child refugees to help run the assemblers, in exchange for dropping all official complaints and inquiries, the Talleyrands were given the rare opportunity to legally adopt a son or daughter of their choice.

Luka remembered Charlie's parents bringing her to the orphanage in China Basin and visiting with the children. Sometimes they left with one for a few hours, then brought him or her back, usually clutching some kind of homemade doll or crude toy. Luka wondered if they would ever visit with him, or maybe even take him out for an afternoon to play at the old Miraloma Park, but they never did, and he still remembered wondering why. He tried to figure out what the differences were between him and the kids they did pick, and how he could be more like them. He wondered what it was about himself that he was not hiding well enough, or what he didn't have that the other kids did, or what exactly they saw—or didn't see—when they scanned the room and their eyes briefly touched on him, and then always kept going. But most of all, Luka wondered if the reasons the family didn't want him were all the same reasons his parents had made the decision to give him up in the first place.

Eventually the couple began visiting with the same little girl repeatedly, and even keeping her overnight. Luka didn't know Valencia, but he had spent enough time watching her that he knew every detail of her appearance. Her skin was the color of the syrup they were sometimes given to sweeten their soy porridge, and her eyes were the color of pure copper. Her lips were full and pink, and from the moment she arrived, she had always clung to some kind of dingy and threadbare purple stuffed animal that Luka couldn't identify. Even when she came back from her visits with new stuffed animals made of socks and buttons and other scrap material, she abandoned them beneath her cot and never protested when they went missing. Finally the little girl went on her last overnight visit with the Talleyrand family, and although Luka waited every day for her to come back, she never did.

Charlie and Valencia were always close, but they didn't always get along very well as children. And according to all the stories Luka had been told over the years, they weren't particularly well-behaved children, either. Rather than competing for their parents' attention, the two sisters seemed to prefer to compete for their disapproval, and Val almost always won. She'd been accepted aboard the *San Francisco* specifically for assembly technician training, but from the moment she saw the terraces and vertical farms in the center of the rig, she insisted that all she would ever be was a grower. After being dismissed from the foundry for excessive insubordination (or, according to the explanation section of the discharge form, "insufferable temper tantrums") only two months after she started, she spent four years training at the Pacific Medical Center. But rather than becoming the doctor or even the nurse that her parents hoped, she was once again dismissed for insubordination. She subsequently spent the next five years working alongside her parents, helping to ensure that the *San Francisco* was never without clean air and water, then four years doing various jobs at the refinery before one of her many requests to the Labor Committee to be transferred to Yerba Buena Gardens was finally approved—probably more to mollify her than out of any real need to rebalance resources. According to Val, she was told by her supervisor on her first day of work that this was her final chance to make herself useful aboard the *San Francisco* above deck. The only place left for her to go was the one place nobody who had any options ever went: down below into the deep-sea mines.

But the ultimatum turned out to be moot. As Luka eventually learned for himself (very much the hard way, as he recalled), by far the easiest way to deal with Val was to simply give her what she wanted. Once she felt she'd been listened to and had her opinions (though some might say "demands") sufficiently respected, she was usually not only extremely cooperative, but in the context of her career, also remarkably industrious. Val proved such a competent grower that after only sixteen months, she was promoted to a junior supervisory role, and then eventually up to foreman. From then on, she was continually turning down promotions that threatened to take her away from the hands-on physical labor that she loved and instead confine her to a desk where she would spend most of her time reducing friends and coworkers to resources; the miraculous harvests that they produced to caloric output; and the families whose lives they sustained to nothing more than quantifiable units of demand.

The better you did your job, Val used to say, the sooner someone tried to take it all away from you.

Meanwhile, Val's sister—then known as Charlene Abigail—did not have it in her to sustain long streaks of rebellion, and therefore got most of it out of the way all at once. She'd been an excellent student and teaching assistant who appeared singularly focused on dedicating her entire life to academics by first becoming a lead teacher, then eventually the administrator of Mission Dolores, and finally—if all went according to her parents' plan—the chairwoman of the Education Committee. But all of that changed on her seventeenth birthday when the application she'd submitted without her parents' or sister's knowledge—the request to transfer down below into the deep-sea mines—was instantly approved. The next day, she cut and colored her hair, and traded her closetful of long synthetic dresses for heavy utility pants and one-piece engineering suits. A week later, on the first day of her new job, standing before her new colleagues and peers, Charlene Abigail Talleyrand introduced herself as Charlie.

While Val might have been willing to indulge her disposition toward oppositional and defiant behavior for longer periods of time, Charlie proved willing to take hers much further. However, like her sister, Charlie had finally found the one place aboard the *San Francisco* where she felt she truly belonged. Education and administration were safe and comfortable, but depth charges, nautilus-class excavators, atmospheric diving suits with self-contained rebreathers, and compression and decompression chambers that allowed miners to survive at depths as far down as it was possible for humans to possibly go were unfamiliar and exotic and challenging, and were the things that still reminded Charlie almost every single day of her life that she was alive.

Mr. and Mrs. Talleyrand's dreams of at least one daughter ascending even a single socioeconomic rung were now hinged entirely on marriage, and were therefore further imperiled first by Charlie's determination to date water rats exclusively, and then by Val's fluke reacquaintance with an assembly technician named Luka. It happened while she was standing outside Yerba Buena one evening during shift change, waiting for a coworker she'd been on several dates with. Luka was maneuvering a calibration cube between loitering pedestrians when Val looked up and caught him watching her. She stopped him with a hand on his arm on his way past—the very first time, Luka clearly remembered, that they'd ever touched.

"Hey," she said with a curious expression. Luka wondered if she'd recognized him from China Basin, but she looked from his eyes to the cube balanced on the hand truck in front of him. "What is *that* thing?"

"It's a calibration cube," Luka told her. "From an assembler."

"What's it for?"

"It's just trash."

"If it was just trash, you wouldn't be hauling it above deck," Val said. "What are you planning on doing with it?"

"I doubt you really want to know," Luka said.

"Why wouldn't I want to know? I asked, didn't I?"

"Because it's a very long story that I don't think you'd find very interesting."

"I have time," Val countered. "And you might be surprised by the things I find interesting."

She told Luka to give her a second while she used a nearby terminal to send a message, then returned and asked where they were going.

When they reached the Millennium Tower lobby, Luka stopped.

"If you really want to know what this is for," Luka said, "you're going to have to come up to my flat."

"Very good line," Val said with mock admiration. "So is this what you do? Use calibration cubes to lure innocent women up into your transpartment?"

"Usually hauling trash around has the opposite effect," Luka said. "I think most people think I'm crazy."

"They do," Val confirmed. "But crazy's good. Let's go."

While Luka shaped the cube, Val picked at a boxed meal of soy cubes and almonds (she explained, at great length, her theory of how evolution had never intended for humans to become insectivores). Every time she tossed one of the shelled nuts into her mouth, she produced a new almond-related fact: how much vitamin E, vitamin B, fiber, and protein they contained; the various uses of almond milk and oil and flour; how their almond tree was genetically engineered to be incredibly small, but to produce 50 percent more seeds than a tree twice its size. Luka didn't eat, but he opened a small flask of pear brandy and divided it between two mugs.

Once he'd finished with the rough cuts on the cube, he turned Val's stool toward the window so she couldn't see what he was doing. He told her, while he worked, that she would have recognized what the calibration cube was if she hadn't gotten herself kicked out of the foundry. Val laughed and wanted to know how Luka knew about that. Luka told her everything he remembered about her from China Basin. He was older than Val and therefore remembered more. He told her about how he used to watch her, and how he'd always wished he'd had something with which to sketch or paint her. And about the family that came in to visit with her, and how they picked her out of all the other kids there, and how one time they took her overnight and never brought her back. He talked about how feisty he remembered her being, but also how generous she was, and how she never minded when the other kids took the new toys that the family brought her. And finally, he described the dingy purple stuffed animal she'd brought on board with her and used to cling to as though it had been a part of herself.

When he turned her around, he did not look at the sculpture along with her, but rather watched her expression instead. She seemed confused at first and Luka wondered if he was remembering it wrong, or if maybe she didn't remember it, but then she drew in a breath and covered her mouth and her big dark eyes filled with tears.

"It's Moocow!" Val exclaimed.

"That thing was a *cow*?" Luka asked. "I always thought it was some kind of mutant bear."

Val stood and circled the object, stepping over the scrap material and running her fingertips along the object's curves.

"In retrospect, I'm pretty sure it was supposed to be a hippopotamus," she said, "but my mother always told me it was a purple cow."

"What do you think?" Luka asked her. "Did I capture its hippopotamus-ness?"

Val looked up from the sculpture and bit her lower lip. "I love it," she said.

"I herby christen it Moocow," Luka said, and it became the first sculpture he ever kept.

CHAPTER TWENTY-EIGHT

EXISTENTIAL THREAT

THE OFFICER LYING IN THE drain was not the first dead body Luka had ever seen. Back in Hammerfest, before his parents brought him to the *San Francisco*, he and his friends had come across several. He'd even seen a dead body in China Basin once—a kid who, for reasons nobody bothered explaining to the children, died in his cot during the night. In Luka's experience, there was no mistaking a dead body. While it was possible to wonder for an instant or two if someone unconscious might be dead, it was seldom possible to wonder if a dead body was just unconscious. It was not unearthly peacefulness or tranquility that made death so apparent, but rather an unnatural or peculiar pose, a chilling stare of terror or bewilderment, or an overall affect of profound and utter abandonment.

Although Luka had never admitted this to anyone, he was thankful that he'd never been confronted with Val's lifeless body.

Luka recognized all four of the officers, but he didn't actually know any of them. The only one he'd met before was the girl. Val had introduced him to her once at the Moscone Theater shortly after they'd started dating. Mandy, her name was. Val never explained how she and Mandy knew one another and Luka never asked. Luka wondered briefly if she recalled meeting him, and if so, what she must think of him now.

He was surprised by their apparent indifference to their dead colleague. They gawked at his pale and limp body as they entered the waterlock at gunpoint, but nobody knelt to check his vital signs—even if purely for show—or to roll him over into a more dignified or peaceful position. He was lying on his stomach, half in the drain and half out, with his head turned too far to the side and his dislocated shoulder creating the impression that his arm had been popped off like a doll's and then reattached backward. There was a massive laceration in his scalp parting his ginger hair, through which a sliver of bright white skull was visible, and one of his steel-blue eyes was missing its gold-threaded contact. When Omicron explained the circumstances of the officer's death to Luka and Charlie—that the other officers had made the decision to sacrifice their commander by flooding the chamber after he had been overpowered—the survivors' detachment suddenly made more sense.

Disarming and sealing the officers in the waterlock was the obvious first step, but now that they all stood together outside the chamber, they weren't sure what to do next. Luka had immediately identified three of the four outsiders as his fellow Hexagon Row inmates, primarily because of the size of the big one. The young Asian girl in the electrode suit was new to him. She wore a complex expression of hate slightly tempered by determination, and although she was by far the smallest member of the group, there was no question that she was also the one Luka would least like to have a disagreement with right now.

Both Luka and Charlie had assumed that the purpose of their rescue operation, once accomplished, would become self-evident, but nothing obvious was presenting itself. Even after awkward self-introductions, nobody seemed any closer to understanding why they'd all been brought together—or even precisely *how* the rendezvous had been orchestrated—and nobody seemed to have any idea whatsoever of how to proceed.

Luka was about to prompt the four outsiders for their versions of how they'd come to be prisoners on the rig (and specifically, what they'd done to very nearly get themselves summarily executed) when an EMATS notification sounded from a nearby endpoint. The terminal was flashing and the panel beside it showed a countdown—currently at eight seconds—indicating the amount of time remaining before the capsule would be automatically returned to its sender.

Luka hastened to the beacon, laid the railgun down on the floor, and used the terminal to authenticate. The curved security panel slid to the side and Luka reached in to remove the hexagonal capsule. The delivery required second-level authentication, and after Luka's personal certificate was transmitted from his contacts to the miniature craft through his bioelectromagnetic field, the lid dilated open.

One of the capsule's six sides was an active display that senders could use to convey short messages to recipients in order to provide some context for the delivery. They were typically used for invoice numbers, simple instructions, salutations, condolences, or expressions of gratitude related to the item within having been borrowed. But rather than clarifying the mysterious dispatch, in this case, the scrolling text only confounded Luka further:

Set this down on the floor and gather around it.

His hand went inside the capsule and emerged with an unfamiliar brushed metallic cylindrical device almost the full length of the capsule. The end that appeared to be the top, Luka noticed, had a series of concentric seams. Luka's companions had assembled around him and he looked around for some sign of recognition, though nobody seemed to have any better idea of what was going on than he did.

"Well," Luka began, "unless someone has a better idea, I guess we set this thing down on the floor and gather around it."

The group opened up in order to give him space and Luka placed the cylinder down on its base. As soon as he backed away, a slightly narrower cylinder emerged from the first, and then a third emerged from it, extending its full height to just below waist level. The tip of the topmost cylinder was a dark, opaque lens that suddenly erupted with light. Luka was expecting a holographic image to resolve, but instead the light formed a bright white, 360-degree scan grid. The lines were sharp and the matrix spread across their bodies from their knees to their chests.

"It must be searching for something," the woman from Hexagon Row said. Her short, black hair was partially dry already, and it was shaggy and uneven in a way that Luka thought somehow worked exceptionally well on her. Ayla, she'd said her name was.

"It's looking for our eyes," her bodyguard said. "It's a VRD."

"A what?" Luka asked.

"Virtual retina display."

The man had introduced himself as Omicron, and something about his articulation had surprised Luka. He'd expected the enormous figure to be little more than a tower of carefully engineered reflexes and muscle, but Luka was gradually getting the impression that he was every bit as intellectually capable as he was physically.

Charlie was running her hand through the projected grid as though it were tangible—a field of waist-high wildflowers. "What does it do?" she asked.

"It uses lasers to project an image directly onto the retina," Omicron explained. "I think we're supposed to be sitting."

The small girl, Cadie, was the first to fully submerge herself into the scan grid. Her companion, Cam, immediately followed. As soon as their heads were within range, the grids constricted around their faces, then further constricted around their eyes, and then finally focused into single rails of light perfectly targeting their pupils. Both their expressions held a look of astonishment as they folded their legs beneath them.

"It's a man," Cadie said. "He seems to be waiting for something."

"Or someone," Cam added.

"It's a recording," Omicron said. He'd lowered himself into the scan grid, as well, and his eyes were similarly connected to the cylindrical lens via dual light rails.

The beams perfectly tracked their eyes as they attempted to make themselves more comfortable on the metal floor. Charlie and Ayla sat, and once the lasers connected their retinas to the projector in the center, the group reminded Luka of a giant spoked wheel. As Luka sat, the scan grid located his pupils, and when the device focused on the backs of his eyes, he saw the same image as the others: a man standing in the center, looking directly at him.

"Holy shit," Luka said.

"It's Two Bulls," Charlie said from beside him.

"Who's Two Bulls?" Cam asked.

"He's on the City Council," Luka said, then decided to leave it at that. He did not mention that Matthew Two Bulls was also the Chair of the Judicial Committee, and the one who had so passionately advocated for Luka's incarceration during his hearing. The man was big—not Omicron big, but certainly big by *San Francisco* standards—his portliness clearly concealing a sturdy frame and probably substantial strength. The skin on his face was both the color and texture of sandstone, and while the sides of his head were shaved, the rest of his glossy, black hair was pulled back into a tight braid that Luka could not currently see, but that he knew sprouted from the back of his head and fell almost to his waist. He wore a long, dark gray shirt that bulged as it hung over his paunch, and his typical darkened visor was clipped to his face. Two Bulls notoriously disliked the quality of the artificial lighting aboard the *San Francisco* and almost always wore some manner of filter.

"Hello, Luka," Two Bulls said. His subdued tone and demeanor were clearly incongruous with the current state of affairs, bolstering the bodyguard's theory that everything they were about to hear was prerecorded. "I know you must have a lot of questions for me. I've tried to anticipate as many of them as possible, but before we begin, there a few things you need to know. First, the moment the projector no longer detects your presence, the entire quantum storage block inside this device will be randomized, and this recording will be irreversibly destroyed. Second of all, you are never to approach me, attempt to contact me directly, or mention me outside of this circle under any circumstances whatsoever." He paused as though giving Luka a moment to consider his terms. "We can start whenever you're ready."

There was a subtle combination jump cut and a crossfade, and Two Bulls now appeared to be waiting patiently.

"I'll start," Charlie said. "What the hell gives you the right to involve Luka in whatever all this is?"

There was another jump cut and crossfade as the device accessed the right time code in the video sequence for the appropriate response.

"I can only answer questions from Luka," Two Bulls said. "From now on, all other voice patterns will be ignored."

"Who is Tycho?" Luka asked.

The response was both preceded and punctuated by the visual transition as the device's playhead changed locations.

"I am Tycho," Two Bulls said. "The account is completely anonymous and untraceable, and after tonight, it is the only way the two of us will ever communicate."

"Why did you want me in the brig so badly?"

"I apologize for the speech I gave during your inquiry, but I needed you to be imprisoned for as long as possible to make sure I had a chance to contact you in total isolation. And I needed to create the appearance of us being adversaries."

"Why?"

"I don't have an answer for that question. Try being more specific."

"Why did you need to create the impression of us being adversaries?"

"To help conceal the fact that we will be working together, and to make sure that I can't be connected to what you and your associates do."

"What are me and my associates going to do?"

"That will be up to you."

"Who are these people?"

"Surely the people around you can speak for themselves."

"What's all this about?"

"I don't have an answer for that question. Try being more specific."

Luka heaved an exasperated sigh. "What should we do next?"

"I will tell you what to do next, but there are other questions you must ask first."

Luka shook his head and the dual light rails tracked his motion. "This thing is obnoxious," he said. "Why were the outsiders brought here?"

"The outsiders were brought here for two reasons," Two Bulls said. "First, the Coronians wanted something they had. And second, the Coronians wanted them dead."

"Why do the Coronians want them dead?"

"The Coronians want the outsiders dead because they are considered an existential threat."

"Hold on," Cam said. "What's he talking about? Who are the Coronians?"

Charlie and Luka looked at one another. There was a period of uncomfortable silence as glances were exchanged among the group.

"They've been in isolation their entire lives," Ayla said. "This is all new to them."

Charlie leaned to the side so she could see past the projection of Two Bulls. "Almost all of Earth's power comes from a space station called *Equinox*," she explained. "The Coronians built and control it, which means the Coronians basically control Earth."

"Not our power," Cam countered. He looked at Cadie, then back at Charlie. "We had our own fusion reactors."

Charlie shrugged. "Maybe that's why the Coronians considered you a threat."

"No," Omicron said. "It's much more than that. It has something to do with the baby. Something about its genetic code."

"Wait a second," Cam said. He paused while he seemed to be playing something out in his head.

Cadie gave him a perplexed look. "What?"

"It's Arik's research they're after."

"What research?" Cadie asked. "His work on artificial photosynthesis?"

"Arik wasn't just working on AP," Cam said. "He was also working on terraforming, and apparently he cracked it. He knew his research would be destroyed if anyone found out about it, so he hid it inside your ODSTAR project."

Cadie was silent for a moment, and then her hand went down to her abdomen. "Oh my God," she said. "His research was encoded inside the baby's DNA."

"What's ODSTAR?" Omicron asked.

Cam reached over and took Cadie's hand. "It was a research project she and Arik worked on together."

"Organic Data Storage and Retrieval," Cadie said. "A technique for using human DNA to store and retrieve arbitrary data."

"I don't understand," Ayla said. "What does any of this have to do with the baby?"

Cam and Cadie gave each other a long look. Cadie indicated that Cam should explain.

"Arik had a very serious accident back in V1," Cam said. "We didn't think he was going to make it, so Cadie was asked to . . ."

He seemed to be searching for the right way to proceed when Cadie interjected. "To propagate his genes," she said.

"And you used his DNA from the ODSTAR project," Omicron suggested, "which contained all his terraforming research."

Cadie nodded.

"Hold on," Charlie said. "How would the Coronians have known all this?"

"They didn't," Omicron said. "But they knew enough. They intercepted Arik's transmission to us from V1, so they knew there was information encoded in the baby's DNA that was capable of transforming the planet. That's all they needed to know."

"So now we know *what* the Coronians know," Ayla said, "and we know *how* they know it. But what we still don't know is why they *care*."

Charlie gave Luka a significant look that the rest of the group seemed to sense. There was a moment of expectant silence while Luka gathered his thoughts.

"Leverage," he finally said. He looked at Cam. "The Coronians don't give us power for free. They give it to us in exchange for the natural resources they need to expand *Equinox*." He looked at Charlie, and then his eyes passed along the rest of the faces in the circle. "Charlie and I have proof that the Coronians are planning on doing their own mining. We believe that means they know that Earth is running out of resources."

"Wait a second," Cam said. At some point, he had released Cadie's hand and he pointed at Charlie. "You said the Coronians live in a space station, right? What's up there for them to mine?"

"Asteroids," Omicron said. "At least at first. The Asteroid Belt is basically the remains of a protoplanet. In fact, it's better than a planet in some ways because it's already cracked open for them. And as they replace their molecular assemblers with assemblers that work at the atomic level, they'll be able to use just about any kind of matter they can sequester. Given that the entire Asteroid Belt is only about four percent the mass of the moon, and obviously much farther away, it's reasonable to assume they'll eventually strip-mine the lunar surface."

"If they're planning on doing their own mining," Ayla said, "why do they care what we do?"

"Because they're not ready yet," Charlie said. "They might be five, ten, twenty years away, and they know that if something eventually happens that decreases our dependency on them—something like widespread terraforming that could allow us to start living in self-sustaining colonies again—they might not have leverage over us anymore. If we stop sending them resources before they can mine enough on their own, they'll eventually die."

"Basically," Luka said, "they want to make absolutely certain that they no longer need us before we no longer need them. It's a race, and whoever loses could go extinct."

"You said you had proof," Omicron said. "What kind of proof?"

"We assemble a lot of mining equipment," Luka said. "Almost all of it we use ourselves, but lately we've been getting orders from brokers, and they want it crated and shipped in a way that only makes sense if it's being launched into orbit. And as far as I know, the Coronians are the only ones up there."

"Maybe," Cam said, "or maybe launching things into orbit is just a faster way to transport them from one side of the planet to the other."

"I doubt that," Ayla said. "I've been in the shipping business for a long time, and I can guarantee you that putting payloads into orbit is the least cost-effective way to move anything. Unless that's your final destination."

"Have you told anyone about this?" Omicron asked Luka.

Luka let out a sardonic laugh. "I tried," he said. "That's what got me thrown in prison."

"Nobody here wants to hear it," Charlie said. "Everyone's basically in denial."

"Not everyone," Omicron corrected. He nodded toward the center of the circle. "It looks like something you did got Two Bulls' attention. Ask him where the baby is."

The projection had been standing idle while the conversation took place around him. Luka looked back up at Two Bulls.

"Do you know where the baby is?"

Two Bulls crossfaded, then replied, "We believe the baby is probably aboard *Equinox* by now."

"Ask him about Zaire," Cam said.

"Who's that?" Luka asked.

"She was with us when we left V1."

"Zaire is Cam's wife," Cadie added.

Luka looked back up at Two Bulls. "Where's the other girl who was brought here? Zaire."

Two Bulls located the correct response. "The Coronians are not interested in Zaire," the projection said. "She is with a man called Jumanne Nsonowa. He has an obsession with anything—or any*one*—with any kind of African heritage."

Ayla and Omicron looked at each other. This time, it was Cadie who reached over and took Cam's hand. Cam's expression was hardened against any demonstration of emotion.

"Ask him how we get them back," Cam said.

"How do we get them back?" Luka relayed.

"Recovering the baby and Zaire is not your mission," Two Bulls said. "Your mission is to recover the data. That's it."

"No way," Cam said. "We're going after them."

"Hold on," Cadie said. "We might already have the data."

"How?" Omicron said.

"Fetomaternal microchimerism," Cadie told him. "Fetal cells."

Omicron watched her for a moment with his heavy brow furrowed, then nodded in consensus. "Yes," he said. "That might work."

Ayla looked back and forth between Cadie and Omicron. "Are either of you going to explain what that means?" she asked.

"Fetal cells are cells from the baby," Cadie said. "Nobody knows why, but a small number of cells from the baby pass through the placenta and establish lineages in the mother."

"How does that help us?" Ayla asked.

"Those cells retain the baby's DNA," Cadie said. "They'll contain all of Arik's research."

"How long do they live?"

"They can persist for decades," Omicron said, "but we'll need a well-equipped lab in order to isolate them and to be able to extract the genetic material."

"Can we build one on the *Hawk*?"

"It would require a lot of equipment," Omicron said. "Luka, try asking Two Bulls about next steps now."

Luka looked back up at the projection. "*Now* can you tell us what we should do next?"

Two Bulls crossfaded. "You and Charlie have both been given almost universal access throughout the *San Francisco*. Charlie should take Ayla and Omicron to their ship, which is ready to be released."

"What about Cadie and Cam?"

"In the bottom of the EMATS capsule, you will find two sets of contacts. Cam and Cadie are now official citizens of the *San Francisco*, but they should stay out of sight as much as possible while you work."

Luka overturned the capsule and two blister packs of ICLs fell into his palm. He looked back up. "Work on what? What should we do?"

"You need to discover what it is that the Coronians fear," Two Bulls said. "And then you need to figure out how to use it against them."

"Ask him about equipment," Omicron said.

"What if we need equipment?" Luka asked.

"Whatever you need, just send a schematic to Tycho. Within an hour, it will be added to your work queue at the foundry with a forged invoice and manifest."

"Good," Omicron said. "That just leaves one thing."

"What?"

"The guards."

Luka watched Omicron for a moment before looking back up at the projection. "What do we do with the officers?" he asked.

"The bridge is waiting for the waterlock to be flushed and for four bodies to be purged," Two Bulls said. "I think you know the answer to that."

Luka squinted up at the projection. "Hold on," he said. "You want us to *kill* them?"

"The missing officers will be the only way to explain the absence of the *Accipiter Hawk*. Communications and financial records have been created to suggest that after executing the prisoners, the four officers defected with their ship. If the officers' bodies are ever found, your cover will be blown."

"No fucking way," Luka said. "We're not going to just *murder* them." He gestured down the corridor toward the waterlock. "Me and Charlie know those people. This is their home. We can talk to them. We can bring them in on this."

"The Lakota have a very old saying," Two Bulls said. "'Force, no matter how concealed, begets resistance.' The Coronians are applying force. The City Council is applying force. The officers had no problem applying force when they needed to. You and your team are the resistance, Luka. Four lives is a small price to pay for all that you can accomplish."

"I'm sorry, Luka," Omicron said. "But Two Bulls is right." The group looked to him and waited for him to continue. "Either all of us leave right now on the *Hawk* and never look back, or the guards have to go."

Luka was on the verge of panic and Charlie placed a calming hand on his shoulder. "Then we all go," he told Omicron. "Whatever we can do from here, we can do from your ship, right?"

"Unfortunately not. We don't have a lab on board, and we don't have access to assemblers. If we're going to take a stand against the Coronians, the four of you will need to be embedded here. If you leave with us, you can save the lives of the guards, but the chances of us ever being able to make a move against the Coronians are essentially nonexistent."

Cadie abruptly got to her feet. "I can't be a part of this," she said. The optical lasers that had been her connection to the projector expanded back out into a broad mesh of light and were once again attempting to locate her eyes. Cam started to stand but Cadie stopped him. "No," she told him. "You need to be a part of this. I don't."

"Luka," Omicron continued, "I know this isn't easy, but it's the only way this is going to work."

Luka shook his head. "I don't care," he said. "I never asked for any of this, and there's no way I'm going to *execute* innocent people."

"I have an idea," Charlie said. She looked to Omicron and Ayla. "Why don't you two take the officers with you? Hold them prisoner until all this is over? Then we can decide what to do with them."

"What about purging the waterlock?" Omicron reminded her.

"We'll just have to purge it with one body instead of four."

"What if the bridge wants to verify that all four prisoners were purged?"

"That's just a chance we'll—"

There was the sudden sound of static from the other end of the corridor—the full-spectral white noise of violently surging water. Luka looked up and saw Cadie watching them from the panel beside the waterlock's sealed door.

"What the hell is she doing?" he said. He stood, and after the optical beams lost his eyes, the entire projector went dark, and the radial extensions retracted.

Omicron and Ayla rose together.

"She's flooding it," Ayla said.

Cam got to his feet and took a step toward Cadie.

"Stay where you are," Cadie said. She extended her hand so that it was poised above the panel, and in response, Cam stopped.

"Please," Luka said. Desperate muted shouts came from the other side of the thick metal door, but Cadie did not seem to notice. Luka could hear Mandy screaming, and inside his head, the audio was matched with images of Val. Somehow he was aware of Charlie covering her mouth with both hands. Luka thought about the railgun on the floor beside him, but he wasn't sure if there was time to pick it up, and even if there was, he knew he wouldn't be able to bring himself to shoot Cadie. "Please," he said again. "Let's just think about this for second. We can figure something else out. I promise."

Cadie shook her head. "There's no other way," she said. "They have to be flushed."

"This isn't even your fight," Luka told her. There was aggression in his voice now, and he took a step forward. The surging water subsided, leaving only the sounds of weakening fists against the walls, and still Cadie ignored them. "Why do you even care about any of this?"

"Because," Cadie said, "I won't let Arik's sacrifice be for nothing."

Luka could see the word "PURGE" pulsating on the poly-meth panel, and then intensify to a bright crimson red beneath the girl's gentle touch.

PART THREE

CHAPTER TWENTY-NINE

HAMMERFEST

LUKA'S EARLIEST MEMORIES WERE of Hammerfest Arkade. The combination port, dry dock, and trading post was only a few clicks northwest of the Hammerfest Pod System, which was rumored to be one of the wealthiest and most secure in the world. Although by most pod system standards, the Arkade was a slum—a kind of parasitic by-product of the much more affluent and technologically advanced enclave that supported it—Luka had never known anything else, and consequently believed that he and his family enjoyed a near-perfect existence.

He remembered the volume of the hermetically sealed pavilion as being significantly greater than that of the *San Francisco*, though he wasn't sure now if it actually was bigger, or if perhaps his recollection was simply the result of typical childhood-scale distortion. The atmosphere inside Hammerfest was good most days—much hotter than the *San Francisco*'s above-deck mean temperature, but generally clean—and there was always plenty of purified if tepid water available to anyone with caps.

The stall Luka's parents ran doubled as their home with two cots in the back, a kind of nest Luka built himself out of scraps of composite construction material and silicone gel packs, an old low-res polymeth surface they used as a table, and a capacitive cooking surface. The shop was a microcosm of the greater exchange that contained it—a miniature bazaar in its own right. Most of what they sold were items that Luka's father had repaired, refurbished, or pieced together himself out of components or material obtained from other merchants, usually through aggressive but almost always good-natured bartering.

Luka's little family also did reasonably well selling an eclectic selection of novelties. Not dirty, tattered, or incomplete trinkets excavated from the age of inexpensive global manufacturing, but truly unique novelties custom-built by Luka and his mother. Some of them were functional like ornate calligraphic capacitive styluses, and intricately carved polymer storage cases. Others were purely aesthetic such as models or sculptures built out of buckets of old injection-molded thermoplastic bricks, and music boxes that produced melodies when wound up and placed against acoustically resonate conductive polymeth.

Luka and his mother originally began their artistic explorations purely as a way to satisfy and indulge their own visual and tactile curiosities, and perhaps to brighten up their sparse living quarters. They never expected anyone to pay good caps for anything that wasn't necessary or practical—anything that couldn't be used to make a repair, to defend oneself, or to preserve or purify consumables. But when they started getting offers on objects they'd inadvertently left lying around, or that they tinkered with in their laps or on a workbench as they ran the storefront, they began to realize that there were others out there who believed as they did: that just surviving wasn't enough; that any life worth living and fighting for had to find ways of incorporating elements of beauty, wonder, and inspiration.

By far the most popular pieces the Mance family sold—and what rapidly became their signature product—was their line of mechanical butterflies. They purchased the various components from several other venders, assembled them, hand-stained the wings with hypodermic needles, and sold them at a very attractive profit. Luka didn't know much about how they worked, but he knew that the light gathered by their wings gave them energy, and that they were somehow able to seek out bright colors while avoiding obstacles. And—as he'd been told by more than one repeat customer—he knew that his work had reached ports, ships, and even pod systems all over the world.

Luka believed he had the perfect childhood. Although it wasn't unusual for him to get into fights with the other kids— and even though he'd gotten sick several times when merchants who ran the distilleries entertained themselves by giving him shots of vanilla or cocoa vodka frozen with liquid nitrogen—Luka generally felt safe and looked after inside Hammerfest Arkade. He typically spent an hour or two a day being home-schooled by his mother, and often had to run errands for his father, but most of Luka's time was spent doing what he loved more than anything else: scavenging and building. With so much opportunity to create, explore, and interact with diverse and interesting people—some of whom he'd seen every single day of his life, and some he would probably only see once and then never again— it was impossible for Luka to think of himself and his family as poor.

The circumstances surrounding his family losing their stall were never explained in detail to Luka, but he pieced together that it had something to do with his mother and the captain of the Arkade peacekeepers. Whatever it was, the allegations were serious enough that they were not only evicted, but everything they owned was confiscated. Luka's parents tried to borrow caps to pay the fine and get their stall back, but every day they couldn't pay, the amount they owed increased. For several days, the Mance family stayed with some of the other families they did business with, and at night, Luka laid in the dark listening to his parents fight and his mother cry.

One night they stayed with the man who sold them the printed solar sheets that Luka and his mother cut up into butterfly wings. Luka heard his father explain to the man that if they did not pay the fine the next day, they would be arrested and probably banished. Once they were forced out through the airlock, Luka's father explained, it would only be a matter of time before they died of exposure, or were captured by subterraneans who would keep them alive as long as possible while consuming them in order to prevent the remainder of the flesh from rotting. The man said that it was all Luka's mother's fault—that their only option was to give the captain of the peacekeepers what he wanted—and then Luka's father and the man began yelling. Luka heard things breaking, and then he heard screaming. Luka's mother was crying when she came in to get him and they spent the rest of the night on the floor of the public latrines where the peacekeepers were not likely to find them.

When Luka woke up the next morning, his father was gone. His mother gave him a tube of soy paste and a bulb of water, and when he offered to share them with her, she told him that she had already eaten and wasn't hungry. When Luka's father returned, he explained to Luka that he would be going to live in a giant floating city where he would be taken care of and be safe. Luka remembered realizing that morning that his life up to that point had been a lie—that the security and community he'd felt inside Hammerfest had been nothing more than a facade. In truth, his entire family had always been just one accusation, one misfortune, or one late payment away from losing everything. As long as you were in possession of caps, or supplies, or anything else that others wanted, there was a place for you in the Arkade, but the moment there was even the slightest imbalance—the moment you needed more than you could immediately produce—everything about your past was instantly unwritten. It was as though his family's misfortune was a highly contagious disease, and the more they needed help, the more grotesque and offensive they became. Luka never forgot the incredible speed with which the faces of those around him went from friendly to contemptuous, and how quickly his family—once valued members of a collective—became condemned outcasts.

At that point in Luka's life, he had not yet heard the term "unconditional love," but when he later became aware of it, he recalled savagely rejecting the notion that any such connection could possibly exist between two living things without the existence of criteria and prerequisites. Just as everyone and everything had its price, all forms of love and compassion had their limitations and conditions, most of which couldn't be known until such time as they were finally breached.

And so began the cycle of disillusionment and cynicism that had become one of the defining themes of Luka's existence. He recalled the very moment he realized that his instructors at the foundry, who he had once believed to be among some of the smartest people he'd ever known, actually knew next to nothing about the machines with which they worked almost every day of their lives, and worse, really didn't even seem to care, preferring to devote their time and energy to forming alliances and positioning themselves rather than improving their contributions. Similarly, there was a short period during which Luka was enamored by the collective specter of the City Council, and truly believed that they somehow tapped into a precious and rare vein of knowledge and wisdom that entitled them to lead, though after a long enough period of observation, he began to realize that those who held the lives of the entire city in their hands were undeniably among the population's most selfish, unscrupulous, and reprehensible. And finally, the first time Luka had allowed himself to be vulnerable enough to reach out to someone other than his mother for comfort—the first time he loved anyone as much as he'd loved her, and as much as he could imagine ever loving anyone—he discovered that their connection was not strong enough to prevent her from taking her own life, just exactly as his connection with his parents hadn't been nearly enough to keep his family together.

Love, like everything else, was absolutely conditional—a collection of hidden triggers that revealed themselves only after the trap had already been sprung.

CHAPTER THIRTY

AQUARIUS

THE CUBICLE WAS JUST BARELY big enough for four people. Luka and Charlie were squeezed in together on one side, and Cadie and Cam on the other. The table between them was brushed stainless steel, as were most of the surfaces and fixtures in the underwater habitat, and one end of it butted up against the largest of the laboratory's heavily bolted viewports. In the center of the table was a vertical slab of transparent polymeth that received power and data through its malleable silicone base, and was the means by which Ayla and Omicron remotely participated from the safety of the *Accipiter Hawk*.

Cadie guessed she probably knew only about two-thirds of the history of *Aquarius*. From the archives, she learned that it had been commissioned by an organization called the National Oceanic and Atmospheric Administration, or NOAA; designed by a team of submarine builders in Florida and built by industrial machinists in Texas; and operated by the science departments of several universities with a little financial assistance from a wealthy Canadian film director and deep-sea explorer. The habitat spent most of its functional life servicing teams of aquanauts who studied the coral reefs of the Florida Keys National Marine Sanctuary before eventually being decommissioned and promised to a maritime museum in Sydney. However, before it could be transported, it was purchased—and soon thereafter, entirely refurbished and significantly updated—by the vacation-ing grandson of a frozen food magnate whose third wife briefly expressed interest in marine biology. From there, the vessel's historical trail went cold until it was resumed by Charlie, who explained that *Aquarius* had been picked up in trade from bro-kers in Cape Canaveral, after which it was lashed to the rig's hull and—while waiting to be sold, retraded, or converted into some kind of submersible mining habitat—essentially forgotten.

Where power and air were once sent down from the sur-face by the LSB, or Life Support Buoy, it was now provided by an umbilical line connecting it to the *San Francisco*. Municipal caps had kept *Aquarius* in functional standby mode for years, but it was now power and illicitly assembled equipment provided by Luka—and several modifications first outlined by Cadie and Omicron, and then implemented by Charlie and Cam—that transformed the underwater habitat back into a fully functional laboratory, though with much more of an emphasis on human biology than marine.

Even for Cadie, a small girl who grew up within the contain-ment of a clandestine pod system, *Aquarius* felt cramped. The structure was an eighty-ton cylindrical steel chamber about thir-teen meters long and less than three meters in diameter. Despite its compact size, it was divided up into four separate compart-ments. At one end was a cabin that, even with four of the six bunks removed, could barely accommodate Cam. The main lock consisted of the galley and a condensed eating and gathering area doubling as a workspace. The entry lock housed the main labora-tory and the toilet, and at the end opposite the cabin was the wet porch and shower, complete with hot water. Entry to *Aquarius* was gained through an open moon pool: an airtight chamber with enough atmospheric pressure to keep the water level flush with the hole in the floor. Charlie and Luka were comfortable putting on dry suits and simply holding their breath while swimming between the *San Francisco*'s much larger pressurized moon pool and the research habitat's wet porch, but Cadie and Cam—having never learned to swim, and in fact, having never even been submerged in more water than it took to fill a hydromill or a tiny bathtub—used both dry suits and rebreathers, and followed the woven polymer line that Charlie strung for them between the two chambers. When only cargo and supplies needed to be transferred, it was usually easier for Charlie to deploy a remotely operated submersible that Cam and Cadie unloaded on their end, then sent back towing crates packed with waste.

The ocean outside the viewport was a drab olive green and the weak light that filtered down through it cast a subdued glow across the dull abraded surface of the table. While Cam hadn't had much trouble transitioning from a diet of stemstock, which sustained them in V1, to the assortment of arthropods that were the main source of protein on the *San Francisco*, Cadie discovered that she was much less gastronomically adventurous, and was therefore making a meal out of a tin of congealed, fermented soy cubes. Luka and Charlie had bulbs of fresh water in front of them and were both wrapped in thermal cloaks after rinsing off back on the wet porch. Luka's short hair was already dry; Charlie had stopped at the sink in the entry lock and borrowed Cadie's brush to get the knots out of her artificially flaxen hair before smoothing it back out of her face.

"I'm coming up on a shift," Luka said, "so I don't have a lot of time, but I want to finalize our plans."

The connection and the bandwidth between *Aquarius* and the *Hawk* were reasonably good considering they were using underwater, line-of-sight acoustic waves at a distance of nearly ninety kilometers. Above-surface radio waves would have been preferable—yielding much higher data rates and better reliability—but they would have also been much easier to detect. Eavesdropping was not so much the concern as the signal could have been adequately encrypted; the real danger was that it might be suspected that the *Accipiter Hawk* was still in the vicinity, which would not only prompt a relentless pursuit of the four defectors, but probably also a local manhunt for the coconspirators that such close proximity implied.

"Go ahead," Omicron said. "We read you."

While they used a digital protocol with flow control and error correction for data transfer, for the sake of simplicity and latency, they used a simple analog signal for communication. Data obviously had to be perfectly reliable, but voice and video glitches could easily be compensated for by the human brain. The multipath interference between the vessels caused phase shifting, which resulted in a quivering ghosting effect in the two faces rendered in fluctuating fidelity inside the polymeth tablet. Coincidentally, Omicron sounded as though he might actually be talking underwater.

"We've discussed two different plans," Luka began. "Sabotaging the Coronians' ability to mine, and using the data recovered from Cadie to start terraforming. All of us agree that either one would loosen the Coronians' grip on Earth, right?"

Cadie, Cam, and Charlie nodded. Omicron transmitted his verbal assent.

"In that case," Luka said, "I propose we do both."

Cam gazed across the table at Luka with obvious skepticism. "How?" he asked. "We don't have the resources to be offensive *and* defensive at the same time."

"You're wrong," Luka said. "I think we do."

Cadie was still trying to decide whether or not she liked Luka. She found herself frequently put off by his brazenness—by his propensity to say whatever came into his head—and by the fact that he was probably about as close to the opposite of Arik as anyone she'd ever met. But at the same time, there was something about him that prevented her from dismissing him entirely. He was far more unassuming than just about anyone she'd known in V1, and he came across as entirely unapologetic about who and what he was. Although it was difficult for her to admit—even to herself—the things that annoyed her most about Luka were also the things she most admired.

It was Charlie who finally prompted Luka to continue. "How?" she asked.

"First of all, we move forward with the plan to smuggle Cam onto *Equinox*."

"No," Cadie interjected. "I don't like that idea at all."

"Hold on," Cam said. "At least let him finish."

"I've tried every hack and work-around I know to try to assemble explosives," Luka explained to the group, "but I'm still not getting anywhere. I can assemble pretty much anything we need, but even Tycho can't get some types of contraband past the assemblers' DRM."

"Wait a second," Charlie said. "We use underwater charges for mining all the time. Why can't we just send a bunch of those up to *Equinox*?"

"Those are depth charges," Luka said. "They're designed to create massive shock waves in high-pressure environments. They're not going to be very effective in a vacuum."

"Can't you just use whatever technique you use to assemble your—" The girl stopped when Luka's expression became a cautionary glare. "That you use to assemble other types of contraband?"

"That won't work," Luka told her. "Bombs are much more than just explosives. You need binding agents, primers, detonators, fragmentation material. And probably a ton of other stuff I haven't even figured out yet since most of the information I need is missing from the archives."

"There *has* to be a way," Cadie insisted. "There has to be *something* you haven't tried."

"If we had enough time, we could probably figure out some kind of recomposition technique that might work, but it could take months or even years to learn how to build something effective and reliable enough to send up there. And it's not exactly easy to experiment with bombs around here without someone noticing."

"What about buying explosives?" Cadie suggested. She looked at the vertical sheet of polymeth in the center of the table. "You two could find some, couldn't you?"

Before Ayla or Omicron could respond, Luka intervened. "Forget the problem of obtaining explosives for a second," he said. "Even if we had all the bombs we wanted—even if we were guaranteed that they'd work, and even if we managed to pack an entire shipment of mining equipment full of them—the chances of us detonating them at the right time and in just the right place are basically zero."

Cadie watched Luka from across the table. Cam was the last link she had not only to V1, but to her entire former existence— the closest thing to home that she had left—and she therefore had no intention of sending him on what she believed to be a suicide mission.

"Then we just have to get creative," she told Luka. She guessed at something she hoped would prove they hadn't exhausted all the possibilities just yet. "We could build a microgravity fuse."

Luka's expression was immediately dismissive. "Then we'd just blow up the rocket," he said.

"We could use a zero-g fuse to trigger a timer, then."

"That's not much better," Luka said. "How would we know we weren't just blowing up a warehouse? Or how do we know payloads aren't kept in orbit for a few days before being captured by the station? The reality is that we need to wait until the equipment is in position to do maximum damage, but we have no way of knowing where or when that is, and even if we did, we'd have no way to get a signal to the detonator. We have to assume that we're only going to get one shot at this—one chance to smuggle something into orbit before the Coronians realize they're under attack—and that means we have to go with whatever option gives us the most flexibility and best shot at success, no matter how dangerous."

"We could build the bomb so that it detonates when the equipment is put together," Cadie tried. "Or the first time it's used. Or we could even—"

"Cadie," Cam interrupted. "It's a moot point. We don't have a way to assemble the explosives, or test them, or make sure they're in position, or detonate them. And even if we had all that, there are still way too many unknowns."

"Like what?" Cadie challenged.

"Like the fact that Haná is up there, which means we probably shouldn't be indiscriminately blowing things up. And like the fact that we need to destroy the Coronians' ability to mine, but not their ability to generate and transfer power down to Earth.

The only way to sabotage their mining capabilities with any kind of precision whatsoever is to send someone up there who can infiltrate the station."

"But why does it have to be you?" Cadie asked him.

"Because I have a background in mechanical engineering," Cam said. "And because everyone else is needed for other things down here. And most importantly, because nobody will notice that I'm missing."

"He's right," Luka said. "We have a much better chance of getting Cam up to *Equinox* than any kind of a destructive device, and he has the best chance of figuring out what to do once he's up there."

Cadie was about to try again, but Cam stopped her. "*And*," he said, "I can try to find out what happened to Haná."

The baby was an element of all this that Cadie had been doing her best not to consider. More than once Cam had tried unsuccessfully to talk to her about her daughter, inviting her to open up, to share with him how she was feeling, to grieve if she felt she needed to. But Cadie would not discuss the subject beyond a brusque acknowledgment that her baby was gone and there was absolutely nothing any of them could do about it. Growing up amid the isolation and protection of V1 had not prepared Cadie—or anyone from her generation, for that matter—for having to deal with any form of significant loss. Therefore, the only way she had to handle being suddenly deprived of not only her unborn daughter, but also her husband, her parents, and the only home she'd ever known was by simply not dealing with any of it at all. But now the prospect of Cam locating Haná—even just the possibility of him being in close proximity to her, and maybe finding out definitively whether or not she was still alive—instilled in her something she was surprised to discover felt even worse than despair. It gave her hope.

When Cadie did not respond, Luka continued.

"I've already started drawing up plans," he said. "I think I know roughly how to get Cam up there."

"How?" Charlie asked.

"All I have to do is assemble the next piece of mining equipment they order so that it can be packed in one less container. That gives us an extra crate for Cam and all the necessary life-support systems."

For the first time, the warped and twisted image of Ayla spoke. "Are we talking about a one-way trip?" she asked. "How is he supposed to get back?"

"She's right," Omicron said from his side of the polymeth surface. "I agree there's a good chance we can get Cam up there, and that he's our best shot at setting the Coronians back. But I don't see an obvious way of returning him safely to Earth."

"Escape pods," Luka said. "We know *Equinox* was originally built with emergency reentry vehicles, right?"

"We know ERVs were in the original schematics," Omicron corrected, "but we don't know if they were ever built. Or if they even function, for that matter. And even if they do, how would we know where he splashed down?"

"I'll take my chances," Cam said. "I'll find a way to get a message to the *Hawk* either before reentry, or once I splash down. If it means stopping the Coronians, and potentially finding Haná, it's worth the risk. Now let's move on to the second part of the plan."

Cadie could tell that Luka wanted to continue before there could be any more objections. "The second part is terraforming," he said. "You guys have Arik's research, right?"

The question was directed at Cadie. "We've extracted most of it," she said.

"So all we need to do is genetically engineer a bunch of seeds and figure out how to spread them all over the world, right?"

Hearing Luka discuss her area of expertise—and her husband's research—so cavalierly and with so much ignorance was unexpectedly infuriating. Not only had he managed to talk the entire group into essentially sacrificing Cam, but he obviously knew nothing about the biology and the mechanics of terraforming. She let her hands drop to the stainless steel surface and her chopsticks leapt from the edge of the soy tin.

"And how are we supposed to do that when we don't even have access to seeds or soil?" she asked.

"We'll get you some," Luka said, unperturbed.

"How?"

"Charlie and I know plenty of people at Yerba Buena Gardens," he assured her. "We'll figure something out."

"And do you know which seeds will be genetically compatible with Arik's research?"

"Nope," Luka said, "but I'm sure you'll tell me."

"And will you be able to get us sufficiently toxic and irradiated soil so we can test under realistic conditions?"

"Nope," Luka said again. "We can get you dirt, but the rest will be up to you. Any more questions?"

Cadie noticed for the first time how bloodshot Luka's eyes were, and she wondered if he'd gotten detergent in them while rinsing down, or if he was having problems with his contacts. It also occurred to her that he very likely felt the same way about her as she felt about him—though perhaps he had not yet located that sliver of admiration that might, in his eyes, make her slightly more tolerable.

"Actually yes," Cadie said. "How do you propose we spread seeds all over the planet from a secret underwater laboratory strapped to the side of a deep-sea mining rig?"

Before Luka could provide her with another insipid, incompetent, and unproductive response, she heard Ayla's distorted voice arise from the polymeth.

"Drones," she said.

Cadie looked at the flickering image of Omicron to try to gauge his reaction, and she saw him nod in agreement.

"Perfect," Luka said, seizing on the girl's initiative. "Drones."

Cadie trusted Omicron's judgment, but the logistics of using autonomous robots for terraforming struck her as absurd.

"Where are we going to get hundreds of drones capable of traveling thousands of kilometers," she asked, "while at the same time dispersing seeds and fertilizing agents—which, by the way, all have to be implanted at a very specific depth and under very specific conditions?"

"We have about a dozen vehicles on the *Hawk*," Ayla said. "That's a start."

"We'll need to assemble new models," Omicron said. "Charlie, Cam, and I can hopefully build a working prototype from what we have, then derive an assembly schematic from it."

"Just make sure they're as discrete as possible," Luka said. "Try to remember I'm the one who has to smuggle all this stuff out of the foundry."

"I'll send out the specs on our fleet," Omicron said. "Let's start iterating as soon as possible."

Cadie was about to stage additional protest but she stopped herself. She could name dozens of reasons why none of this would work—hundreds of details they were conveniently ignoring—though it occurred to her that the same could almost certainly be said for just about any scientific endeavor of true consequence. She recalled the excitement and optimism with which she and Arik approached the ODSTAR project even though their academic adviser had discouraged them from even attempting it. And how they'd solved artificial photosynthesis only by throwing away almost everything everyone believed they knew about the problem and trying something completely new and unproven. And finally, she recalled the extent to which Arik was ridiculed—even persecuted—for wanting to research terraforming, and how determined he'd been to do what almost everyone else believed to be impossible. Doing great and important things, Cadie realized, was not always about being practical, logical, and realistic. Perhaps there was something to be said for selective myopia; for childlike resolve and willfulness; and perhaps even for the occasional touch of insanity.

"OK," Cadie said. She looked around at everyone in the group. "I'm with you," she told them. "I have absolutely no idea how we're going to pull all this off, but I'm with you."

"We don't have to know how we're going to pull it all off," Luka said. "We just have to know what we're going to do next." He maneuvered himself out from behind the table and stood. "Let's meet again at the same time tomorrow. I have to be on the line in fifteen minutes."

"Hold on," Charlie said. "There's one more thing."

Luka began folding his thermal cloak. "What are we forgetting?"

"We're forgetting about the *San Francisco*."

"What about it?"

"Even if both of these plans work," Charlie said, "they won't necessarily change anything here."

"So?" Luka said. "I'm done with this place."

The girl was clearly accustomed to Luka's impudent disposition and didn't appear particularly phased by it. "You may be," she told him calmly, "but I'm not. This place is my home. And it was your wife's home, too."

Luka dropped the folded cloak onto the brushed steel surface and looked down at Charlie.

"In case you forgot," he told her, "Val and I were brought here as child slaves. This place was never a home to either of us."

"I know that's what you'd like to think," Charlie said, "but it isn't true. Val loved it here once she found her place. You know she loved working in the Gardens, and you know she loved being married to you."

"Maybe *she* found her place," Luka said. "But I never found mine."

"Then why'd you send that note?" Charlie asked him. "Why'd you shut down the power? If you hate it here so much, why didn't you just leave? Why'd you even start all this?"

Luka finished his bulb of water and made a fist to compact it. "Because I was stupid enough to think that I could change it," he said. He turned and threw the crushed bulb into a refuse bin beneath the counter behind him. "Now I know better."

"I don't think so," Charlie said. "I think you did it because you know how much potential the *San Francisco* has under the right leadership. And because whether you like it here or not, it's the only home you have."

"Whatever you think my motivations were," Luka said, "they're irrelevant now. We have to think bigger than the *San Francisco*. I'm already taking way too many chances. I can't take on trying to fix this place, too."

"Maybe you can't," Charlie said. "But I think I can."

CHAPTER THIRTY-ONE

CHEMILUMINESCENCE

CADIE SELDOM LEFT *AQUARIUS*. IN accordance with Two Bulls' warnings, she and Cam usually kept themselves confined to the cramped steel cylinder, experimenting with genetically modified seeds and spores, iterating on drone design, and trying to figure out how to turn a reinforced shipping crate into a one-man spacecraft. They generally stayed awake as long as progress could be made, and slept when waiting on results, materials, or equipment. Except in the cabin, task lighting constantly burned, and the amount of natural illumination that reached the vessel's eight viewports was not nearly sufficient to promote any kind of true circadian rhythm.

The risks of Cadie leaving *Aquarius* were statistically small, but the repercussions were potentially catastrophic. The problem wasn't that nobody would recognize her since the population of the *San Francisco* was high and dynamic enough that one did not expect to recognize every single person one saw; the far bigger problem was the opposite: that the population was simultaneously small enough that she could run into Dr. Abbasi, or someone else who had seen her between the time she was removed from her cryostatic chrysalis, and the time she was escorted down to the waterlock where she was supposed to have been executed.

Initially Cadie didn't think that confinement to *Aquarius* would be a problem given that she and Cam grew up in V1.

However, she rapidly became acutely aware of the differences between the two environments. Most of the individual pods that made up V1 were small, but at least there were enough of them—and enough variety, due to their specialized nature—to accommodate the need for changes of scenery. Additionally, there were long stretches of uninterrupted metal-grate walkway beside the maglev track that one could use not only to enjoy some exercise, but also to get away from everyone and everything, and to clear one's head without having to resort to the maddening litany of pacing. And finally, after working in the Life Pod, Cadie essentially had unrestricted access to the dome—by far the most voluminous structure in V1—in which she could experience not only the natural beauty of the thousands of tulsi ferns that provided the colony with oxygen, but even a small amount of natural light, weak and refracted as it was. Cadie wondered how the aquanauts who once lived aboard *Aquarius* kept themselves from losing their minds, then realized that most of them probably spent as much time as possible outside the habitat, exploring the exotic forests of coral reefs around them.

It wasn't just the familiarity and the closeness of the space that made Cadie stir crazy—and, at times, even borderline claustrophobic—but also her proximity to Cam. To be fair, she told herself, it probably wasn't so much about Cam specifically as it was about having to share such a cramped environment with any other human being. Cadie was an excessively introverted girl, and although she had always enjoyed the limited company of close friends like Cam and Zaire, about the only person she could imagine living with for so long in such confinement was Arik.

There were times, therefore, when Cadie felt she simply had to leave *Aquarius*. Luka and Charlie tried to talk her out of it initially, but it quickly became apparent to them that they were much better off supporting her in her determination to experience a little novelty (and put some distance between her and Cam) than risk her doing something impulsive and reckless. Preparations consisted of Charlie cutting Cadie's long, black hair into a perky bob and coloring it a milk-chocolate brown that matched her irises, and Luka asking Tycho for a detailed account of Farah Abbasi's whereabouts over the course of several weeks. Everyone was surprised when, from the list of places it appeared Abbasi was least likely to ever be, Cadie chose Kacis, a Turkish hookah lounge located on the lower level of the retail structure known as Union Square.

Although Luka and Charlie agreed to help Cadie get out of *Aquarius* and explore a little of the *San Francisco*, they only did so under the condition that she would not go alone. Luka met her at the moon pool, provided a circuitous escort to Union Square (by way of Yerba Buena Gardens, per Cadie's request), and then sat across from her in one of the U-shaped padded chairs arranged in the corner of the lounge. Cadie wore a double-breasted black jacket buttoned across her chest and a cinnamon-colored newsboy-style cap low down over her eyes. Luka was wearing his usual cargo scrubs with a fitted, long-sleeve microfiber shirt printed with geometric shapes in various shades of dark gray. Docked to the table between them was the flared and ornate multistemmed hookah. Cadie clutched one of the hoses, and although she'd sniffed at it once or twice, hadn't yet put it in her mouth. Luka, on the other hand, drew on his liberally and with obvious relish.

Technically, Kacis Hookah and Coffee Lounge violated several *San Francisco* ordinances, yet as long as the proprietors agreed to maintain certain standards, the Public Health Committee allowed it to operate. The filtration and air circulation systems were custom-designed, and since Union Square was on the south side of the city—and Kacis was in the southernmost corner of the structure—a special hexagonal PVC duct carried vapor over Alemany Boulevard and allowed it to vent directly through an opening in the dome. The shisha they smoked was shisha in name only, and in fact was a liquid solution synthesized from several chemicals that Kacis had special permission to have assembled, and which was vaporized by simple heating elements in the base of the pipes. Apparently Luka's favorite selections were vanilla and a sickeningly sweet flavor known as whipped cream.

Despite the sophisticated atmospheric conditioning system, there were still enough vaporized chemicals in the air to give Cadie a feeling that she did not find entirely unpleasant.

The establishment was dim and bathed in a serene violet glow from walls coated in chemiluminescent paint. Although Cadie turned out not to be much of a smoker (beyond the secondhand variety), there were two things that drew her to Kacis. The first was the Turkish coffee, the smell of which brought her back to the office of one of Arik's favorite teachers, Rosemary Grace. Rosemary worked for Arik's father in the Water Treatment Department, or the Wet Pod as it was commonly known, and in order to promote organic collaboration and communication among her reports, she always had a pot of fresh coffee available (even though she preferred tea). Rosemary was an environmental and hydraulic engineer by trade, but she taught Gen V about much more than just computational fluid mechanics. Not only did Rosemary introduce Cadie and her peers to the elegance of economy in scientific thought and problem solving embodied in the principle of Occam's Razor—or the importance of cutting away as many assumptions from one's hypotheses as possible—but she also taught Gen V what Cadie now believed was the single most important lesson Arik ever learned: *Question Everything.*

The second thing that attracted Cadie to the hookah lounge was also something that reminded her of Arik: just about everyone in the establishment was wearing a BCI, or a noninvasive Brain-Computer Interface. Cadie wasn't sure what they were called here (mindmouse? wavecap? neuroprosthetic? headcrab?), but they were much more refined than the one Arik had used, and given what they were being used for, they appeared several generations more sophisticated. Everyone's chair but Luka's was turned toward a polymeth wall that showed several perspectives on the same football match, but rather than everyone simply watching, rooting, and boisterously editorializing, they were actually participating. While Arik used his BCI for interacting with his workspace, the people around Cadie were using theirs to play a full football match with all of its complex elements and dynamics: penalties, referees, facial expressions, hand signals, attack and defense strategies, and no doubt dozens of additional subtleties that Cadie lacked the domain-specific knowledge to recognize. What was little more than a diversion to the patrons of Kacis was probably one of the most impressive and technologically spectacular things Cadie had ever seen.

"Before I forget," Luka said. He released his mouthpiece, allowing the hose to retract gently into the body of the pipe, then removed something from the shoulder bag that hung from the back of his chair. "More dirt."

The container he passed across the table was the plastic shell left over from a boxed meal. Cadie bent down and slipped it into the watertight pouch at her feet.

"Thanks," she said.

"And Charlie will bring you more protein cubes tonight."

Cadie was back to watching the game. Luka turned to look behind him.

"Football fan?" he asked her.

"Not at all," Cadie said. "I'm interested in the technology."

"What about it?"

"Was it developed here?"

"Yes and no," Luka said. He extended the hose from the body of the hookah and drew. When he spoke, vapor rose from his mouth and nose, combining into a single rapidly dissipating cloud. "It's old Coronian technology that a bunch of engineers adapted in their free time."

"What else is it used for?"

"You're pretty much looking at it," Luka said. "You can jack your brain into most of the systems around here if you want, but not that many people do it."

"Why not?"

"Most people don't have the patience to get good at it. Unless it's for gaming. Then they'll spend every waking moment trying to master it."

Cadie's eyes wandered over the people around her. At least twenty-five of them were actively engaged in the game—twenty-two players and three referees—yet they were also conversing, sipping coffee, and smoking as effortlessly as though the match were a replay.

"I'm worried about sending Cam up there," Cadie said.

Luka expunged vapor through his nostrils as he lifted his cup of thick Turkish coffee. "I know you are," he said. "You haven't exactly made that a secret."

"I mean I have other concerns," Cadie said. "New ones."

"Like what?"

The team in crimson broke away. Cadie could feel the tension in the room rise as patrons began getting to their feet and shouting. The shot was wide and an anticlimactic uproar ensued.

Cadie waited for the noise to subside. "The Coronians have much more sophisticated BCI technology than this, right?"

"That's the rumor," Luka said. "Apparently anything electronic they can control with their brains."

"Have you ever thought about what would happen if Cam were to be captured?"

Cadie could feel Luka trying to read her. Behind him, a goal kick sent the white glistening ball on a long and graceful arc that she watched from multiple perspectives.

"I think we both know the answer to that," Luka said.

"I mean other than the obvious," Cadie said. "What if they interrogate him? Or worse, what if they don't *need* to interrogate him? What if they can just take what's in his head?"

Luka squinted at Cadie through a curtain of vapor. He reached down and ejected the shisha cartridge from the pipe, then took a fresh one from the box on the table, popped the cap off with this thumb, and loaded it into the pipe's receiver.

"You're worried they'll find out about the terraforming, aren't you?"

"Think about it," Cadie said. She leaned forward and lowered her voice. "If this stuff is child's play to the Coronians, even if they can't extract information from him directly, they'll at least know if he's lying to them."

Luka rocked his chair with a deep mellow nod. "Probably," he said. "I have to admit, that hadn't occurred to me."

"Me either," Cadie said. "Until now."

"So what do you think we should do?"

"I don't know," Cadie said. "But it makes me wonder if maybe we're going about this whole thing wrong."

Luka was about to draw on his mouthpiece, but stopped. "What's that supposed to mean?"

"Luka," Cadie began, "what if we misunderstood Two Bulls?"

"Misunderstood *what*?"

"The Lakota saying. 'Force begets resistance.'"

"What is there to misunderstand?" Luka asked. "It's pretty clear, isn't it? The Coronians and the City Council are exerting force, so we have to be the resistance."

Cadie shrugged. "That's one interpretation."

"Well what's *your* interpretation?"

"What if it means that the resistance is the *result* of the force—that the force actually *causes* the resistance, and conversely, resistance will just cause *more* force?"

Luka's eyebrows went up as vapor rose from his lips. "You're going to have to be a little less abstract," he told her.

Cadie closed her eyes and shook her head subtly enough that she didn't think Luka would notice. This was perhaps not a conversation to be having over a hookah. "I think it means that if we push back on the Coronians, it will only make them push harder."

"The point is to make sure they *can't* push harder," Luka said. "If we destroy their ability to mine, they'll continue to need us as much as we need them."

"Maybe for now," Cadie conceded. "But don't you think it will just increase their resolve to stop relying on Earth? Don't you think it will just validate what they already think of us?"

"That resolve is already there," Luka told her. "Someone has to lose in all of this, and we need to make damn sure it's the Coronians instead of us."

"I don't know if I agree with that," Cadie said.

"Agree with what, exactly?"

"That someone has to lose."

"How else can this possibly play out?"

"I don't know," Cadie said. "But there's something about all this that doesn't feel right to me."

"Well, you better start getting used to it," Luka told her. "It's a little late to change direction now."

"Is it?" Cadie asked. "We have a chance to reboot the entire planet, right? To basically rebuild human civilization?"

"If you and Omicron say so."

"So what if instead of promoting competition this time, we promote cooperation?"

Luka looked at her over his cup. He sipped his coffee and shook his head. "I'm sorry," he said as he placed the cup gently back on its saucer, "but I'm having a hard time hearing this from you."

Cadie sat back. "What's that supposed to mean?"

"It means you're the one who couldn't wait to purge the waterlock."

Cadie narrowed her eyes at him. "That *had* to be done," she said. "You have to let that go."

"I *have* let that go," Luka told her. "It *did* have to be done because it was us or them. That's the nature of competition. Life has *always* been about competition, and life always *will* be about competition. I've never seen anyone do a goddamn thing that wasn't ultimately in their own best interests, and I'm sick of being the one to always play by different rules. I'm sick of being the one always at a disadvantage because I happen to give a shit about other people." Luka leaned forward and watched Cadie carefully. "Listen to me," he said to her. "It's us or them. It will *always* be us or them."

On a whim, Cadie pulled the mouthpiece on her side toward her, placed it between her lips, and inhaled. Luka leaned back in his padded chair and watched. Cadie felt instantly warm and serene, and although she felt she might be on the verge of getting sick, she also felt something else rise up from within her—some kind of bright white power achieved through the clarity of unexpected alignment.

"Maybe that's the way it's always been," Cadie said through the vapor escaping her lips. It rose and rolled luxuriously over the rim of her hat and continued on up toward the ceiling. "But that doesn't mean we can't do better."

CHAPTER THIRTY-TWO

UNPLANNED OBSOLESCENCE

AS FAR AS LUKA WAS CONCERNED, Charlie still lived at home with her parents. Charlie disagreed. Technically, she lived just below her mother and father in the transpartment she once shared with Val. Whether the vertically stacked flats were in fact two separate transpartments, or simply two levels of the same living space, was a matter of both interpretation and occasional debate.

What made the matter ambiguous was the fact that, although there was no direct access between the two levels, they still shared a kitchen, toilet room, and a shower stall. Any of the three common rooms could be raised or lowered via recessed vertical hydraulics on an as-needed basis, either providing occupants with their intended services, or temporarily freeing up anywhere from 10 to 25 percent of total living space. The design was intended to be an improvement on the concept of communal living, and back when the Talleyrand family lived on the lower floors of Paramount Tower, they shared their utilities with a total of ten families across five floors. But with both Charlie and Val working, they were able to move up to where conveniences were divided among fewer residents, and were therefore much more readily available.

The kitchen was currently present and Luka helped himself to a caffeinated chocolate protein shake. They'd chosen to meet in Charlie's transpartment because it contained, in addition to modular utilities, another peculiarity: a display known as a poly-vid. Polyvids were loud and bulky devices capable of rendering three-dimensional holographic models between two volumetric plates, and were once considered such novelties that it seemed inevitable that they would become the future of both work and entertainment. For a short time, enthusiasm around polyvid technology was such that they were designated standard house-hold appliances by the Urban Planning Committee, and there-fore built into all new transpartments.

But for reasons nobody seemed able to entirely agree on, the polyvid revolution was short-lived. Some self-proclaimed cul-tural and technology pundits blamed the fact that the opposing, concentrically laser-etched plates took too long to warm up, that the arrays of optical micromirrors were too finicky and too dif-ficult to calibrate, and that the stray magnetic fields the devices produced caused a harmonic buzzing right at the very edge of human perception that tended to put some people on edge. Others said it was because the images—refreshed at a relatively low frame rate—gave between 10 and 15 percent of the popu-lation headaches. One faction cited evidence suggesting that polyvid-rendered scenes were too realistic and therefore made viewers unconsciously anxious, and another insisted the exact opposite: that the disembodied slices of action were not quite realistic enough, and therefore did not represent a sufficient advantage over much larger, brighter, and cheaper high-density 2D material to justify the additional power, maintenance, space, and general hassle. Luka's personal theory was that believable 3D content was too hard to generate, and existing content simply too laborious to port, so once everyone got sick of rewatching the same dozen or so demos, shorts, and films—and once they'd played through the same two or three games several times and experienced all the possible outcomes—they never turned their polyvids on again. Whatever it was, by the time Luka's transpartment was finished, volumetric displays had already fallen out of favor and engineers were experimenting with the promising field of ferrofluids instead.

Such semipermanent but disused amenities fascinated Luka. How could something that once seemed so innovative and utilitarian become suddenly so quaint and idiosyncratic? Even after centuries of humanity relegating domestic apparatuses to abandoned anthropological fetishes (bell pulls for summoning servants, root cellars, coal chutes, phone boxes, dumbwaiters, milk doors, laundry chutes, central vacuum systems, intercoms, heated driveways, etc.)—either because newer technology rendered them obsolete, or because their benefits did not ultimately outweigh the costs of maintenance, repair, and upgrade—the lessons of modular design as a safeguard against unplanned obsolescence still had not been fully internalized. The result was that one corner of Charlie's transpartment would probably be forever occupied by two built-in, one-meter-diameter holographic plates that were already too outdated to be useful, too expensive to remove, and too unpredictable to know whether or not they would even work.

But for the first time since Charlie used her polyvid as a kind of high-tech bait to lure a toolpusher named Benthic back to her flat (only to be walked in on soon thereafter by Val and Luka), she was glad she had the device. She'd been using the space between the floor and ceiling volumetric plates as an auxiliary closet, so while Luka rummaged through the kitchen, she relocated stacks of clothing and a honeycomb-shaped shoe rack to the corner beneath the currently absent toilet room and shower stall. Once the obstructions were removed, she used the panel on the wall to switch the polyvid on. Luka had never seen one booted up cold before and he was surprised by how long it took for the plates to get warm, for the micromirrors to calibrate, and finally for the standby image (a randomly morphing and spinning polyhedron) to fully resolve.

The timing of Luka and Charlie's lunchtime rendezvous was designed to correspond with the reply they were expecting from Tycho, and while they waited on the polyvid's temperament, an incoming message notification appeared in the corner of Luka's vision. He reached over and authenticated on the wall beside the futon on which he reclined and his workspace sprang forth from his touch. As requested, there were two annotated, three-dimensional model files attached: the *San Francisco* as it currently was, and the next phase of development as formerly revealed to Luka by Khang Jung-soon.

"Got them," Luka said.

"Good," Charlie replied. "Bring them up. Let's see if this stupid thing still works."

Luka reached the bottom of his shake and maneuvered his straw into the corner of the carton to slurp up the remains. "How do I move the files over?"

"I don't know," Charlie said. "Don't you see the polyvid on the network?"

Luka flicked through the list of all the endpoints his workspace was currently aware of.

"What's it called?"

"I think I named it *transporter*."

"Nope," he said. "Don't see it. I don't see anything on your network requesting three-D models. When was the last time you updated this thing's firmware?"

"I don't know," Charlie said. "Probably never. Are you sure you're on the right network?"

"I'm on Deep Core."

"That's me," Charlie said. "Here, forward the files. Let me try."

Luka forwarded the attachments. Charlie brought up her workspace and found that she, too, was unable to locate the polyvid on the network. Eventually she rummaged through a long, shallow drawer beneath her futon until she found an old solid quantum storage block, blew dust out of its contact, and copied the files over. Despite being surrounded by hundreds of kilometers of twisted-light fiber optics, aura-nets uniting millions of individual nodes, the equivalent of tens of thousands of electron computing cores, terabits of bandwidth, and zettabytes of storage capacity, in the end, Charlie stood up, walked to the other end of the room, and copied the two files over manually.

"I love technology," she said from the polyvid's panel.

"But just think how much harder that would have been fifty years ago," Luka said.

"That's true," Charlie admitted. "I would have probably had a much bigger flat and had to walk at least twice as far."

The volumetric plates began to hum as the first schematic resolved. Charlie reached in to rotate it but there was contention somewhere in the rendering pipeline, and until all the textures were cached, the animation stuttered. Once it was able to rotate fluidly, she used both hands to move it out of the way, then brought the second model into view.

"Oh my God," Charlie said as it resolved.

The second-phase model similarly stuttered at first, then began responding smoothly to Charlie's gestures. She zoomed in on the new Paramount Tower, and although Luka couldn't see her expression from where he was sitting, he knew what she was thinking. The building in which she and her sister had essentially grown up was now entirely unrecognizable, and in fact, could no longer be legitimately referred to as a tower at all. While significantly wider, it was only about half as tall, and not much more than a nondescript block. Judging by the spacing of the windows, the flats were no bigger than they were on the first few stories of the current Paramount Tower, and possibly even slightly smaller. Although there was none of the decay and dilapidation one typically associated with the term "slum," beside Millennium Tower—and especially in the shadow of the clover-shaped quatrefoil of The Infinity—the new Paramount structure conveyed the distinctive impression of institutionalized poverty.

"Welcome to the ghetto," Luka said.

"This is absolutely sickening," Charlie said. "Not just Paramount, but the loss of the gardens. We have to have some kind of natural habitat—even if it isn't for food."

"Apparently not as much as we need luxury flats."

"We can't let this happen," Charlie said.

"Still glad you became a water rat?" Luka asked. "If you'd stayed a teacher, you might be over in Millennium with me. Hell, once you were head of the Education Committee, you might even be able to afford something in The Infinity."

Charlie was quiet for a moment as she watched the model rotate with the inertia of her last gesture. "Actually, yes," she said distractedly.

"Actually yes, what?"

"I *am* still glad I'm a water rat," Charlie said. "Because that's exactly how we're going to stop this from happening."

"What do you mean?"

She turned around, and Luka could see that she was more determined now than upset. "I need you to assemble both these models."

"*What?*" Luka had allowed himself to sink down into a slouch amid the plush cellular foam of the futon, but he once again pushed himself up straight. "How big?"

"Big," Charlie said. "Big enough to draw a crowd. Big enough cause a spectacle."

"How the hell am I supposed to do that?"

"The same way you've been assembling everything we need. Ask Tycho to create a fake order."

"Don't you think these are a little blatantly subversive? How do you expect me to get them out without anyone noticing?"

"Assemble them while nobody's there."

"There's *always* somebody there," Luka said. "The assemblers never stop. You know that. We're not talking about the refinery here. There's no night shift."

"*Shit*," Charlie said. She turned toward the window and looked out over the gleaming green globe of Yerba Buena Gardens. "I can't imagine how Val would react if she saw this."

"Why are you bringing Val into this all of a sudden?" Luka asked her. "Is that your way of trying to guilt me into doing this?"

The look Charlie gave Luka was a combination of astonishment and hurt. "I can't believe you think I'd try to manipulate you like that."

Luka set the empty shake carton down on a shelf behind the futon, closed his workspace, and stood. "What do you have in mind for these things anyway?" he asked. "And how soon do you need them?"

"Never mind," Charlie said. "It doesn't matter now anyway."

"It might," Luka said.

"Why?"

"Because in case you've forgotten," Luka said, "assemblers aren't the only way to make things around here."

CHAPTER THIRTY-THREE

TRIPLE SEVEN

IN THE SIX YEARS SINCE she stowed away aboard the *Accipiter Hawk*, Ayla Novik had seen the world. Maybe not as much of it as born traders like Costa, but Ayla was pretty certain that she'd seen far more of the planet than the huge majority of those who remained to populated it.

Although she'd never been particularly interested in history, Ayla knew that before the invention and proliferation of trains, cars, steamers, and various forms of air travel, most people relocated only when they had to—either when their lives depended on it, or when sufficiently motivated by opportunity. But over time, advances in transportation technologies allowed humankind to become much more transient, and to wander about the globe for no other reason than to experience the novelty of it. Eventually those with means were just as likely to leave their homes and their families forever as they were to die in the same villages or cities in which they were raised.

But the end of the Solar Age also brought with it an end to widespread migration. If you were born in a location that was stable, secure, and prosperous enough to allow for the conception and delivery of a healthy baby, chances were pretty good that your family would do everything it could to stay there for as long as possible. Anyone in a position to carve out an even remotely comfortable existence was much more likely to protect their home with their lives than risk seeking out a better one.

Ayla knew that she would have probably never left her home on the southern tip of Greenland permanently. As unhappy and as hurt as she was—and as determined as she was to get her father's attention—she'd always envisioned herself returning. But now, while she would do or give anything to have her family back, she realized that even if it were possible, she could never live in Nanortalik again. Even during times throughout human history when generations upon generations were born and died on the very same land—when migration happened at the protracted pace of soil or groundwater depletion, drought, or the redistribution of wild game rather than at the speed of magnetically levitated trains and supersonic passenger jets—there were probably always those few who made their living by wandering, and now that Ayla had become one of them, she didn't think there was any going back.

Over the last six years, Ayla had seen things that she could never have even imagined before leaving Nanortalik: ports and pod systems cobbled together out of dry-docked vessels and shipping containers connected by poorly welded corrugated tubes; rust-streaked supercarriers permanently moored after their decaying nuclear reactors were hastily ejected; enclaves of former ballistic missile submarines, berthed and interconnected by complex matrices of enclosed catwalks; bunkers blasted into the bases of mountains once used as data centers, fallout shelters for dignitaries, and as vaults for secret church records; at least a dozen different abandoned and repopulated coal mines, some of which had collapsed and been re-excavated as many as four or five times; former private spaceports carved out of coral and hardened magma from extinct volcanoes; a network of titanium capsules and glass tubes that once formed an exotic and sprawling undersea luxury resort; supermax prisons surrounded by fenced yards still littered with the corroded remains of thousands of long-dead inmates; voluminous sports stadiums, hermetically sealed with patched composite-weave air domes; entire vertical cities built out of tiers of old twine-bound bamboo scaffolding and decking inside disused nuclear reactor cooling towers; pod systems that used sophisticated atmospheric distribution systems to ration the oxygen their genetically enhanced geodesic greenhouses struggled to exhale beneath an anemic trickle of sunlight; and now, a floating mining rig as big as four square city blocks with the near-magical ability to produce just about anything out of seemingly nothing. Each harbor, marketplace, pod system, and metropolis required its own unique combination of environmental and personal protection before it could be safely approached and negotiated—a process determined through research, rumor, and through the harshest and least forgiving teacher of all: experience.

Ayla had seen a lot of innovative and resourceful communities in her life, but probably the most unique, interesting, and just plain unexpected was the port known as Triple Seven. Triple Seven was located on Bouvet Island, which, at more than 1,700 kilometers north of Antarctica's Princess Astrid Coast, enjoyed the distinction of being among the most remote natural land masses on the planet. Ayla had originally assumed that Triple Seven's location would have ensured that it remained one of the more obscure and underdeveloped destinations along the *Hawk*'s normal circuit, but she was both surprised and delighted to discover that the islanders had learned to use their desolation to their advantage.

Triple Seven, it turned out, was one of the best places in the world to buy and sell electronics. It was roughly equidistant from the coasts of South America, South Africa, and Antarctica, and it was reachable by most decent-size vessels in the South Atlantic and Southern Oceans. Since the overwhelming majority of the world's population relied on technology to sustain itself, the trading of hardware, systems components, assembly schematics, and even collections of algorithms was just as reliable an enterprise as protein, supplements, water, oxygen, and weaponry. Not only was Triple Seven right at the heart of at least 25 percent of the world's technology demand, but due to the island's strict regulations and well-trained peacekeeping force, it was also considered one of the most secure marketplaces in the world.

The name of the system was derived from its principle composition: dozens of old Boeing 777 wide-body jet fuselages that had somehow been loaded into a massive hexagonally tessellated rack and connected to one another via steel and silicone bulkheads. As one approached the island from the southwest, the tableau was truly otherworldly: a monstrous honeycomb of pointed metallic larva suggesting swarms of vast and grotesque robotic insects; a perfectly symmetrical block of what should have been impossibly heavy and unwieldy aircraft neatly shelved like children's toys. Rather than appearing colossal, the structure had the curious effect of making anyone who stood anywhere near its base feel minuscule and existentially insignificant.

How so many old planes had been assembled in one location—and how anyone had managed the logistical feat of stacking and so meticulously connecting them—Ayla had absolutely no idea. The system was far too elegant and intricate to be mistaken for a renovated airplane graveyard. Whoever had done this—especially in such a fantastically remote location—must have had the determination and resources of a modern-day pharaoh. The first time Ayla had ever seen Triple Seven, Costa recalled the rumor that the structure had once been the final refuge of an eccentric British airline and private space tourism mogul who commandeered his company's entire fleet before abruptly changing his mind and deciding to take his chances up in the thermosphere instead. It was said that the remains of his ancestors still languished inside one of the many long-expired, private single-stage-to-orbit spacecraft that, until their orbits sufficiently decayed over the coming centuries, would continue to whisper secrets of a foregone era into the infinite emptiness of space.

Ayla passed this oral history along to Omicron as the *Anura* transitioned from water to land, lowering its open-sided polymer mesh wheels and starting up the flattened path that served as the main approach to Triple Seven.

"It's possible," Omicron conceded, leaning forward so he could see the structure at the top of the rise before them. "Unfortunately, all the paint has dissolved so there's no way to know if they bore common insignias."

"The other theory is that it was done by aliens from another dimension with gravity guns."

"That," Omicron said as he checked the air quality on the panel in front of him, "sounds somewhat less plausible."

The *Accipiter Hawk* had broken away from the *San Francisco* for the purposes of obtaining fresh components to build more drone prototypes. Omicron and Cam had cannibalized just about every auxiliary vehicle on the *Hawk* other than the *Anura*, but they still hadn't finalized a design capable of supporting a global terraforming effort.

"Radiation levels are remarkably low out here," Omicron observed.

"What about contaminants?"

"About as good as it gets."

Ayla was looking out the window rather than at the environmental metrics being reported through the *Anura*'s dash. "We used to get away with just respirators."

"I think we still can," Omicron said. "What about self-defense?"

"No weapons of any kind," Ayla said. "Not even shocksuits."

They slowed as they approached the wall that divided the shore from the vertically stacked city behind it. The partition was assembled out of alternating 777 wings welded together into a single, extremely formidable structure that was held upright by a framework of pillars anchored deep into the rock. Although they couldn't see the ground level of fuselages from where they were, Ayla knew that they had the points of their noses clipped off, and just inside were airlocks, decontamination chambers, and security checkpoints.

"Wait a second," Ayla said.

"What?"

"Something isn't right."

Omicron stopped the *Anura* before they'd reached the gate. "What's wrong?"

"It isn't busy enough," she said. "We shouldn't be the only ones here."

Omicron touched the dash and superimposed an infrared overlay. The honeycomb structure on the other side of the wall lit up in reds, yellows, and greens—even a few concentrated regions of white.

"There's plenty of life up there," Omicron said.

"Up there, maybe," Ayla said. "But what about down here?"

"Only one way to find out."

Before Omicron could continue forward, an incoming communication notification appeared on the panel before them. Omicron used his fingers to expand it so he could peek at the underlying metadata.

"It's a high-priority, spectrum-wide hail," he said. "Someone really wants to talk to us."

"Good," Ayla said. "Let's find out what the hell's going on."

Omicron opened the channel and a heavily bearded face resolved on the polymeth dash. The man's whiskers were dark, as were his eyes, but his long and disheveled hair was blond. There was a moment of silence while the man studied the two occupants on his own display.

"What do you want?" he finally asked.

There was overt suspicion in the man's tone and menace in his eyes. Omicron looked at Ayla.

"We were hoping to do some shopping," Ayla said. "Is Triple Seven still open for business?"

The man squinted at them. "It's been a while since you've been here, hasn't it?" he said. Something about the Afrikaans inflection in his speech was familiar to Ayla.

"A little while," Ayla admitted. "Why?"

"How long?"

Ayla took a moment to add up the time in her head. "Probably close to twenty circuits."

Circuits were the preferred unit of time for those who either spent the majority of their lives at sea, or for those who often did business with them. One circuit was the amount of time it took to circumnavigate the globe on a straight path at an average of twenty knots—about 61.75 days.

"I thought so," the man said. "The exchanges have moved."

"Moved *where*?"

"The middle of the island," the man said. "The approach is from the north now."

"Oh," Ayla replied. "Well, shit."

"Didn't you hear the beacon?" The man looked away briefly while he checked something on a panel to his left. "It's broadcasting."

"I thought I knew what I was doing," Ayla said. "My mistake. We'll go back."

"It's all right," the man said. "You can get there from here. Just follow the road up ahead to your right."

Ayla and Omicron both checked the external view and verified the turnoff.

"Thank you," Ayla said. She looked up from the dash at the massive rack of fuselages on the other side of the wall. "So what do you use this place for now?"

The man leaned forward and watched her for another moment. "You're Costa's girl, aren't you?" he asked.

Ayla's surprise—both at being recognized, and at hearing Costa's name—was such that she was fully conscious of not being able to conceal it.

"Yes," she said. "I mean I was."

"He was a good trader," the man said. "A good man, as well. I was sorry to hear about what happened to him and his crew."

Ayla could see that there was sincerity in the man's dark eyes, and perhaps even genuine empathy. "He was," she agreed.

"We're keeping an eye out for the *Resurrection*," the man told her. "We have a pretty good cross-section signature. If we find it, we'll sink her."

Ayla was silent for a moment and found that she was suddenly blinking back tears. "Thank you," she finally got out. "Really."

"You know there's always a place for you here, don't you?" the man said. His eyes flicked over to Omicron, then back. "For both of you. Any friends of Costa's are friends of mine."

Ayla could not respond beyond nodding. Her hand went up over her mouth and then the tears finally spilled, pooling up momentarily against her fingers and then continuing down.

"That's a very generous offer," Omicron said on Ayla's behalf. "Thank you."

The man gave a single, curt nod. "Be safe," he said, and then he was gone.

Omicron pulled the *Anura* forward, then turned right along the wall. He followed the turns in the road cautiously, and for a time, maneuvered in silence. Eventually, Ayla was aware of him glancing over to check on her.

"I wish I could have known him," he said.

Ayla sniffed. She was wearing a liquid-cooled polymer suit with thumb loops in the sleeves, and she used the back of her hand to wipe her cheeks. "It's not that," she said.

"Then what is it?"

"I don't know," Ayla said. She turned and looked out of the window beside her and saw the ocean dash itself spectacularly against the black cliffs below. "I guess it just surprises me sometimes how beautiful the world still is."

CHAPTER THIRTY-FOUR
FRICTION COEFFICIENT

BOUVET ISLAND WAS AN EXTINCT volcano with a yawning, low-lying crater at its heart. The *Anura* had been climbing its rocky crags by assiduously following a narrow and serpentine path for close to an hour. When he needed maximum traction, Omicron put all six of the amphibian's nonpneumatic polymer tires in contact with the terrain, and when he needed to maximize maneuverability, he retracted the two center wheels, leaving four independently powered pivot points. The vehicle was finally nearing the ridge when Omicron looked down at his wrist and swore.

"*Damnit,*" he said.

The device he wore on his arm was neither subtle nor particularly elegant. Ayla had been calling it his wrist station, though it extended several centimeters past his wrist and up his forearm, constituting more of a high-tech cuff. The polymeth display was curved to approximate the contour of his arm and concealed most of the bulky internals that were built into a thickly padded sleeve and secured with two polymer straps. Had Ayla slipped her own arm through it—even all the way up to her bicep—the device would have made her look like a child playing with her father's watch, though on Omicron, the device was well proportioned.

He'd started wearing it back on the *Hawk* in order to keep in constant contact with Cam, and to have easy access to reference material while also keeping both his hands free. When Ayla first noticed it on his arm, she thought Omicron was controlling it with a BCI, but she couldn't see any kind of electrode netting over his scalp. When she asked him how it worked, he showed her the sensor array he wore high up around his neck like a collar. He called the technology ST, or Synthetic Telepathy, and explained how the nanometer circuitry detected subvocalizations and speech impulses, then transmitted them to the device on his wrist. The technique was inherently less powerful and flexible than a brain-computer interface since input was necessarily serial as opposed to being highly parallel as it was with a BCI, but the trade-off was that it was much easier to configure, calibrate, and maintain. And it required far fewer hours of conditioning to master.

"What's wrong?" Ayla asked.

"We lost another prototype," Omicron said.

He'd stopped the *Anura* so he could focus on the crisis. Ayla saw the map on his arm transition into a table of numerical data that he simultaneously studied and scrolled.

"How?"

"Same as the others," Omicron said. "My best guess is an electromagnetic pulse weapon."

"The Coronians defending their airspace?" Ayla suggested.

"Probably. Their sentinels don't seem to like anything they can't control."

"Can you fly above them?"

"We can't go much higher," Omicron said. He was selecting data points for a 3D scatter plot using his finger in order to leave his voice free for talking. "We need enough atmosphere to generate lift, and we're already cutting back on shielding to reduce weight, which means we have to start worrying about exposing payloads to radiation."

"What about flying lower?"

Omicron shook his head. "Then we have the opposite problem. Too much atmosphere. And weather. We wouldn't have sufficient power to cover the required distances unless we completely redesigned the capacitors, and even then, I don't know if it would work."

Ayla never knew what the right thing was to do or say in situations like these, when she felt she had nothing to contribute but emotional support. She was happy to continue making suggestions as long as she thought they were useful, but she knew she wasn't likely to come up with anything that Omicron and Cam hadn't already considered and dismissed. This kind of thing had always been easy with Costa. She'd listen as long as he needed to vent, and when it was clear that he was winding down, she would hug him, pull back and kiss his cheek, then his neck, and then gradually move to his lips. He sometimes resisted, but she always felt his opposition eventually melt away into desire, and when he was ready, she would pull him down to the floor, or into the nearest isolated compartment big enough to accommodate two bodies, and then regardless of how vexing the problem was, his mood was always better when they were done, and a solution was usually not far behind.

After several minutes of uncomfortable silence, the *Anura* began moving forward again, and the mood remained somber for the remainder of the ascent. But when they crested the final ridge, the despondency of setbacks and seemingly insurmountable obstacles unexpectedly lifted as they were both drawn in by what revealed itself below. The crater in the center of the island was an incredibly intricate patchwork of nautical splendor. The entire northern barrier of the island had been blasted away to accommodate the new approach and replaced with a series of locks designed to permit safe passage for just about any sized ship, and probably also control the depth of the entire marina. On either side of the canal were walkways that, just inside the basin, transitioned into floating docks that ran in opposite directions, following the general contour of the inner wall, and eventually meeting to form a complete loop. The circular pier served as anchorage for multiple offshoots and spokes around which were moored almost every type of small-to-medium-size ship, boat, and yacht Ayla had ever seen, and probably at least a dozen she hadn't. There was only enough slip space for maybe a quarter of the vessels that occupied the cove with the remainder being accessible mainly by networks of gangplanks, or via a long stride between hulls. The cumulative effect was an almost uninterrupted surface of independently undulating ship deck supporting swarms of humanity constantly rebalancing the delicate social and economic equilibrium of Triple Seven.

They both sat there in silence for some time as they looked down into the crater. Ayla imaged Omicron was analyzing, parsing, calculating—perhaps considering all the engineering required to build and maintain such a complex operation, and almost certainly incorporating this wealth of new empirical data into his constantly shifting and expanding worldview. But Ayla was in a very different place. She was simply taking it all in and letting it all happen. To her, it was far more interesting to experience novelty and unfamiliarity and complexity as a coherent and elegant whole rather than attempting to discover and explain its individual constituents.

While Omicron was scrutinizing, Ayla was just being.

"It makes sense," Omicron eventually said.

"What does?"

"That they'd switch from aeronautical salvage to boats."

"Why?"

"Easier to find, easier to repair. And far easier to transport."

Ayla nodded absently, only partially listening. But then she felt a connection abruptly establish itself somewhere just below the level of consciousness, then begin fighting its way up until it was a fully formed idea so obvious and elegant that she couldn't believe she hadn't seen it earlier.

"Wait a second," she said. She sat up straight in the *Anura's* passenger seat. "That's it."

"What's it?"

"Boats," she said. "You and Cam shouldn't be building aerial drones. You should be building boats."

When Omicron looked at her, Ayla expected him to dismiss her revelation, but he didn't. Instead, he lowered his heavy brow in apparent contemplation.

"What about power?" he asked. "Water produces a much greater coefficient of friction than the stratosphere. They might be safe from the Coronians, but the capacitors would have to be massive."

"Boats have all the free power they could ever want," Ayla said. "As long as they know how to capture it."

That's when Omicron finally got it. "Not just boats," he said. "You mean *sail*boats."

"Sailboats," Ayla confirmed.

"Ayla," Omicron began, "I want you to remember this moment."

"Why?"

"Because you might have just single-handedly changed the entire future of the planet."

Ayla's mind went instinctively to Costa. She often conjured him in moments like these so that, in her mind, they could enjoy the experience together. But perhaps for the first time since she'd lost her husband, she consciously stopped herself. Instead of willing the present to be haunted by the apparitions of her past, Ayla looked back down over the marvel of the new Triple Seven marina and just tried to appreciate what was.

CHAPTER THIRTY-FIVE

RECONSTITUTED NATURE

As MORNING DAWNED AGAINST THE *San Francisco*'s mighty white canopy, so too did the serene warbling of songbirds. The melodies originated from the park in the southeast corner of the platform and skittered along the composite weave as far as the rig's bridge, drizzling crisply down among the morning commuters.

The City Council had recently approved a proposal to start broadcasting simulated birdcalls from acoustic panels angled down over the Embarcadero. The songs were algorithmically generated by software that used as reference material hundreds of thousands of digital recordings harvested from the ship's archives. Luka reflexively dismissed the initiative as inane in the extreme, and hypothesized that next, condensers would bring fog to the city, and in order to spawn a market for umbrellas and hydrophobic outerwear, even the occasional rain shower. However, he was surprised to find that the chirps and trills and chatter were much less offensive than he expected, and that he was even compelled to skirt the perimeter of the park whenever the opportunity presented itself. Luka suspected that, just as mankind was drawn to the color green because of its association with the sustainment of life (hence the historical obsession with suburban lawn care, he'd once read), perhaps buried somewhere deep in the human psyche was also some lingering and heretofore dormant archetypal appreciation for the magnificent symphonies that once emanated from the secret worlds above.

Luka was not alone in his unexpected appreciation for reconstituted nature. Since everyone on the *San Francisco* lived either in Millennium or Paramount Towers—and since the Embarcadero was positioned right between the two—the recently installed auditory ambiance drew, over the course of the day, just about everyone on the rig who did not make a concerted effort to avoid it.

The Embarcadero was therefore the perfect location for Luka's newest creative triumph. Not only was the site logistically sensible because of its central location, but positioning the installment directly between the two residential towers lent it a certain measure of symbolism that helped it to accomplish that which Luka believed all true works of art ultimately sought: the elevation to something more than what it actually was.

Luka remembered very clearly how much was made of the fact that Millennium and Paramount Towers were identical— how much their equivalence was held up as a symbol of social and civil responsibility. Of course it wasn't technically true that the two buildings were entirely indistinguishable. "Interchangeable" was probably the better term. In reality, transpartments at the top of Millennium tended to be a few degrees warmer due to the use of slightly less efficient microfiber insulation, and roughly a third of the flats in Paramount were stuck with tacky, disused polyvid systems. Additionally, water pressure in Millennium was every-so-slightly (but nonetheless noticeably) lower due to a minute change in the diameter of the lines without anyone thinking to make a corresponding adjustment to the water pumps. And finally, although the conductive polymeth dividers in both towers used frictionless maglev tracks, there was something slightly different about the formulation of the silicone gaskets and lubricants used in some hinges and sealed bearings in the Paramount that made them more prone to squeaking. As a result, on one side of the Embarcadero, it was considered extremely poor etiquette to do any major living space reconfigurations after ten p.m., while on the other side, no such taboo existed.

Trivial variations aside, the floor on which you lived had a much greater impact on your living arrangement than which of the two towers you occupied, though even the discrepancies implied by elevation were kept intentionally moderate. While those who lived on higher floors did indeed enjoy more space and privacy than those below them, even the smallest and most communal of flats provided their occupants with more than adequate amenities, and a standard of living far above that which the overwhelming majority of the rest of humanity was forced to endure.

Such was the promise of the two great towers—the unwritten contract that had made the razing of China Basin a largely celebratory event rather than one marred by controversy or gloomy nostalgia. Similarly, the promise of the Embarcadero was to serve as a free and open public space uniting the two halves of the city's population forever—or at least for as long as anyone at the time cared to plan.

But now, the carefully honed socially engineered philosophy that had for so many years helped to maintain a perhaps slightly imperfect, but still highly functional, balance between equality and upward mobility was about to undergo a dramatic transformation. And Luka and Charlie were going to make absolutely certain that everyone aboard the *San Francisco* knew it.

Forty-five minutes before the morning shift, and thirty minutes before a scheduled task awoke the bytecode that would begin the slow crescendo of randomly synthesized birdsong—working beneath the spread of simulated stars, galaxies, and planets projected against a sapphire-blue canopy—Luka and Charlie used self-balancing hand trucks to maneuver one calibration-cube sculpture depicting the *San Francisco* as it currently was (labeled *Our Present*), and another one depicting the rig as it would be after the next major overhaul (labeled *Our Future*), right out into the middle of the Embarcadero's main cricket pitch. The intention was to position the installment somewhere it could not be missed or ignored, and there was probably no better way to attract attention than by blatantly disrupting the second-shifters' early morning competition. The theory was that Luka and Charlie were guaranteed a minimum of thirty water rats, refinery workers, and assembly technicians standing together in a tight cluster, projecting a combination of unmistakable befuddlement and irritation. And since nothing attracted a big crowd like a smaller one, within an hour, they were likely to have achieved critical mass: enough witnesses that the sculptures could not be whisked down to the waterlock, purged, and subsequently disavowed.

Both Luka and Charlie were stunned by how impeccably it all came together. Neither had views of the Embarcadero from their transpartments so they watched side-by-side and crosslegged from a window at the end of Charlie's hall. They dubbed an imbecilic sound track over the silent and distant scene as team rivalries were temporarily put aside for the sake of trying to solve the enigma of the sculpted calibration cubes. What started out as an abundance of shrugging, head shaking, and mystified glances at one another rapidly evolved into frantic beckoning and what appeared to be impassioned debates. As the crowd swelled, they somehow even began self-organizing queues so that everyone could get a better look at what lay at the center of the attraction.

As soon as the assembly grew so large and so loud that Luka and Charlie could hear the commotion from all the way up on the eleventh floor of Paramount Tower, they looked at each other and found that neither of them were smiling anymore. It wasn't necessarily the size or the sound of what seemed to be escalating into a rally, or even the intensity of the rising tumult; rather, it was the realization that what they had just started was no longer even remotely within their control.

Luka saw a notification appear in the corner of his vision. He initially assumed it was a message from Tycho until he noticed the icon indicating it was a video communication—something Two Bulls would probably never risk. When he called the stream up on the polymeth window in front of them, they were greeted by the smiling face of Khang Jung-soon—somehow simultaneously endearing and vitriolic, as was characteristic of the councilwoman. Khang promptly congratulated Luka for providing her with precisely the excuse she needed to open a brand-new investigation into his activities, which she was certain would eventually result in a conviction of high treason, the penalty for which, as he well knew, was exile. In the meantime, in order to ensure that he could not pursue any additional illicit activities, all of his assets were to be immediately frozen.

Luka couldn't tell what Charlie was thinking as they sat there alone and silent at the end of the hallway, but he found himself looking out over the crowd in the park below them and contemplating, unexpectedly, sports. Perhaps what drew people to organized competition, Luka mused, was its distinct lack of ambiguity. Cricket and football and boxing matches might be frequently and painstakingly analyzed, but they were rarely disputed, and even when they were, rulings were usually swift and decisive. Each individual match lasted a predefined amount of time, and when they were over, everyone involved—players, fans, coaches, and bookies—knew exactly where they stood.

But outside of organized competition, the line between victory and defeat was far less distinct. Events appearing to culminate in your favor one minute could be your undoing the very next—if not today, then perhaps tomorrow, or next week, or next year. In fact, the very definition of what constituted a victory was prone to amendment over time as repercussions continued to compound, and as beliefs and sentiment and popular opinion evolved. But perhaps most unsettling of all was the realization that real-life competition did not occur as discrete, time-boxed events with results fastidiously recorded in some universal ledger the moment a whistle blew, or a buzzer sounded, or a bell rang. Rather, most struggles were open-ended and indefinite processes that had to be constantly watched over and tended to and fiercely protected, lest those achievements perceived as victories eventually be seized by those who prove themselves willing to go to increasingly greater lengths to obtain them.

Luka wondered if the type of conflict in which he now found himself embroiled might be less about ultimately winning, and more about simply trading defeats.

CHAPTER THIRTY-SIX

BALANCE OF FORCES

THE LAST PLACE ON THE PLANET Ayla expected to go was back home.

She captained the *Hawk* between Triple Seven and the ninety-click perimeter they agreed to maintain around the *San Francisco* while Omicron researched and built miniature sailboats. He didn't have as much to learn as he'd originally feared since, as he explained it to Ayla, the type of sailing he was interested in was essentially just aeronautical engineering literally turned on its side. Sails and keels, as it turned out, were really nothing more than wings that happened to generate lift along the surface of the earth rather than away from it.

Old square-rigged ships worked by raising as many as thirty-four trapezoidal sails on as many as four separate masts set perpendicular to the hull where, at their most efficient, they worked together to harness the combined energy of a tailwind to push the ship forward. Ironically, the ancient principle was not all that much different from the most modern manifestation of sailing technology: solar and beam propulsion. Before the end of the Solar Age, spacecraft used sails of various shapes and diameters only fractions of a micron thick to harness pressure exerted by photons emitted either by stars, or by carefully directed lasers.

But between the oldest and the newest surprisingly simple sailing techniques was an entire world of intricate aerodynamics.

Like an airplane wing, a fore-and-aft rigged sail—a curved sail set along the length of the hull rather than perpendicular to it—forced air to travel around it at different speeds. Wind moved at a higher velocity over the convex side, resulting in a local low-pressure system that the air from the other side was compelled to fill, generating lift in the process. The boat's keel—essentially its underwater wing—used the forward motion of the boat to generate its own lift with the resultant vector being momentum. The dynamic could be thought of as a complex but undeniably elegant balance of forces where, when everything was optimally configured, the net direction was forward.

Fortunately schematics for both military and hobbyist UNVs, or Unmanned Nautical Vehicles, abounded in the *Hawk*'s archives, as did various algorithms for optimizing operations like tacking, jibing, trimming, heeling, and reducing sail. Omicron even found what his automated testing verified to be extremely stable, robust, and well-optimized software implementations of those algorithms—libraries that took as inputs decimal floating-point values collected by onboard sensors like accelerometers, multiaxis gyroscopes, magnetometers, anemometers, barometers, and extensometers designed for measuring line tension. The final problem of navigation was easily solved by decrypting signals from the Coronian-controlled geostationary constellation of sixty-four high-definition GPS satellites.

By the time the *Hawk* rejoined the *San Francisco*, Omicron had what he believed was a viable prototype and a set of reverse-engineered assembly specifications. But although the UNVs were ready for production, according to Cadie, the payloads were not. The seeds Luka and Charlie had provided were proving problematic. Not only were the quantities they were able to liberate from Yerba Buena without anyone noticing insufficient, but the species of flora they had access to didn't have all the characteristics on which Arik's research was partially predicated. Over the underwater acoustic link, Cadie and Omicron proceeded to discuss dominant and recessive traits, genotypes and phenotypes, genetic isolation, and things like recombination and synthesis. Ayla half listened to their conversation while initiating routine ship-wide diagnostics. While they ran, she cleaned the dust off the wings of her butterfly using the ultrasonic vibration filters Omicron installed, which removed contaminants from around the solar cells by vibrating at around fifty thousand hertz. Although she was unable to follow the discussion in detail, she could tell that the two of them were going around in circles, and every time they arrived back where they started, they seemed slightly more frustrated. Eventually they were in agreement that if they were going to maximize their chances of success, Cadie would need a much wider variety of botanical samples to work with. But in stark opposition to the general darkening mood, after a long moment of silent reflection, Omicron announced that he knew exactly where to find them.

The good news, according to Omicron, was that GSV, or the Global Seed Vault, would undoubtedly have exactly what Cadie needed. The bad news was that the price was certain to be exorbitant. On the polymeth surface in front of which Omicron stood, Ayla could see the defeat in Cadie's expression as she informed them that there was more bad news: Luka's caps had been frozen. He was still working at the foundry and earning his regular salary, so between he and Charlie, they had the watts they needed to keep *Aquarius* online, but if the GSV dealt in the currency of caps, they were going to have to find another source.

Omicron turned, sat at the terminal behind him, and brought up a map. He had the navigation system plot a course, then compared the results against a summary of the ship's status. The problem, Omicron explained, wasn't just currency. It was also *current*. The vault was on the other side of the planet; almost exactly at their hemispheric mirror image; well over fifteen thousand kilometers away. He was confident that he could negotiate with the seed keepers—figure something out that they wanted, which he and Ayla were uniquely positioned to obtain—but the *Hawk* only had enough of a charge to get there, and then maybe 15 to 20 percent of the way back. And that was assuming a relatively direct course with no major deviations—a premise that was unlikely to hold true across such a vast distance. It had been months since Ayla and Omicron had done any for-hire work, which had left them entirely dependent on Luka. Without his caps, the *Hawk* wasn't going to Svalbard—or at least, it was not coming back. And without going to Svalbard, there would be no more seeds than what remnants and miscellany Luka and Charlie could smuggle out of the gardens.

Ayla was paying attention again. She'd never herd of the Global Seed Vault before, but she definitely knew of Svalbard. It wasn't all that far from her home pod system in Nanortalik. In fact, if there were any kind of permanent settlement around the vault (which, Omicron assured her, there was), they would have almost certainly done some trading with her people in the past. Both Omicron and Cadie watched her and waited as she arranged the pieces in her mind, and when Ayla continued, her fervency was fueled not just by idle talk of home, but the sudden and unexpected prospect of possibly even seeing it again.

Nanortalik, she explained, had a detailed and comprehensive evacuation plan in the event of any type of catastrophe, the apparent ineffectiveness of which Ayla had spent many hours reflecting upon. Part of the pod system's emergency provisions were a series of silicon and graphene industrial-scale power cells buried beneath the loading bay, and could only be charged and drawn from inductively. Unless someone had the right equipment—or got absurdly lucky by inadvertently setting an inductive capacitor down directly on top of one of the concealed contact patches— there was probably still at least a gigawatt of juice up there on the tip of Greenland, entirely free for the taking to anyone who knew how to find it.

Omicron considered Ayla's proposal, and when he finally responded, she was certain he would dismiss it. Although she was still technically the captain of the *Hawk*, the reality was that she and Omicron had become partners, and it was rare that anything happened without full consensus between them. And it was even rarer for Omicron to endorse a plan so fraught with uncertainty.

But to Ayla's surprise, his somber tone was more to make sure she understood the risks of what she was proposing than to try to talk her out of it. If they weren't able to gain access to the power cells, they would be out of options, and would have to put in at the nearest port—probably Hudson Strait or St. Lawrence— and look for any kind of work they could find. It might even mean having to do a job on credit—which, of course, would mean the worst possible terms. Additionally, if they were to get sidetracked, it would be a very long time before they caught up with the *San Francisco*, and it was even possible that their paths might never intersect again. But the point Omicron seemed most determined to make was that the expedition would in no way be about revisiting Ayla's past. With the amount of traffic Nanortalik used to get, there was no way the pod system was still uninhabited, and there was no telling what they would find once they got there. This was a salvage operation, he emphasized, and absolutely nothing more. Under no circumstances whatso-ever should Ayla make the mistake of thinking that the place they were about to go was anything like she remembered. Her home was gone, Omicron told her with unexpected solemnity, and nothing they could do would ever bring it back.

CHAPTER THIRTY-SEVEN

PARADOXICAL THINKING

IN EXCHANGE FOR HIS REGULAR compensation, Luka had been granted the privilege of continuing to fulfill his responsibilities at the foundry. That's how the Judicial Committee worded it in the formal Notification of Investigation that followed Khang's smug missive. The reality, Luka knew, was that they couldn't spare him, and had in fact fallen significantly behind quota as a result of his former extended vacation on Hexagon Row. The *San Francisco* was no different from any other burgeoning economy that borrowed elements from capitalism wherever it was convenient to do so, in that its long-term survival was predicated on indefinite and perpetual growth. And the foundation of that growth, at this particular moment in the course of its evolution, was molecular manufacturing.

The last thing he should be doing right now, Luka knew, was bootlegging curious yellow. He'd already assembled and smuggled all of Cadie and Cam's UNVs, but they still needed a way to get Cam up to *Equinox*. And there was no telling what else they might need to obtain between now and the moment their plan had advanced far enough that nobody—not the Judicial Committee, the City Council, nor the Coronians—could contain it.

Yet somehow he ended up with an envelop of yellow powder anyway. Once again, Luka did not willfully perform the code injection and then carefully sequester the yield, but rather watched as it happened from the perspective of a detached outside observer. And when he got back to his transpartment, he again stepped outside of himself and watched as he cut it into lines, accepted it into his nasal passage through the slightly flared glass tube, performed that spectacular and sumptuous act of balance, and then, having skipped dinner, laid down on his carefully calibrated silicone mattress, and for the very first time that day, simply enjoyed the experience of being.

Now that his mind no longer had to occupy itself with the problem of achieving his next high, there was room to think about how long he would be able to keep this up. One way or another, it was almost certain that he would not be an assembly technician for very much longer. In fact, he was frankly surprised it had lasted this long. Most people who knew Luka assumed that he had learned to operate forklifts and liftsuits—and subsequently insisted on keeping all his certifications current—because he had a passion for powerful industrial machinery. That wasn't entirely untrue, but his primary motivation was one he'd never shared with anyone: Luka was very aware of the fact that he needed a backup career.

There were several reasons why the City Council originally approved the proposition to bring hundreds of thoroughly screened and hand-selected orphaned children aboard and train them as assembly technicians. The most obvious was the sudden labor shortage that was inevitable as soon as construction of the foundry was complete. While there were certainly plenty of highly skilled adult workers available in any port, pod system, or broker post who would happily give up everything they had for a chance to live aboard a vessel like the *San Francisco*—even prior to the spoils of molecular assembly—it wasn't skilled adult laborers that the City Council was interested in. Adults brought with them established criminal and violent tendencies, sexual dysfunction, and possibly even the individual components for what one day might, under the right circumstances, coalesce into mutiny.

Children, on the other hand, were much more predictable and pliable. Not only were they easier and safer to control physically, but they were far less likely to require physical control in the first place. It was much more straightforward to mold a child into a productive, responsible, and functional citizen than a mature and established adult, and certainly less trouble to dispose of one who, for whatever reason, didn't take to the conditioning.

But the initiative wasn't entirely motivated by behavioral considerations. As predicted by the teams of engineers who, in cooperation with the Coronians, designed the foundry and oversaw the installation of the brand-new assemblers, it turned out that children were actually far more adept factory technicians. The first generation of assembler technology required a great deal of constant attention in the form of both maintenance and repair, therefore there were clear advantages to employing a staff who could easily fit into constrained spaces (without protesting or complaining) and had small enough hands and fingers to reach material lines fed through narrow gaps, adjust inconveniently located valves, and retrieve accidentally dislodged hardware. Left to adults, such tasks would have invariably meant extraneous safety procedures and lost productivity that, cumulatively, might have set the *San Francisco* back as long as years. When swiftly and unreservedly attended to by children, though, mishaps could often be resolved without so much as filing a report, requesting an inspection, or even pausing production.

But there were other, far subtler advantages to putting children in charge of the rig's material destiny. The models, paradigms, and workflows introduced by the combination of Coronian-designed molecular assembly hardware and the various levels of software that gave them life had a tendency to challenge the expectations and preconceptions of even the cleverest and most mentally adroit adults, very often resulting in frustration, rejection, and flat-out ineptitude. To children, however, almost everything they encountered was already unfamiliar, so there was almost no limit to the diversity and novelty they were capable of accepting and incorporating into their worldviews. Since children had not yet formed very many expectations about how the world should work, they could function—and indeed even thrive—within an astonishingly broad range of realities.

There was a period of time during which Luka believed that growing up right alongside the technology that an entire city had rapidly come to rely on would result in the ultimate job (and hence life) security. However, he eventually began to realize that one man's security was inevitably another man's vulnerability. Just as he and his peers really began to understand and internalize the power they yielded, so too did the City Council, who responded by assigning a team of inspectors, observers, and foremen to the task of penetrating—and eventually, methodically dismantling—what had become an opaque assembly technician culture. But the first step was understanding exactly what it was that an assembly technician did.

A typical day at the foundry involved starting a shift with a thorough review of overall quotas, and then breaking them down into individual purchases (newly initiated, in-progress, paused, recalled, and stalled) along with their requested delivery dates and their relative priorities (standard, preferred, high, and critical). The next step was to carve off a block of orders and break them down further into discrete components for which various assemblers were optimized, subtract what were referred to as "commodity components," which were preassembled in bulk (after verifying that they were indeed in stock), look for opportunities for parallel assembly (it was faster to assemble multiple identical components if you could do so during the same run), and then commence with the equally artistic and scientific process of task scheduling.

Three things made task scheduling complex: order of assembly mattered; any given technician might be juggling as many as thirty separate jobs concurrently; and finally, every technician was competing for the same limited resources (both the assemblers themselves, and the medium that fed them). Therefore, almost all task scheduling occurred through AX, or the Assembly eXchange board.

AX was an unauthorized piece of software that was hacked together and deployed to the foundry's local network by a team of technicians, and was designed to support and coordinate the trading of assembler and medium access. Because of malfunctions, bugs, unscheduled maintenance, the continuous addition of new jobs, changes in priorities, and fluctuations in the supply of medium, tasks were always changing and resources constantly being rebalanced. AX, therefore, had a permanent place on every technician's workspace, and constantly flashed with updates, warnings, notifications, and the occasional impertinent witticism. When individual components were fully formed, the best and most vigilant technicians were always right there ready to crack open the receiver, perform initial visual inspections, run diagnostics to ensure operation consistent with specifications and within designated mechanical and/or electrical tolerances, and finally to encase the newly spawned article in the gelatinous embrace of a silicone shipping pack. When entire orders were complete, they were bundled according to shipping manifests, transferred to the cargo hold, lowered down to level three, and finally distributed via forklift or liftsuit to their final destinations, where they awaited either further fabrication or final installation.

Luka could recall at least half a dozen attempts to automate almost the entire assembly workflow and thus reduce technicians' individual contributions to little more than maintenance, diagnostics, and transport. And he distinctly recalled how every such attempt resulted in a complete shutdown of the entire foundry—and sometimes even the refinery—usually within half an hour, though in a few cases, as quickly as thirty seconds. In every instance, the newly installed systems were rolled back and every assembly technician required to work overtime in order to make up for lost productivity, each and every one of their jobs—which only moments prior, had been right on the cusp of being designated obsolete—freshly validated and secured.

What the City Council didn't realize—and indeed still refused to accept—was that the *San Francisco* was a living, breathing organism. The crew was the cells that delivered nutrients to where she was starving, attacked the pathogens that constantly tried to invade and disable her, and built subsystems that were the organs that combined to keep her healthy and strong. And as a complex organism, the only rational way to make sense of her was in the context of long-term evolution rather than the delusion of spontaneous generation. It wasn't feasible to simply shut down complex and critical systems that had evolved organically over long stretches of time and replace them with unproven solutions with little more to recommend them than economically and politically motivated mandates. Just as the human brain had to add additional structures and layers to itself in order to grow ever-more sophisticated rather than simply bestowing an entirely new and untested neurological design upon a future generation, the cost of the *San Francisco*'s adaptation to a rapidly changing world was layers of subtlety, intricacy, and convolution—a general complexity that, if it were to be successfully reimagined and ultimately replaced, would need to be dismantled with a level of respect and thoughtfulness few policymakers seemed capable of demonstrating.

Nobody denied that there were obvious disadvantages to complexity. The human brain, in its attempt to synthesize disparate evolutionary fragments into coherent models of reality, suffered from countless phobias, disorders, obsessions, and addictions. Humanity's endless demonstrations of hypocrisy, duplicity, and paradoxical thinking were not anomalous character flaws, but rather biological inevitabilities. However, it was also the case that the hundreds of billion of neurons, and the trillions of synaptic connections, and all of the layers and lobes and cortices and hemispheres contained within the brain were precisely what made possible everything about being human that was held most dear.

Almost all complex systems embody that which is valued and that which is not, and the *San Francisco* was no different. While it was probably true that, if done properly, removing as many humans as possible from the foundry workflow could theoretically increase productivity, it was also undeniably true that the foundry existed for the sole purpose of serving humans, and in more ways than just providing a consistent supply of tools, technology, and trinkets. Equally important were the by-products of pride and self-worth that almost all the assembly

technicians—no matter how jaded they presented themselves—
clung to after having mastered their trade, become part of a community, and made the long and often terrifying journey from the
unwanted of the world to the needed, the respected, and in some
cases, even the loved.

But perhaps the most important thing the foundry ever produced was one almost nobody thought to credit them with: the
creation of a true middle class. Whether the City Council liked
it or not, assembly technicians were indispensable and nearly
irreplaceable, and with every failed attempt to contain them,
not only did their compensation increase, but so too did their
purchasing power. It was the assembly technician—that mysterious amalgamation of highly skilled professional and brute-force
physical laborer—who early on became the *San Francisco*'s main
economic engine, and thereby inspired the engineers, doctors,
teachers, administrators, and gradually all those who would
come to think of themselves as professionals rather than inden-
tured servants to exert their newfound influence. In the end, not
only did the foundry produce the machinery that razed China
Basin, and then every last component that went into the construction of both the Millennium and Paramount Towers, but
it also inadvertently manufactured the underlying philosophies
that motivated them.

The complexity of the *San Francisco* was far too much for
Luka to hold in his head all at once. He hated the unfettered
materialism, the cultural hypoxia, and the seemingly instinctual
inclination toward self-destruction that the rig somehow seemed
destined to cultivate. Yet he couldn't deny that, more than once,
he'd proven himself perfectly willing to risk everything to try to
preserve it.

Luka was beginning to realize that it was possible to simultaneously hate something and to take comfort in it—not unlike an abusive relationship, or a debilitating but familiar mental disorder, or an addiction that, while making no apologies whatsoever for ruthlessly and systematically dismantling your life, was also somehow the very best friend you had.

CHAPTER THIRTY-EIGHT

SANITY CHECK

USING AYLA'S INTIMATE KNOWLEDGE of the Nanortalik Pod System, Omicron prepared for every contingency he could think of. He anticipated everything from EMP mines, to various configurations and patterns of snipers, to swarms of unmanned sentinels. He even verified that the old steel teardrop-shaped depth charges with magnetic anomaly detectors for going up against submarines—munitions that, according to their stamps, had expired tens of circuits ago—would probably still function. The fundamentals of all of Omicron's plans were essentially the same: go in slowly and quietly, and should they encounter any significant resistance, release everything at their disposal, then turn and run. The only variation was the order in which their defenses were deployed, and the direction of their attempted escape. It wasn't that the *Hawk* couldn't hold her own in a fight, but one ship against an entire potentially well-fortified pod system was not what Omicron considered to be particularly favorable odds. And the *Hawk*'s biggest asset was, by far, its speed.

Unfortunately the one thing Omicron really felt he needed, he no longer had: at least one functioning medium- to long-range reconnaissance drone. Instead he used every onboard sensor, sonar, radar, and lidar system at his disposal to see as far into their future as he possibly could, and scanned every frequency in the radio spectrum, hoping to stumble upon some form of prognostic chatter. He continued decreasing their speed until they were creeping forward at a barely perceptible dead slow ahead, and that's when Ayla realized that they were up against the one and only obstacle that Omicron had not planned for: absolutely nothing. Although it seemed impossible that Nanortalik could still be uninhabited, every indication was that nobody was home.

Ayla's former residence of seventeen years was essentially an archipelago of geodesic domes connected by underground passages. The southernmost pod was designed to be the initial approach as it housed the loading dock as well as the system's primary decontamination chamber and airlock. Very much in opposition to Omicron's advice (which fell just short of insistence), Ayla stood fully suited and helmeted at the rail of the forward deck with a centrifugal pistol clipped to her thigh by its acceleration disk. Although Omicron made it clear that he preferred that they both remain below (his biggest fear was thermal-cloaked snipers), he stood beside her—likewise fully suited—holding a remote polymeth panel in both gloved hands, and with his rifle slung over his shoulder.

The feelings of nostalgia and sentimentality that Ayla expected were conspicuously absent at first, and she realized that it was because she barely recognized her home from the outside. The first and only time she'd ever left Nanortalik was aboard the *Hawk*, and therefore the southern approach never had an opportunity to imprint itself upon her. Omicron maneuvered the vessel beneath the loading bay, which was a long, fully enclosed stone cove, blasted out and shaped with a hydraulic breaker, then reinforced with buttresses and arches of steel trusses. All the slips were empty and the main cargo bay doors were lowered, leaving only a few meters of empty dock. When Ayla was growing up, unless a ship was either inbound or outbound, the artificial cave was usually sealed and the main loading bay doors raised, creating a single massive open space where winches and cranes constantly loaded and unloaded cargo and freight. The environmental and water circulation systems had kept the area mostly free of contaminants so Nanortalik's primary airlock—off to the side where the loading bay doors ended—was seldom used. The dock, as Ayla was accustomed to it, had always been indicative of vibrancy and commerce and purpose, but its current state made the entire pod system feel shuttered and abandoned. As deserted as the loading bay was, though, just being inside the dim and damp cavern proved to be catalyst enough, and Ayla began to sense the emotional charge that can only be induced by returning to the one place in the world that one forever thinks of as home.

In the ensuing barrage of memories, there was no accounting for chronology. Suddenly there was the collective reverberant cacophony of children swinging from the loading bay winches; her mother's clearly feigned calm when Ayla told her she'd gotten her first period; the smell of the detergent her father used every evening to remove grit and lubricant from his hands and from beneath his fingernails; the texture of the six stitches on the inside of her lip that she couldn't stop feeling with her tongue after she ran into an air intake duct; the tiny pictures all the kids drew in the corners of their tattered silicon paper notebooks, which they flipped through to create primitive animations; the reaction of her mother and her entire Queen of Spades card group when Ayla and her best friend walked in after lopping each other's hair off with the curved beaks of tin snips; the nests she used to build at the top of the warehouse shelving where she wrote stories by the faint green light of stolen glow sticks; the salty soy broth her mother brought her when she was in bed for three days with a urinary tract infection; the first time she boarded the magnificent vessel with the mysterious and regal moniker of *Accipiter Hawk*; and finally, the look on the crew's faces—and especially the profound regret in Costa's eyes—when they returned from investigating the unexplained radio silence, and the moment Ayla realized that almost everything she'd ever known was gone forever.

Omicron was the first on the dock. His rifle was raised and he was trying to detect movement through the walls using the 3D radio reflection scope he'd attached. Ayla followed him down the gangplank, holding in each hand a suitcase-size inductive capacitor. By the time Omicron had traversed the length of the dock, he had a detailed model of the entire space beyond the bay doors. Not only was there no movement, but his acoustic and infrared sensors were coming up empty, as well.

"I think we're clear," he said, though his tone indicated that he wasn't sure he believed it.

Ayla stood on the dock in front of the lowered bay doors. "The contact patches are this way," she said.

Omicron turned his rifle on Ayla. His finger was safely up along the receiver, above the trigger guard, and she knew that he was simply performing a sanity check. He wanted to make sure that something he knew was there appeared on his scope before he was willing to bet their lives that they were actually alone. After a moment, he seemed satisfied that his instruments were indeed working, and he lowered his weapon.

Ayla moved the cases around to different locations on the dock. She loosened her grip on the handles and allowed them to magnetically align themselves with the contact patches embedded in the siliconcrete floor, then paused, watching for a reaction from the charging indicators, shaking her head when the displays remained dark. Initially she refused to believe that anyone could have found the stash, and even questioned the viability of her capacitors, but as she began to feel increasingly like a physician desperately looking for a heartbeat in a patient she already knew was dead, her entire perspective shifted. Maybe the equipment to detect such a substantial store of power really wasn't all that complicated or unusual after all. The architects of Nanortalik, Ayla suddenly realized, probably got the idea for hidden capacitors from other pod systems, which meant there were almost certainly thousands of people who knew right where to look. Perhaps concealed current was among the very first things raiders and scavengers looked for when they came across an abandoned or insufficiently guarded outpost. Maybe the entire trip had been for nothing, Ayla thought, and her judgment had been skewed by an unconscious desire to see her home one last time.

Ayla stopped moving the cases and looked up at Omicron.

"Anything?" he asked. He was on the opposite side of the dock now, but his voice—resonating from the spheroidal polymeth of her helmet—made it sound as though he was standing right beside her.

"I'm sorry," Ayla said. "This was a stupid idea."

"It wasn't stupid," Omicron said. "It was the best shot we had."

"No, it wasn't. It was stupid and selfish and naive. What are we going to do now?"

"Continue on to Svalbard," Omicron said. "That's all we can do."

"How are we going to get back to the *San Francisco*?"

"We'll worry about that when we have to."

Ayla looked down at the two handheld graphene power blocks—dark and cold and empty—then looked back up at Omicron. "Hold on," she said. "Let's go inside."

"Ayla," Omicron began. Even from across the dock, she could see both caution and concern in the narrow slits of his eyes. "We already talked about this. You can't think of this place as your home anymore. There's nothing left for you in there."

"I'm not saying I want to take a tour," Ayla snapped. She knew she was taking her disappointment and anger at herself out on him, but at that moment, she didn't care. "Maybe there's something in there we can salvage. Maybe we can find something worth enough caps to get us back to the *San Francisco*."

"You understand how unlikely that is, don't you?" Omicron asked her. "If someone was able to find capacitors buried in a meter of siliconcrete, they'd easily find anything else of value. It's even possible all the cabling has been ripped out of the walls. That might be why nobody's here."

"I don't think so," Ayla said. She nodded past Omicron at the airlock behind him. The outer door was circular and set back into the wall next to the loading bay door about half a meter. The curved polymeth panel in front of it was dimmed, but clearly still powered.

Omicron did not turn to look behind him and Ayla realized that he'd already made the same observation, probably long before she did. And then she realized that he was almost certainly hoping that she wouldn't notice.

"Come on," Ayla said. "What do we have to lose? We're already here. We might as well take a quick look around. That thing will tell us if anyone's coming. It's worth the risk."

"The risk is our lives," Omicron said, "and there's almost certainly no reward. I'm not sure I agree."

Ayla watched the enormous Neo standing between herself and the airlock. She considered issuing him a direct order—even tried it out a couple of times in her head—but ultimately decided she couldn't sell it. She knew that it was her own safety and well-being that Omicron was concerned with rather than his own, just as it had always been since the moment they met in the Maldives and just as she believed it always would be until, for reasons as inevitable as they were unknowable, it was finally time for them to part ways.

"*I'm* the reason we came all the way up here," Ayla finally said, "and *I'm* going to do everything I can to make sure that we leave with something. *Anything.*" She set the capacitors down on the dock and drew her sidearm from its clasp on her thigh. "I'm going in there," she told Omicron. "I'm not asking you to agree with me that it's the smartest decision, and I'm not asking you to like it. But I *am* asking you to come with me."

Ayla hadn't realized what a defensive posture Omicron had assumed until she noticed him relax. He turned and looked at the airlock behind him, then back at Ayla.

"I'll go on one condition," he said.

"What?"

"You let me go first."

Ayla watched him for a moment, then smiled. "I wouldn't have it any other way," she said.

The panel in front of the airlock detected their presence and the screen brightened. Omicron touched it and a massive disk-shaped door pivoted outward toward them, spilling a red warning glow from within. Omicron checked the integrity of the twin orange O-ring seals recessed in the edge of the door—seals that Ayla knew would expand into place as they inflated after the door closed—and, apparently satisfied that they hadn't dry rotted, stepped into the chamber. Ayla followed, and after Omicron touched the panel inside, the door swung closed behind them with a metallic rasp and a final deep, resonant rumble. After a moment of stillness, there was the sound of the seals inflating and air exchanging while Omicron swung the rifle back and forth, trying to detect movement or heat signatures on the other side.

The decontamination instruments were all housed inside the dull metallic walls, so the only features were ventilation openings and air fins. The red glow overhead transitioned to a rich indigo blue, and then the exchange of air stopped.

"Still clear," Omicron said. He crouched and placed the rifle gently on the grate at his feet, then unclipped his helmet and pulled it off. "I suggest we leave our suits here. If something goes wrong, we're better off taking a few rads on our way out than trying to run in these things."

Ayla nodded. She secured her pistol, then reached back behind her neck and lifted her helmet latches, rotated the gasket ring, and lifted the dome up over her head. She set it down at her feet and started unthreading her gloves when she was suddenly aware of Omicron's stillness.

"Wait a second," he said. He looked at Ayla for a moment, then made a sudden movement toward her helmet on the floor. "Don't breathe!" he yelled.

Ayla froze while Omicron got her helmet over her head again and rocked it into position. She was aware of him rotating the gasket ring, and she remembered him turning her roughly, then slapping the latches down. Whether or not he ever got as far as activating the helmet's purge, Ayla never knew.

CHAPTER THIRTY-NINE

SUPERUSER

LUKA FREQUENTLY STARTED HIS workday from home. He liked having an entire wall of polymeth across which to spread his workspace while planning out his shift, and so long as he remembered not to accept any incoming two-way video requests, he liked that he could do it all in nothing but his underwear. There were certainly plenty of pixels available at the foundry, but there was also too much competition for large, uninterrupted swaths of display real estate in quiet, secluded corners. And this morning—as evidenced by the hacked and modified cupcake decorator on the kitchen counter, along with the yellow-tinged glass tube and eviscerated envelope—Luka was in neither the mood, nor the condition, for distractions.

In his hand was a cup of sweetened and caffeinated soy porridge, prepared just thin enough that he could drink it without needing a spoon. It was his second cup, and though he was feeling jittery, the effects of the synthetically crystallized stimulant were not translating into anything like alertness or vigor. On mornings like these, Luka found he sometimes had to resort to the drastic measure of exercise in order to perk himself up enough to get through the day. A few invigorating laps through the swimming tubes at the Noe Valley Rec Center almost always made him feel somewhat less somber and lethargic, but if he was going to have time, he would need to have several tasks spooled up well in advance. After confirming that there were no urgent communications awaiting him, he brought up his own personal mash-up of the foundry's general order queue and the assembly exchange board.

There were any number of workspace shells available to *San Francisco* citizens, and new ones—generally forks or derivatives—being made available all the time. The rig's information and computing architecture was entirely service-oriented, which meant that any piece of code, as long as it contained implementations of the right protocols, could interact with anything for which it could construct well-formed requests and, of course, provide valid credentials. How the input to those services was gathered, and how the resulting output was subsequently presented, was entirely up to the workspace program, and of no concern whatsoever to the underlying infrastructure.

The workspace Luka used most often was an early version of something called DesignSpace. It was less of an operating system and more of a creative authoring environment, but rather than panels of drawing tools and editing options, the interface primarily supported the visual design of workflows across thousands of discoverable services, data providers, and remote sensors. Of course DesignSpace could execute the precompiled bundles of bytecode usually referred to as applications, but it was more common for its users to piece together their own interfaces and data visualizations, or to import and modify someone else's.

DesignSpace is what powered the sound track to Luka's morning. Several months ago, he'd spent a moderately intoxicated evening connecting an archive crawling service to a service capable of audio recognition and analysis that he'd trained to identify downbeat ambient electronica (original compositions only—none of that algorithmically generated crap). A third service analyzed the waveforms, and still another harmonically overlapped the tracks, seamlessly stitching them together into an infinite stream. Whenever Luka's "Fusion" workflow was running, all of his notifications were fed into yet another service that buffered them until they could be worked into the soundscape in a way that was just prominent enough to get his attention, but still subtle enough not to take him out of his zone.

There were those who found DesignSpace daunting to use, and Luka had to admit that if he'd been presented with it as an adult rather than from the time he began his technician training shortly after arriving on the *San Francisco*, he might have given up on it, as well. Like the majority of those on the rig, he would have likely opted for a workspace predicated more on constraints than on flexibility, intent, and creative expression. Existing within such traditional operating environments was comforting to most people, allowing them to feel productive almost immediately, however whenever Luka was in them, he couldn't help feeling like it was the computer using him rather than the other way around.

In exchange for increased complexity, Luka and his peers had the ability to optimize workflows as they became more familiar with particular tasks; to connect workflows in novel and creative ways; to experiment and iterate; and to customize their experiences so that they personally resonated as opposed to being designed for users of the lowest common denominator. By no means was Luka a computer scientist—and in fact, he had very little interest in the mysterious binary universe that lay beyond the analog-digital barrier—but by virtue of having been encouraged to explore the versatility of technology at an early age rather than be hindered by its limitations, he was undeniably part of an elite but expanding demographic that was frequently referred to aboard the rig as the nontechnical superuser.

Almost all of the visuals shared across the *San Francisco*'s computing infrastructure were multidimensional vectors (.mdv files), which meant they were comprised of equations and mathematical instructions that could be interpreted and rendered at any size, scale, rotation, and resolution. They could also contain an unlimited number of references to other .mdv files, which meant that they were essentially infinitely and seamlessly zoomable. It was theoretically possible, therefore, for Luka to bring up a schematic of something as large as the *San Francisco* itself, and not just zoom in on its individual structures, and then on the individual mechanisms housed within those structures, and then on the individual components housed within those mechanisms, but indeed continue gesturing and zooming either until his arms got tired, or he got lost in the relatively vast expanses of space between atoms. He supposed it was even possible to go subatomic, all the way down the current limits of humanity's understanding of the quantum-scale universe, where he would probably eventually find the broken asset icons that indicated data was either missing or malformed.

The model that Luka was evaluating this morning was a massive industrial ice auger, but rather than considering the most efficient and parallelized approach to assembling it, he was reflecting on how bold the Coronians had gotten. At least with the conveyers, grinding mills, and various types of drills and power shovels, there was some pretense—some amount of investigation or even interpretation involved in deciding whether the equipment was bound for orbit or not. Before Luka could be certain, he would run the packaging and shipping specifications through a suite of equations Omicron had prepared between excursions to Triple Seven and the Global Seed Vault, research the invoice and manifest details, and finally run everything by both Charlie and Tycho for second and third opinions. In reality, it was pretty easy to just eyeball which shipments were likely to be headed up to the Coronians versus which were staying aboard the *San Francisco* or intended for other terrestrial destinations, but if they were going to use mining equipment as a way to smuggle Cam up to *Equinox*, they needed to be as certain as possible.

But the Coronians seemed increasingly less concerned with covering their tracks, and the commission of a massive industrial ice auger didn't really leave very much room for interpretation. Luka was pretty certain that there hadn't been any natural ice formations on Earth in many decades, and even if everything Cadie was planning worked perfectly, it would probably still be centuries before any natural ice formed again. Therefore, the final destination of an autonomous, radiation-shielded, multibit tank driven by six independent snow tracks had to be worlds far more distant and exotic than any Luka knew.

Omicron's equations further bolstered Luka's theory: the components for the ice auger were to be distributed, packaged, and balanced in such a way as to be optimized for transport into orbit. This wasn't the first opportunity they had to try to sabotage the Coronians' mining operations, but it was possible that it could be one of their last. Luka already knew that the inquiry into how he and Charlie had obtained the schematics for the next major phase of the *San Francisco*'s development would almost certainly not conclude in their favor—regardless of what evidence was actually uncovered—and that their only hope was that Two Bulls could find a way to obstruct the investigation. Luka's fallback position was to claim that he had sculpted the model purely from memory after his meeting with Khang around the vat of ferrofluid (which she would undoubtedly deny ever took place), possibly steering the prosecution more toward misdemeanor charges of vandalism or inciting minor civil unrest rather than high treason or attempted mutiny. Regardless, if it came down to an official arraignment, Luka was pretty certain that he was gone, and the best they could hope for was that Tycho would go undiscovered, and that Charlie—after a little time in the quiet room and a few tearful sessions with her own custom instance of Ellie—would be allowed to stay and finish what they'd started.

Luka moved the ice auger into his queue, and then forwarded the schematics on to Charlie and Tycho to get their feedback. In his opinion, if they were ever going to make a move against the Coronians, the time was now.

COMPARISON OPERATOR

WHEN AYLA REGAINED CONSCIOUSNESS, she knew immediately where she was. The polymer surgical hood suspended from the ceiling told her that she was back aboard the *Hawk*, in the medical bay, lying on one of the two foldable cots. The muscles in her right shoulder were sore, and when she saw the jet injector in Omicron's hand, she understood why.

"It's OK," he told her. He was sitting on the cot opposite hers, and he set the pneumatic syringe down on a stack of crates next to two bulbs of water. The med bay doubled as a storage room for emergency rations, and inside the boxes were cartons of Ayla's least favorite sources of protein—mostly cured cockroaches and giant water bugs—which is why they were designated for emergency use only, and placed down here where they were well out of sight. "You're safe now."

She tried to judge the passage of time. Her intuition told her she wasn't out for all that long. Omicron was wearing the same mesh thermal lining he had on under his environment suit when they left, and when she looked down, she saw that she was still wearing her liquid-cooled polymer thermal wear. It had to be hours as opposed to days or weeks.

"What happened?" she asked.

"How's your breathing?" Omicron wanted to know.

She drew in a deep, experimental breath. "Normal, I think," she said. "God, I'm thirsty."

"Can you sit up?"

"I think so."

Ayla gathered herself into a sitting position and swung her legs around. She accepted a bulb of water from Omicron, and as she sucked on the jointed straw and swallowed, she realized that she had a vital band across her chest. There were two empty glass vials on top of the steel drug cabinet in the corner.

"Headache?" Omicron asked.

"A little," Ayla said. "Not bad."

"Good. It should be gone in a few minutes. Keep drinking."

Ayla sucked again at the straw. "So," she said through a tone of contrition, "I guess going inside wasn't such a good idea after all."

"You've had better," Omicron admitted.

"It was a trap, wasn't it?"

"It was."

"Why didn't it work on you?"

"The gas was some kind of a synthetic opioid aerosol," Omicron explained. "It was intended to immobilize rather than be fatal. The dose was much too small for me."

Ayla frowned as she sucked the cool, fresh water through the straw and swallowed. "That's kind of strange, isn't it?"

"What?"

"Immobilizing. If they really wanted to keep people out, why not go a step further?"

"I don't know," Omicron said. "Let's just be thankful they didn't."

"Where are we now?" Ayla asked. She leaned to the side so she could see past Omicron, to an auxiliary terminal in the wall.

By default, it showed a summary of the ship's status. She could see that they were headed east at a full thirty-five knots—close to top speed for the *Hawk*—and then she saw something else. She leaned forward and squinted to make sure, then looked back at Omicron.

"What the hell?" she said. "Where'd we get all the power?"

"It turns out you were right," Omicron said. "I found full capacitors inside."

"Where?" Ayla asked him. She wasn't sure why that was important, but for some reason, it was. Perhaps it was just a way to get something more out of him about what had become of her home.

"Just inside on the loading dock."

There was something about Omicron's story—and something about the subtle reluctance with which he seemed to be doling it out—that didn't feel right to Ayla. "There were just a bunch of completely full, completely unguarded capacitors right inside the airlock for anyone to take?"

"I wouldn't exactly say they were unguarded," Omicron countered.

"Why are we moving so fast?"

Omicron glanced behind him at the terminal, then looked back at Ayla. "We need to get to the GSV and back as soon as we can."

"I understand that," Ayla said, "but we can't sustain this kind of speed for long."

"I'll back it down," Omicron said. "I'm just trying to make up for lost time. You lie back and get some rest."

"Omicron," Ayla said. "What aren't you telling me?"

The Neo gave her a perplexed look. "What do you mean?"

"I mean there's something you're clearly not telling me. We stumble into a trap meant to knock people out rather than kill them. You just happen to find a bunch of full capacitors right inside the airlock. And now I wake up to find that we're obviously running away from someone or something. Now I'll ask you again: what aren't you telling me?"

"I'll slow us down," Omicron said. "You're right. We don't need to be moving this fast."

There were still several milliliters of water left in Ayla's bulb, and when she threw it against the med bay hatch, it erupted.

"*Damnit!*" she screamed. "Stop treating me like a fucking child and tell me what's going on. This is *my* ship, and I don't appreciate you keeping things from me."

She stopped and clenched her eyes shut. Her fingertips went up to her temples and pressed.

"Are you OK?" Omicron asked.

Ayla took a deep breath through her nose, let it out her mouth, and opened her eyes. "I'm fine," she said with forced composure. She saw that Omicron was looking at the panel on the wall above the cot, probably evaluating her vital signs. "Now tell me what's really going on before I turn us around and go find out for myself."

Omicron watched her for a moment as though weighing her threat. "OK," he eventually said. "I'll tell you, but you need to be prepared. It's going to upset you."

"I've been through a lot more than you know," Ayla said. "I'm a lot tougher than you think."

Omicron took the second bulb of water off the stack of crates and handed it to Ayla. "The trap set off a beacon," he began. "That's why I'm trying to put some distance between us and Nanortalik."

"Why would it set off a beacon?" Ayla asked. She sipped from the second bulb, then held the cool receptacle against her forehead.

"So whoever set it would know to come back."

"Obviously," Ayla said. "But come back for what?"

"For collection."

"Collection?" Ayla repeated. "Human trafficking?"

"No," Omicron said. "Not human trafficking."

"Then what?" Ayla pressed.

"For power."

Ayla shook her head. "I don't understand."

"There's a great deal of chemical energy stored in the human body," Omicron said. "Especially when it's still alive."

Ayla's expression changed from confusion to horror. "Oh my God," she said. "Tell me what you found in there."

Omicron hesitated while he appeared to search for the right word. "Machinery," he finally said.

"What *specifically* did you find, Omicron? What *kind* of machinery?"

"Vats," Omicron said. "Decomposition vats. Full of . . . human remains. Connected to capacitors."

Ayla's eyes flicked away from Omicron to the terminal behind him, then back. "You didn't," she said.

"Didn't what?"

"Please tell me that's not where you got the power, Omicron. Please tell me we're not running on electricity that came from human remains."

"I told you you didn't want to know."

"My God, Omicron," Ayla said. She shook her head. "How could you do that?"

"Do *what*?" Omicron shouted. He stood suddenly and Ayla flinched. She realized at that moment that he wasn't as indifferent to what he'd just witnessed as he'd been trying to convey. "Take free caps just because of where they came from? It's done. Those people are dead. I could have left it there for someone else to take and probably use to kill more people, or we could use it to try to change the world. I'm sorry if that doesn't meet your standards of morality."

Ayla was sitting up straight on her cot now, eerily composed. She did not look like a girl who was about to cry, yet when she blinked, tears spilled from both eyes.

"I'm sorry," Omicron said. He sat back down, closed his eyes, and breathed. "I didn't mean that. I'm sorry for what I said, and I'm sorry for what happened to your home. That's why I didn't want to tell you."

"I swear to God, Omicron," Ayla said. "As hard as I try, I just don't understand this fucking world we live in."

"I know," Omicron said. "I know."

"I mean how can places like Triple Seven exist where they're willing to take us in and protect us just out of respect for Costa, and places like the *San Francisco* where we were almost drowned as part of a business transaction? How can people like you and Costa and Cadie and Luka and Charlie all exist in the same world as people like Nsonowa, and all the human traffickers and raiders and cannibals out there, and people who use other people as sources of energy?" She paused and gave Omicron a piercing and imploring look. "I don't know how to make sense if it all, Omicron. I honestly don't."

Omicron looked down at the floor for moment, then leaned back against the wall. "Do you remember how the UNVs work?"

It took Ayla a moment to grasp the non sequitur. "The sail-boats?" she asked him. "Why?"

"Do you remember how I explained that the sail generates lift in one direction, and the keel generates lift in another direction, creating a resultant vector of momentum? A sort of balance of forces that moves the boat forward?"

"I guess," Ayla said. She wiped her cheeks with her palms and sniffed. "So?"

"That's how I make sense of humanity," Omicron said. "There are millions of individual dynamics out there moving in all different directions. Some of them compound, and some of them cancel each other out, but in the end, you're left with a resultant vector—a balance of forces that moves us all forward, no matter how slowly and how painfully."

"But is it really *forward*?" Ayla asked. "Sometimes I can't tell which direction we're moving. One day I think things are getting better, and the next day I honestly think it would be better if something finally just wiped us all out and the world started over again without us."

"I don't know," Omicron said. "I think all you can do is contribute your own force in whatever way you can and just hope that it helps to move things in the right direction."

Ayla stared at a spot on the floor for a moment, then looked up. "Omicron," she said. "We have to go back."

"Back where?"

"To Nanortalik," she said. "We can't leave it like that. We can't let more people die."

Omicron watched her for a moment, and Ayla could tell he was trying to decide how much of something else to reveal. "Don't worry," he finally said. "I took care of it."

Ayla's eyebrows went up. "What does that mean?" she asked. "What did you do?"

Omicron turned to check the status of the ship, then turned back to Ayla. "The device they used to hack the airlock," he said. "It was right inside. It was just an old sixty-four-bit microcontroller. No encryption, no security. They were obviously assuming nobody would ever make it through."

"And . . ." Ayla prompted. "What did you do?"

"I inverted a comparison operator."

"What the hell does that mean?"

"Whoever did this injected a condition into the decontamination and air exchange algorithms," Omicron began. "It compares the biometric signatures of the people in the airlock to a set of hard-coded signatures. If any of them match, nothing but nitrogen and oxygen are exchanged. But if there are no matches, in addition to nitrogen and oxygen, they introduce just a few parts per million of a colorless and odorless synthetic opioid from a tank they spliced into the ducts."

"What are you saying?" Ayla asked. "You mean the people who set the trap can't spring it?"

"That's what it *used* to mean," Omicron said. "But after inverting the comparison operator in the condition—just by adding one little exclamation mark to the code—it means the exact opposite. Now the people who set the trap are the only people in the world who can spring it."

Ayla's eyes widened. "Holy shit," she said. "Omicron, that's brilliant. But won't it just knock them out? Won't they just change it back after they wake up?"

"Well," Omicron said, "I also redefined the atmospheric ratios. I guarantee whoever set that trap will never wake up again."

Amusement suddenly broke through Ayla's somber mood, and she surprised herself by laughing. But just as quickly, she covered her mouth.

"I guess that's not funny," she said. "I mean we're talking about people's lives."

Omicron shrugged and allowed a subtle and mischievous grin to spread across his heavy features. "I don't know," he said. "I think it might be just a little bit funny."

Ayla hadn't realized how much she needed the endorphins until she started laughing again, and despite the pounding in her head, found that she could not stop.

CHAPTER FORTY-ONE

PSYCHOLOGICAL TRIAGE

THE NOE VALLEY REC CENTER was the newest building on the *San Francisco*, and probably also the boldest and the most advanced. It was built diagonally opposite the quantum battery bank, which was neither by coincidence nor by accident. Every flywheel and resistive mechanism housed within the orderly formations of eclectic exercise contraptions drove a compact generator connected to a superconductive cable that ran down through the floor panels to a series of junctions eventually terminating on the other side of Sunset and Market, feeding what amounted to mostly symbolic quantities of wattage into the mining rig's power grid—enough to fuel plenty of political bluster, but not nearly enough to offend the Coronians.

When the arrangement was initially proposed, so too were citywide minimum exercise quotas that supporters touted as a way to both improve general health and wellbeing, and boost the per-citizen municipal power allocation (which, at the time, was far too low for anyone to live off of, and was now only modestly less inadequate). While construction of the new rec center and its quantum battery bank umbilical were both approved, the exercise mandates were not. A nutritionist at the Pacific Medical Center showed that forcing everyone to be regularly active would inevitably result in them consuming more calories, which, in turn, would increase pressure on Yerba Buena and ultimately end up costing more energy through expanded food production than it could possibly hope to generate. Of course the study was commissioned by a self-assembled panel of council members who, if their physiques were any indication, could easily be counted among the most sedentary of the entire crew. No serious objections were raised, though, since those with physically demanding occupations usually didn't have the energy to exercise regularly anyway, and many of those with less active careers lacked the volition, positioning both parties squarely in the unfamiliar territory of consensus.

Luka did not have a regular workout routine. To him, a routine implied obligation, and obligation implied demands, and demands felt just a little too much like authority. Even from himself, Luka did not easily accept orders.

Instead of a regular schedule, Luka stopped by the rec center whenever he felt like it, and when he got there, he did whatever he felt like doing. Sometimes that was strength training, sometimes it was cardiovascular, occasionally it was rock climbing or boxing, and every now and then, it was screwing around with the virtual reality cubicles that made you feel like you were running through fields of wildflowers, or biking spiraled ridges carved into mountain slopes, or rowing against the current of the Amazon river. But when Luka was feeling especially dull and languid and irritable—usually after a night of intoxicated sculpting, solitary brooding, or both—the best thing for him was a few laps through the cool blue swimming tubes.

The swimming tubes both originated from, and terminated in, the aqua center on the top floor, but in-between, they snaked among all five floors of the rec center, and occasionally even veered outside among the cantilevered decks. They reminded Luka of an image he once found in the archives of a cast someone made by pouring molten aluminum into an ant nest, producing a beautiful piece of natural sculpture that seemed to work out quite well for the artist, though decidedly less well for the ants. The water in the tubes was kept well oxygenated for the sake of swimmers' full-face gill masks, and distributed throughout the tubes at regular elevation intervals were pressure-bearing wet locks that both helped to keep one's ears comfortable, and alleviated any concerns about decompression sickness.

Luka sometimes did surface swimming, as well, but there was something about being completely submerged for as long as forty-five minutes that was an entirely different kind of workout. And, as he had reluctantly admitted to Ellie while serving time on Hexagon Row, the experience was also a form of surrogate socialization. While meandering throughout the building, the turquoise passages brought Luka into close proximity with as many as several hundred fellow *San Francisco* citizens while, at the same time, serving as an impenetrable barrier. The insight Ellie showed by labeling his behavior as "social and emotional voyeurism" had both stunned and impressed Luka.

The aqua center was busy and, as was typical in the mornings, reverberantly cacophonous. There always seemed to be someone shouting about something from somewhere around the pool, but the acoustics of the room usually made it impossible to locate the source. Luka kept his head down and looked at the tile as he skirted the heated lap lanes in order to avoid any awkward acknowledgments, or worse, empty and meaningless conversation in which neither party had any real interest. He didn't need to take a very good look around him to know that he was being watched. After having finally recovered from the infamy of sending out cryptic prophecies about the Coronians and shutting down all the power on the entire rig, he had once again become a curiosity, and one of the primary topics of the ceaseless stream of ship-wide gossip. At least this time, he had Charlie to share the distinction with.

Luka stood at the edge of the swimming tube pool and hiked his trunks up on his bony hips. The silicone strap of the gill mask he'd taken from the cage in the locker room was around his wrist and the apparatus bumped against the back of one leg while the two short-blade fins he was carrying bumped against the other. One of the advantages of being an assembly technician was that Luka knew all about almost every single new product available on the rig (whenever technicians came across anything novel, they usually posted it to the exchange board for everyone to make snarky comments on), therefore he was aware that his simple synthetic drawstring shorts were considered hopelessly obsolete athletic apparel. Had he been more concerned with both function and fashion, he'd purchase a full-body suit coated in tiny synthetic hydrodynamic denticles, inspired by the skin of fast and sleek and long-extinct oceanic predators.

Gill masks had to soak for several seconds before they were maximally efficient, so Luka tossed the contraption into the pool ahead of him to give it a head start on the saturation process. He managed to maintain his balance while slipping the fins over his feet and working the straps over his heels, then he got the soft silicone frog palms untangled from the inside of his pockets and pulled them on over his fingers. After taking a moment to brace himself, Luka reached down and grasped the edge of the pool, then dropped into the chilly water beside the mask.

The swimming tubes weren't heated, so Luka's skinny body always experienced a slight shock at the sudden temperature change. His first time in, as he shivered and hyperventilated, he was incredulous at having to endure not just the initial cold, but then the slight thermocline beyond the first wet lock that reduced the temperature of the water a few degrees more. But he quickly realized that whoever designed the system actually knew what he or she was doing. Negotiating the network of tubes required pretty significant effort, so had the water been heated, within minutes you would have felt as though you were swimming through a giant, boiling chemistry experiment.

When Luka saw the oxygen patch on the mask turn blue beneath the surface, he took and held a deep breath, went under, pulled the mask down over his head, and tightened the straps. His finger found and depressed the purge valve between the gill fronds, and when he felt the pocket of air form in front of his face, he opened his eyes and blinked away the moisture. Even though gill masks were relatively simple devices (Luka had assembled several variations of them over the years) and generally considered extremely reliable, as always, he took several experimental breaths and confirmed that the oxygen patch remained blue. The capillary-scale technology could be susceptible to deterioration if exposed to dry heat for too long, but from what Luka understood, as long as a gill mask worked during your first few breaths, it was pretty much guaranteed to keep working for the rest of your swim. And even if it didn't, as long as you were paying attention to the color of the patch, and as long as CO_2 was being properly vented, there would be plenty of residual oxygen to keep you alive until you got back up to the surface.

Luka descended headfirst through the wet lock into the even colder water below. He followed the path he had memorized, which he knew would result in the longest possible circuit and maximum coverage of the building. Each lap would take him along the perimeter of the cardio floor and directly above the track where he could race against the runners below him; briefly outside the building where he could see into the lush green helix of the Yerba Buena Gardens shrouded in thick morning aeroponic nutrient mist; directly through the focus of the circular strength training center and amid dozens of individuals struggling against complex and highly customized distributions of dynamic resistance; alongside the most technically challenging climbing walls with their coarse molded textures, their polygonal overhangs, and their strategically spaced grips and holds; discretely through the corners of the heated yoga studio, the dojo with its synthetic tatami floor, the racquet courts with their configurable glass walls, and the muted salon throughout which the tube cast serene undulating shadows; and finally, before heading back up, the café where members exhibited their physical achievements while attempting to conceal all signs of effort.

Luka negotiated the tubes with the agility of a dolphin. Swimming, he discovered, was more than just a form of exercise for him. After his time with Ellie on Hexagon Row, isolating himself underwater had become a critical cognitive exercise—a way of achieving a completely placid mental surface, and then waiting to see what bubbled up to the surface. A form of meditation, perhaps. There was certainly no shortage of challenges from Luka's past that he could use the time to explore and process, but through the mysterious logic of psychological triage, he found that it was events from the last several months that tended to take precedence now.

During other recent swims, Luka had reflected upon the fact that he was now under constant threat of being arrested, tried, and very likely exiled, and even if Khang couldn't get rid of him in the short-term, he knew that his time aboard the *San Francisco*, one way or another, was probably coming to an end. He'd thought about how they were all making big short-term bets on shifting the balance of power between *Equinox* and Earth, but the payoff—if it came at all—was likely to be so far in the future that it was possible none of them would ever get a chance to see it, and might never even know whether or not it worked. And finally, he had tried to reconcile the fact that the only relationship that didn't make him feel like he was cheating on Val was, for reasons he did not understand, whatever it was he had with Charlie, and yet it was Ayla who he now found himself fantasizing about.

But these were not the things Luka found himself dwelling on this morning. As he propelled himself through the café, and then on through the wall into the serenity of the salon, he realized that what was bothering him more than anything else was the ice auger.

Until this morning, sending Cam up to *Equinox* had been an abstract notion—something that, as long as you didn't think about it too much, seemed to have a reasonable chance of success. But now that it was actually happening—now that Tycho and Luka had modified the shipping manifest in such a way as to leave an entire crate free for Cam and all of his life-support equipment—the whole idea suddenly seemed ridiculous. Even if he survived orbital insertion, there was no guarantee that anyone or anything would come pick him up before his consumables ran out. It might be years before the Coronians needed the auger, and it probably made more sense to leave it in orbit than to store it on or near *Equinox*. Even if they retrieved it right away, instead of bringing it into the station for inspection and giving Cam a chance to slip away and infiltrate their mining operations, the Coronians might decide to send the payload directly to its final icy destination millions of kilometers away. And finally, even in the tremendously unlikely event that everything just happened to unfold exactly as they needed it to, there was still the extremely uncertain question of not only getting Cam home, but then of finding him again before his capsule sank, or before he was captured or murdered by the crew of a nearby vessel drawn to his location either by the energy signature of the splashdown, or by Cam's subsequent beacon.

The idea of smuggling Cam onto *Equinox* had evolved a great deal over time, and Luka could no longer distinguish exactly who was responsible for which aspects of it, but there was one thing about it that seemed particularly perplexing. Initially Cadie had been entirely opposed to this part of their plan—extremely reluctant to allow her final connection to her home and to her former life to be exposed to so much risk. But at some point, her attitude had dramatically shifted. Perhaps it was the prospect of Cam locating her daughter, but from the timing of it, that wasn't the impression that Luka got. Her transformation seemed to have occurred in isolation rather than in response to debate or discussion, and although at times it was subtle, both Luka and Charlie agreed that it was undeniably there. One day Cadie was determined to do everything in her power to hold on to Cam, and the next, she acted as though absolutely everything depended on him successfully boarding the space station that, directly or indirectly, held every human being left on the planet captive.

CHAPTER FORTY-TWO

BLACK TEARS

THE POLYCARBONATE CYLINDER CONNECTING the port on the southern tip of the Norwegian island of Svalbard to the Longyearbyen Pod System two hundred kilometers away was not intended solely for comfort and convenience. Rather, the reduced-pressure tube—along with the pressurized capsules that were conveyed through it on top of a millimeter-thick cushion of air—was the only safe mode of passage. It was technically possible to get as close as one and a half kilometers to the Global Seed Vault by sailing up the Isfjorden inlet. However, all six kilometers of its mouth had been blockaded by a braided, galvanized, electrified mesh, and the entire body of water behind it was well stocked with thousands of variable-depth mines retrofitted with magnetic anomaly sensors that steered them resolutely toward anything with a metal hull. The vault was easily within walking distance of the airstrip to its north, but all two and a half kilometers of the runway were secured beneath nets of a type of synthetic spider silk sticky and strong enough to ensnare vertical takeoff and landing aircraft, and sharp enough to shear aircraft attempting traditional landings into long strips of titanium ribbon. Enough of the island was patrolled by sentinels and littered with booby traps of various levels of sophistication and brutality that the only sensible way in or out was by a combination of hypertube and express invitation.

During the trip from Nanortalik to Svalbard, Omicron explained to Ayla the justification for all the surveillance and security on and around the archipelago: the Coronians badly wanted what the Longyearbyen Pod System had. The Svalbard Global Seed Vault was established before the Solar Age, and started out as a type of backup seed bank funded by a combination of philanthropic software tycoons and government entities. It was a remote and secure location where samples of the world's most nutritious, productive, and therefore calorically critical agricultural products were kept frozen as contingencies against drought, flooding, fungus, swarms of locusts, civil war, nuclear war, asteroid strikes, ecophagy, or anything else that could permanently wipe out entire strains of crops. Over time, though, it became more of a generalized gene bank and a mecca for the world's top geneticists, who greatly accelerated their curation efforts as the Solar Age came to an abrupt end, struggling to stay one step ahead of mass extinction events, and aggregating the world's databases of gene sequences and preserving DNA samples with the hope that the technology would one day exist to not only re-terraform the entire planet, but possibly even repopulate it with a significant portion of its former biodiversity. The project could best be conceptualized as a kind of genetic and cryonic Noah's ark, and as such, was of tremendous interest to the Coronians.

Of course, nobody doubted the Coronians' ability to completely obliterate the GSV—or, more likely, have it completely obliterated on their behalf—but nobody believed they would do so until they somehow gained access to everything inside. Svalbard security, therefore, was not so much intended to prevent a catastrophic attack as it was to prevent the theft of the data and physical specimens that was guaranteed to immediately precede it.

Stopping the Coronians from buying what they wanted, coercing others into procuring it for them, or remotely gaining access to databases and helping themselves to sensitive information was far from a simple matter. Primary protection against hackers came in the form of the tried-and-true air gap: computers physically disconnected from any and all types of networks. However, air-gapping a machine—as system administrators were constantly learning the hard way—wasn't quite as easy as it sounded. First of all, none of the hardware could contain any type of peripheral port through which an infiltrator could surreptitiously connect a transmitter or receiver. Second, machines that were potential targets needed to have their speakers and microphones removed so that they couldn't be infected—and subsequently infect their nearby peers—by high-frequency binary chatter. Third, they could contain no optical sensors whatsoever through which vulnerabilities could be exploited with a simple line-of-sight laser, or even cleverly encoded flashes of ambient light. And finally, they had to run on isolated batteries with redundant pulse suppressors to ensure that malicious instructions weren't being injected directly into CPU cores using minute power fluctuations. It wasn't enough anymore to simply pull the network cable out of the back of a server and assume it was safe; rather, for systems to be considered secure, they needed to be hand-built with verified components and spend their entire functional lives rigorously quarantined inside biometrically secured, acoustically dampened, and electromagnetically impervious Faraday cages.

Ironically, physical access security—while logistically intensive—was actually much simpler. It was mostly a matter of manpower, checkpoints, body scans, redundant authentication, and the quantum randomization of routines and schedules. The primary challenge was keeping entire garrisons sharp day to day, minute to minute, and even second to second. The enemy of virtual defenses is often the exotic and the unknown, but the enemy of physical security is usually just boredom.

It tended to help that the lives of everyone in the Longyearbyen Pod System—and indeed everyone on the entire Svalbard archipelago—depended on their impeccable and uncompromising success. But just for a little extra incentive, the stewards of the Svalbard Global Seed Vault took additional precautions. No less than 10 percent of all traffic in and out of the GSV was a deliberate and staged attempt at penetration, and anyone associated with any lapses in security were—along with his or her entire family—escorted to the European mainland on the very next ferry, provided with a few days' worth of rations, and left to fend for themselves against the subterraneans known locally as "muldvarp mennesker," or the mole people.

Ayla had seen security implemented in all kinds of ways since she left home, but nothing quite like this. They couldn't drop anchor off the Sorkapp shore because they weren't allowed to get close enough that any of their anchors would be able to reach anything, so they virtually anchored the *Hawk* to coordinates transmitted to them over the radio and, as instructed, waited on the forward deck, fully suited and unarmed. There was a viscous black rain falling that day, so Ayla suggested they use the *Anura* to shuttle themselves ashore in order to make everyone's lives a little easier, but her proposal was tersely rejected, and instead she and Omicron were conveyed via a heavily armed tender, then escorted to the hypertube terminal by men in black environment suits with tinted visors wielding long, slender electromagnetic pistols.

The terminal was a round and elevated carousel beneath a transparent geodesic dome that, due to the current weather, looked to Ayla like it was weeping black tears. The airlock was housed inside an adjacent silo and raised them to the level of the platform during multiple cycles of high-pressure sanitization and thermal sublimation, and then eventually the final air exchange. Upon exiting, they were instructed to remove everything they had on and leave it in side-by-side lockers, and to do so without any form of communication whatsoever. Ayla looked at Omicron for confirmation, and he responded with a single reassuring nod.

After a series of scans, they were handed thin, waxy, dark gray outfits similar to surgical scrubs and directed through another secure door. There was a bench in the room along with a young nurse who drew blood and placed the vials into a fractionation centrifuge, closed the lid, and waited. Ayla noted that the two guards watched the nurse carefully as she did her job, and each verified the results independently before using their combined biometric signatures to open the next door. The nurse followed them out of the room, and Ayla guessed that her work was not yet complete.

Once they were on the platform, Ayla understood the reason for the carousel. There was the hiss of rapid pressurization as a translucent hatch rolled aside and the hypertube capsule finished transitioning between the airlock and the terminal. It slid into a set of gates, and then the giant turntable began rotating it so that it would be able to go back in the direction from which it came. The front of the capsule was fashioned as a single angled air scoop that gave the entire vessel an aggressive and almost angry disposition, and while it turned, Ayla wondered why it hadn't been designed to simply operate in reverse. She knew just enough about engineering to know that every additional moving part meant additional wear and maintenance, along with an increased likelihood of failure, and a giant rotating platter seemed like just the kind of thing that would love to malfunction. But as the rear swung into view, she saw that its operation did not allow it to be designed symmetrically: the back of the capsule was a giant recessed and bladed turbofan.

The capsule door pivoted upward on its hinge, and inside was a single occupant. Ayla assumed that the man was Claus Odegaard, the geneticist with whom Omicron had been corresponding. He was an older man with thinning, shoulder-length hair that still had some blond interspersed among the gray, and a full and somewhat matted beard that continued well down into the neck of his shirt. His lab coat was khaki rather than white, which made him look slightly more formal than academic, and when he released a strap that dangled from the ceiling and stepped out onto the platform, Ayla was surprised to discover that a man with access to so much technology would choose to wear perfectly round wire-framed spectacles. There were clearly many years of hard-earned fatigue evident in the old man's slate-gray eyes, deeply furrowed face, and stooped posture, but not yet enough to entirely dampen a smoldering of passion somewhere beneath—an ember that clearly flared at the sight of Omicron.

By the old man's side was a small, black, thermal-molded box that he clutched by a hinged handle. As he approached, the nurse appeared from behind Ayla and received the case as it was extended toward her, the old man's gray but gleaming eyes never leaving Omicron's.

"Astounding," Odegaard breathed with an unmistakable tone of wonder. A smile spread beneath his whiskers as he extended his hand toward Omicron. "I'm Dr. Odegaard," he said, then abruptly corrected himself. "*Claus* Odegaard."

There was a subtle Nordic cadence to his voice that reminded Ayla of home. Omicron's giant hand enveloped Odegaard's and the old man looked down, seemingly pleased with the spectacular mismatch. He took a few additional moments to inspect Omicron's features before finally relinquishing his grip. It was only then that he seemed to notice Ayla.

He apologized and remade his introduction, this time with much less gawking. The nurse had unlatched the case and removed a pistol-like device that reminded Ayla of a jet injector, but bigger and clearly more complex. The nurse stepped toward Omicron but the doctor intervened.

"No no no," Odegaard objected. "Please. I will do it myself."

The device, Ayla realized as the doctor took possession, was a genetic core sampler. It used a hollow cylindrical scalpel to collect a plug of hair, skin, fat, muscle, blood vessels, and possibly even a few tiny chips of bone. The price for the seeds that Cadie required was nothing less than fresh genetic material so rare that the GSV had thus far been unable to add it to their stores: complete and viable DNA from a living *Homo neanderthalensis*—courtesy, no less, of their chief enemy and rival.

Omicron rolled the tight sleeve of his scrubs up over his thick bicep, and then the bulk of his shoulder. There was a layer of fine, dark hair over the pale skin, and below, an immense mass of muscle. Once the old man had the core sampler set, he watched Omicron rather than the incision site. There was a high-pitched whirring interspersed with pneumatic suction and for the very first time, Ayla saw pain register throughout Omicron's heavy features. He didn't flinch, but it was clear to Ayla that it was only with great effort that he suppressed his instincts to pull away, and probably to retaliate.

Odegaard lowered the sampler and Ayla glimpsed a dark purple hole in Omicron's shoulder. It began to spill blood but the nurse was quick to catch it and apply pressure. She lifted the gauze and directed a thin stream of fluid from a syringe into the wound while catching the pinkish runoff. The fluid eventually turned clear as the coagulant closed the incision, and when the nurse applied a new patch of gauze, securing it with an adhesive wrap around Omicron's entire arm, the dressing remained clean and white.

The old man watched the display on the core sampler, and his smile broadened.

"Thank you, Omicron," he said as he handed the device back to the nurse. "Sincerely."

Omicron nodded as he gently unfurled his sleeve and worked it down over the wrap. Whether it was bleeding or not, Ayla couldn't imagine that his arm wouldn't be extremely tender for several days.

"Are we clear?" Ayla asked the doctor.

"Yes, of course," the old man said. "Please, come."

He turned and crossed the platform, then stepped back into the hypertube capsule. The back of his khaki coat was wrinkled and his wiry, white hair tangled—the look of a man who was in the advanced stages of withdrawing into his own internal world. The nurse and two guards waited for Omicron and Ayla to board before stepping in, as well. One of the guards moved to the panel at the front of the vessel and touched the polymeth surface.

The door lowered on its hydraulic cylinders. When it was nearly flush, something caught the latches at the bottom and pulled it the rest of the way in, hardening the door's seal. Ayla could tell from the feeling in her ears that the capsule was pressurizing. They began to move, and although the acceleration was gentle and their movement perfectly smooth, when she saw the old man reach up and grasp an overhead strap, she knew to do the same. They stopped again—just as fluidly as they'd started—and Ayla envisioned the outer airlock hatch rolling closed behind them and the seal being set. The windows in the capsule were long horizontal strips, but there was nothing to see at the moment except the thick steel wall of the airlock. The capsule started moving again, exiting the chamber and beginning a smooth but constant acceleration.

Ayla was hoping for better visibility, but the black rain clung to the outside surface of the tube and left an ashy film, though from what she could see, she decided she probably wasn't missing all that much. There was little more out there than dark peaks of desolate crags piercing a sheath of smog as thick as the ice sheets had probably once been. As she continued to peer through the viewport, searching for signs of civilization, she experienced a mounting sense of disorientation caused by what she identified as an incongruity between her internal sense of motion, and the incredible speed at which the landscape was passing. It made her wonder if the old man had grasped the strap not because the ride might be bumpy or jerky, but because it was actually so smooth.

It seemed Omicron was having similar thoughts.

"If I may ask," he said, "what kind propulsion system does the hypertube use?"

"Not at all," the old man said. Omicron was stooped forward so he could see out the viewport and the old man was looking up at him, watching his expression intently. "Linear induction motors."

"What about the turbofan in the back?"

"Purely for moving air from in front of us to behind us while siphoning off just enough to maintain a cushion underneath."

"Interesting," Omicron said. "But why not just create a vacuum and use a combination of electromagnetic levitation and propulsion?"

"Indeed," the doctor replied, and Ayla could tell that it was not the discussion of hypertube transport theory that was exciting him, but rather the experience of having a technical conversation with an actual living, breathing Neanderthal. "That was the designers' original plan, but they found it impractical to maintain a near-perfect vacuum over such a distance."

"So it's a *reduced*-pressure system," Omicron hypothesized, "and you use the air to your advantage to create a cushion and offset friction."

The old man's eyes smiled behind his spectacles. "Correct," he said.

The windows instantly blackened as they entered what Ayla assumed was a tunnel. Other than the quality of the light inside the capsule, there were no other discernible changes.

"How much pressure do you maintain in the tube?"

"An average of one millibar," the old man said.

Omicron squinted for a moment, and Ayla knew he was probably snapping together a quick virtual prototype in his mind. "You must not need very many induction motors then," he said.

"How many do you think?" the old man challenged. His scrutiny of Omicron intensified.

"Over a span of two hundred kilometers?" Omicron said. "Probably just two. One to accelerate and one to decelerate."

"Three, actually," the old man said. The pattern of his whiskers indicated that he was grinning beneath. "One in the middle—just in case we get stuck."

The viewports brightened again and Ayla could see that visibility was slightly better now. They were rapidly decelerating, and once again she felt disoriented. The sensation was a kind of dizzying mental parallax—a disquieting discrepancy between what she was seeing with her eyes, and what her inner ears were reporting.

The windows turned the same dull metallic tone as the airlock in the southern terminal and Ayla believed she felt the capsule stop. A moment later, it crept forward into the carousel gates and began its rotation. Ayla countered the movement by turning in the opposite direction so she could keep an eye on the structure that was just barely visible in the distance through the transparent geodesic dome: a massive concrete block that looked like a wedge that had been pounded into the surrounding sandstone. The Svalbard Global Seed Vault.

Her view was interrupted by a small procession on the platform. The door lifted and Ayla experienced a moment of panic when she saw that at least half a dozen armed guards were waiting for them. But their weapons were not raised, and the one in the middle stood behind a steel-blue thermal molded case at least twice as big as the portable inductive capacitors she kept on the *Hawk*. It was bulky enough that it could not be easily lifted by a single person, but there was a handle protruding from the top and wheels recessed into its base. Ayla had seen—and in fact both handled and transported—similar environmentally stable crates several times, and therefore knew that it probably contained valuable biological material. In this case, a small sampling of some of the last seeds in existence on the entire planet.

Omicron was the first one out of the capsule. The guards on the platform stirred, and although their weapons remained in a natural and nonthreatening position, Ayla could see them adjust their grips. Ayla and Odegaard followed, as did the two guards. The nurse carried Omicron's core sample through a set of secure folding doors in the back of the terminal that snapped shut behind her.

The old man presented the case. "Everything we discussed," he said.

Ayla was less interested in the case than she was in the building outside, and she looked down through the dome's semitransparent weeping panels at the GSV below them. Rather than the structure having been built into the side of a mountain, it now looked to her as though it had somehow always been there, and that the surrounding stone only needed to be chipped away to reveal it.

"Aren't we going in?" Ayla asked.

"I'm afraid that's impossible," the old man said. "This is as far as you go."

Omicron looked down at the stooped doctor. "How do we know everything's here?"

"You're free to take an inventory, of course," he said. "However, I would very much recommend you keep it sealed. Everything is in perfect cryogenic stasis, and from what I understand, she has a long journey ahead of her."

Ayla looked at the old man, then up at Omicron, and what she saw made her entire world tilt. Instantly she recognized the very same expression of pain and regret that had preceded some of the very worst moments of her entire life.

"What is he talking about?" Ayla asked him. She could feel everyone watching her and she tried to maintain as much composure as she could. "Omicron. What is he talking about?"

"Ayla," Omicron began. "I'm sorry."

"Sorry for *what*?"

"I'm not going back with you."

Of all the emotions Ayla might have experienced at that moment, she was surprised that what she felt more than anything else was stupidity. She felt stupid for not knowing what everyone else seemed to know; stupid for thinking that Omicron would be happy staying with her for any longer than he absolutely had to; stupid for once again allowing herself to get attached to someone when she should have known by now that nothing ever lasted, and that nobody ever stayed. It was impossible at that point for her to contain her emotions, and her eyes filled with tears.

"This can't be happening," she said as much to herself as to him. "Please tell me this isn't happening."

"The price of the seeds wasn't the core sample," Omicron told her. "That was just for verification. That was just to get us this far. The price of everything in this case—everything Cadie needs to give the planet a fresh start—is me."

Ayla looked at the old man, and when she shook her head, tears fell from her cheeks. "You can't do this," she told him. "You can't have him. He isn't *property.*"

The old man's expression had grown disturbingly neutral. His hands were in his coat pockets and all traces of excitement from having just gotten a new toy were gone. He looked over his glasses at Omicron as though to indicate that this was between the two of them, and that she should be left out of it.

"It's more complicated than that," Omicron told Ayla. "This is my choice."

"But *why*?" Ayla asked. She took a step back as though suddenly fearful of the man who had saved her life so many times. It wasn't his physical presence that intimidated her, but rather his unexpected ability—and his apparent willingness—to be so careless with her emotions. "Why would do you this? Why wouldn't you at least *tell* me?"

"Because this is almost certainly the most important thing that you and I will ever do," Omicron said. "And I knew if I told you, you wouldn't have come."

"That's *bullshit*," Ayla spat out. "This is just an excuse to get rid of me, isn't it? You have better things to do with your life now than babysit."

"That's not it at all," Omicron insisted. "I owe you everything. I owe you my life. I owe you my *freedom*."

"So you repay me by *abandoning* me?"

"I'm not abandoning you," Omicron said. "I'm just exercising that freedom."

Ayla knew that freeing Omicron would one day lead to this moment. She knew that eventually he would feel that his obligation to her had been paid, and would start making plans for himself that did not include her. She just didn't expect that day to be today, and for that moment to be now.

"Please don't do this to me," she begged him. She hated herself for resorting to pleading, but she was otherwise powerless. She knew she had nothing to lose at this point, and there was no sense in holding anything back. "Please. Come back with me. We don't need this place. We'll figure something else out."

"Ayla," Omicron said, "there is no other way. The seeds in this case don't exist anywhere else on the entire planet. We have to do this. Both of us. I have to stay here, and you have to get this crate back to Cadie. Everything depends on the decisions we make right now."

"I can't do it," Ayla said. She put her hand over her mouth and shook her head. "Omicron, I can't do it by myself."

"You can," Omicron said. "You're much stronger than you think. You've been on your own before, and you can do it again. All you have to do is get the case back to the *San Francisco* and then you're finished with all of this."

"And then what am I supposed to do?" she said. "Where am I supposed to go after that?"

"Triple Seven," Omicron said. "Start a new life. You'll be safe there."

"Start a new life," Ayla repeated. She sniffed and nodded and smiled sardonically. "Again."

"Ayla, I'm so sorry."

"Stop fucking saying you're sorry!" Ayla screamed. Her outburst reverberated off the dome's panels and then the room fell eerily silent. "It doesn't make any difference if you're sorry, Omicron. It doesn't change a goddamn thing."

"I know it doesn't," Omicron said. "But unfortunately, neither of us has a choice right now. *This* is the force that we can apply to make sure we all keep moving forward, Ayla. *This* is the most important contribution either of us will *ever* make."

Ayla looked up at the black rain falling on the roof of the dome and shook her head with a scornful laugh. "You know, that's the irony of all this," she said. "I never wanted any of it. I never wanted to save the world, or to be a hero, or even to make a difference, really." She stepped forward, took the handle of the crate, and tipped it onto its wheels. "All I ever wanted was to stop feeling so alone."

PART FOUR

CHAPTER FORTY-THREE

ESCAPE VELOCITY

CAM WAS IN COMPLETE AND total darkness. He had a plasma lantern that he could turn up to as high as a thousand lumens, but at this point, the tedium and familiarity of his compact surroundings were worse than the pure blackness. According to the chronometer strapped to the outside of his pressure suit that auto-illuminated when he looked down at it, he'd been inside the crate for a little over three days now, though to him, it felt more like three months.

At last check, about a third of his consumables were gone (air, water, tubes of protein paste, supplements, and the antinausea pills he took in preparation for a launch he was beginning to think might never happen). Other biological necessities had been addressed through indiscreet germicidal receptacles that were accumulating in the bulging refuse pouch behind him.

His seat was mounted on a triple-axis gimbal that kept him in an optimal launch position regardless of which way the crate was stacked. Cam was thankful for the arrangement since he had indeed been rotated several times during transport, though the contraption left him little room to stretch. And despite regularly kneading freshly oxygenated blood into his hamstrings, quadriceps, and calves, they'd begun seizing and spasming with increasing regularity.

When at last Cam was awakened by the sound and feel of multiple colossal engines igniting somewhere beneath him, there was an instantaneous upwelling of emotional dissonance. This was the point of no return—the moment beyond which it was impossible for him to change his mind. Even though the reality was that it had probably been too late from the moment his crate had been loaded into the cargo bay, he knew now that no amount of screaming or banging could possibly alert anyone to the fact that he was inside, and that cracking the hatch or blowing the explosive bolts and trying to get out would, at this point, almost certainly be suicide. What only moments ago had been by far the most dangerous thing Cam had ever done was now the only hope he had for survival.

There was another reason why the sensation of immensely powerful rocket fuel combustion was a relief. When they were working out the details of how to get Cam up to *Equinox*, Omicron had explained that there were three widely used methods for launching objects into orbit: Single-Stage-to-Orbit spaceplanes (SSTOs), hypervelocity mechanical mass acceleration rings (or "hammers" as they were usually called), and traditional rocket technology. Since nobody knew which spaceport was assigned to ultimately receive the ice auger components, it was impossible to know for sure which method would be used. Cam's capsule was designed for either an SSTO (which was unlikely since spaceplanes were far better at quickly inserting small objects into orbit than delivering heavy payloads to a space station), or just about any kind of expendable, multistage, vertical-launch system. But had the brokers built a hammer big enough to launch industrial-scale equipment—and somehow found a way to counter the effects of massive amounts of centripetal acceleration on mechanical cargo—anything organic inside would be reduced to protoplasmic gelatin long before it ever got off the ground.

Cam began to sense movement, and then shortly thereafter, the gradual accumulation of g-forces. That was the moment when he knew, absolutely, that despite all the brave optimism, and all the contingency plans he was forced to memorize consisting of coordinates and radio frequencies and survival techniques, he would never see Cadie or Zaire ever again. Even if he survived the launch and somehow managed to make it to *Equinox*, the chances of him getting back down to Earth without being discovered, or before he ran out of consumables, or before he perished in any number of other ways, were laughably minuscule. And even if he did manage to complete his mission and get himself on a homeward trajectory, the chances of him surviving reentry and being picked up by someone more interested in rescuing him alive than waiting for him to die and then salvaging his capsule were probably even lower.

Cam knew as well as anyone that this had always been a one-way trip.

But rather than fear or desolation, what Cam felt more acutely than anything else was a sense of relief. As soon as someone suggested attempting to infiltrate *Equinox* as a way of sabotaging the Coronians' mining operations, Cam knew that this was his best way out—perhaps the only way left for him to fulfill his obligations to the people he loved, and then, one way or another, to finally move on. Living with Cadie inside *Aquarius* had gotten to be unbearable. He hated that he watched her sleep, and that he looked for opportunities to brush up against her so that he could feel and smell her, and that he even enjoyed holding her hair back out of her face as she vomited from seasickness their first few nights aboard the research vessel. Yet never once did she respond to him in the way he wanted her to. As hard as he tried, he could not stop thinking about the request she'd made of him back in V1—her plan to try to preserve something of her dying husband—and how badly he had wanted it to be something physical between them rather than just a dispassionate procedure that occurred in isolation inside a laboratory. He could not forget how he had tried to turn the whole thing into something that it was not; tried to use his best friend's accident to his advantage; how much he hoped that comforting Cadie would eventually grow into something much more.

But now he could see how impossible it had always been. Everyone had his or her place in V1, and his place was with Zaire. Somehow—he couldn't even remember exactly how anymore—the two of them had been matched up and expected to marry in the communal ceremony that had been celebrated as the biggest wedding in the galaxy, and then both had been assigned to work in the Wrench Pod. Cam knew that being with Cadie had always been unrealistic—that he was not good enough for her, not smart enough, and that he would never be or have the things that she valued in a partner. Even when they had nothing left in the entire world but each other—when their home was gone, and Arik and Zaire were both gone, and even the baby was gone—even then Cadie had not responded to him, not even in one single helpless and desperate attempt to cling to something familiar, something of their past that nobody else on the entire planet shared with her but him. When Cam watched Cadie, he could see that the source of her passion would always be her past, and never the potential for a future with him.

Yet somehow it had been possible for Cam to love Zaire. Somehow he both loved her and hated her for not being Cadie, and loved his best friend, but also hated him for having the only thing in the world he'd ever wanted. And now the only way he knew to reconcile all the contradictions of his past was to give the only thing he had left—his life—in service of something that he hoped was bigger than himself, big enough to shift his perspective and make everything in his past feel so small and so insignificant that, if even for a few hours or minutes or seconds before he died, he could finally put it all behind him.

The velocity a spacecraft must achieve in order to escape Earth's gravity was enormous. Cam was told that a typical cargo rocket burning highly refined kerosene and liquid oxygen would likely take between eight and nine minutes to reach orbit, and along the way, accelerate to between three and four times Earth's gravity. By no means was such strain trivial, but it was easily survivable. He was also told that those who had not been conditioned, or prescreened for tolerance, or who weren't wearing a g-suit designed to squeeze the blood from their legs and abdomen back up into their brains, might very well lose consciousness along the way.

Cam had spent most of his life believing that he had already left Earth behind forever. The last thought he had as he closed his eyes and surrendered to the forces of escape velocity was that now he actually had, and even though he was terrified of what lay ahead, he hoped more than anything else to never have to go back.

CHAPTER FORTY-FOUR

JETSAM

OVER THE LAST SEVERAL MONTHS, Cadie had learned all kinds of new things about herself, but the one that probably surprised her most was that she was terrified of insects. She'd never seen one in person before being brought aboard the *San Francisco* (nor, for that matter, any other form of complex multicellular organism other than her fellow humans), but as a competent and even accomplished biologist, it never occurred to her that she might find other living things so repulsive and somehow menacing.

It was Cadie's second encounter with an insect that was the most traumatic. After she met Luka in the Turkish hookah lunge, she'd decided to postpone returning to the confines of *Aquarius* so that she could see a little more of the *San Francisco*. As she turned from Market onto Mission, she came upon something long and sleek and iridescent that turned out to be a set of wings cloaking what seemed to her an impossibly large cicada with enormous, beady, bulbous red eyes. It had somehow escaped from the broods raised by the growers in the center column of the Yerba Buena structure, and had attached itself right at eye level to the outside of the electrolysis station. In an attempt to acknowledge and emphasize her curiosity over her fear and rising disgust, Cadie leaned toward the unfamiliar creature to get a better look, and when it suddenly buzzed with the intensity of a fire klaxon, she shrieked, spun, and immediately returned to *Aquarius*, where she did not complain about cabin fever or claustrophobia again for almost a month.

However, *Aquarius* was not entirely impervious to entomological infiltration, either, and in fact the tiny research habitat had been the setting of Cadie's very first—though thankfully much less dramatic—insect encounter. Charlie had brought Cadie one of her own favorite boxed meals, which happened to be quinoa and ant stir-fry, and it wasn't until Cadie was about to put the first bite into her mouth that she realized what the little bristly black curls actually were. Charlie apologized profusely at having forgotten that there were cultures out there who found the consumption of insects offensive, including the one from which her own sister originally came. The meal did not go to waste, though, since curiously, Cam had none of the same culinary misgivings as Cadie, and in fact, benefited more than once when boxed meals meant for his roommate were mislabeled, or when Luka or Charlie simply forgot about Cadie's self-imposed dietary restrictions. Ever since those little articulated legs and pointy abdomens and crooked antennae and pincer mouthparts had come so close to her lips, Cadie had been subsisting primarily on nutrients derived from almonds, black beans, and soy—along with capsules of probiotics to help her digest them, and lots of vitamin supplements.

That was what led Cadie to a second discovery about herself. She'd never given much thought to food before she'd come to live aboard the *San Francisco*, and in fact, had always found eating to be more of an inconvenience and a distraction than a form of pleasure. But now that she'd probably lost close to five kilograms since leaving the medical center, she found she was thinking about food almost constantly, and specifically, nice big hot boxes of stemstock. There was a long-standing debate in V1 about whether consuming meat synthesized from the stem cells of long-dead bovine or fowl (and sometimes both simultaneously) qualified one as a true carnivore, or whether the intersection of food production and modern genetics merited entirely new dietary categories. Cadie had never cared to argue semantics and paid little attention to how those around her chose to label themselves, though she now knew unequivocally that whatever she was, she was no vegetarian, and that she desperately wanted some meat.

According to Luka, there was sometimes an item called black pepper chicken available in the Union Square food court for up to a week after the *San Francisco* left a broker post. He didn't much care for stemstock himself, but apparently those who did were constantly raving about the dish to anyone they could get to listen. Cadie would have probably asked Luka or Charlie to bring her an order or two rather than risk leaving *Aquarius*, but the food court held another draw: it was on the top floor of Union Square, and apparently the higher up on the rig you were, the more you could feel the flushing of the waterlock.

Cadie and her team had explored several methods for launching the UNVs. Their initial plan was to fill them with ballast, drop them through the moon pool, then after some interval of time, have them jettison their weights so that they would bob up to the surface, deploy their sails, and begin their long journeys around the globe. The main problem, according to Luka and Charlie, was that someone on the bridge might notice a trail of sixty-four solid-sail hydrofoils wandering off in different directions in the *San Francisco*'s wake. The next idea was to transport them all over to the *Accipiter Hawk*, where Ayla and Omicron could launch them in safety a few hundred kilometers away, but for reasons Ayla still hadn't explained, Omicron did not come back from their trip up to the Global Seed Vault, and although Cadie knew that Ayla was perfectly capable of launching the UNVs on her own, without Omicron, she seemed to lack the confidence.

That was when Charlie—just before being put on saturation rotation—had the brilliant idea of simply throwing them all away. There were records of everything that came aboard the *San Francisco*, and records of everything that was assembled and distributed throughout the rig, but nobody ever paid any attention to what got dumped. Additionally, though the UNVs' hulls were assembled from self-healing polymers, the team really had no idea how much punishment they could withstand, and launching them through the refuse chamber would probably result in less structural stress since the rig slowed down significantly before releasing its waste. And finally, as long as the UNVs did not deploy their sails too soon, they would easily blend in with the other jetsam and just float away with the rest of the garbage.

Cadie was sitting in a secluded corner of the food court, absently watching a cricket match on a massive overhead panel— presumably a classic rivalry from the archives. She'd never really been a fan of any sport, and in fact only knew enough about cricket to be able to follow the matches that were sometimes held in the Play Pod pitches in V1, but it was a convenient distraction from the skewers and pans and platters of insects for sale all around her. On her way in, she'd seen a stall with a Japanese theme offering compressed rice-substitute pillows garnished with grubs, beetles, and roaches, and now she was actively trying to unsee them.

Since Tycho had made her an official citizen of the *San Francisco*, Cadie's cap repository was automatically credited at regular intervals. Although she didn't really have a good sense of the economics aboard the rig, her impression was that the allocation was a paltry and primarily political sum, but lacking any other financial responsibilities, she found that it was more than enough to get her not just one plate of black pepper chicken, but a second one, as well. It was just as she was gathering her first bite of seconds with her chopsticks—and reflecting on how this was probably one of the very best meals she'd ever sat down to—that she finally felt it.

Cadie considered the gyroscopic stabilizers that Luka and Charlie claimed made the rig feel as solid as dry land to be closer to motion dampeners rather then eliminators. The closest Cadie had ever come to floating on anything before being brought aboard the *San Francisco* was the maglev that connected all of V1's pods, and she suspected that her inner ears had a far more solid baseline for sensing movement than those who'd spent most or all of their lives at sea. In fact, even though *Aquarius* inherited most of the motion compensation from the hull to which it was lashed, she'd spent her first few nights aboard vomiting into the stainless steel receptacle in the entry lock with Cam standing behind her, holding her then-long hair back out of her face. Therefore, the sensation that Luka had said she *might* be able to detect from the top floor of Union Square (the tallest building she had access to, and where she would remain relatively anonymous and inconspicuous) was, to her, unmistakable. She looked around at the other patrons who continued carrying trays from stalls to tables, or animatedly conversing over elaborate presentations of exotic invertebrates, or interacting with their workspaces in solitude without the slightest acknowledgment of what just occurred.

Cadie figured that continuing to eat would help her to blend in better, so she wrapped her mouth around the bite of black pepper chicken and looked back up at the cricket match while she chewed. A few moments later, she felt the same sensation again, but this time in the opposite direction, and she knew that it was done.

It was strange, and perhaps even a little unfair, how anti-climactic the world could sometimes feel. Sixty-four solid-sail unmanned hydrofoils—each one christened with a unique species of extinct flying fish, and known collectively among the team as "gliders"—had just started the gradual process of entirely changing the course of humanity. Using decrypted signals from Coronian navigation satellites, they would eventually disband and dynamically plot courses toward multiple coasts of every continent on the planet, propagating not only genetically engineered and fully automated terraforming technologies, but just as important to Cadie, also finally realizing and actualizing her husband's legacy. Yet the only indication was a subtle sway in the level of the tea in her cup; a delicate, seemingly magnetic inclination to lean slightly forward toward the table, and then a few minutes later, slightly back; a sensation so deeply ingrained into the psyches and equilibria of everyone around her that not a single person even paused to take notice.

Cadie wondered how many other scientists had experienced disappointment at the incongruent coexistence of profound paradigm shifts and insipid normalcy. She wondered if Gregor Mendel, having just discovered the entire field of genetics by recognizing the pattern of inheritance in pea plants, was soon thereafter called inside from his garden to eat his lunch before it got cold. She thought about how newspapers were far more interested in the gossip of the day than in printing a single factual account of the Wright brothers having just invented controlled, powered, and sustained heavier-than-air human flight. And how Buzz Aldrin, having participated in one of the most daring adventures in the history of humankind, returned to Earth to face the suicide of his mother, multiple failed marriages, depression, and alcoholism. Finally, she thought about her own husband, and how solving artificial photosynthesis and figuring out how to terraform an irradiated and sterile planet were simply means to an end, and that they might never have the opportunity to be widely celebrated as scientific revolutions in their own rights.

Whenever Cadie was feeling small and insignificant, she tried to remember the moments that had profoundly changed her own life: the first time she and Arik witnessed the successful writing of binary data to human DNA, and the subsequent error-free decoding; the day of the wedding, and how after the ceremony and the reception, she and Arik had returned together to their very own brand-new home pod; the moment she discovered that her experiment had worked—that she was, in fact, pregnant with Arik's baby, and that she would make sure that something of him lived on whether he ever woke up or not. And she thought about how much everything would have changed the moment the baby was born—how suddenly being solely responsible for another human life would have made the world exhilarating and mysterious and terrifying all at the same time.

But now the baby was gone and the result was simply numbness. And after months of determination and persistence, the gliders had finally been launched, yet she sat alone and isolated among the oblivious prattle of strangers. Cadie's life sometimes felt to her like a constant and confusing vacillation between feeling nothing, and feeling more than it seemed a single human being could possibly handle.

CHAPTER FORTY-FIVE
NULL VOLUME

CADIE DIDN'T KNOW MUCH ABOUT architecture other than what she casually observed around her. She was much more interested in the life sciences than in design, but there was one thing about the arrangement of public spaces that she found fascinating: no matter how carefully structures were planned, if you looked closely enough, you could almost always find little patches of dead space; spatial by-products of load-bearing or utility infrastructure; dim eddies of dust around which foot traffic consistently flowed, but never actually penetrated.

Several such areas existed back home in the maglev terminals where vertical beams occasionally occurred close enough to walls that it would have been awkward—even, for some reason, childlike—to pass between them. Or around the perimeter of the geodesic dome enclosing the greenhouse where the ceiling was too low for one to stand, and the steep angle of the slope made storage more trouble than it was worth. Cadie had reflected on these observations one evening while playing four-handed chess with Arik, Cam, and Zaire, and together they came up with the expression "null volume" to refer to areas that remained undefined, empty, and meaningless.

Even though she hadn't seen all that much of the *San Francisco*, she'd noticed an emerging hexagonal theme, which indicated an acute awareness of the principle of null volume and a desire—maybe even a civic mandate—to limit it as much as possible. But as far as she could tell, some amount of unused space within any type of structure, no matter how carefully planned, was probably unavoidable. It might even be that, over time, areas that were once highly trafficked became null volume as the priorities, motivations, and the habits of those who frequented them evolved.

Cadie guessed that the area under the steps in the northeast corner of Union Square where she now sat, cross-legged and meditatively, had once been a kind of attraction—a deliberate vista or overlook from which to behold the splendor of molecularly assembled gentrification. Through the two windows converging in a seamless right angle, she could see the Noe Valley Rec Center, occasionally perforated by meandering luminescent turquoise swimming tubes like a monstrous radioactive serpent rising from the sea below; the giant green screw of the vertical gardens impeccably preserved inside the Yerba Buena snow globe; and the gleaming distended facade of Millennium Tower, a forty-two-story sail petrified in microlattice and silicon glass. To her, the view was spectacular—a high-end amusement park, or a luxury resort, or an artist's interpretation of a microcosmic utopia—and perhaps it had once been considered spectacular by the citizens of the *San Francisco*, as well. But she could tell from the unperturbed layer of dust around her that any enchantment the panorama once offered no longer registered for those who came here in search of novelty in the form of the newest conveniences and unfamiliar exotic cuisine.

Cadie had been expecting an incoming call notification, and it finally appeared in the corner of her vision. She watched it flash for a moment while she gathered her thoughts, then after authenticating against the polymeth window, Luka's face resolved, superimposed over Sunset Boulevard.

"Did you feel it?" he asked by way of greeting. She could sense his exhilaration, and she could tell from his eyes that he was probably also intoxicated. It was a variation of the look her husband sometimes had in his final weeks and days, which Cadie now understood to be the combined result of stimulants and painkillers.

"Yes," she said. She was still trying to fully make sense of the anticlimactic experience she'd just had upstairs in the food court; still dreading returning to the isolation of *Aquarius* without anything to work on anymore, and without any idea of what she was supposed to do next; and still unsure of how she was going to convince Luka to do something she knew he would outright reject.

"Where are you?"

"Union Square."

"Can you talk?"

Cadie checked behind her and confirmed that she was still alone. "Yes."

Luka turned and looked behind him, as well, then looked back at Cadie. The background was dark enough that she couldn't tell where he was, but she guessed a secluded corner of the foundry. "It worked!" he mutedly exclaimed. "They're all deployed! We did it!"

"I know," Cadie said. She tried to smile, then realized that the expression was probably worse than if she'd remained impassive.

Her reaction—or distinct lack thereof—immediately tempered Luka's elation. "What's the matter?" he asked her. "I thought you'd be celebrating."

"There's something I need you to do," Cadie said.

"What?" Luka asked her. "What's wrong?"

"Do you have any way of getting in touch with the Coronians?"

"*Getting in touch?*" Luka repeated incredulously.

"Sending a message."

"How the hell would I be able to send a message to the Coronians?" he asked. "Why would I even *want* to send a message to the Coronians?"

"What about Tycho?"

Luka watched her for a moment, then shrugged. "I don't know," he finally said. "I assume he can. But you still haven't told me why."

"We need them to know that Cam's up there."

Luka looked at Cadie with a combination of suspicion and disbelief. "Why the hell would we do that?"

"Because," Cadie said, "it's his only chance of survival."

"If the Coronians know he's there, he has *no* chance of survival," Luka countered. "What's to stop them from deorbiting the entire shipment and burning it up in the atmosphere?"

"The gliders," Cadie said.

"What about them?"

"Tycho needs to tell the Coronians about the gliders, as well, and that Cam helped design them. That will give them incentive to capture him alive."

"What the hell are you talking about?" Luka blurted out. "That puts *everything* in jeopardy. That absolutely *guarantees* Cam gets captured, *and* that the gliders get destroyed."

"It's the only way Cam will survive up there, and it's the best way to make sure he gets aboard *Equinox* unharmed. From there, it will be up to him to figure out what to do."

"But what about the gliders?"

"The Coronians can't stop them now," Cadie said. "Even with Cam's help. At least not all of them."

"Are you positive about that?" Luka asked her doubtfully. "There's a hell of a lot we don't know about Coronian technology."

"Positive enough."

"What if they demand that *we* stop the gliders in exchange for Cam's life? Have you thought about what you'd do then?"

"It doesn't matter," Cadie said. "At this point, we can't stop the gliders, either."

"That's a hell of a big gamble," Luka said. "What you're talking about puts everything we've worked for at risk."

"That's one way of looking at it," Cadie admitted. "But another way of looking at it is that it's the only way any of this could possibly work."

"You're a long ways from convincing me of that," Luka said.

"Is it even worth trying?"

"If you want me to relay a message to Tycho, I think you'd better."

"OK," Cadie began. "Let's think this through. Terraforming is a long-term strategy. It could be decades before the earth sees any benefit from the gliders, *if* they end up working at all."

"As you've repeatedly made painstakingly clear," Luka said. "How does that change anything?"

"Compare that timeline to the pace of Coronian innovation," Cadie said. "Look around you at everything you have because of Coronian technology, and now consider how all of it—the assemblers, the power cells, the buildings, the atmospheric conditioning systems, the contact lenses, the BCIs—every piece of technology aboard the *San Francisco* is completely obsolete relative to what the Coronians are keeping to themselves."

"So what's your point?" Luka challenged.

"My point is that they could be much closer to doing their own mining than we originally thought."

"I seriously doubt that," Luka said. "Considering how much raw material they still buy from us, I think we still have plenty of time."

"I don't," Cadie said. "You're thinking linearly. To figure out where technology will be in the future, you have to think exponentially."

"What's that supposed to mean?"

"It means you can't necessarily base future predictions on the past. It means in addition to thinking about change, you have to factor in the *rate* of that change, and how technology recursively changes *itself*. We know the Coronians probably already have atomic assemblers rather than just molecular. Think about the kinds of things they can build now—the kinds of new assemblers they can build using the old ones. If they're ordering a giant ice drill from the *San Francisco*, that probably means two things: First, they have bigger and more important things to assemble themselves; and second, they're probably already thinking about mining on Europa or Titan. All they need is one reliable source of matter and there's basically nothing they can't build and nothing they can't do. At a certain point, they might even be able to reuse matter they already have—essentially recycle what's already up there to build whatever they need at that particular moment, and then once they're done with it, turn it into something else. We know the Coronians want to become self-sufficient, but they might also be close to becoming self-*sustaining*."

Cadie could see that her argument was not being well received. Only moments ago, Luka had been in a celebratory mood, and now he looked as though he was about to put his fist through the polymeth.

"Listen to me," Cadie said. "We're still on the right track, but this isn't an either/or proposition anymore. We need the gliders to work, *and* we need Cam up there doing what he can to delay the Coronians' progress. And unfortunately, the only way to make sure he gets aboard *Equinox* alive is to tell the Coronians he's there."

Luka glared at her for a moment, then shook his head. "I don't even know why I got involved in any of this in the first place," he finally said. "I'm about to get myself thrown out of here, and the reality is that none of this is probably going to work, anyway."

"Luka," Cadie began, but before she could make any further attempt to reassure him, he was gone.

Although his last words were obviously spoken in anger, Cadie found that she could not dismiss them. *None of this is probably going to work, anyway.* He could very well be right. It was impossible for any of them to predict with any accuracy or confidence whatsoever which way things were going to go at this point. The only thing Cadie believed was universally true about the future was that it almost never turned out like you thought it would. The collection and analysis of data points and variables was useful up to a point, but the complexity of the world seemed to have a way of increasing in direct proportion to the extent to which you tried to measure it until the only sane way to make sense of anything at all was ultimately through instinct and intuition rather than cold and objective calculation.

Unfortunately, her instincts were every bit as inconclusive as the facts.

Cadie's philosophy about anyone's ability to accurately predict the future was heavily influenced by a conversation she once had with Arik on the nature of probability. In retrospect, she now believed the discussion was prompted by Arik somehow

discovering the truth about V1. It was during dinner one evening, and she recalled how he'd slid his boxed meal forward to
make room for his elbows, and how he never ended up eating
anything at all that night.

He began his argument by naming several of the things that
kept them alive inside of V1: a substantial inert metal alloy shell
designed to stand for at least a thousand years against the harsh
atmosphere; the greenhouse where genetically engineered tulsi
ferns produced massive amounts of ozone twenty-four hours a
day that rapidly disassociated into breathable dioxygen; the protein synthesized from the stem cells of long-extinct livestock.
Then there were those factors that were slightly more subtle: the
atmospheric administration system that controlled the distribution of oxygen and removed pathogens from the air; the filtration
systems that enabled them to recycle almost all of their water;
the fusion reactors that were the lifeblood of every piece of technology they relied on.

Arik went on to point out that it was also possible to state the
reasons for their survival in the negative. For instance, they were
alive because a coronal mass ejection *hadn't* struck in precisely
the right place at precisely the right time, frying the constella-
tions of satellites they relied on; and a gamma ray burst emanat-
ing from a super or hypernova *hadn't* fatally irradiated all life on
the planet in the span of just a few milliseconds. As Arik continued to demonstrate, it was possible to keep parsing the individual elements enabling their existence into increasingly specific
dependancies—both in the positive and in the negative—until it
seemed there were an infinite number of things keeping them
alive, and an infinite number of things preventing them from
perishing, each one with a mathematical probability attached
to it. Some of those probabilities were high (that the shell of V1

would continue to remain structurally sound for the foreseeable future), and some were extremely low (that the beam of deadly energy released from the brightest electromagnetic event known to occur in the entire universe would be directed at precisely their minuscule location in the galaxy), but the reality was that every moment of every day, an almost infinite number of dice were constantly being rolled, and no matter how many sides each one had, given enough time, eventually one of them would hit, and then something that you always believed was either immutably true, or unconditionally false, or simply mathematically and statistically impossible, suddenly wasn't.

CHAPTER FORTY-SIX

THE ABYSSAL PLAIN

AFTER THE *SAN FRANCISCO* SLOWED enough to flush its most recent accumulation of refuse and scrap, it sped back up just long enough to clear the debris, then slowed down once again. It continued on for about another hour at somewhere between fifteen and twenty knots, then came to a dead stop, dropping both of her thirty-ton anchors. The rig was almost directly above an area of seabed that the fleet of ROVALEs (Remotely Operated Vehicles for Advance Long-range Exploration) had identified as rich in polymetallic nodules, manganese crusts, and sulfide deposits.

Mining operations conducted by Metropolis-class rigs usually occurred at three separate depths. The shallowest portion of the operation took place aboard the rig itself, on decks four through six, which miners referred to as "topside" (a relative term since topside was still well below sea level). That was where filtering chambers separated minerals from silt and slurry, pumping the isolated ore up to the refinery and the tailings back down to the ocean floor.

The deepest portion of the operation—referred to as the mining site, or usually just "the site"—was the mining location itself where semiautonomous robotic cutters worked in collaboration with collecting machines at between eight hundred and six thousand meters, depending on the types of deposits they were gathering. Miners occasionally operated "on-site"—down alongside the massive excavation machines themselves; however, due to the extreme depth, it was necessary to do so inside of an ADS, or Atmospheric Diving Suit. An ADS was essentially a human-shaped, articulated, fully pressurized and powered submersible that, while extremely robust and relatively safe, was also fairly cumbersome and unwieldy. Using one of four different tools that could be rotated into position at the end of an ADS appendage (variable-digit pinchers, a multibit drill, a worm-drive saw, and a power hammer), divers could conduct crude repairs such as dislodging obstructions or untangling fouled lines. However, anything more complicated or delicate than that had to be done in an area between the mining site and topside, usually referred to as "staging."

Staging generally occurred right around five hundred meters of depth—just about as deep as it was possible for humans to go without an ADS—and was therefore by far the most dangerous portion of the entire operation. It typically consisted of three dry diving bells—colloquially known as shacks—where, for up to twenty days, two technicians per shack lived amid the exact same ambient pressure as the ocean outside, enduring such hardships as excessively lumpy cots, a mere trickle of tepid fresh water that passed as a shower, blue chemical toilets behind tattered three-sided curtains, and usually cold and overly acidic coffee of which there was never enough. In fact, it was Charlie's cumulative time spent inside various shacks over the years that was principally responsible for her lack of sympathy for the numerous grievances expressed by Cam and Cadie at being confined to *Aquarius*, which, by comparison, was practically palatial and luxurious.

In order to survive such a high-pressure environment without the protection of an atmospheric diving suit, there was a constant rotation of miners who spent weeks inside topside compression chambers until they were "saturated," or sufficiently acclimated to high-pressure breathing gasses, allowing them to safely transfer down to the shacks where, when called upon to do so, they could operate inside standard, nonpressurized, radiation-shielded drysuits. While such relatively lightweight equipment meant that shack miners couldn't go much deeper (and in fact wore redundant depth alarms on both wrists to ensure they didn't inadvertently descend), it also meant that they had the agility and dexterity necessary to conduct much more complicated and intricate maintenance and repair procedures than could be attempted from inside an ADS. Having access to several wire traps full of all kinds of tools, and the use of all ten fingers with which to operate them, meant that most glitches, malfunctions, and failures could be fixed "on the fly" rather than having to reel equipment back up to dry dock on the rig. Staging was where final diagnostics and, if necessary, any last-minute tweaks, optimizations, and repairs were conducted on all heavy machinery before it was cast into the medium-rich void below, and before it was brought back up to the rig at the end of a job and stowed.

Charlie wasn't due to be back in the saturation rotation for another month, which was one of the reasons she initiated her plan when she did. Coordinating a ship-wide labor strike—shutting down all the mining operations, the refinery, and the foundry until the City Council agreed to scrap its new housing plans, and then subsequently organizing unions as a contingency against further abuses of power—would take a huge amount of coordination that she obviously couldn't orchestrate from inside a hyperbaric chamber, or while trying not to electrocute herself as she welded broken cutting teeth back into place, or from inside an ADS a kilometer or more down on the seafloor. And with as closely as Luka was being watched, he couldn't risk any more direct participation. But unfortunately, a friend of Charlie's—a miner by the name of Benthic, whom she fondly remembered as one of her very first crushes—wasn't responding well to compression mixtures this time around, so when he was pulled and sent to the Pacific Medical Center, Charlie was put into the saturation rotation to take his place, and all plans for once again bringing the *San Francisco* to a standstill were temporarily put on hold.

If a miner was lucky, the hardest part of working the shack was enduring the boredom. Once all the heavy equipment was deployed, an ideal tour was three weeks of sitting around the miniature flickering moon pool between routine maintenance tasks, configuring and then consuming a few algorithmically generated romance or mystery novels, playing backgammon with your shack mate while a relaxing generative sound track reverberated in the background, and watching old cricket or football matches from the archives—all the while bathed in the beautiful green glow of nominal indicators. But never in her career had Charlie experienced such a deployment, and this one, as it turned out, was no exception.

Having been the one to serve as the original inspiration for a new generation of female miners, and since shack mates were always paired by gender, Charlie was almost always the senior technician in her shack. But she was also frequently the senior technician across all three shacks since, as an early gender pioneer, she'd been forced to work extra hard to prove herself, which meant that she'd accumulated more hours in an ADS than anyone else her age, male or female. As the current active senior staging technician, Charlie could have used her authority to assign the task of getting a better look at a shaped cutter that had seized almost a kilometer below them to her shack mate, Kimberly, or to another more junior technician in some other shack. However, anxious to get her mind off the postponement of the strike, she decided to take the assignment on herself.

Kim ran through all the regular obstruction clearing procedures while Charlie prepped the suit, and after thirty minutes of relaying commands down to the cutter through the network of ROVs (Remotely Operated Vehicles) with no change in status whatsoever, Charlie finally called it.

"Forget it," she told Kim. "I could've been halfway down there by now. Back it up from the wall, shut everything down, and help me get into this thing."

Charlie really didn't mind the ADS itself. It was pressurized to the level of the shack, which meant there were no additional risks of dysbarism, or various serious medical conditions arising from changes in ambient pressure, and it was assembled from some kind of molecular structure that was supposed to be so strong that as long as you didn't step in front of a Nautilus-class cutter running at full tilt, nothing was going to get through it. It wasn't even the physical exertion of working on-site that bothered her, or the inevitable dehydration (nobody wanted to drink so much that they had to urinate inside the suit), or all of the raw, pink, slippery blisters she would emerge with from pushing against actuators with worn padding. More than anything else, what Charlie disliked about stepping over the precipice and descending down into the blackness below was the fact that there was probably no colder, lonelier, and more desolate human-reachable location on the entire planet than the deep-sea abyssal plains.

Charlie tied her traditional *hachimaki* around her forehead to keep the sweat out of her eyes, then climbed into the ADS from the ingress hatch in the rear. Once she was locked up tight inside her own personal anthropomorphic submarine with all of her diagnostics reporting green, she and Kim did a comms check, then Kim used the crane's remote to maneuver the heavy suit out over the moon pool, lower it into water, and set it down on the staging platform below.

The ADS had a widely diffuse ring light embedded around the perimeter of the faceplate as well as two adjustable socketed spotlights protruding from the rebreather on the back of the suit, but even at full intensity, they weren't nearly enough for the voraciousness with which the ocean consumed all forms of radiance. That's where Tinker Bell came in. Tink was a sleek, flat, hydrodynamic autonomous submersible with two primary modes: hover and tow. In hover mode, the bot oriented itself above the ADS it was linked to at either a default or specified distance, providing as much as a hundred thousand lumens of task lighting from the individually adjustable plasma panels on its underside. In tow mode, it descended and oriented itself directly in front of a linked ADS, waiting for the suit's pinchers to mate with its two rear port hooks before gradually powering up its magneto-hydrodynamic propulsors and smoothly delivering its payload to a set of predetermined coordinates. Most divers developed a strange form of affection for their ATCs, or Autonomous Task Companions, since the bots were usually the only company they had down in the trenches.

Charlie took several powered but sluggish steps across the platform until she had cleared the shack above her and was beneath Tink's column of illumination. While constantly relaying to Kim what she was doing (in full accordance with the *San Francisco*'s dive-mining regulations), she used the toggle switch under her thumb to navigate the menus of her heads-up display, selecting ATC > Link > Tow. She watched the light above her both narrow and intensify as the bot floated down into the range of her viewport and waited for its next command. Kim had already fed Tink the coordinates of the faulty cutter, so all Charlie had to do was hang on.

Shaped cutters were the most intricate and complex of the Nautilus-class excavators. Their primary component was a twenty-six-meter articulated telescopic boom terminating in sixteen individual flat bits with sixty-four retractable teeth. Each bit could be independently pivoted and rotated, resulting in an almost infinite number of shapes, from a tapered bore for drilling directly into a surface, to a polygonal disk for planing, to a flared cone for consuming entire ridges or outcroppings all at once. In an exterior cutting configuration (one in which the teeth pointed outward), material was gathered by a flanged collection collar, and while in an interior cutting configuration (one in which the bits were pivoted so that the teeth pointed inward), anything that was chewed up was sucked down the machine's whirring mechanical gullet.

It had only been a little over a week since Charlie had worked on the cutter in staging, but every time she saw a piece of Nautilus-class equipment up close, she was freshly impressed by its scale. Tink set her down beside the excavator's starboard track, which was half again as tall was she was, even in the ADS, then kicked up twin clouds of sediment as it ascended into a hover position from which to both illuminate the scene, and serve as a relay in Charlie's communications back to the shack. For the first time, as Charlie looked up at the cutter beneath Tink's murky glow, she realized it was the only thing she'd ever seen down there that made the ocean feel just a little less vast. Of course, the inverse of her observation was also true: that it made her feel correspondingly insignificant, and just being in its presence increased the sensation of utter desolation and triviality.

Charlie turned a full 360 degrees to see what else was around her and found that there was nothing but the usual suspended greenish-brown clumps of insoluble particles within the range of her lights. When she looked back up at the cutter looming over her, she confirmed what the telemetry data had already reported: the bits had seized in an interior cutting configuration that looked to Charlie like images she'd seen from the archives of a brand-new tulip blossom just about to burst forth. But inside, instead of delicate flower parts, were the carbon-hardened teeth of a beast born to chew through absolutely anything that divided man from medium.

All Nautilus-class excavators had extremely sophisticated instrumentation infused through their structures and subsystems, so Charlie already knew that the source of the contention was deep inside one of the machine's driveshafts. She even already knew which of the eight access panels to remove in order to expose the corresponding site-serviceable gearboxes. However, SRP (Standard Regulatory Procedure) dictated an initial visual inspection of the disabled region prior to initiating any repairs—a policy represented by the mnemonic acronym IDEA that, during training, every technician had thoroughly drilled into their heads (pun very much intended by every one of Charlie's instructors, each of whom believed himself both witty and original):

Inspect the site. Be aware of all equipment and other potential hazards around you. Plan primary and secondary escape routes and communicate them to your shack mate.

Decide on an approach. Talk it over with your shack mate. Do not proceed with any form of maintenance or repair until a consensus has been reached.

Evaluate your surroundings. Before attempting any form of maintenance or repair, make sure any loose debris or other hazards have been removed. *Remember: 98 percent of accidents can be prevented through proper site evaluation!*

Address the problem. It is now safe to attempt an on-site repair. Remember that all procedures must fully comply with the latest approved maintenance manuals, field guidelines, and safety regulations.

Charlie had never understood why such painfully obvious common sense required not only a mnemonic device, but one that was so redundant, generic, and verbose that it was far more confusing than it was instructive. She ultimately decided such policy was simply one more way in which the HR and curriculum departments attempted to justify their continued pathetic existences.

Charlie knew that clearing debris from around a repair site was more for the sake of the machine than for the safety of the technician, but it was still sound procedure. The last thing you wanted was to remove whatever obstruction was causing the contention, move off to a safe distance (usually all the way back up to shack depth), start everything back up, and have something else go wrong. Although these machines were capable of masticating even the densest layers of the planet, because of all the additional torque required to function at such incredibly high pressures, they needed to achieve a certain number of RPMs before they were more destructive than they were vulnerable. According to the cutters' engineers, Nautilus-class excavators functioned a little like air-breathing ramjet engines in that the faster matter moved through them, the more matter they could process. Once they reached a certain speed, there wasn't much that could stop them, but while they were initially starting up, they were surprisingly easy to bind and stall. Charlie thought of them a little like a boulder at the top of a hill. If you could get to it early enough on the curve, you could probably stop it pretty easily. But once it reached a certain velocity, the best you could hope for was to get the hell out of its way.

"OK," Charlie transmitted to Kim. "I'm going up to take a closer look."

"Roger that," Kim said.

Charlie used the two joysticks beneath her thumbs to maneuver herself into position. The joystick on the left activated the horizontally oriented propulsors that controlled her depth, and the one on the right distributed power among the two vertically oriented propulsors that controlled either her orientation (by moving water in opposite directions), or her movement forward or backward (by moving water in the same direction). She powered them up gradually so as to reduce the amount of sediment she stirred up, and as she rose and rotated, Tink adjusted its position to ensure optimal illumination.

The bad news was that since the bits were in an interior cutting configuration, Charlie's options were limited. If she discovered large amounts of debris inside the parabolic jaws, there wouldn't be much she could do from where she was. The opening was easily big enough for her to enter, but no matter how many safeties the machine had, or how many reassurances the shack gave her that it would not start up, there was absolutely no way she was crawling down its throat. With the right tools, the cutter's hydraulics could be operated manually from an access panel, which meant that the bits could be opened up into a far safer configuration—one in which most of the debris would probably just fall away on its own. However, that was a level of repair that would have to be done up at staging.

But the good news was that the bits looked clear. Charlie rolled her socketed lights over the entire interior of the dark carbon-barbed cavern, and although there was plenty of sediment inside, she couldn't see anything nearly big enough to stop the machine from starting back up. Assuming she could reach the obstruction through an access panel, it probably wouldn't be much more than an hour or two before she was back up in the shack with a lukewarm shower stinging her blisters and complaining about cold, overly bitter coffee.

"Bits are clear," Charlie reported. "We might just get out of this without having to reel it back up."

"Roger that," Kim said. "The repair plan recommends starting with panel four and working your way up from there."

"Roger that."

It was unsettling to be positioned directly in front of something so enormous and so menacing. The diameter of the aperture was greater than the height of her suit, and from her perspective, the machine looked like a monstrous worm rooted to the seabed, lured out of its tube by the passing of oblivious prey, eerily frozen in midlunge. Each individual tooth was at least the size of Charlie's helmet and they spiraled hypnotically down the machine's gullet, terminating in a complex enmeshment of gears designed not for transferring power, but for pulverizing rock into slurry. Charlie stared directly into the beast's maw, and then—as though believing it had her sufficiently lulled—the machine struck.

At least that's how it felt to Charlie. The movement wasn't actually all that fast, but the effect of so much machinery—every visual point of reference she had—simultaneously stirring was so jarring and disorienting that it felt like her entire world had slipped.

Charlie thought she screamed something, though she wasn't sure what. She could hear Kimberly's voice in her helmet, but there was no comprehension; no real communication; nothing but noise and the turning of the teeth in front of her. Instinctively she used her right joystick to move herself away, and as she did, she watched the rotation of the teeth increase so rapidly that they blurred, becoming a thick haze that coated the inside of the massive barrel. And then fear and shock turned to horror when she realized that her distance from it was no longer increasing. There was enough debris and sediment around her to give shape to what she already knew was there: a vortex forming between herself and the furiously rotating cavern of teeth and gears she was being pulled toward.

An equilibrium had formed between the pull of the cutter and her suit's propulsors. Her instincts screamed for her to try to break free of the funnel by moving to the side, but she deliberately disobeyed them out of fear of diverting any power at all away from the counterbalance. She could feel herself pushing against the back of the ADS with her feet and her palms, and she pulled back on the joystick so hard that she felt crushing pain in her thumb as though her suit's inability to access more power was simply a function of the joystick's limited range of motion. The gyroscopes in Charlie's suit sensed the rotational momentum of the vortex, and opposing lateral propulsors were engaged in order to ensure that she did not succumb to the increasingly energetic storm before her. However, remaining vertically oriented came at a price, and power was automatically diverted from other propulsors. She could hear the pitch of the beast's whine rise in greedy anticipation of their violent unification.

"Shut it down!" she heard herself scream. And then repeat, over and over.

As she watched the cutter grow larger and felt herself diminish, Charlie found herself pleading to some greater force that her terror would finally just yield to resignation, but it would not, and then some other part of her brain registered that the light around her was changing—that Tink was still somewhere above her, impassively tracking her progress toward being ripped apart and ground into silt. Conscious of the fact that this could very well be the last thing she ever did, Charlie desperately began navigating the menus of her HUD with her left hand while maintaining as much back pressure on the joystick as she could with her right. As soon as she reached the end of the hierarchy and selected the final option, the intensity of Tink's light began increasing as it descended, gently easing itself down into the diminishing gap between Charlie and the cutter, though before it could stop and wait for Charlie to attach herself to its tow hooks, it was gone. In the harsh illumination of Charlie's suit lights, she watched the bot spin with the force of the vortex and briefly bounce amid the blur of teeth before exploding and becoming a whirlpool of finer and finer particles.

But Charlie had never intended to take hold of Tink. As soon as she heard the pitch of the cutter change—the moment the little bot caught, and the spinning momentarily slowed with the stress of cannibalizing another extremely robust and highly pressure-resistant machine—Charlie clenched her eyes and bit down and screamed through her teeth as she pushed so hard on both joysticks that the pain shot all the way up into her shoulders.

When she finally opened her eyes again several seconds later, she had never been so happy to see nothing but darkness.

CHAPTER FORTY-SEVEN

INFINITE CAPACITY

THE TRIPLE-AXIS GIMBAL IN WHICH Cam's seat was mounted didn't do him much good in zero-g. Since the concept of "up" was entirely arbitrary, the best he could do was maneuver himself into an orientation that positioned the things around him, from his perspective, more or less upright: the tanks of compressed air, the twin redundant CO_2 scrubbers, the water lines and tubes, the plasma lantern strapped to the wall, the pockets in which blister packs of protein and medication were stored. And the electromagnetic rifle Luka referred to as a railgun, secured to one wall of the cube by three padded clasps, its trigger guard sawed off and filed down in order to accommodate a thickly gloved finger.

Since he regained consciousness, the pressurized crate had been transported and repositioned several times with an efficiency and precision that Cam knew had to be robotically orchestrated, sending the nucleus within the three concentric rings of the gimbal twirling. The last time it was moved, the maneuver ended with the cubical vessel making contact with something far more massive and solid than it was, and the image that formed in Cam's mind was that of being stacked, or otherwise secured, inside some sort of zero-g warehouse. Now that he had been stationary for over an hour, he hoped that establishing a frame of reference—even an artificial one—might help him feel less nauseous, though if it was helping, he certainly couldn't tell. The timing of the launch was such that he was caught right between antinausea treatments: the patch on his arm had worn off, and the pills he swallowed soon after orbital insertion took too long to absorb in zero-g, and therefore came back up before they had a chance to take effect. All he could do now was ride it out.

Prior to today, Cam had only vomited one other time in his life. He and two other boys—Syed and Seth—had filled an aluminum canister with a cloudy white liquid from a complex borosilicate glass still Syed's father set up in the back of the Code Pod, then proceeded to pass it around until it was half-gone. He remembered thinking that throwing up must be the worst physical feeling that it was possible for a human being to experience, though enough time had passed that the memory of the sensation had mostly dulled. However, now that Cam was experiencing it all over again—the sweating, the quivering, the gagging, and the violent involuntary retching—he realized that, all those years ago, he'd been right.

His helmet was off and meandering about in a leisurely cir-cuit of apparent perpetual motion so that he could safely vomit into a wet-trash sealable pouch (vomiting into a helmet, Cam knew from his experience with environment suits back in V1, could easily be fatal, and doubly so in zero-g). He had already thrown up several times and found now that there wasn't much left to come up—not even gastric acid. Although Cam was unable to clearly articulate any of Newton's three laws of motion, he suspected that the spinning that resulted from his heaving was probably evidence of one of at least one of them.

A fresh patch on his shoulder would probably see him through what remained of his bout with space adaptation syn-drome, but he was hesitant to get far enough out of his pressure suit that he could peel the old one off and get a new one into position. Although things had been quiet around him for some time, he was worried about the crate being structurally compromised or otherwise suddenly opened in a vacuum. Cam was confident that he could get his helmet back on and sealed in time (it was designed for rapid emergency pressurization), but if the capsule depressurized while he had too much of his suit dismantled—both of his gloves and perhaps even the upper torso assembly—he was pretty sure he wouldn't be able to get them back on before either freezing to death, or succumbing to ebullism as all of his bodily fluids began boiling simultaneously.

After a short nap, Cam awoke feeling much better, and even a little hungry. He had rotated while he was asleep, so he reached out and oriented himself again in the direction he'd decided was up, then stowed the unused wet-trash pouch he was holding in an elastic pocket in front of him. His consumables would easily last him several more days, but psychologically, Cam could tell that he was approaching some kind of internal threshold, especially now that his stomach was settling. Protein, water, supplements, and oxygen would not be enough to sustain him for much longer; whether it was danger, fear, or failure, Cam needed stimulation.

There was no way for him to know exactly where he was except by formulating a hypothesis around eliminating the obvious. The fact that he was experiencing weightlessness told him that he was neither on Earth, nor on the inner ring of *Equinox* which, according to Omicron, was supposed to have close to 90 percent of the gravity of home. And since he wasn't detecting any centrifugal forces, he couldn't be accelerating out toward a more distant orbit. Given the interval of time between when he launched and when he regained consciousness, it was possible that he was in a detached but stable low-earth orbit, although that seemed unlikely since his crate had clearly been through some sort of receiving or docking procedure. Cam's best guess was that he was right where he wanted to be: somewhere on the outer ring of *Equinox*, very likely in close proximity to the Coronians.

He looked down at the chronograph strapped above the threading of his glove, and had just decided that he would wait one more hour before cracking the hatch and taking a look around when he heard something beneath him. Cam immediately reoriented himself into a position that his eyes told him was facedown, but that his inner ears seemed entirely indifferent to. The sound was clearly that of something attaching itself to the crate at multiple points, but this time, it was not followed by the centrifugal sensation of movement. There was a moment of silence, and then the whine of very precise, high-speed machinery—something like the probing of a fine, diamond-tipped drill bit. Cam had managed to bring his level of anxiety down to a manageable baseline so he could focus on getting past the nausea and on making reasonable decisions, but now it appeared that decisions were about to made on his behalf, and his adrenaline once again surged.

The drilling paused, then started again in a slightly different location. Cam could tell from the depth of it that the intention was not to penetrate the capsule, though it wasn't until the whining came from a third and then a fourth location that he was able to detect the pattern: every one of the points so far seemed to correspond to the locations of the capsule's pyrotechnic fasteners—the emergency explosive bolts that would, at Cam's command, violently blow the hatch. Whatever was out there wasn't probing at all, but rather knew exactly what it was doing, and exactly where to do it. The initiators inside the eight bolts were triggered by pulsed laser diodes, and would probably respond to coordinated bursts of light from fiber-optic strands inserted from outside the crate.

The Coronians were about to blow the hatch.

Instinctively, Cam snatched his helmet from the air, flipped it around, and brought it down over his head. He rocked it until it was properly seated, lifted the two sealing levers, then used the console on his wrist to confirm that he wanted pressurization. When he saw green on his heads-up display, he rotated himself 90 degrees, reached forward, and released the three railgun latches. Nudged by the rotation of the final clasp, the rifle drifted toward him, and Cam grasped it by its stock, pulled it into his lap, then swung himself back toward the hatch. The whining of the drill bit was muted by his helmet, but Cam could still hear it, and for some reason, he reached up and turned the plasma lantern off as though he might be able to hide in the dark from whatever was out there. As he tightened the seat's webbing against his chest, he tried to remember how many more bolts there were, but realized that in his panic, he had lost count. When the whining stopped and did not start back up again, he knew that all eight had been drilled out, and that he probably had only seconds left before the hatch was blown.

Cam had no way of knowing what kind of environment was outside—whether it was pressurized, or whether it was a complete vacuum—but when the moment came, he knew instantly. He heard the eight simultaneous detonations, but only for a tiny fraction of a second before there was no more air to propagate sound, and then all he could hear was himself groan and gasp as he was thrown against his restraints, and then his own rapid breathing. He'd seen the brief flashes and expected the hatch cover to simply be gone, but it wasn't. Instead, it spun away for a moment, and then something folded over it—a type of elastic netting—cinching itself tight with the momentum of Cam's violently expelled environment. Although he was terrified, Cam still had the presence of mind to understand that whatever was out there was conscious of high-velocity litter. Or perhaps it never passed up an opportunity to collect any form of matter that could be transformed into viable assembly medium.

Cam did nothing but sit and breathe. His arms were crossed over his chest, pinning the rifle to his torso, and he could feel it rise and fall with his heaving. He was beginning to feel dizzy, and he closed his eyes for a moment, took a deep breath through his nose, held it, then let it out gradually through his mouth— a conscious attempt to slow his oxygen consumption, and keep himself from hyperventilating. When he opened his eyes again, he found himself gazing out over an infinite black void before him, but embedded in the darkness were hundreds of points of light—clusters of photons that had traveled decades, centuries, and even millennia to reach him. For the very first time in his life, Cam was looking at stars.

The darkness outside the capsule was not the result of a complete absence of light, but rather the absence of anything to reflect it. The hatch and the netting were gone, but now something maneuvered down from the top left-hand corner of Cam's field of view. It was compact and industrial, and although it was partially concealed in the glare of two spotlights, Cam could see that it had four dull metallic arms. The two major appendages on top were long and complex, comprised of several segments connected by servo-mechanical joints, terminating in what appeared to be as many as eight highly dexterous and surgically precise digits. The two minor appendages below were less well articulated and more crudely prehensile in nature—more like vices or pinchers—and

Cam could tell from their gearing and exposed pistons that they were capable of generating immense amounts of crushing torque. Behind the appendages was a thick and thoroughly scored white carapace in which were set three bluish lenses in a triangular pattern. The one on top had an enormous aperture—at least twenty centimeters—and appeared fixed in place. The two below, which Cam had initially mistaken for spotlights, were in fact individually socketed cameras with sturdy protracted housings and ring lights. With the eerie reflexive shifting of human eyeballs, the two lower lenses used their circular illumination to inspect the inside of Cam's capsule while the wide-diameter lens in the center stared directly through his faceplate.

The machine appeared to bristle with the vapor of dozens of tiny gas jets silently adjusting its pitch, yaw, and roll. Cam couldn't tell if it was explicitly weaponized, or whether its potential for destruction was implied by its appendages, but he decided he didn't want it thinking that he was entirely defenseless. Far clumsier than he would have liked, Cam raised the railgun and placed the stock against his shoulder. He powered up the device with his thumb, though since he did not know how sensitive the trigger was—nor how steady his hands were at the moment—he kept his finger along the outer housing of the device's electromagnetic track rather than down on top of the trigger.

The machine had no discernible reaction to Cam's threat. When the inside of the crate had been thoroughly scanned, the movement of the two smaller lenses locked in binocular synchronicity, illuminating Cam and holding steady except for an occasional, oddly muscular tic. Cam heard the transducers in his helmet crackle, and then there was a male voice, speaking to him in what he believed was probably a dialect of Chinese. There was a pause and Cam wondered if he'd been asked a question. The next sentence was in Spanish, or possibly Portuguese, and then another pause. Cam couldn't tell whether the voice was synthesized or organic until it finally spoke to him in English, and then he knew without a doubt. While it was a seemingly perfect reproduction, the vocalization lacked any trace of emotion appropriate to the situation: no threat, hatred, curiosity, and certainly no empathy.

"Do you speak English?"

"Yes," Cam said as calmly and steadily as he could manage. He assumed the Coronians would be listening on the same frequency on which they'd discovered he was able to receive. "Yes. I speak English."

"Do you require medical assistance?"

Cam hesitated. He thought about the danger of him vomiting in his helmet in zero-g, and the headache he was getting from dehydration since he hadn't been able to keep any water down. But ultimately he decided that he was not yet ready to appear in any way weak or vulnerable.

"No," he told the drone. "I'm fine."

"Please lower your weapon," the machine said. "You are in no danger."

"How do I know that?"

"Because if we wanted to kill you, you would already be dead. And if we decide to kill you in the future, you will not be able to stop us. The unintended consequences of discharging that weapon currently pose far more danger to you than we do."

Cam knew that this might be his only opportunity to stage any kind of resistance, so he took a moment to consider his options. He felt confident that he could destroy or disable the machine in front of him, but he suspected that it wouldn't do him very much good. There were likely hundreds if not thousands more just like it, and the reality was that it was probably far more effort on the part of the Coronians to keep him alive than to kill him, or to simply isolate him and let him die on his own. And finally, the drone was probably right: As far as Cam knew, the railgun had never been fired, so there was no telling what might happen in an extremely confined space where his life depended on the integrity of his pressure suit. With visible resignation, Cam cut the power to the railgun and took it down off his shoulder.

One of the machine's upper arms extended and rotated, wrapping its fingers delicately around the railgun's barrel. Cam released the weapon as it was gently withdrawn, and he watched as it was deftly passed down to one of the lower arms where it was securely clamped. He waited for the machine to crush it, or snap it in two, or otherwise render the weapon inoperable, but it did not. Perhaps they would take a few moments to make sure they understood how it worked before disabling it, and then probably reducing it to assembly medium and eventually turning it into something entirely different.

"Please come with me," the machine transmitted. "Your quarters are fully pressurized."

"My quarters?" Cam repeated. He did not move. "Wait a second. You mean you knew I was coming?"

"Yes," the machine said. "Your capsule was isolated from the remainder of the shipment until we were prepared for you."

"How did you know?"

"Your people alerted us."

Cam shook his head incredulously. "What do you mean *alerted*?"

"What we mean," the machine explained, "is that you were betrayed."

Cam was about to challenge the allegation, but something stopped him. First of all, he realized that there was no point in trying to convince the Coronians that his team would never give him up. And second, he wasn't even entirely convinced of that fact himself. He hadn't known Luka and Charlie long enough to have a good feel for whether or not they might trade his life for whatever rewards there were to be had aboard the *San Francisco*, and Tycho or Two Bulls or whoever he was was an even bigger unknown. The only person left in the entire world he was certain would never betray him was Cadie.

"What do I do?" Cam asked.

A complex pattern of gas jets fired as the machine rotated in place a full 180 degrees, then backed toward Cam so that it was just outside the capsule. On the rear of the machine was a thick bar with enough clearance for gloves, and below it, a retractable tether.

"Please secure yourself and let me know when you are ready."

Cam released his restraints and pushed the webbing aside. He moved tentatively forward in his seat toward the machine and reached for the tether. As he pulled it toward him, jets in the rear of the drone fired to compensate.

Cam knelt in the narrow space between the chair and the hatch. It took him a few tries to get the safeties on the carabiner open and to connect it to the ring anchored to the waist of the torso assembly, but when he released it, the spring-loaded mechanisms clamped tightly and securely shut. He gave the tether several yanks until he was satisfied with its integrity, then inched closer to the rear of the machine, the black and yellow belt retracting to take up the slack. Cam wrapped both gloved hands around the handle in opposing grips, then breathed deeply as he looked out into the blackness.

"OK," he said. "I'm ready."

"You are perfectly safe," Cam heard through this helmet. "Just hold on and relax. We will start off slowly."

Jets began firing and Cam felt himself being lifted and pulled through the hatch. He looked down into the blackness, searching for points of light, and although his hands were tightly clenched—and although he could hear his breathing quicken inside his helmet—he discovered that he'd internalized the concept of weightlessness fairly well. It wasn't so much the fear of falling that concerned him as much as it was the incomprehensible vastness into which he was being pulled. Having spent almost his entire life within the confines of V1, Cam had no experiential references, or even remotely suitable mental models, from which to draw. As part of his work in the Infrastructure Department, he'd spent plenty of time outside of V1, but visibility was always so poor that one was more likely to report feeling claustrophobic upon leaving the outer airlock than agoraphobic. The concepts of wide-open spaces, vistas, and horizons simply never had the opportunity to imprint themselves upon Cam's brain, so although he could clearly see what was was happening to him, the neurons and synapses he needed to help him make sense if it were simply not there to fire, or were too weak to register anything of consequence. But then Cam wondered if anything could truly prepare one for something like this. Maybe it was simply impossible for the human brain—regardless of how richly and complexly and intricately sculpted by past experience it might be—to truly comprehend the vastness of the cosmos. As Cam stared into the abyss that surrounded him, he did not feel, as the famous quotation went, that the abyss stared back into him, but rather that it absorbed his gaze with infinite capacity, and that if he were not careful, the universe might slowly drain him of everything that he was.

But when the drone began to rise and to rotate, the trance was broken, and Cam was suddenly aware of what an incredibly limited perspective he'd had. Relative to Earth's orbital plane, he had been looking down, and now that he was outside the capsule and could see several more degrees of what was around him, he discovered that what the machine was actually pulling him through was absolutely anything but open and empty space.

The sudden shift in scale was the most disorienting experience Cam had ever known. He was suddenly a speck among what could only be described as a vast multidimensional cargo dock, but at such a magnitude as to be seemingly no easier for him to comprehend than infinity had been just a moment before. Cam's capsule (which he'd already lost track of) was just one of thousands, then tens of thousands, then hundred of thousands, and perhaps even millions. There were dozens of appendages protruding in every direction of the outer ring of the space station, each one entirely enveloped in layers upon layers of crates and shipping containers of all sizes and colors, stacked and organized in impossibly complex configurations. Moving throughout the slips like bees among blossoms were thousands of drones not unlike the one to which Cam now clung with a renewed sense of both marvel and misgiving. His perspective was first that of a mite among the bristles of a caterpillar, and then, as they gained more speed and distance, he felt as though he was looking down upon a section of a round, statically charged tube brush that had just emerged from a vat of glitter, the light from the sun illuminating million of individual calico surfaces.

As they continued distancing themselves from the docks, the digital polychromatic patterns of the shipping containers dissolved into the orange and yellow atmospheric bands of the planet below. The only pictures Cam had ever seen of Earth from space were of the "Blue Marble" variety—the cool, cloud-swirled aquatic world of decades and centuries past. But what he saw below him now did not glow azure with clean habitual atmosphere, but rather burned amber and angry beneath the sun. Cam knew as well as anyone that Earth had always contained within it the potential to become another Venus—a world far closer to being Earth's sister planet than Mars ever had been— and that all it needed for that potential to be unlocked was the initiation of certain self-perpetuating and exponentially accelerating processes.

Cam was trying to discern whether the patterns he was studying below him were indications of surface features barely detectable beneath the atmosphere, or whether they were in fact the sinuous borders between chemical interactions, when he felt a sudden shift in the drone's orientation. He refocused from Earth back to *Equinox* and was surprised to find that the portion of the outer ring below him was still much more scaffolding and lanky offshoots of golden solar arrays than complete and functional space station. After everything he'd been told of the Coronians, Cam was expecting a bustling, high-tech, orbital metropolis, populated by artificial intelligences and sleek transports piloted by the exotic and unsettling derivatives of *Homo sapiens*, yet everything he could currently see was still mostly just trusses, substructures, and various configurations of photovoltaic panels. His eyes continued to follow the outer ring's curved frame until they landed and focused on a set of distant features that immediately explained exactly why *Equinox* was still so incomplete.

The formations were far enough away that they were small, but unmistakable. Cam had no way of judging distance or size, but there was no question that what he was looking at were two massive ships docked with the outer ring, both far bigger than anything that could possibly be lifted off the surface of the planet. They were long, relatively flat, multideck structures, intricate and cantilevered. One looked to be about three-quarters complete with about half of it aglow with power, while the second was mostly still skeleton and hull with only hints of outer plating. The more complete of the two vessels was crowned with several masts, and even at such a great distance, Cam could make out patches of antennae and parabolic communication dishes.

Equinox, Cam realized, was not so much a space station anymore as it was a hangar. And judging by the size of the ships the Coronians were constructing, they were not only planning on severing ties with Earth, but were in fact planning on leaving it behind forever.

CHAPTER FORTY-EIGHT

FALSE BOTTOM

THE BEST PART ABOUT COMPLETING a mining tour was that you got to leave the shack. The worst part was that you went directly from the shack into decompression.

If you got pulled out of the saturation rotation midcycle—usually due to an accident, an injury, or some other kind of medical complication—you'd probably have to do most of it in isolation. That usually meant between one and three weeks of being completely alone inside an enormous white and nautical-blue accented metal cylinder with nothing but your workspace to keep you company, and with amenities only modestly superior to those from which you just ascended.

But the only thing worse than decompressing alone was decompressing with five other miners. Each chamber was enormous as far as hermetically sealed hyperbaric capsules went, but once you partitioned off a quarter for a toilet, basin, and a shower, another quarter for a galley, and then filled the remaining space with six recliners (three to a side), storage racks (packed with blankets, towels, and standard-issue gear sacks), and then filled just about every remaining cavity with hoses, lines, valves, and oversized anachronistic analogue gauges, what little living space remained tended to make one long for the vast and seemingly boundless expanses of luxurious transpartment living.

When you decompressed as a team, there was typically a honeymoon period during which you enjoyed the company. You were kind of giddy just to be topside again, and everyone usually had some stories to share about pranks played on shack mates, or topics to debate like which players throughout history would have made the most unstoppable football squads, or descriptions of bizarre cultural remnants from before the Solar Age, dislodged from a collector's gearbox with the pinschers of an ADS. But the camaraderie usually only lasted for the first few days, after which the lack of personal space—along with various hygienic, digestive, and nighttime respiratory idiosyncrasies—eventually created an atmosphere only marginally preferable to the alternative of dissolved gasses forming microbubbles in your blood stream and soft tissues, leading to any number of unpleasant complications and symptoms up to and including an allegedly extremely painful death.

All things being equal, Charlie preferred to decompress alone. She loved being a miner, but as much as she tried to reject her former identity as an academic, the older she got, the more she realized she was better off coming to terms with her past rather than trying to disown it, and long periods of seclusion were ideal for both self-reflection, and for indulging in the kinds of activities for which she was otherwise usually too tired. In the past, she had used her time in isolation to write, to dig up some old pieces of short fiction from the archives, to sketch, and even to occasionally experiment with writing little bits of code that—as terse and elegant passages meant to move the souls of machines rather than those of human beings—she found curiously satisfying. There were so many things Charlie had been interested in when she was younger that she sometimes wondered if becoming a miner had been a way for her to give up on everything she was afraid of before she had a chance to fail at it. The only way not to let the people you loved down—the people who expected you to succeed at everything you ever tried—was to simply not try at all. That way, the disappointment could be spread out over long periods of time and more easily integrated into one's life like the slow-growing, low-grade chronic pain of a stress fracture rather than the shock of a compound break.

But right now, all things were not equal. After what she'd just been through, she wanted company—if not to comfort her, at least to distract her. She wanted her parents, her friends, and she wanted Luka. And as long as she was wishing, more than anything else, she wanted her sister, Valencia. All of the arguments and rivalries of their teenage years now felt like privileges neither of them had adequately appreciated and respected.

• • •

Charlie learned early on that your average deep-sea miner was not a big fan of authority, and few things throughout the course of modern human existence symbolized the expectation of subordination quite as purely as the closed-circuit surveillance camera. As long as she'd been a part of the saturation rotation, none of the cameras mounted in the corners of any of the decompression chambers worked, supposedly due to the number of times they'd been disabled by stir-crazy miners. According to water-rat lore, the first cameras had relatively soft acrylic lenses that were easily abraded into wide, white-cataract eyes using disassembled disposable razors. Between decompression rotations, the lenses were replaced with hardened borosilicate glass that stood up to razor blades, but succumbed to the tips of case-hardened screws laboriously removed from whatever equipment inside the capsule looked as though it probably wasn't critical. The synthetic sapphire replacements managed to maintain their transparency for a full rotation until diamond-tipped drill bits were smuggled inside each chamber, at which point the medical staff finally conceded defeat and accepted that remote monitoring of vital signs was as invasive as they were ever going to get.

The lack of visual surveillance opened up all kinds of new possibilities for passing the time. No alcohol was allowed inside the hyperbaric chambers since time spent decompressing was considered time on the clock, but there was a long tradition of maintaining a small hip flask beneath the false bottom of a storage compartment in the armrest of the recliner across from Charlie. The substance tended to mutate over time as it was topped off with the by-products of whatever it was Yerba Buena could spare that proved distillable. Charlie wasn't usually much of a drinker, but she'd already taken a few warm swallows of the fruity and nutty liqueur, hoping that it would give her the two things she felt she really needed right now: a little solace, and a lot of courage.

Her workspace was up on the polymeth surface suspended from the ceiling, but she wasn't using it. She'd already confirmed that Luka and Tycho had delivered on what she'd asked for before reporting for saturation rotation, which was a list of every single person who worked in the foundry, refinery, or who was in any way involved in the rig's deep-sea mining operations. In the process of trying to assemble such lists from memory, Charlie and Luka had been surprised to discover that they were only able to name between fifty and seventy people each over the course of several days—a startling reminder of how big the *San Francisco* actually was—and therefore they finally appealed to Tycho for official manifests. Two Bulls had indeed delivered, and Luka merged all three lists into one before forwarding them to Charlie.

People used all kinds of different forms of input aboard the *San Francisco*, from devices as sophisticated as noninvasive neural interfaces to as old-fashioned as keyboards with maddeningly cacophonous mechanical switches. But Charlie often used the oldest and most primitive of them all: handwriting. When she was a teaching assistant, she occasionally requested (she would not have the authority to insist until she was a lead teacher) that her students turn in at least one handwritten assignment per unit. Although Charlie was by no means a neophyte, she had serious reservations about completely abandoning—essentially overnight, on a relative timescale—a portion of the brain that humans had so fastidiously developed over the course of thousands of years. When Charlie had something important to say, she found she preferred to write it out by hand. And what Charlie was about to write was the most important thing she'd ever needed to express.

She worked on the horizontal retractable surface in front of her that, as evidenced by the bulb-shaped crater in the corner, was assembled more with eating in mind than composing longhand. With her magnetic pen poised above the surface of her silicon paper—held unconsciously askew in order to avoid the blood blisters that resulted from the amount of pressure she'd applied to the joystick inside her ADS—she tried to recall exactly what it was that Luka had sent out through the EMATS tubes just before cutting the power.

> *The time is coming when the Coronians*
> *will no longer need us.*
> *This is how it will feel . . .*

Although the cryptic dispatch had succeeded in getting Two Bulls' attention—and possibly the attention of others who he might now be collaborating with—Charlie knew she needed a very different approach. The economy of Luka's warning had been an appropriate harbinger of something as dramatic as the *San Francisco*'s first total power failure in their lifetime, but she needed to make a case; rally over half the population of the the entire city to an urgent and incredibly dangerous cause; establish a political and cultural movement that would change the lives of every last soul aboard the rig.

Charlie wrote.

She knew that it was too risky—and probably too conceptually foreign, without far more context—to describe their plans for sabotaging the Coronians' mining ability, or to reveal their ambitions around rebooting the planet's oxygen cycle by terraforming. Instead she focused on facts that she knew were easily compatible with her audience's own experiences, starting with what she thought of as the beginning of it all, and then working her way forward to the present.

She laid out all the evidence that she and Luka had that strongly suggested the Coronians were preparing to do their own mining, and what they believed that meant not just for the *San Francisco*, but for all of Earth. She presented the results of the analysis she'd done of all the rig's archives as far back as mining records went, clearly demonstrating a gradual decrease in yields, and despite constantly improving exploratory and surveying technology, a subtle but verifiable increase in the amount of time between locating new, highly productive sites. She recounted Luka's meeting with Councilwoman Khang Jung-soon during which he learned of the city's plans to raze Paramount Tower in order to free up mass to build The Infinity—a clear violation of the *San Francisco*'s long-standing social contract. She described how Luka had been imprisoned and repeatedly threatened with exile simply for telling the truth, and then outlined the deal the City Council had made with the Coronians securing the first generation of atomic assemblers in exchange for secretly executing several people the Coronians perceived as a threat, including a young woman whose unborn child had been forcibly taken from her, placed into stasis, and essentially sold. Finally, Charlie told of how she herself had been only seconds away from being sucked into the open bits of a shaped cutter despite the fact that it had every one of its safeties engaged—safeties that had never once failed in the entire history of Nautilus-class equipment.

When she was done, she found that she had filled six full sheets of silicon paper. She read through the letter several times, opening up gaps so that she could further elaborate on the points she hoped would strengthen her case and make her audience more receptive to what she was asking them to do. On the day she was to be released from decompression, she was requesting the simultaneous shutdown of all mining, refining, manufacturing, and production on the entire rig until a group of three representatives was appointed, a list of demands was drafted and ratified, and negotiations with the City Council had reached a satisfactory conclusion.

She brought up the menu at the top of the first page, then copied the letter to her workspace. After reading through it one last time without making any changes, she merged the document with the list of names that Luka had forwarded, took one final nip from the flask, levered the stopper back down into place, and told her workspace to send it.

There was an error.

The *San Francisco*'s network was robust enough that failures were extremely rare. After several more unsuccessful attempts, Charlie brought up the standard diagnostic utility, which needed only a few milliseconds to complete an inspection of her workspace instance and report back that while 100 percent of incoming packets were verified, every attempt to reroute outbound packets was failing. Charlie was about to increase the resolution of the `traceroute` command so she could inspect the individual hops between nodes when she felt the pressure in her sinuses suddenly change and heard something land on her writing surface. When she looked down, there was a disk of blood on the top sheet of silicon paper, perfectly round but for the halo of fine radial ejecta like the crimson corona of a tiny star.

She passed the back of her hand beneath her nose and saw that it was streaked red. The pressure was behind her eyes now, and for a moment—as she tightened her grip on the arms of her recliner—she thought the capsule had been toppled from its base and was rolling before she realized that what she was experiencing was vertigo. And then came the searing pain erupting from somewhere deep inside her skull. That's when it occurred to Charlie how incredibly stupid and careless she had been; how she had willingly allowed herself to be sealed inside a machine every bit as deadly as an industrial-scale cutter; and how all of this had been orchestrated, probably starting with the manipulation of Benthic's mixture to get him out of the rotation.

She knew she probably only had seconds before she blacked out—enough time to commit to one response. She looked at the emergency pull beside the hatch and tried to calculate the chances that the explosive bolts would function; tried to anticipate whether they were designed to be fail-safe, or whether they could be remotely disabled by anyone with sufficient permissions. Both of Charlie's hands went up to her temples and her eyes cinched themselves shut. She wanted nothing more than to pull her legs up into her seat and submit to whatever was happening—to will it all to be over as quickly as possible—but she knew she still had one more thing to do.

She slid out from behind her writing surface with the flask in one hand and the stack of silicon paper in the other. As soon as she was clear, she fell forward, though not toward the hatch. Instead, Charlie lunged toward the storage compartment with the false bottom. From the floor, she reached up and deposited the flask, then folded the stack of silicon paper as best she could and stuffed it down on top. With the last of her resolve, Charlie replaced the false bottom, closed the compartment, then curled up on the floor around a human-size ball of bright white pain. The last thing she experienced before losing consciousness was a peculiar but beautiful proximity to what she believed was the aura of her dead sister.

CHAPTER FORTY-NINE

EQUILIBRIUM BETWEEN FORCES

Luka discovered that cupcake decorators were much easier to assemble than they were to take apart.

These types of trinkets and novelties were seldom designed with servicing in mind, since it was far faster and cheaper to simply assemble a brand-new one and have it delivered free of charge via EMATS than it was to fix an old one that had been knocked off a counter, or neglected for long enough after use that it had become hopelessly clogged. Not only was replacement a more practical policy from a time-and-caps perspective, but assuming it had been at least a month since your previous purchase, there was a good chance the replacement model would represent a significant upgrade. New and cleverly refined schematics for all types of gadgets were constantly being traded among merchants at broker posts and ports; algorithmic engineering heuristics were always suggesting innovative new ways in which devices and components could be both enhanced and optimized; and millions of physical testing simulations were constantly being run across dozens of kilocores, ensuring that new or modified products would probably function acceptably over a minimum number of applications.

All this, even for a cupcake decorator.

It was precisely this culture of disposal that accounted for Luka's struggle to penetrate his multiaxis confection embellishment appliance. He had already exposed (and ingested) all the residual curious yellow that was accessible by removing the components that were designed for easy cleaning, but he knew there had to be more. He had finally taken to smashing the entire contraption with a mallet he used for sculpting, and was now fastidiously inspecting each and every chip, shard, fragment, and splinter for any sign whatsoever of a golden tinge.

Luka would have never guessed that house arrest would be so much worse than Hexagon Row. Aside from the quiet room, his time beneath the Pacific Medical Center had not been nearly as bad as it could have been. His cell had been surprisingly comfortable, the food mostly the same as it was at home, and although he would probably never admit this to anyone but himself, there were worse ways to pass the time than talking with Ellie. If one was going to be unexpectedly thrust into withdrawal, one might as well go through the process in the presence of an infinitely patient emulated psychotherapist.

House arrest, in contrast, placed incarceration entirely out of context. Luka felt strongly that prisons should look and feel like prisons instead of looking and feeling exactly like your transpartment. They should be separate, distinct, isolated locations that you entered with the belief—no matter how unrealistic or remote—that one day you will be allowed to go home again. Counterintuitive as it might seem, turning one's home into one's prison was far crueler. Luka believed now that one should never be detained or confined without ritual or ceremony—a rite of passage that inherently suggested an eventual rite of return. To simply wake up one morning and find a recorded message from the Judicial Committee, and then subsequently discover that one's front door refused to open, was to be sentenced to more than just time; the real punishment was a lifetime of wondering whether every room you entered would be the one from which you were never allowed to emerge.

Luka now understood house arrest to be as psychological as it was concrete. While his front door was now programmed to ignore both his presence and his commands, he had devised at least half a dozen ways he could probably escape: ask Tycho to let him out; set off the fire alarm, which would probably override whatever access directives were in place; use his sculpting tools to force the door open, probably without causing any more disturbance to his neighbors than reconfiguring his walls; rappel down the refuse chutes until he reached a maintenance hatch, then kick out the slats and find the nearest shower. *Et cetera.* But he also knew that it wouldn't do him any good. In anywhere from a few minutes to a few hours, he'd probably just end up back on Hexagon Row, which, while preferable to house arrest in many ways, would also mean giving up access to his workspace, and more importantly, any prayer whatsoever of excavating even just a few milligrams of curious yellow residue.

So instead, Luka focused on distracting himself while trusting that Tycho would continue finding ways to delay his inevitable exile long enough for Charlie to get off saturation rotation, organize a rig-wide labor strike, and arrange for a full pardon. He'd sculpted the same refrozen block of ice several times, and even incorporated the melting of his self-portrait into a kind of melancholy performance art when played back at high speed; disposed of most of his material possessions—or at least those that fit through his refuse chutes—expecting, at some point, to suddenly attain some form of metaphysical enlightenment (and secretly hoping to find a forgotten, unopened envelope of powdered synthetic opioid); slept as much as his body could tolerate; committed to, and subsequently abandoned, strict regimens of meditation and yoga; made significant progress toward his goal of doing one thousand push-ups, pull-ups, and sit-ups over the course of ten days, though he was pretty sure he'd lost count of all three; somehow found himself exploring the esoteric but surprisingly broad domain of furniture made out of old recycled boat wood in the archives; and, of course, used a mallet to smash a device designed to spread, spray, deposit, or otherwise arrange an infinite spectrum of condensed sweetener through an array of dynamically shaped nozzles, then proceeded to sort and scour every last fragment, touching each side to the tip of his tongue and then rubbing whatever came off against the roof of his mouth.

While Luka sat bent over his work, a notification intentionally similar to the warbling birdsongs of the Embarcadero emanated from the front of his transpartment. Although the door was completely nontransparent, the inside polymeth surface displayed an image of what was on the other side, applying a type of Gaussian blur filter and combining it with just enough opacity to suggest translucent frosted glass. Although the visitor could, of course, see nothing from his or her side of the door, the effect was designed to allow the resident to retain a sense of privacy while still discerning who had come calling.

It was Matthew Two Bulls.

Luka straightened himself. His speculation around why Two Bulls would risk coming to his flat—especially while he was under house arrest—was interrupted by his realization that the door might not even open, and that he might not even be able to admit the man behind the seemingly omniscient Tycho persona.

"Come in?" he tried. The doors parted, and Luka involuntarily registered yet another potential way to subvert confinement.

Two Bulls checked both sides of the hallway outside before stepping hurriedly through. The doors eased closed behind him, presumably recommencing Luka's detention. Luka's most recent impression of the substantial Lakota tribesman came from the virtual retina display that had made Two Bulls seem much taller and more authoritative than he looked now, perhaps because Luka had been sitting on the floor and looking up at the projection. Or maybe it was the distress in the man's expression that made him appear a little more earthly and mortal, apparent even though his eyes were not visible.

"Luka," Two Bulls acknowledged with a nod. His hair and wraparound visor were equally dark and lustrous, both agleam in the bright white light of Luka's entry.

Luka stood. "What are you doing here?"

"We can't communicate electronically anymore," Two Bulls said. He gave the flat a rapid appraisal. Luka had the impression that he was both verifying that they were alone, and satisfying his curiosity about how one of the *San Francisco*'s most notoriously eccentric citizens lived. "I believe Tycho's been compromised."

"Well, that's suboptimal," Luka remarked. "But then what makes you think it's safe to communicate in person? Don't you think someone might be listening?"

"I'm the Chair of the Judicial Committee," Two Bulls reminded Luka. "I arranged for some cover."

"Cover for what, exactly?"

Two Bulls allowed himself farther into the room, placing his broad hands on the back of the chair opposite Luka. "For talking about what we do next."

"What do you mean?" Luka asked hesitantly. "We wait, right?"

Two Bulls shook his head. "I'm sorry about this, Luka," he said, "but it's too late to prevent your exile. The best we can do now is find out where they're taking you and make sure the *Accipiter Hawk* is there to pick you up."

"Wait a second," Luka said. "Back up. Why is it too late to stop my exile? What about the strike? What about shutting down the city, and demanding a pardon, and all that?"

"The strike isn't going to happen."

"*What?*" Luka exclaimed. "Why the hell not?"

"Because . . ." Two Bulls began, then faltered. He bent and rested his forehead against his hands on the back of the chair.

"Because why?" Luka prompted. "What's going on?"

Two Bulls straightened up and watched Luka for a long moment. "Because Charlie is dead."

Luka heard and understood Two Bulls' words, but he wasn't able to make sense of them. It was like understanding that there must have been a time before the beginning of the universe, but running up against your own cognitive limitations before being able to comprehend or internalize the fact. Or believing that, after you died, your consciousness simply ceased to exist, but then having that consciousness refuse to truly contemplate its own extinction. It seemed simultaneously feasible that the City Council would feel so threatened by a labor strike that they would have someone killed, and entirely impossible that that someone could be Charlie—the only person left on the entire planet who Luka truly cared for and loved.

"I'm so sorry, Luka," Two Bulls said. "But we don't have much time. I need you to focus."

"Oh I'm focused," Luka said. He watched Two Bulls with eerie placidity. "I'm focused on finding out who did this and ripping their fucking throats out."

"Revenge is not the answer right now," Two Bulls said. "That's what I'm here to make you understand. You have to accept your exile and never come back."

"I'm not going anywhere," Luka explained to Two Bulls. "Not until I send this entire fucking city to the bottom of the ocean."

"Listen to me carefully, Luka," Two Bulls said. Luka saw his eyebrows rise from behind his visor. "If you're anything other than one-hundred-percent compliant, they will kill you. All they need is an excuse."

"Then I'm happy to give it to them."

"*Damnit!*" Two Bulls said, lifting the chair by its back and slamming it down into the sound-dampening silicone mat beneath their feet. "This isn't a goddamn *game*, Luka. They *will* waterlock you."

As they stared at one another across the table, it suddenly occurred to Luka how absurd all of this was.

"Wait a second," he said, shaking his head. "Why would they kill Charlie? It doesn't make any sense. Why wouldn't they kill *me* and exile *her*? The whole reason she took the lead on the strike was because *I'm* the one they perceive as the bigger threat."

"Exactly," Two Bulls said. "Charlie wasn't enough of a threat to justify exile so they needed another way to neutralize her. If you were the one suddenly killed in an accident, it would look suspicious, but everyone knows how dangerous the life of a water rat is."

"So I'm the one who gets to live," Luka said. "Again."

"*If* we play this exactly right," Two Bulls stipulated. "But make no mistake. Although the City Council would prefer to keep up appearances, that doesn't mean they won't hesitate to put a bullet in your head or waterlock you at the slightest provocation."

"So you think we should just let this go," Luka said. "Just let them get away with murdering Charlie."

"I'm suggesting *you* let this go," Two Bulls said. "Let me deal with this in my own time."

Luka smiled a touch maniacally. "You should know me better than that by now," he told Two Bulls. "If you didn't want me to do anything, then you shouldn't have come here and told me. There's no way I'm letting this go."

"Then you'll be dead, too," Two Bulls said plainly. "Probably by the end of the day."

Luka shrugged. "I accept that," he said. "It's not like I have anyone or anything to live for, anyway."

"I'm sorry that you feel that way," Two Bulls said. "Because from where I'm standing, it looks like you have *everything* to live for."

Luka narrowed his eyes at the man across the table. "Like what?"

"Like everything you've accomplished," Two Bulls said. "Think about it. Without you, there wouldn't be any gliders. Without you, we couldn't have infiltrated *Equinox*. Luka, *you're* the one who started all of this. The day you made the decision to shut the power off might just be remembered as the day that changed the entire course of human history. Don't you want to see how all this turns out?"

Luka didn't answer. Once again, he'd heard everything Two Bulls said, but he was fixated on just three words: *made the decision*. Luka had always thought of his life as a series of events that had happened to him without his input or intervention—circumstances over which he'd never really had any control:

being forced to leave Hammerfest; being separated from his parents; his life in China Basin; becoming an assembly technician; the loss of the baby; Val's suicide; and now, Charlie's murder.

Maybe things were different for people who were born on the *San Francisco*, but Luka had figured out a long time ago that the best he could do with his life was just try to get through it—distract himself with sculpting, and keep the endorphins surging with curious yellow, and just hope he was lucky enough not to see the end coming, whatever form it took. But now there was evidence that this was not necessarily the truth of his life's narrative. He had made the decision to invite Val up to his flat that evening; he'd decided to go down to deck two and shut the power off that day; and he'd made the decision—all on his own—to rescue Cadie, Cam, Ayla, and Omicron from the waterlock, and then support their plans to try to contain the Coronians. While it was certainly true that his life was not something he had entirely dictated, it was equally untrue that his life had simply happened to him without any conscious volition. He was starting to see that there was an equilibrium between the forces that defined his life, some of which were under his control, and some of which lay outside. Life was neither preordained nor entirely arbitrary, but rather the aggregate of infinitely complex dynamics, forces, and vortices to which you were free to contribute as much or as little energy as you yourself chose.

When Two Bulls spoke again, Luka realized that he had been looking down at the ruin strewn across the table.

"Luka, we both know that exile is a death sentence," he said. "But we can get you a reprieve. I can find out where they're taking you, and I *will* make sure Ayla is there to pick you up. And then once things have blown over, I'll figure out how to get Cadie to you, as well. Luka, this is your chance to finally get out of here—to start an entirely new life. This doesn't have to be the end. It can be an opportunity."

Luka looked up at Two Bulls and nodded. "OK," he said. "I'll go."

Two Bulls did not smile, but Luka could see the satisfaction and the relief in this features. The big man took his hands off the back of the chair, straightened himself up, and walked around to Luka's side. Suddenly the man once again seemed as big as his projection had been, and when he reached out and grasped Luka's shoulder, a feeling of warmth seemed to flow throughout Luka's entire body.

"I promise you that Charlie's death won't be for nothing," Two Bulls said. "You have my word on that."

All of the loss in Luka's life began to rise up inside him, triggering the familiar instinct to suppress it. He had just made the decision to let it happen—perhaps for the first time in his entire life—when the front doors slid apart.

Two Bulls remained composed as Luka's transpartment filled with officers, their compact assault rifles raised and sighted. He gave Luka a final nod as he let his hand drop to his side and stepped back.

"It's OK," Two Bulls announced. "Lower your weapons. He will go peacefully."

Luka did not resist as his arms were gathered behind him and he was roughly cuffed. The commander of the unit stepped into the space between Luka and Two Bulls, and looked down at his prisoner. The man was unshaven, but in a way that came across as well groomed, the length of his stubble blending nicely with his receding hairline. He sharpened his look by lowering his heavy brow and squinting his intense, amber-flecked eyes.

"I'm glad to hear that," he said with an accent that Luka identified as British, but not the highborn kind. The man then turned around to face Two Bulls. "But what about you?"

Even with his visor, Luka could see the confusion in Two Bulls' expression. But before he could respond, the commander struck somewhere down low, and Two Bulls—after a sickening, guttural heave—was silently doubled over.

The commander turned back to Luka, and Luka recoiled.

"The bad news is that there won't be anyone waiting to rescue you," the commander said. He turned once again and watched as Two Bulls was forced upright and cuffed. "But the good news is that you won't die alone."

CHAPTER FIFTY

FEEDBACK LOOP

CAM DID NOT EXPECT TO HAVE the best meal of his life four hundred kilometers above the surface of the planet.

He wasn't entirely sure what it was, though he suspected that the firm and fleshy little pink curls were extinct crustacean scavengers once commonly known as shrimp. How the Coronians were able to provide him with a sterile but fresh vacuum-sealed packet of them, he had absolutely no idea, but every time he spun another one in the air, wrapped his mouth around it, and chewed with great relish, he was positive that he was experiencing the very pinnacle of Coronian achievement.

The drone had towed Cam to one of several interconnected hexagonal habitation capsules, each equipped with its own tiny airlock. Even after living inside *Aquarius* for months, the module felt small, and Cam was astonished to discover that it had once been a dormitory designed to accommodate as many as half a dozen technicians. In the back of the capsule, recessed into each one of the six sides of the hexagon, were individual sleep stations—quilted cubbies with anchored sleeping bags, inoperable terminals, dimmable plasma lighting, and folding doors. Just beyond them was another folding door with a crescent moon drawn in black indelible marker, and inside, a small toilet and urine collection tube with a plastic yellow attachment, both of which produced light suction which Cam quickly learned was critical for ensuring that everything flowed in the correct direction. (On the wall were pockets of paper, wipes, and even latex gloves just in case escape velocity was unexpectedly achieved.) In front of the sleeping pods were shelves of towels, several detachable mirrors, and pouches of toothbrushes, toothpaste, razors, water bags with resealable straws, and various types of no-rinse soap and shampoo. A portion of the capsule's ceiling was reserved for the galley with racks of vacuum-sealed food pouches (which is where Cam was told to look for the shrimp-like meal), a water terminal (which could be used to fill drinking bags, or to rehydrate various forms of ancient nutrients that Cam did not recognize, bearing labels in languages he did not know), and a small table surfaced with woolly loops designed to mate with their hooked counterparts. Folded up into the walls were various forms of exercise equipment: a type of stationary bike with toe clips, but no seat; a treadmill with an elasticized shoulder harness to create downward force against the belt; and a device labeled ARED (and below, in a smaller font, Advanced Resistive Exercise Device), which was a collection of bars, hinges, and pneumatic cylinders probably capable of facilitating a wide variety of strength-training exercises for anyone with proper coaching or sufficient patience. Most of what was intended to be thought of as the floor was treated as stowage and filled with canvas-covered crates and steel canisters secured beneath elastic webbing.

Every other available surface that was more than a few square centimeters served as an anchor point for an assortment of miscellaneous objects visually coalescing into an intricate collage of convenience and utility: powerless terminals mounted on segmented articulated appendages; nontoxic fire suppression canisters; plastic bags marked "Contaminated Cleanup Kit" with masks, eye protection, and heavy, chemical-resistant gloves inside; at least three pairs of scissors, Velcroed and leashed; sockets and outlets designed for unfamiliar configurations of plugs and pins; cameras with extremely long lenses mounted beside the airlock door; a miniature Go mat strewn with magnetic stones; variously angled handgrips, toeholds, and straps; patches, labels, stickers, and a speed limit sign marked "17,500," probably hung by an American since the units were in miles rather than kilometers. The sound in the capsule was not unlike the environmental systems on *Aquarius* or in certain sections of V1: static white noise that, when you first heard it, you thought you'd never get used to, but that within minutes you forgot about entirely until the next time you experienced the peculiar sensation of silence.

Cam's pressure suit was in the airlock, but his chronograph was on his wrist, the excess strap floating rather than hanging. Over the course of nearly twelve hours, he'd managed to re-oxygenate his cramped muscles by getting a little exercise on the stationary bike (which he kept trying to lower himself onto, surprised each time to rediscover that there was no seat), get some sleep (dreaming of free-falling and waking with a violent start several times before finally being able to relax), clean himself up (noticing in a mirror that his face was getting puffy from the fluids in his body becoming more evenly distributed), change his clothes (dressing in what looked like fern-green pajamas and white tube socks that he found sealed in a bag in one of the sleep stations), have his first taste of shrimp (realizing he might now be the only member of his species who could claim to have enjoyed such a delicacy), and in-between it all, drink several liters of water (and as a result, gain a great deal of experience with the urine collection tube).

He spent some time trying to spot something of interest though the airlock windows, but from his angle, even through the long camera lenses, all he could see was the occasional drone drifting by, gas jets bursting to correct its course. He was pretty sure that the airlock was still pressurized, and he thought about opening the inner door so that he only had one window to look through (thereby widening his visual range), but ultimately Cam decided it was probably best not to tamper with an unfamiliar airlock—especially one built so long ago and probably disused for so many years. Instead, he searched the sleep stations for something he hoped might entertain him while he waited, and behind a sliding panel, he found a small, cobalt-blue, hollow rubber ball that he discovered rocketed nicely—if somewhat perilously—around the capsule.

The first game he played involved identifying surface area devoid enough of clutter to accommodate the ball's contact patch. The challenge was not just hitting his target, but also recapturing the projectile on its way back. He then noticed that the top of a crate in the floor was almost exactly parallel to the surface of the table on the ceiling, so he played a game with himself to see how many times he could get the ball the bounce between the two surfaces. A perfect round would be one where the friction of the environment stopped the ball before the gradual accumulation of misalignment put an end to the volley, but unfortunately that was not to be.

Cam wasn't just distracting himself. He was also problem solving in the way one sometimes tried to figure something out by not thinking about it directly, like attempting to detect faint traces of light or movement by intentionally looking away and placing the area of interest in your peripheral vision. There was, of course, an established procedure for capture—a plan they'd all agreed on should the Coronians take Cam prisoner. Sitting around the cubical in *Aquarius*—Omicron and Ayla participating via line-of-sight acoustic link and a slab of polymeth—the consensus had been that concealing the gliders was top priority. Cam was to tell the Coronians absolutely nothing, look for every opportunity to escape and complete his mission, and above all else, do whatever he had to do to in order to protect their terraforming plans.

But he and Cadie had, privately, come to a very different understanding. The night before he was smuggled up to deck three and sealed inside the modified crate—the night he'd wanted, more than anything else, to share his bunk with Cadie—the two of them had secretly established a new protocol. Cadie believed there was a good chance the Coronians would already know about their attempts to terraform. There was no question that they would have studied her daughter's DNA carefully, and therefore would have already come across not only the image known as Blue Marble, but all of Arik's research. Cadie also believed that the Coronians very likely had—or could rapidly develop and assemble—technology to ensure that Cam would not be able to conceal anything from them. That meant any opportunity to make a deal with the Coronians would likely be brief, and that the longer Cam was in custody, the less leverage he would have. The gliders, Cam and Cadie agreed, were not top priority after all, and neither was Cam's mission to sabotage the Coronians' ability to mine. Should Cam be captured, he was to use the gliders as a bargaining chip for the things that, to them, mattered most: the lives of Zaire and Haná—and, of course, his own life, as well. There would be other opportunities to terraform, and other opportunities to set the Coronians back, but they would almost certainly never again be in a position to directly affect the lives of the ones they loved.

It was not difficult to imagine a scenario where Cam was able to negotiate safe passage for himself and Zaire, but Haná was not nearly so straightforward. She'd probably already been in zero-g long enough that she would not be able to return to Earth, and the Coronians might consider her enough of a prize—a genetic and possibly even cultural link to their distant past—that before they agreed to terms that might jeopardize that which they'd worked so hard to obtain, they would probably find other ways to take what they wanted from Cam. Therefore, it was not Haná's release that Cam was to negotiate, but something that, if Cadie was right, could ultimately be of much greater importance.

Cam had just decided that he might take another look at the airlock after all when every terminal in the module suddenly lit up simultaneously. Appearing on each of the capsule's screens was a young girl who Cam—despite his circumstances—couldn't deny was stunningly seductive. She had straw-yellow, bed-tousled hair; almost unnaturally wide, sapphire-blue eyes that penetrated through long, heavily made-up lashes; a petite, slightly upturned nose; and very full, flesh-colored lips. She wore a low-cut and fitted white tank top, and she seemed to be leaning against a simple gray-blue gradient backdrop. The girl watched Cam with great interest, but also with a self-awareness that suggested he should be watching her with an interest even greater.

"Good morning, Cam," she said. Her voice was young, sweet, slightly groggy. All of the display panels in the capsule must have been acoustically resonant as her voice came at him from multiple trajectories. "How are you feeling?"

Cam looked from screen to screen. "Who are you?"

"My name is Angelia," the girl said. "Do you have everything you need?"

"I don't mean your *name*," Cam said. "I mean who *are* you? Are you Coronian?"

The girl blinked and dimples formed in her cheeks as she smiled. "Think of me as your personal liaison," she said.

Cam used a handhold to pull himself closer to the screen in the galley. As convincing as she was—as subtly and perfectly as her expression transitioned from one to another, and as closely as her voice matched the movement of her lips and larynx—the illusion dematerialized as soon as Cam noticed that she was changing. Her flaxen hair was now strawberry blonde and slightly neater, and her eyes were transitioning from blue to hazel.

"What's going on?" Cam asked.

"You're changing me," the girl said, less flirtatiously and more as a simple statement of fact. "Please keep watching."

She continued to morph, more rapidly now, but still fluidly. Her hair lengthened until it finally stopped—full and slightly wavy, and in a simple off-center part—just above her breasts, a shade somewhere between brown and black. Her face was rounder and her eyes—lashes shorter and makeup gone—were narrower and a dark copper brown. Her lips were pink, but naturally so, and her nose a tad broader. Her shirt was now a charcoal-gray V-neck that was still suggestive, though more modest than the tank top had been, and her posture was straighter—more attentive than evocative. Once her new form appeared finalized, she reached up with both hands and tucked her hair behind her ears, and Cam realized that she had gone from classically alluring to everything that matched his own personal and highly specific definition of pure, breathtaking beauty.

"My God," he breathed as he unabashedly leered. "How did you do that?"

"Feature randomization combined with a physiological reaction feedback loop," the girl said. Her voice was still feminine, but more mature now—confident rather than coquettish. "We want you to feel as comfortable as possible."

"Who exactly is *we*?" Cam asked.

"All of us," the girl said elusively. "How are you feeling?"

"You tell me," Cam said with a hint of resentment. "You probably know better than I do."

"Yes," the girl said plainly, "but we are attempting to convey empathy in order to establish trust."

Cam's eyebrows went up at the girl's candidness. "At least you're honest."

"We will not attempt to deceive you," the girl said. "And attempting to deceive us will be ineffective."

Cam shrugged. "Fair enough."

"Did you enjoy your meal?" the girl asked. "Please describe how you are feeling."

Having already tried to make sense of his seclusion in various ways, a new possibility suddenly occurred to Cam. He wondered if the habitation module—rather than temporary accommodations or a prison—was in fact a laboratory. Perhaps for the very first time, the Coronians had among them a mature specimen of the species from which they arose. Maybe they'd never considered Cam a threat so much as a research opportunity.

"What was it?" Cam asked. "Where did it come from?"

"*Pandalus borealis*, previously known less formally as the northern prawn, pink shrimp, deepwater prawn, deep-sea prawn, great northern prawn, and the northern shrimp. They are a relatively primitive decapod crustacean that—"

"Where did they *come from*?" Cam interrupted. "They're *extinct*, aren't they?"

"*Pandalus borealis* no longer occur naturally, if that's what you mean by extinct. But we have successfully reconstructed more than two hundred extinct multicellular species using genetic biological assemblers."

Cam's eyes left the screen as he thought about what the girl had just told him. When he looked back, it was with an expression that combined horror and intrigue. "Are you telling me you *assembled* them? You can assemble *life*?"

"We can assemble organic matter," the girl clarified. "The samples you consumed were exact clones of the specimen from which the DNA was originally extracted several decades ago. But none of them was ever actually alive."

"Why not?" Cam asked. "I mean, what's the difference? If you can assemble an exact biological duplicate, what is it that make them *live*?"

The girl smiled in a way that, for the first time, seemed a genuine expression of emotion. "Unfortunately we have not yet figured that out," she admitted, "but we will."

"Is that why you brought me here?" Cam asked. "To experiment on me?"

"No," the girl said. "Determining whether you are able to derive nutrients from a genetically assembled life-form was purely opportunistic. That is not the primary reason you are here."

Although he was was relieved by the girl's response—glad to dismiss the images of experimentation and invasive examination that had involuntarily started forming in his head—he was also back to being confused. "Then why *am* I here?"

"We know that you came here to attempt to sabotage our mining capabilities," the girl explained. "And we know about the devices you refer to as gliders. We recovered Arik Ockley's terraforming research from his daughter's DNA, and we have determined that it is not only viable, but that it constitutes a genuine and imminent threat to us."

"Why?" Cam asked. "Why do you feel like you have to maintain such tight control over Earth?"

"Coronians cannot survive Earth's gravity," the girl said. "We must ensure that we continue to receive resources until we are able to obtain sufficient quantities ourselves."

"But why do you assume that we'll abandon you?"

"Because abandonment was the very genesis of our species. We will never forget the Lessons of Genevieve. The First Coronian Law states that independence and self-sufficiency are to be valued above all else."

Cam found the girl's response unsettling in a way he hadn't expected. Having been raised in the godless and engineered environment of V1, he'd never really been exposed to religion, but there was clearly a cultlike fanaticism to what he'd just heard. He wondered if the portion of the human brain that somehow enabled faith to coexist with logic and empirical observation had been retained by the Coronians—perhaps even amplified or enhanced—and he wondered what horrors a culture of internalized martyrdom combined with an obvious emotional detachment and such advanced technological and scientific achievement might ultimately give rise to. Suddenly the girl's name—Angelia, she'd said it was—took on an entirely new significance, as did the Coronians' apparent obsession with assembling life. Even the massive carriers Cam had seen on his way to the habitation module took on a new meaning for him, evoking perhaps the only biblical story he knew other than Adam and Eve: the building of an enormous ark designed to escape an imminent existential threat.

"The ships," Cam said. "What are they for?"

"For ensuring our survival," the girl replied.

"Are they for mining?"

"Yes," the girl said. "But we don't just intend to mine the solar system. We also intend to explore and populate it."

"Why?" Cam asked her. "Why dedicate all your resources to building ships instead of just expanding *Equinox*?"

"Because we know that it is only a matter of time before your species once again attempts to eliminate ours. Genocide is a persistent theme throughout all of human history, and to assume the future will significantly differ from the past would be naive. It is imperative that we keep ourselves out of Earth's reach. As your presence here clearly indicates, four hundred kilometers above the surface is not nearly far enough."

Cam did not respond right away. He'd already given a great deal of consideration to how realistic it was for him to escape captivity—already looked around for objects that, should he decide to put his suit back on and step out through the airlock, might provide him with thrust (the fire suppression canisters, the pneumatic cylinders inside the exercise equipment, some kind of improvised water jet). But even if attempting to complete his original mission didn't feel entirely futile at this point, he realized now that ever since he and Cadie had agreed on a contingency plan, his actual mission had changed.

"That's not why I'm here," Cam said. "I'm not here to destroy anything, or to kill anyone."

The girl watched Cam for a moment, blinking. "Your neurological imagery indicates that you believe you are telling the truth," she said. "Why *are* you here?"

"I'm here to help you," Cam said.

"How?"

"By telling you how to stop the gliders."

The girl tilted her head and looked at Cam with genuine curiosity. "In exchange for what?"

"Not *what*," Cam said. "*Who*."

"Your wife," the girl postulated. "The girl called Zaire."

"That's right. I know you have influence over whoever has her. I want passage to wherever she is, and I want her returned to me. And there's someone else."

"Haná," the girl said.

Cam hesitated while he prepared himself for the answer to the question he now had to ask. "Is she alive?"

"Yes," the girl told him. "However, she has proven to be a tremendous asset to us, and we are unwilling to release her. Even if we did, it is no longer possible for her to return to Earth. Haná is one of us now. She is a Coronian."

"I'm not asking for her back," Cam said. "How long before your ships are ready to leave orbit?"

"At the rate we are currently receiving material from Earth, we estimate that all four carriers will be ready to leave orbit in approximately sixty thousand cycles."

"Cycles," Cam repeated. "I don't understand."

"A cycle is the amount of time it takes for the outer ring of *Equinox* to complete a single rotation. Sixty thousand cycles is approximately ten-point-five years."

Cam nodded. "OK," he said. "Then all I ask is that a conversation be allowed to take place between Haná and her mother before you leave."

The girl was not ready with a response. While her expression never conveyed confusion or perplexity, her silence suggested that she—or more likely *they*—were busy conferring, consulting, and, Cam imagined, calculating.

"We don't understand," the girl finally said.

"There's nothing *to* understand," Cam told her. "I want Cadie to have the opportunity to say good-bye to her daughter. That's it."

"Even if we were to accept your terms, what makes you believe we will ultimately honor our agreement?"

"Because Zaire means nothing to you," Cam said. "And because what Cadie has to say to Haná, I promise you every Coronian will want to hear."

CHAPTER FIFTY-ONE

AFTER-HOURS JUSTICE

Two Bulls' visor was snatched violently off his face as though it was something the commander had been waiting a very long time to do. Luka watched the isolation mask go over his coconspirator's head, and correctly anticipated his own imminent sensory deprivation.

He knew what the device was because of a prototype that had been passed around the foundry about a year ago. Nobody had ever seen one before, and they experimented with it until it finally broke, at which point they tagged it as defective, shoved it down a refuse chute, and promptly assembled a new one.

An isolation mask was an extremely lightweight carbon shell not unlike a high-speed hydrofoil helmet, but constructed as two separate components. The first fit snuggly over the head and was held in place with a strap beneath the chin, and the second module pivoted down over the face, compressing the entire form factor in the process and locking it tightly closed around the head. When activated by the switch in the back, arrays of sensors on the outside monitored the external environment while inside, destructive interference patterns were constantly being generated, effectively phase-canceling all light, sound, and electromagnetic waves before they could be perceived either organically by the senses, or mechanically by implants or wearables. Active isolation masks tapped into the same omnipresent ambient radio waves that powered an increasing number of devices aboard the *San Francisco*, and had a soft layer of silicone on the outside that Luka suspected was intended to limit the potential damage of a head-butt, and to prevent a prisoner from attempting suicide by blunt trauma during transfer.

Although the isolation mask effectively deprived Luka's senses of all light and sound, it could not counteract the forces of gravity on the fluid of his inner ears, so he knew that they had descended twice: once to the lobby of Millennium Tower, and once again only a few seconds later, almost certainly down to deck three where he and Two Bulls could be escorted without causing a spectacle. From there, it was impossible to tell exactly where they were headed, but from the number of steps they took, Luka knew that they were traversing the length of the entire rig, which meant they were probably either going to City Hall to satisfy a few statutes or regulations with a quick mock-trial, or—dispensing with formalities altogether—directly to the hangar. It wasn't until Luka was gruffly stopped, and then moments later shoved forward again, that a third possibility occurred to him: the waterlock. He sniffed, trying to detect moisture in the air, but could sense nothing beyond the ammonia crystals in the isolation mask's vents, designed to undermine olfaction by irritating the nasal passages. He was relieved when he once again felt hands grasp his biceps and sensed the smooth ascent of an electromagnetic lift.

By the time the face shield of his isolation mask was raised, Luka was pretty sure he'd already figured out where they were. As he expected, they were inside the *San Francisco*'s one and only tribunal chamber—the same room in which we was sentenced to time on Hexagon Row. However, this time, there was the unmistakable feel of after-hours justice. Both the galleries behind them and the jury box to his left were empty, and from the way he and Two Bulls were positioned—standing in front of the bench, surrounded by the same officers who had stormed Luka's transpartment—it seemed pretty evident that the trial phase had already occurred in their absence, and they'd arrived just in time for sentencing.

In Luka's opinion, the room was inappropriately elegant. Most of the lighting was provided by giant artificial luminescent crystals jutting dramatically down through the ceiling. The walls were overlapping tapered panels channeling all attention forward toward the three-tiered, marble-assembly bench. At the peak of the pyramid, where Two Bulls once sat, was Khang Jung-soon. The rest of the Judicial Committee sat below her (minus one), and below them, the remaining four members of the City Council. Behind them was a backdrop of irregularly cut glass block supporting a relatively understated version of the city's polygonal phoenix crest, each surface a subtly varied shade of white.

Luka knew everyone on the bench by sight, and even remembered a few names: Sutro, Alvord, Lapham. They were dressed according to a mode Luka would describe as high-fashion judicial with complexly woven pastel tie knots peaking through the tops of shimmering robes, and luxuriously draped capes secured about the shoulders with wreaths of platinum herringbone chains. Khang's robe—checkered in two different shades, or perhaps textures, of black—was by far the most conservative. Although the garish attire was probably an attempt to project individualism and self-determination, Luka felt that the City Council's embellishments served only to reinforce what each member truly was: a barely sentient tentacle that existed only to extend the reach and influence of the chairwoman who presided above them.

Khang greeted the defendants with her disarmingly warm smile.

"I think we can probably make this quick," she said in a tone that would have been far too casual for formal proceedings, but seemed appropriate for whatever this actually was. "You have both been found guilty of plotting to overthrow the democratically elected council of a sovereign Metropolis-class vessel. Such charges constitute treason, the punishment for which, as you both know, is mandatory exile. Does either of you have anything you want to say?"

"I do," Luka said. He rolled his shoulders, hoping to get some blood to flow down into his cuffed hands. "Why don't you just tell us what you want so we can skip all the theatrics?"

Khang seemed perplexed by Luka's suggestion. "What makes you think I want anything from you?"

"The fact that we're here," Luka said. "We're obviously not getting a fair trial, so why else would you bring us here if not to try to strike a deal?"

Khang smiled down at Luka. "I've always appreciated your outspokenness, Luka," she said. She leaned forward and interlaced her fingers. "Allow me to be equally forthright. Each of you has one chance, and one chance only, to change our minds. We know about the strikes you were planning, and the unions you hoped to organize, and the list of demands you intended to present to us under the threat of mutiny. And we know about the Tycho user account that the two of you have been using to communicate." She paused, squinting at the two prisoners, possibly looking for signs of acknowledgment. "But what we haven't figured out yet is what *else* you two have been up to. Luka, we know that you've received hundreds of fraudulent assembly orders, and Matthew, we know that you were the one who arranged them. But what we don't know yet is what was assembled, or why. Now I want you two to consider your positions very carefully before you answer. I want you to tell me exactly what you assembled, why you assembled it, and who else is involved in your conspiracy. If you choose to cooperate, your sentences will be commuted, and after some time on Hexagon Row, you will each report to your new positions as grade-one deep-sea miners. If you choose *not* to cooperate, we go directly from here to the hangar, and both of your sentences will be carried out today. Now . . ." She paused while contemplating the accused. "Which one of you would like to go first?"

Two Bulls did his best to straighten himself before the bench. He was still trying to blink away the brightness he was unaccustomed to, and probably still sore in the gut. Luka could see that his eyes were narrow but heavy, and that he looked significantly older without his visor.

"How do we know you'll keep your word?" he asked Khang.

"You don't," Khang replied. "But from where I'm sitting, it doesn't look to me like either of you has much to lose."

"Then we have nothing to say," Two Bulls stated. "Not without a guarantee."

"Matthew," Khang began. "Believe it or not, I have a great deal of respect for everything you've done, not only for the council and for the city, but for me personally. Please don't throw everything away like this. Please. Let me help you."

Two Bulls glanced at Luka, then looked back up at Khang. "Let's try this," he said.

"I'm listening."

"There's a ship called the *Accipiter Hawk* that maintains a perimeter of about a hundred kilometers from the *San Francisco*."

Luka turned to Two Bulls. "What the hell are you doing?"

"Trying to save your life," Two Bulls said. He then looked back up at the bench. "Forty-eight hours after I know Luka is safely aboard that ship, I'll tell you everything you want to know. I'll even tell you things you didn't know you wanted to know."

Khang leaned back and looked up at the crystals in the ceiling while she contemplated Two Bulls' offer. She tapped her fingertips together in front of her face, then looked back down.

"No," she said simply. "I reject your offer."

This was obviously not the response Two Bulls was expecting. "Why?" he asked. "That's more than fair, and you know it. Everyone gets what they want."

"Quite frankly," Khang said, "because I don't have to. Whatever you two are plotting will almost certainly perish along with you, so I have no intention of setting either of you free. Either both of you stay here where I can keep an eye on you, or we take both of you ashore and leave it up to the subterraneans. As much as I respect your attempted sacrifice, Matthew, there are no other deals to be made here today."

"You're making a huge mistake," Two Bulls said. "Killing us won't stop what we started, and I won't tell you anything until Luka's safe."

"You never were very good at negotiating," Khang observed. "You want to know why? Because you don't understand the concept of leverage. You have something I want—information—but I have something you want far more: your lives. That means *I* dictate the terms, not *you*. Now I'll ask one last time: Does either of you have anything to tell me, or should we all go on a picnic?"

Luka bent to the side and did his best to raise his cuffed hands from behind his back. Khang smiled sweetly.

"Yes, Luka."

"I just want you to know that it doesn't matter where you take us," he began. He watched Khang for a moment, then regarded each council and committee member in turn. "It doesn't matter how far away you take us, or how deep of a hole you throw us into, or how tightly you tie us up. I'll never forget what you did to Charlie, and I promise each and every one of you one thing."

"What's that, Luka?" Khang prompted.

"That you will see me again."

Khang looked down at Luka with a patronizingly disappointed smile, and then she stood and smoothed her checkered robe. "And I think *you* should know," she said, "that as much as I admire your tenacity, I find that extremely unlikely."

CHAPTER FIFTY-TWO

ERROR CORRECTION

THE BRAND-NEW, CUSTOM-ASSEMBLED pressure suit that had been drone-delivered and left tethered in Cam's airlock was of an entirely different design from the one he'd worn on his trip up to *Equinox*. The suit Luka had illicitly assembled on Cam's behalf from somewhat antiquated but proven schematics was essentially a personal, human-shaped spacecraft. Its primary jobs were to maintain a pure oxygen environment, create enough localized atmospheric pressure to keep the fluids in Cam's body in a liquid state, insulate him from temperature extremes, protect him from the odd micrometeoroid, and remove carbon dioxide using lithium hydroxide canisters housed in a bulky life-support pack.

Cam's new suit obviously needed to accomplish all of the same things (except micrometeoroid protection—it appeared that the Coronians kept their local vacuum spotless), but it did so in a seemingly far more sophisticated and elegant fashion. Rather than encasing Cam in a ponderous and pressurized anthropomorphic bubble, the surprisingly supple skintight material simulated one atmospheric unit through dynamic mechanical force. As Cam moved, the material redistributed tension so rapidly and intelligently that he hardly felt burdened at all. If he needed a way of quantifying how much thinner this new suit was, his chronograph strap had been sized to the old wrist coupling, leaving only a few centimeters of overlap for the self-aligning fasteners to mate, but when he strapped the miniaturized atomic clock above his new left glove, there didn't seem to be all that much less excess than there was when he wore it against his bare skin. In principle, the helmet was not substantially different from the one he'd worn previously, however this one was shaped like an elongated sphere and was entirely transparent, which meant that his peripheral vision (where all of his suit's readings were some-how unobtrusively projected) was not at all obstructed. As far as Cam could tell, the neck coupling housed the suit's computers, comms, and redundant power sources.

Life support was distributed throughout a series of linked rubberized packs that hung down Cam's back and around his waist, concentrating and distributing most of the mass around what would have been his center of gravity had he not been in a state of constant free fall. The design made Cam wonder if the suit had originally been intended for use on the inner ring of *Equinox*, where, through some of the most daring engineering in human history, gravity was said to be experienced very much as it was on the surface of the planet below.

On behalf of all Coronians, Angelia had accepted Cam's terms, but she explained to him that there was one more thing they wanted. To understand what it was, he would need to travel to a different section of *Equinox*. On the way, Cam was to explain how the Coronians should go about stopping the gliders, and if they felt as though trust had been sufficiently established (with the aid of some form of noninvasive cognitive verification, no doubt), he would be shown something that no one on Earth had ever seen before, and that no member of the *Homo sapiens* spe-cies would ever be allowed to see again. The details of what would happen should Cam fail to establish a sufficient level of trust were not offered, and Cam decided not to ask.

When the outer airlock door opened, Cam was expecting another clawed, robotic escort, but what he found instead was something best described as a kind of swooping, glossy, ultra-modern chariot—something that made his habitation module look clumsy and archaic. The body of it bore a clear resemblance to the drones he was already familiar with—its outer shell being a similar curved white carapace, but without any of the scoring or blemishes he remembered from the machine that pulled him from the crate. In fact, it looked to Cam like the vehicle was brand-new, and might very well have been assembled specifically for this task. A sparse framework extended below the body and connected to a small oval platform with integrated boot clamps. Extending to either side of the chassis were handles that appeared to house no controls whatsoever.

There were minuscule bursts of jets as the device closed the remaining gap to the airlock, and Cam held on to either side of the bulkhead as he stepped out and clipped his boots into place. They were, as he expected, a perfectly engineered fit, and the handles he wrapped his gloves around were exactly the right height for him to stand comfortably.

"Are you fully situated?" Angelia asked. Her voice came from inside the helmet coupling and resonated such that it seemed to come from everywhere and nowhere simultaneously—almost as though it were inside Cam's own head.

"I think so," Cam said. "Go slow, though. I don't want to see what happens if I fall off this thing."

"You are already falling around Earth at a rate of almost eight kilometers per second," the girl said. "Falling off the conveyor would probably be relatively inconsequential."

Cam wondered if this was an example of Coronian humor. "You know what I mean," he said.

He reflexively tightened his grip when he felt the inertia of silent acceleration. When he looked down, he saw the surface of the ring below him both speed up and fall away simultaneously— and then, a moment later, he saw nothing at all.

"What the hell just happened?" Cam asked. He spoke as steadily as he could in an attempt—futile as it probably was—to conceal his anxiety. "Why can't I see anything?"

"I'm sorry," Angelia said. "There are elements of *Equinox* that you are not allowed to see. I've had to temporarily dim your visor."

"A little warning would have been nice."

"Are you comfortable?"

"Not really," Cam said. "I'm flying blindly through space at tens of thousands of miles per hour wearing nothing but thermal underwear in a vehicle I can't control and I have no idea where I'm going or what's about to happen. So no—I wouldn't describe how I feel right now as particularly comfortable."

"Please try to relax," the girl told him. "You are perfectly safe, and your destination is not far."

"*How* far, exactly?"

"That depends."

"On what?"

"On how long it takes for us to discuss the gliders."

"I should have guessed," Cam said. "Are you sure you can talk and fly this thing at the same time?"

"We are very good at multitasking."

"You better be," Cam said. "What do you know about the gliders so far?"

"Very little," the girl said. "Although it's only fair to inform you that we are skeptical of your ability to stop them."

"Why?"

"We haven't detected any form of unusual or unexpected electromagnetic radiation anywhere close to where they were launched, nor any definitive radar signatures. Therefore, we believe it is unlikely that we will be able to reliably track them."

"You're not picking up any signals because they're not broadcasting any signals," Cam said. "They're almost entirely autonomous. And they're probably too small for you to see with radar from all the way up here. The whole point was to make them as hard for you to stop as possible. That's why we went with little toy sailboats rather than aircraft."

"Yes," the girl agreed. "Yet you claim to know of a way."

"Not just claim," Cam said. "I can tell you exactly how to stop them. Whether it's something you're willing to do or not is up to you."

"We are listening."

"If the gliders aren't broadcasting anything, and if you're not picking up any unexpected electromagnetic radiation in the area, then how do you think they're navigating?"

"The only logical conclusion is that they are able to navigate without the aid of any external guidance."

"Or . . ."

There was a moment of silence before the girl responded. "Or you have broken our GPS encryption and are using our own navigation signals."

"Exactly," Cam said. "Well, not me personally. It was actually one of your Neos."

"Thank you," the girl. "I believe that is all we need to know."

"Is it?" Cam asked doubtfully.

"Is there more?"

"You tell me. Now that you know how the gliders are navigating, how do plan to stop them?"

"All we have to do is increase the complexity of our encryption."

"And what will that accomplish?"

"That will prevent the gliders from determining their latitude and longitude, which will in turn prevent them from reaching their intended destinations."

"That will prevent them from knowing their *exact* latitude and longitude," Cam corrected, "which will probably prevent *some* of them from reaching their intended destinations. But they still have plenty of other onboard sensors. Some of them will probably still get close enough to release their payloads."

There was another moment of silence, and then, "What is your recommendation?"

"You can't stop the signal," Cam said. "You have to change it."

"We don't understand."

"Introduce an error," Cam said. "Alter the signal such that everything using it will end up navigating to the same location, then just send someone out to that spot to destroy them for you."

"That would be an effective method for both concentrating and capturing the gliders," Angelia observed. "However, tens of thousands of other vehicles rely on the accuracy of that signal. Causing all of them to malfunction would be an unacceptable loss."

"Tens of thousands of *your* vehicles, right?"

"Yes."

"That *you* control."

"That's correct."

"That presumably you can transmit software updates to."

A pause, and then: "We think we understand now."

"Understand what?" Cam asked. "Explain it to me."

"Before introducing an error into the navigation signal, we update the software of all the vehicles we wish to remain in normal operation so that they are able to compensate for that one specific error. Therefore, once the signal is altered, the only vehicles that will rendezvous at the designated location are those over which we have no control."

"There you go," Cam said. "It's that easy."

"Cam," the girl began, "you have surprised us with your cognitive abilities. You seem to have a gift for reason."

"That wasn't reason," Cam countered. "That was creativity. You guys should look into it."

"Before we return you to Earth," the girl said, "we would like to do some higher resolution neurological scans. With your consent, of course."

"One thing at a time," Cam said. "First, I want to know what you're about to show me."

"Of course," the girl said. "I am about to show you my own personal biological manifestation."

"What does that mean?" Cam asked. "You mean I'm about to see *you*?"

"Yes," Angelia confirmed. "For the first time in history—and perhaps for the last—our species are about to meet."

CHAPTER FIFTY-THREE

GROUND EFFECT

LUKA AND TWO BULLS WERE strapped into side-by-side jump seats bolted to the bulkhead that divided the forward airlock from the main cabin. They were both in full, sapphire-blue emergency membrane suits, their hoods hanging limp down their backs. In addition to harnesses across their chests, their wrists and ankles were bound with a material called recoil cord: a type of polymer that, past a certain threshold, released energy at a rate faster than it was generated or absorbed, meaning that it not only arrested any sudden movement, but violently reversed it. Recoil cord let you walk, but not run; lift something, but not strike with it; fully comply, but never catch your captors off guard. Luka felt like he was in a dream where all of his movements were impeded by some kind of invisible viscosity, while those who were after him moved with infuriating fluidity.

About midway down the long, narrow fuselage, a total of eight officers, including the commander, were divided between two rows of four seats. They wore proper environment suits, fully powered and armored, minus their helmets, and they held carbines across their laps. Beyond the unit of officers, among what appeared to have once been the vehicle's aft cargo hold, were the seven remaining members of the City Council, facing one another across an expanded folding surface. Above them, angled downward, was a massive sheet of polymeth bearing the rising phoenix of the *San Francisco* interpreted in steely grays against a vignetted graphite background.

The inside of the *Pelikan* was much more industrial than Luka imagined it would be. Old recessed LEDs provided harsh cones of slightly bluish light, leaving wide wedges of shadow in-between. There were long stretches of exposed, neatly bound cabling along the ceiling, and the metal floor—obviously designed to accommodate modular seating and various cargo configurations—was crisscrossed with patterns of pill-shaped grip tape. The walls were lined with quilted, soot-colored padding, and black hash marks just below the ceiling counted off meters from the rear of the fuselage forward, probably to help make the loading of vehicles more efficient.

Luka wished he were experiencing the inside of the *Pelikan* under different circumstances. He'd seen the GEV, or Ground Effect Vehicle, several times while hauling cargo from the foundry to the hangar, and had been intrigued enough by the eccentric machine that he'd spent several hours researching it and its predecessors in the archives.

GEVs looked like planes, but they didn't fly. Most of them floated, but they weren't boats. Resolutely defying classification as aircraft, watercraft, hovercraft, seaplane, or hydrofoil, ground effect vehicles were truly their own unique, and somewhat mysterious, mode of transportation.

As their name implied, GEVs leveraged a principle known as "ground effect." Ground effect was caused by airfoils generating lift in very close proximity to a parallel horizontal surface, causing an air ram to form between the ground and the wings, and consequently providing a nice, low-friction cushion on top of which the vehicle could comfortably travel. As altitude was gained, the ground effect rapidly dissipated, requiring true aircraft to employ much longer wings in order to continue generating sufficient lift, and to counteract drag. But by staying close to the ground, GEVs could preserve the precious and fleeting phenomenon, floating on a high-pressure buffer that allowed them to travel much faster than ships, and much more efficiently than planes.

The downside of GEVs was that they required long swaths of uniform and predictable topography, which is why, for most of their existence, they'd seldom moved beyond the curiosity, novelty, and research phases. But now that there were entire human populations whose energy-constrained worlds were surrounded by thousands of kilometers of just such uniform and predicable topography (oceans, seas, and massive freshwater lakes), ground effect vehicles had finally found their place in history. It also didn't hurt that the GEVs' relatively short wingspan made them much easier to store in confined spaces than high-altitude airplanes or gliders whose wings usually had to be folded, retracted, or disassembled.

The *Pelikan*'s lines were reminiscent of an old aesthetic Luka knew as Art Deco. It had a long, rounded snout, and beneath it, a strong, sloping chin riveted with curved hydrodynamic waves to help it channel water before it had generated enough thrust to lift it up off the ocean surface. Behind the cockpit were two beams, each supporting four wire-caged engines, and behind them— about halfway back along the fuselage—were the two straight and stubby wings. The tail rose dramatically and proudly, and was topped with a massive, boomerang-shaped horizontal stabilizer. To Luka, it was one of those rare technologies (not unlike pneumatic tubes) that was simultaneously futuristic and obsolete—a captivating symbol of what the future once was.

The *Pelikan* was many things, but quiet was not among them. Before lifting itself up above the water and forming an air ram, the GEV was both thunderous and turbulent. But now that it was floating, the ride was much smoother, and the noise from the electric engines, while still a harmonized roar, was at least consistent enough that Luka and Two Bulls could effectively communicate above it, yet still loud enough that there was no way their voices would carry all the way down to where the officers sat.

The two of them agreed that the only explanation for staging such a spectacle was that Khang was still hoping to extract information from them. The only reason to prolong the inevitable—to bring the entire council along on the excursion; to let Luka and Two Bulls conspire in relative privacy; to not just shoot and/or waterlock them back on the *San Francisco*—was to continue to build foreboding and fear until one or both of them were willing to bargain for their lives. But they also agreed that nothing they could possibly tell Khang would make any difference at this point. If she was willing to have Charlie killed just for planning a labor strike, there were obviously no circumstances whatsoever under which Luka and Two Bulls would ever be allowed to return to the rig. The longer they kept quiet—the longer they kept the City Council guessing—the longer they probably had to live. Their best and only chance at survival was to force the Judicial Committee and City Council to follow through with the banishment. The faster they could get away from the *Pelikan*, the more breath they would likely draw.

Having agreed to remain silent—and, at their first opportunity, to run in a zigzag pattern intended to make targeting them as difficult as possible—they fell into a grim and meditative silence for the duration of the voyage. Luka was surprised by how numb he felt toward the whole experience, and he wondered if perhaps it was a good thing that he was more preoccupied with curious yellow than the fact that, at this time tomorrow, one way or another, he and Two Bulls would almost certainly be dead. He wondered vaguely how much of his state of mind was the result of addiction and withdrawal, and how much of it was a defensive response to the trauma of facing his own mortality. Or maybe his apathy was genuine. Maybe now that both Val and Charlie were gone, he truly didn't care anymore whether he lived or died.

But even in his desensitized state, Luka realized that there was more to the acceptance he was experiencing than just pure defeat. As young as he was, he had managed to accumulate a disproportionately large portfolio of regrets—the kinds of regrets that could not be undone or made up for—and he knew that living a long life only meant spending more time trying to endure his past with no way of reconnecting with the people he loved. Some part of him was also very aware of the fact that, no matter how much longer he lived, he'd probably already done the most important things he would ever have the opportunity to do: save the lives of Cadie, Cam, Ayla, and Omicron; orchestrate a campaign to sabotage the Coronians' mining capabilities; help launch an effort to terraform the planet that, if successful, could change the entire course of human history. Luka wondered whether if, in a way, he was lucky to have been given opportunities to participate in events much larger than himself, and to have the clarity to recognize that he probably wasn't of much use to humanity anymore. Before his thirtieth birthday—or at least the day that had been randomly chosen as his birthday by the Immigration Committee—Luka's legacy was already complete.

• • •

Setting the *Pelikan* back down on the water was something of a controlled crash and Luka felt himself get pressed hard against the back of the jump seat while he watched the officers in front of him pitch forward against their harnesses. The GEV taxied for about another minute, and when the engines abruptly stopped, the cabin was filled with a sudden and almost insufferable silence. The speed and efficiency with which the operation subsequently unfolded told Luka that every detail had not only been premeditated, but probably also rehearsed.

All eight officers unclipped and retracted their harnesses, then rose to their feet, legs shoulder-length apart to help them absorb the vehicle's swaying. Half of them moved past Luka and Two Bulls into the airlock while the remaining four—including the commander—stood guard. Luka leaned to the side to try to see what Khang and the rest of the council were doing. They continued to talk among themselves, deliberately oblivious to what was happening around them.

Luka heard and felt the airlock cycle behind him. Although he had no intention of telling Khang or anyone else what they wanted to know, he wished somebody would say something. Any kind of communication—even threats or intimidation or coercion—would have been better than silence. Of course, the City Council was well aware of this, which, Luka knew, was precisely why they insisted on feigning disinterest.

The commander's wrist pad illuminated, and he took one hand off his carbine long enough to check its status. He used the same hand to make a gesture, and two officers immediately stepped forward, releasing Luka and Two Bulls from their harnesses.

"Let's go," the commander said, lifting his unshaven cleft chin.

Luka and Two Bulls stood. One of the officers opened the inner door of the airlock and stepped aside, waiting for the prisoners to pass. There was a moment of hesitation while both Luka and Two Bulls cast one last look toward the back of the cabin, and once again were met with nothing but calculated detachment.

The recoil cords imposed an especially painstaking mode of shuffling. As soon as they were finally both inside the airlock and surrounded by the remaining four officers, the inner door was closed, the prisoners' hoods were brought up over their heads and sealed, and their membrane suits were activated. One of the officers knelt to remove Luka's and Two Bulls' restraints, which he then gathered and tossed into the bottom of an equipment locker. The officers took turns detaching their helmets from the rack on the wall and getting them seated and latched into their collar rings while the other three guarded the prisoners. Once everyone was fully suited up, the commander initiated a comm check, and Luka was surprised that he—and presumably Two Bulls, as well—were on the same channel. Even though nothing about their circumstances had changed, the fact that the City Council was still leaving open the possibility of communication gave Luka unexpected—if illogical and baseless—comfort.

The outer airlock door swung away and Luka looked out toward the multicolored bands of miasma outside. The first party of officers waited on a platform that seemed to be hooked into the fuselage below the hatch. All four of them glanced back momentarily, then rapidly turned their attention back outward. A long, emergency-yellow inflatable gangplank had been deployed in order to connect the platform to the shore, and at the end of it, obscured in the thick atmospheric particles, were dozens of humanoid figures, gaunt and suit-less and eerily still. They were either the homeless (scavengers and cannibals who had somehow adapted to the extreme temperatures and high levels of aboveground radiation), or subterraneans (underground colonies usually brought to the surface by external vibration, but about whom almost nothing more was known).

"Clear?" the commander wanted to know.

"Clear!" an officer responded.

"Anything try to make an approach?"

"No, sir," the same officer said without turning. "So far, they've all been very obedient little mutants."

"All right, then," the commander said. "Out you two go."

Luka and Two Bulls ducked through the opening and stepped out onto the platform. Luka could feel the surface beneath his feet dip with the change in weight. The commander and one other officer followed while the remaining two stayed behind inside the airlock, their weapons pointed safely downward but ready to be raised. Luka looked around, trying to understand as much about their situation as he could, but there was nothing more to see other than the black water beneath the inflatable bridge, and the tall, slender figures patiently awaiting their sacrifice.

The commander's voice filled Luka's hood. "If you're looking for your mates' ship," he said, "you won't find it. The *Peli*'s way too fast to be tracked. It's just us out here. And the ghouls, of course."

Luka sensed Two Bulls watching him. He turned his head, hoping to find signs of reassurance behind the soft plastic of his partner's hood—some subtle indication of a conspiracy not yet revealed—but the man's expression was a heavy mask of somber resignation.

"Hang on," the commander said. "Message from the boss." Both Luka and Two Bulls turned toward the commander and watched his eyes wander as he listened. "Roger that," he said, then touched his wrist. "Her highness in there wants to know if either of you have anything to say that might change her mind."

Luka and Two Bulls looked at one another, but neither spoke.

"Right," the commander said. "In that case, I've been authorized to make you one last deal. The first one of you to tell us who else you've been working with, and to give us a list of all the contraband you've been assembling, gets to go back inside."

"What happens to the other one?" Luka asked.

"The other one walks the bloody plank," the commander said. "Ready. Set. Go."

"Neither of us has anything to say," Two Bulls said.

"Sure about that?" the commander asked. "Going once. Going twice."

"Actually, I have something to say," Luka said. He was looking up at the commander and could feel Two Bulls beside him, watching him intensely. "Tell Khang she's a psychopathic bitch, and tell the rest of the City Council they're a bunch of pathetic cowards for not standing up to her." He looked at the rest of the officers around him. "Now, if everyone's done trying to intimidate us, can we please hurry up and get this over with?"

The commander watched Luka for a moment, then smiled. "You want to get this over with, do you?" he asked. He turned to the officer beside him. "Give me your sidearm," he said.

The officer hesitated for moment, then slung his carbine over his shoulder, withdrew the pistol from the holster on his thigh, and passed it to his superior. The commander received it, and when he raised his arm toward Luka's chest, Luka took a step back. Nobody moved and there was a moment of silence before Luka looked down and saw that it was not a threat, but an offer.

"Take it," the commander said. He was holding the pistol by its slide so that the grip was facing out.

Luka tentatively reached up and accepted the weapon. After handling the railgun he built, and the rifles from the officers in the waterlock, he was surprised by how light it was. The commander drew his own sidearm, turned it around, and offered it to Two Bulls.

"And one for you, too," he said.

Two Bulls accepted the weapon, then looked down at his hands.

The commander gestured down the gangplank. "You're going to want to try to make a hole," he told them. "Don't try to kill them all. Conserve your ammo. You only got twenty rounds each, and you're going to want to save one for yourselves, just in case. So keep count. Just drop enough of them to make an impression. Then get to high ground. You'll still have the homeless to worry about, but not the subs, and believe me, they're the worst. Try to hide in the fume. The homeless are half-blind, and about as dumb as my nuts, so even in those clown suits you got on, you might be able to throw them off. If you make it that far, you're going to want to head northeast." He made a chopping motion with his arm to help get them oriented. "You're only about two hundred clicks from the Otago Pod System. They're a bunch of cock-ups, if you ask me, but who knows? You might be able to charm your way in. Tell them you're an assembly technician. If they got any Coronian technology, they might just not kill you. But you," he said to Two Bulls. "Whatever you do, don't tell them you're a career politician. They wouldn't even waste a piece of lead on a talker like you. If I were you, I'd play up the whole Native American angle. If they got any geneticists, you might just be worth experimenting on. Got it?"

Luka and Two Bulls watched the commander, awkwardly handling their weapons. Two Bulls finally broke the silence.

"Why are you doing this?" he asked.

"Because I don't like that silly cunt in there anymore than you do," the commander said. "I just know how to pick sides, is all. Now if I were you, I'd get started. The longer you wait, the more of them you're going to have to pop to get through."

Luka turned and checked the end of the gangplank. The commander was right. There were at least twice as many figures waiting for them now as there had been.

"Come on," Luka said to Two Bulls. "Let's get this over with."

One of the officers inside the airlock leaned out. "Sir, we're getting a transmission from the *San Francisco*."

"From home?" the command said. "You sure about that?"

"Yes, sir."

"Put it through to my HUD," the commander said.

"Yes, sir."

Luka saw a notification appear in the corner of the commander's visor. The commander looked down and touched the curved polymeth panel on the inside of his wrist, and then his faceplate went opaque. Enough light still got through that Luka could see that he was talking to someone, though he couldn't tell who it was, and no sound escaped from the commander's helmet. Luka looked down at the pistol in his hand. He'd been thinking about using it against the officers since the commander handed it to him, but he knew he wouldn't be able to get the safety off and get it raised before someone dropped him. But now that everyone was watching the commander instead of him, the dynamics had changed. Luka put his thumb on the lever above the grip. Nobody reacted, so he rotated it down, and beneath it was a bright orange dot.

"Un-fucking-believable," Luka heard the commander say.

When he looked up, the commander's faceplate was transparent again, and he seemed somehow both amused and annoyed.

"What's going on?" Two Bulls asked.

The commander held out both his gloved hands. "If you give me those two pistols back," he said, "I'll take you inside and explain."

CHAPTER FIFTY-FOUR

INVICTUS SOL

AFTER SEVERAL FLUCTUATIONS IN SPEED and what felt to Cam like a series of delicate maneuvers, his conveyor slowed to a stop, then docked with a silent, definitive jolt. As his visor began to clear, he saw that he had landed within the circumference of a diffuse cone of light. And that he was not alone.

The conveyor had set down beside a wall of dull, graphite-gray, hexagonal panels, each about a meter in diameter. A second, seemingly identical wall ran parallel to the one he was next to—probably about as far away as the *San Francisco* was wide—each exhibiting a slight fish-eye bend from the curvature of his helmet. The scale of each plane was such that Cam could not see how far or high either stretched off beyond the perimeter of illumination maintained by the single overhead drone.

The woman stood at a hospitable but cautious distance. She was tall and slender, her arms at her sides, her posture expectant. She was a collection of sleek white body parts—some of them the same glossy, armor-like finish as the conveyor and the drones, and some of them a soft, matte, semiopaque silicone impregnated with flecks of gold—all bound together by flat black and gleaming chromed hinges, joints, and sockets. Her wasplike waist was an exposed mechanical spine, and her neck was an elongated bundle of delicate pistons, servos, and cables.

The only thing even remotely human about her, other than her general form, was her face. It was incongruously flesh-colored and so lifelike as to make the rest of her look like a life-support system for a transplanted human head. Even without hair, Cam recognized the girl instantly as Angelia's avatar—the face of a stunningly attractive, intelligent, empathetic young woman, peeled off its host and grafted onto an impossibly complex synthetic skull. She blinked a little too deliberately as she watched him, and Cam could see her copper-brown eyes subtly shift in their sockets. Although obviously entirely robotic, her body swayed with the unconscious nervous motion of the living.

Aspects of the girl seemed so alive that Cam had to double-check the external atmospheric composition on his heads-up display. It confirmed that they were still in a near-perfect vacuum—final proof that no part of her—or of *it*—could possibly be organic.

The avatar smiled, and when she spoke, her lips were perfectly synchronized with the voice in Cam's helmet.

"Welcome," she said, seemingly inside Cam's head, "to the *Invictus Sol*."

It suddenly occurred to Cam that the girl was standing rather than floating in microgravity. His feet were still clamped into the conveyor, and the conveyor seemed securely planted on the floor, though there was no other evidence of gravity, or anything remotely *like* gravity. He wondered briefly if they had traveled to the inner ring of *Equinox*—if what he was seeing were the results of a reduced gravitational field—but he dismissed the theory after raising his arms, relaxing them, and finding that they remained, as he suspected they would, perfectly suspended.

"Where are we?" he asked.

"Unclip your boots and step off," the girl encouraged.

The flexibility of Cam's suit enabled him to look down and see his feet. "How?"

"Pivot your heels outward."

Rotating on the balls of his feet broke his boots free of the clamps. By now he was certain there was no gravity, yet as one boot approached the floor, he felt something take hold of it and yank it down until it was firmly attached. After experiencing the sensation a second time with his other foot, Cam realized that the illusion was achieved through simple electromagnetism, though whether the field-generating mechanism was in the soles of his boots or in the floor, he couldn't tell. The effect was really nothing like gravity—not even a particularly good imitation—but he had to admit that the implementation was practical. While magnetism could never counteract the long-term physiological complications of microgravity, it did provide a useful frame of reference. And in wide-open spaces like this one, there was a great deal of benefit to being rooted to a surface. Cam took a few experimental steps and found that the best way to break the bond was by lifting from his heel in a motion that was an approximation of a natural gait, though greatly exaggerated.

Cam looked at the wall beside him and took in as much of it as the drone's illumination allowed. "Hexagons," he commented absently.

"Yes," the girl replied. "Hexagons are the highest-sided regular polygon capable of tessellation—"

"I know, I know," Cam interrupted. "I already got my geometry lesson back on Earth. Hexagons are very fashionable there, too. They even have prisons made out of them."

"Were you imprisoned on the mining platform?"

"Among other things," Cam said. As he watched the girl, he found that his perception kept shifting, his brain oscillating between trying to make sense of the avatar before him as an actual human, and as a machine wearing an eerily convincing human mask. He would have preferred that she'd chosen one form or the other—something he could either fully relate to, or that he could address as an inert, lifeless object. "I don't quite know how to ask you this," Cam continued, "but what exactly *are* you?"

The girl blinked at Cam, then began to approach with a perfectly natural, elegant stride not remotely influenced or encumbered by the magnetic field beneath her. For the first time since he'd seen the machine, it occurred to Cam how powerful it must be—how swiftly she could probably move, and just how much force an impeccably engineered and assembled collection of polymer muscles, carbon tendons, and graphene bones could generate.

The girl stopped. "I'm simply another manifestation of Angelia," she said.

"And the *Invictus Sol*," Cam prompted. "What's that?"

"It means: *The Sun Unconquered*."

"Not the translation," Cam said. He used his arms to indicate their surroundings. "I mean what is this place?"

The machine's head tilted a degree. "You haven't figured it out yet?" she asked. There was neither condescension nor superiority in her tone—only genuine curiosity. Something about the way she was always observing and evaluating made Cam think of Arik. "It's something you've seen before."

Cam examined both of the hexagonally plated walls; looked down at the dense, slightly textured floor beneath him; attempted to find the ceiling beyond the glare of the drone's spotlight, but couldn't. The shape of the structure was unlike anything he could recall having seen. It was extraordinarily tall, relatively narrow, and seemingly very deep—by far the largest enclosure Cam had ever experienced, if indeed it was fully enclosed. But then he began to wonder if what he was seeing might actually be an optical illusion of sorts, at least from the perspective of someone with the concepts of up and down indelibly imprinted upon his psyche. What if, Cam considered, instead of standing on the structure's floor, they were in fact attached to its wall?

"We're on one of the ships, aren't we?" Cam guessed. "We're standing on the wall of one of the carrier's decks."

The girl seemed pleased, as though Cam were a personal experiment that had just validated a hypothesis of hers. "Yes," she said. "The *Invictus Sol* is the first of our Centauri-class carriers."

"Is this what you wanted to show me?" Cam asked, clearly perplexed. "Another avatar, and the inner hull of your ship?"

"No," the girl said. She took a few more steps toward the wall then stopped, placing the soft white silicone fingertips of one hand gently against one of the hexagonal panels. "Before we send you back to Earth, I want you to see me." She looked from the wall back up at Cam. "The *real* me."

Cam could feel her watching him as one of the panels began separating itself from the rest—ejecting with a smooth, linear motion. A pale golden glow spilled out over the texture of the surrounding panels as a translucent prism emerged. It looked at first like a massive yellow sapphire crystal with its own embedded light source, but then Cam realized that it was a capsule filled with a type of fluid, or more likely, a viscous, luminous, semi-transparent gel. There was something solid suspended inside of it, and Cam bent closer to get a better look. When he finally realized what it was—when the shape suddenly and unexpectedly took the form of what he interpreted as a giant fetus—Cam gasped and pulled his feet up off the floor, stumbling back.

The figure looked like a genetic mishap fossilized in amber. It was on its side, facing Cam, oriented with its head toward the wall. Surrounding its broad crown was a halo of light—probably some kind of optical-neural interface—its intensity muted and its shape distorted by the depth of the gelatinous material. The figure appeared emaciated and severely deformed, its spine twisted, its legs bowed and drawn up toward its torso, its arms bent and wrapped around itself in a protective and self-soothing embrace. The head was disproportionately large and hairless, its eyes sunken and clenched, its nose a pair of asymmetrical slits, and its distended lips parted as though paralyzed midsentence.

"You find me unsettling," the girl observed.

Cam looked back at the machine, his face contorted by a combination of astonishment and revulsion. "That *can't* be you," he said. His head shook inside his helmet. "How can that thing even be *alive*?"

"The human body develops very differently in microgravity," the girl explained. "But I assure you that I am not only alive, but perfectly healthy." She indicated the other hexagonal panels around them. "As are the rest of us."

Cam looked at the walls with a renewed sense of awe, reinterpreting their scale in the context of what he now knew lay behind them.

"*This* is the Coronian race?" he asked with unabashed disbelief. "*All* of you live like this?"

"Not all on the *Invictus Sol*," the girl said. "However, we are all maintained within similar centralized habitation capsules. The honeycomb structure is an extremely efficient configuration since it allows us to consolidate and minimize life support, as well as reduce the total amount of area requiring heavy radiation shielding."

A new thought suddenly occurred to Cam, replacing the consternation with an unexpected flare of aggression.

"What about Haná?" Cam demanded with more hostility than he'd intended. He took a moment to breathe; to let his emotions subside; to remind himself that, having already given the Coronians what they wanted, he no longer had any leverage. "Please tell me you didn't do this to her."

Cam had the sense that the girl had no trouble registering his anger, but that it simply did not concern her. "This is not something that we *do*," she replied. "This is how we've had to *adapt*."

As he continued to breathe, Cam could feel his animosity melt into resignation. Both he and Cadie knew that there was nothing they could do about Haná now. She was probably no more capable of returning to Earth at this point than any other Coronian. Cam looked down at the still and silent figure entombed within its nutrient-rich cocoon.

"So this *is* how she lives," Cam said.

"This is how her body is sustained," the girl the corrected. "How she actually lives is very different. You should know that Haná is being extremely well cared for and is developing and progressing extraordinary well. I promise you that she will have a far fuller and richer life here than she could have possibly had on Earth."

The indignation and rage flared once again as Cam looked up at the machine, but just as quickly, he felt it subside. He was about to argue that Haná belonged with Cadie—that nobody could give the child a more loving, stimulating, and rewarding existence than her own mother—but two things occurred to him simultaneously: first, the argument was pointless; and second, it might not even be entirely true. The reality was that Cam had no idea what Earth's future would be like once the symbiosis between the two species was permanently severed. In fact, given that Cam did not even know where he and Zaire would end up— much less what the future held for Cadie and everyone else aboard the *San Francisco*—it was entirely possible that Haná was better off up here. The revelation brought to mind something about the relationship between Earth and *Equinox* that Cam still did not fully understand. Why would the Coronians choose secession from humanity over reintegration when it was clearly much more work to leave than to figure out how to stay?

Cam looked back down at the capsule and once again shook his head. "This doesn't make any sense to me," he said. He looked up at the machine. "You can fix all of this," he told her. "You know that, right?"

The girl regarded him with uncertainty. "Fix what?" she asked.

"Fix . . . *yourselves*," Cam said. "You have access to the inner ring. You can re-acclimate your species to gravity. Coronians could eventually return to Earth."

"Why would we want to return to Earth?"

"*Why*?" Cam repeated. "So you don't have to live like *that*. So you can have a *normal* life."

"Our lives *are* perfectly normal," the girl countered. "Normal to us, just as your lives are perfectly normal to you."

"But how can you possibly call that normal?" Cam asked. "The human body *needs* gravity. That's how millions of years of evolution designed us to work."

"Yet we are thriving without it," the girl countered. "Your species has no idea what a prison gravity actually is."

"A *prison*?" Cam repeated incredulously. He pointed down at the capsule protruding from the wall between them. "*That's* a prison."

"Your perspective surprises me," the girl said. "*Homo sapiens* can only survive within a very narrow range of gravitational variance, which limits the ratio of the universe you can inhabit to an almost incalculably insignificant proportion. Conversely, Coronians will be capable of inhabiting the overwhelming majority of the solar system within two decades, and eventually, other solar systems, as well, and then other galaxies."

"But you can't explore the universe from inside little bubbles," Cam said.

"Why not?" the girl asked.

"Because you can't *experience* anything," Cam said. "That's your *real* prison. Not these pods, or life-support modules, or whatever they are, but *yourselves*."

The machine lifted her arms, gracefully presenting her current form for Cam's consideration. "Do I look as though I am imprisoned to you?" she asked him. "We can take whatever form we wish. *Be* whatever we wish, and soon, we will even be able to *go* wherever we wish. What you perceive as a prison, we experience as the ultimate form of liberation."

"But it's not really *you*," Cam countered. "It's just an avatar, or a . . ." He searched for the right word. "A *prosthetic*. You're *puppets*. You can't actually *feel* anything."

"Why do you assume that we cannot feel?"

"Because you're a *machine*," Cam asserted. "You're completely *synthetic*."

"It is true that this manifestation of me is a machine," the girl conceded, "but it is a machine with billions of receptors, every one of which is far more sensitive, and to a far greater range of stimuli, than any of your sensory organs. Not only can we gather several orders of magnitude more input than you, but we are constantly expanding our neurological capacities with which to actually interpret and experience it."

"Then why don't you act like it?" Cam asked her with clear exasperation. "Why do you act like some old, failed, personal assistant AI?"

The machine's gaze sharpened. "Do not mistake the Coronian affect for a lack of feeling," she warned. Her look assumed a level of intensity Cam hadn't realized her facial structure was capable of conveying. "If we seem numb or placid to you, it is only because we feel far more than you could ever imagine, and as a result, have had to learn far greater restraint."

Cam watched the machine for a beat in silence. His next words were more measured—less incredulous and accusatory, and more neutrally inquisitive. "If you can really experience the universe remotely, then why leave? Why not just stay here and send probes? Wouldn't that be a lot easier and safer?"

"It would not make us any safer from you," the machine replied. "And even if it did, the distances are far too great, even within the solar system. At its closest, Mars is approximately four light-minutes away, and at its farthest, as long as twenty-four minutes. We wish to live as much in the present as we can. For us, even four minutes can feel like an eternity."

Cam looked back down at the amniotic pod. His initial shock had waned significantly and he found that he was able to peer at the distorted organism suspended inside with much less aversion, and even a touch of empathy.

"Do you worry about being too dependent on technology?" he asked. "About relying on life support, and assemblers, and whatever else you rely on?"

"No," the machine answered simply.

Cam waited for her to elaborate, but she didn't. "Why not?"

"Because we've never known an existence without technology," she said. "Technology is as much a part of us as our circulatory or nervous systems are."

"But don't you feel like that makes you vulnerable?"

"Vulnerable to what?"

"I don't know," Cam said, shrugging in his pressure suit. "Failures. Crashes. Accidents. All the ways in which technology has a tendency to fail."

"No more so than you," the girl said. "How long would you survive without life support?"

Cam was about to object to the machine's analogy, but he paused. After a moment of contemplation, the machine took the liberty of answering for him.

"In low-earth orbit," she began, "you would be unconscious in approximately ten to fifteen seconds, and almost certainly dead in less than two minutes. On Earth, you might survive for a few days—perhaps even as long as a week—but you would eventually succumb to dehydration, asphyxiation, or acute radiation poisoning. The reality is that humankind hasn't been able to survive without advanced technology for centuries, and without primitive technology for millennia. While it is true that the price of increasingly sophisticated intelligence and knowledge has always been a dependency on the technology it inevitably gives rise to, one should never mistake such a correlation for weakness or vulnerability."

Cam looked at her skeptically. "Why not?" he asked.

"Because eventually, technology becomes the ultimate evolutionary advantage. But not because of things like food production, shelter, transportation, or communication. As crucial as all of these things have been for humanity's advancement, they represent relatively infinitesimal stepping-stones toward what technology is now finally about to become."

Cam squinted at the machine standing across from him. "And what exactly is that?"

"The power to determine our own evolutionary paths," she said. "The ability to finally and absolutely become the architects of ourselves."

Cam took a moment to think about what he'd just heard. "I'm not convinced that's entirely a good thing," he finally said.

"It is only a good thing for those who have come to understand their place in the universe."

Cam raised his eyebrows. "Oh?" he said. "And what place is that?"

"Humanity is the only way we are aware of whereby the universe attempts to understand itself. Do you understand?"

Cam looked up into the spotlight above them while he repeated the machine's words to himself, then looked back into her copper eyes. "I guess so," he said. "We're part of the universe, and we try to understand the universe, therefore it makes sense that we're an attempt by the universe to understand itself."

"Correct," the girl said. "We believe that absolute comprehension of the universe is the ultimate enlightenment, but we also recognize that we are not yet neurologically or emotionally capable. Nor will we ever be capable if we continue to put our evolutionary energy into pointless competition, and to rely on random mutation and natural selection. But we can, and are, changing the way we evolve. The Coronians will eventually become the ultimate expression of the universe. We will be the one and only path through which the universe will finally be able to understand itself, even if it takes us millions of years. Do you see now why it is so critical that we continue to receive material from Earth until we are entirely self-sufficient? We are on the cusp of the ability to build and become whatever the universe needs us to be in order to truly and absolutely know itself, and there can be no greater calling for any form of life."

Cam did not immediately respond. He watched the machine, and thought about what she'd just told him. The religious undertones that Cam had detected earlier suddenly made much more sense. It wasn't blind fanaticism that motivated the Coronians, but rather their insatiable longing for knowledge, and more importantly, the inevitable result: the desire to not just know about, but to truly comprehend, literally *everything*. What other definition of enlightenment could possibly evolve among an abandoned and isolated population of humanity's bravest, brightest, and most curious members if not total comprehension of the cosmos?

"Is that why you showed me all this?" Cam eventually asked. "So that I'll go back to Earth and convince everyone not to abandon you again? So I'll tell everyone how important your work is?"

"No," Angelia said. "We don't expect you to respect, or even fully comprehend, our ultimate purpose."

Cam shook his head. "Then what *do* you want?"

"The same thing as you," the robot said. There was genuine warmth and grace in the machine's smile. "To be remembered after we're gone."

CHAPTER FIFTY-FIVE

SCAR TISSUE

LUKA'S PARTY WAS THE FIRST to cycle back through the airlock and reenter the *Pelikan*'s cabin. The sheet of polymeth angled down from the ceiling was now in use, and the entire City Council was standing, looking up.

The face on the screen belonged to a friend of Charlie's known as Benthic (that was apparently some kind of a call sign; Luka couldn't remember ever hearing his actual name). Benthic was probably one of the toughest-looking miners Luka had ever met, but paradoxically, probably also one of the kindest. He was of Filipino descent, and both of his arms (and, according to Charlie, his back and chest) were covered in the intricate symbols and patterns of Polynesian tribal tattoos. His bronze head and cheeks were perfectly smooth from daily shaving, but he left a thin film of black stubble on his delicately chiseled chin.

"Luka," Benthic said by way of greeting. "Councilman Two Bulls. Are you two OK?"

"We're fine," Luka said. He looked at the seven members of the City Council and saw that they were all as confused as he was—perhaps slightly more so. "What's going on?"

The airlock and decontamination chamber cycled again, and the second party of officers entered the cabin behind Luka.

"In short," Benthic began, "the City Council may have succeeded in stopping a strike, but they bought themselves an uprising."

"Benthic," Two Bulls said, "tell us exactly what happened."

Benthic's eyes shifted to Two Bulls. "Charlie left us a note in the decompression chamber," he said. "It explained everything. But instead of organizing a strike, we decided to organize a mutiny. We're now in complete control of the *San Francisco*."

"This is obviously some kind of a hoax," Khang intervened. She turned to look at the prisoners and at her officers, then looked back up at the screen. "You couldn't possibly have taken control of the *entire* city."

Benthic's eyebrows went up. "Three thousand of us?" he countered. "It took us less than an hour to occupy City Hall without a single shot being fired, or a single injury on either side."

"Prove it," Khang challenged.

Benthic smiled with half his mouth, then leaned to the side and showed them the interior of a bright white office with rich woodgrain accents. An interpretation of the *San Francisco* phoenix appeared splayed against the background of rough-hewn, wood-assembly blocks.

"Would I be able to access your office if we didn't have complete control of City Hall?" he asked Khang. "Would I be able to broadcast on this channel?"

"Benthic," Two Bulls said, "listen to me. Some decisions need to be made here very quickly."

"I agree."

"What happens to Luka and me?"

"The interim council has granted both of you full pardons. As of now, you're completely free men."

Khang took a step toward the polymeth. "You do *not* have that authority," she admonished. She turned to the commander. "Commander Greer, take these prisoners outside and shoot them. *Now*."

"Commander Greer," Benthic interjected, "ignore that order. Instead, place the entire City Council under arrest. With the exception of Councilman Two Bulls."

Khang squinted at the commander. "Don't you *dare*," she warned him.

Unperturbed, the commander looked up at Benthic. "Gladly, mate," he said. "But the real question is, what'll we do with the lot of them?"

"I'll leave that up to Councilman Two Bulls," Benthic said.

"No," Two Bulls said. "I'd like this to be Luka's decision."

"Your call," Benthic said. "Whatever decisions you feel you need to make out there, we will support."

"So, Mr. Mance," the commander said. "What'll it be?"

Luka watched the commander for a moment, then turned to look at the City Council. He found the sudden shift in the situation's dynamics—and more importantly, the new distribution of power—unexpectedly intoxicating. Where only moments ago there had been nothing but apathy and resignation, a calm and quiet rage now smoldered. Some part of Luka wanted to see every single member of the council executed. He thought about the faceless and cowardly and horribly painful way in which Charlie was murdered, and then he thought about having Khang and the rest of them lined up against the hull and shot through the backs of their heads; blood and brains and slivers of skull and matted clumps of hair dripping and rolling down the curved surface; slick pools of thickening red, and boot tracks overlapping the sparkling black grip tape.

While Luka truly believed, at that moment, some part of him could have taken pleasure in ordering a massacre, he couldn't help but think about what Charlie would have him do. And, although the memory was less fresh and buried much deeper, what Val would want him to do, as well. There was no question that both of them would demand justice, but justice tempered by empathy and humanity and restraint. Justice by objective consensus. He could hear each of them whispering to him that murdering Khang and her followers would not bring either of them back, or change anyone's past, or reunite Luka with his parents. It would only open more wounds that he would one day have to work hard to close, and result in still more layers of tough, sinewy scar tissue that would leave him even more emotionally disfigured than he already was.

But although Luka could hear their voices, and even see the compassion in their conjured expressions, he knew that it was ultimately his own voice and his own consciousness talking to him, clearly terrified of the power he now wielded, and of the decision he was being asked to make. He knew he could not allow the City Council to return to the *San Francisco* any more than the City Council could have allowed his own return, or the return of Two Bulls. Luka realized that he was being called upon to lead, and that being a true leader was not about doing what was easy or popular, or even necessarily what was humane. Being a true leader meant having to make the right decisions in circumstances where—no matter how you tried to take them apart and put them back together—there simply were none, and then having to live with the consequences, and with yourself, for the rest of your life.

Luka looked back at the commander.

"Do we have any more membrane suits?"

"Yes, sir," the commander said with an approving nod.

"How many?"

"Plenty," the man said, then shrugged. "Give or take."

Luka nodded, somehow simultaneously contemplating while also doing his best not to think at all. "Do it," he finally said.

"Luka," Khang said cautiously. "Please. Think about what you're doing here. You don't have to do this."

"No," Luka said. "I don't have to do this. In fact, none of this had to happen at all, did it?"

Khang watched him for a moment, then shook her head passively. "What do you want me to do, Luka?" she asked him. "Do you want me to apologize? Do you want me to beg?" She took a step forward and narrowed her eyes. "Well I *won't*," she hissed. "I know you think you've had a difficult life, but let me tell you, what you've been through is *nothing*. You have *no* idea where I came from. *No* idea what I've been through. *No* idea what happened to *me* and *my* family and the people *I* loved. I won't apologize to you or anyone else for the things I've had to do to get to where I am and to protect what I've built. And I will *not* take responsibility for yours, or for anyone else's, past."

"This isn't about anyone's past," Luka told the councilwoman. There was neither malice nor vengeance in his tone. "For once, the only thing I'm thinking about is the future."

CHAPTER FIFTY-SIX

BLACKSAIL

THERE WAS ONLY ONE PLACE where the captain of the *New York*—one of only two remaining Metropolis-class mining rigs—felt she had complete privacy: the uppermost deck of the bridge known as "the nest." She'd annexed the space many years ago, designating it her own private office over the protests of exactly no one. In order to ensure security, the captain had the quick-release hatch cover in the floor replaced with one that sealed biometrically, and the only personnel she permitted on the bridge below were officers personally vetted and authorized by no one but herself.

The weight of the structure was borne by a series of steel struts, the shapes and angles of which gave one the impression of standing beneath the belly of an immense insect, the gaps between its bolted metallic appendages filled with several fused layers of filtered inductive polymeth. Although the nest had windows all around, it did not afford much of a view. It was the only structure that extended above the *New York*'s dome, so rather than a breathtaking panorama of the bustling float-ing city sprawling below, when visibility was good, the captain might occasionally glimpse an expanse of dark and featureless open water, or perhaps even a distant rocky crag, shrouded and desolate. More often, though, she found herself surrounded by multicolored bands of haze—dark and wispy and foreboding where they swirled together in unstable interaction—and the flashes of stroboscopic cloud-to-cloud lightning that frequently discharged when radiation concentrated in the upper atmosphere.

Other than the windows and the biometric hatch, the captain had never allowed the nest to be updated. While the rest of the rig—and even the main bridge below—continued to benefit from Coronian construction, material, and technology, she kept her office as close to original as possible. The floor was a type of prickly green astroturf with paths worn pale and bare, illustrating her tendency to pace when in contemplative moods, and the beams showed signs of corrosion coming through the layers of paint, which the years had turned from white to a muted shade of surgical green. At either end of the room were identical sloping consoles strewn with dozens of dials, switches, knobs, and gauges—most of which still functioned thanks to an analog-digital conversion interface she had installed on the bridge below. But the captain's favorite anachronisms—and the instruments through which most of her communication still flowed—were the two heavy plastic black handsets suspended in their spring-loaded cradles, attached to their consoles by thick glossy cords that had once been neatly coiled, but over the years had been stretched into wayward kinks. There were swivel chairs bolted to the floor in front of each console, their yellowed foam guts held in with several strips of fraying gray duct tape.

The focus was currently on the center of the room where the captain, her commander, and her first lieutenant all stood around an expanded brushed steel surface. In front of them was a single solid-sail hydrofoil—the designation "Blacksail" emblazoned across its hull—that had recently been netted from among the dozens that maintained their positions in the surrounding waters below. It had been smuggled up to the nest inside a hastily assembled crate just large enough to conceal it, and just small enough to fit through the hatch in the floor. In front of the first lieutenant, there was also a slip-sealed jar of thick green sludge.

"The first thing I need to know," the captain began, "is how much the Board of Supervisors knows."

The captain wore a fitted black vest over a white shirt with baggy sleeves and loose cuffs. She was a tall woman with long, black hair that remained obediently tucked behind her ears, and prominent arching eyebrows that gathered all immediately available attention and channeled it directly into her wide-set, upswept, almond-brown eyes. Not only was she usually the most dynamic presence in the room, but she was almost always the tallest, as well. Even her first lieutenant—a stocky Neo who had accompanied the first generation of assemblers, and whom she had promoted rapidly up through the ranks as he continued to demonstrate his loyalty—was a few centimeters shorter.

"They don't know anything," the commander replied. "But we're not going to be able to keep it that way for very long."

As the captain's younger brother, the commander had similar dark and well-honed features, though he was smaller and seemed better suited to a deferential role. These were the two men the captain trusted above anyone else, and on whose allegiance she felt her leadership depended.

"Then tell me what *we* know," the captain said.

The commander looked across the table, deferring to the first lieutenant.

"Just as the Coronians indicated," the Neo began in his powerful baritone timbre, "this is one of an entire fleet of extremely sophisticated hydrofoils."

"Sixty-four?" the captain asked.

"We've counted fifty-eight so far," the lieutenant said. "We believe six were lost."

"And how did the Coronians get them all to gather in one spot?"

This question, the commander fielded. "Do you remember the software patch we received from the Coronians for our navigation system?"

"Yes."

"It contained an algorithm to compensate for an error they intentionally introduced. An error that caused everything without the patch to navigate to the same spot: right here."

"Very clever," the captain conceded. "And what about all this talk of terraforming technology? Is it real?"

The first lieutenant and the commander exchanged looks.

"That's the thing," the commander said. "Either the Coronians were lying, or they have no idea what the hydrofoils are actually for."

The captain regarded her younger brother. "What are you talking about?"

The Neo took over. "They were never designed for terraforming," he explained. "They don't contain seeds or catalysts. They contain spores. I would estimate several billion each."

"*Spores?*" the captain repeated. "Spores for *what?*"

"For algae," the Neo said.

"They aren't terraforming," the commander explained. He picked up the green jar in front of him and presented it to the captain. "They're *aqua*-forming."

"Oh my God," the captain said. "Are you telling me that's *algae? Actual living algae?*"

"We're surrounded by it," the Neo told the captain. "The spores are not only viable, they're thriving. There's no competition out there—nothing whatsoever to slow them down."

"But why?" the captain asked. "Why algae instead of trees and plants?"

"Because the potential habitat for algae is vastly larger," the lieutenant said, "and once it gets started, it's almost impossible to stop."

"In other words," the commander added, "if you wanted to reboot the planet's oxygen cycle, algae is by far the fastest and most efficient way."

The captain took a moment to consider her brother's remark. "Back up for a second," she said. "Explain to me why the Coronians are so threatened by oxygen production?"

"It isn't the oxygen *production*," the Neo said. "It's the oxygen *cycle*. The more habitable the planet becomes, the faster the atmosphere will allow solar energy to penetrate again."

"Which means," the commander continued, "the sooner we go back to the Solar Age, and the less dependent we are on Coronian energy."

The captain nodded her head deliberately. "And the less incentive we have to keep providing them with raw materials," she concluded.

"Exactly."

The captain squinted at the drone in front of her, partially capsized on the steel surface. "Then this is exactly what we need to weaken the alliance between the Coronians and the Board of Supervisors."

The commander and the lieutenant looked at one another before the lieutenant responded. "That's the conclusion we came to, as well," he said.

"How much of the planet's surface have they covered?"

"Unfortunately there's no way to know that," the Neo said. "As far as I can tell, the logs aren't geotagged."

"Speculate."

"It's possible they could have covered as much as five to ten percent before they were redirected."

"*But*," the captain's brother interjected, "if it was the right five to ten percent, their influence could be much greater."

"How?"

The commander deflected the question back to the Neo.

"Currents," the lieutenant said. "Whoever did this was smart. They probably knew they couldn't cover the entire planet, which means they would have probably tried to maximize their effectiveness by targeting the most prominent and wide-reaching currents within range."

The captain took the jar from her brother and held it up to the light. As she peered into the flourishing and self-contained ecosystem, her pallid complexion inherited some of its verdant illumination. "Where the hell did they get spores?"

"We have no idea," her brother said.

"Are there any left?"

"That's the most interesting part," the captain's brother said, then prompted the lieutenant to elaborate.

"We think the hydrofoils have already released most of their payloads," the Neo said, "but there's a way to make more."

"*Make more?*" the captain repeated. "How?"

"I haven't had time to go though all the data yet, but we know the hydrofoils contain schematics for assembling more hydrofoils. *And* cultures for producing more spores."

It took the captain a moment to put together the implications of what her first lieutenant was telling her. When she did, her eyes narrowed and she lifted one side of her mouth into an admiring grin. "They knew someone was going to find them."

"Not only did they know the Coronians would send someone to collect them," the Neo said, "but they correctly assumed that anyone so closely affiliated with the Coronians would have assemblers *and* decent laboratories."

The captain put the jar back down on the metal surface. "Who are *they*?" she asked. "Do we know?"

"Yes and no," the commander said. "For obvious reasons, whoever did this didn't want to be directly identified, but there is a kind of . . . I'm not quite sure what to call it. A kind of *epitaph*."

"For *who*?"

"Someone named Arik Ockley."

"Since you're calling it an epitaph, I suppose that means you know he's dead?"

"Apparently, which I guess is why they felt it was safe to acknowledge him. It was his research that all this was based on."

The captain turned away from the table, clasped her hands behind her back, and followed a worn strip in the floor to the front of the nest. She ran a finger down the curvature of the plastic handset while she deliberated.

"Here's what we're going to do," she said. When she turned, her eyes were wild and her smile was as amused as it was cunning. "The Coronians want the hydrofoils, right?"

"They do," the lieutenant confirmed. "They want them delivered as soon as possible to the nearest broker post."

"OK," the captain said. She addressed her brother as she moved back toward the table. "I want you to gather a small team of people you trust. Bring all the hydrofoils aboard, then strip them of anything that might hint at what they were actually for. Once they're crated up and ready to go, *then* inform the Board."

"Yes, ma'am."

The captain looked at her first lieutenant. "I want you to start figuring out how we can create more spores from the cultures without anyone knowing, and how we can assemble more hydrofoils. Can you fix their navigation systems?"

"Yes," the Neo said. "I should be able to apply the same software patch we used to fix ours."

"Good," the captain said. "Do it."

"How many?" the lieutenant asked. "Another sixty-four?"

"No," the captain said. "That's too risky. We're going to do this one at a time. We're going to target whatever currents we happen to be near at the time we're ready to release them, and we're going to keep doing this for as long as we possibly can. And I want every single one to contain fresh cultures and instructions for how to assemble more hydrofoils. I want these things spreading across the planet like a goddamn pandemic."

"Yes, ma'am," the Neo said.

"What about the epitaph?" the commander asked. "Do you want it included, as well?"

The captain took a moment to consider the question. "Absolutely," she decided. "Whoever this Arik Ockley was, he deserves to be remembered."

CHAPTER FIFTY-SEVEN

HALF-LIFE

Luka sat on the bridge of the *Accipiter Hawk* and watched the butterfly raise and lower its wings. It was delicately perched amid a bouquet of synthetic blossoms sprouting from a spent liquid oxygen canister with its top plasma torched off—one of several Omicron had distributed across various surfaces in order to keep the artificial insect engaged enough that dust and other particles wouldn't accumulate on its solar cells. The butterfly's wings were a type of electroactive polymer that flapped through the manipulation of electric fields rather than by pure mechanical means, and Luka knew that as long as the device remained active and stimulated, it would probably last for decades—perhaps even an entire lifetime.

The key to survival, Luka mused, was to keep moving.

The butterfly's name was *Lykke,* which meant "happiness" in Danish. Apparently Ayla had named it in her head the day it was given to her by Costa, but for some reason, she'd never told anyone. Maybe it was because she was afraid people would think she was childish for giving a toy a name, or maybe it was simply because nobody had ever bothered to ask. But then Luka—before even revealing that he or his mother had probably hand-built the creature years ago back in Hammerfest—wanted to know what she'd decided to call it, and he'd sensed that there was a great deal of meaning in her saying its name out loud for the very first time.

As Luka watched the butterfly, he thought about how life-times were not really defined as the period of time between birth and death. That was life*span*. Each lifespan, it seemed, was capable of containing multiple life*times*. Luka's first lifetime was spent with his parents in the Hammerfest Pod System. His second was aboard the *San Francisco* with Val and Charlie, and as an assembly technician, a forklift operator, and an eccentric and reclusive sculptor. It was obvious to him that he was about to embark on a third lifetime, but this early on, it was impossible to tell who or what would ultimately define it.

Luka was relieved to be moving on—emotionally and physically—but he also knew that the primary problem with the past was that it never stayed where it belonged. No matter how many barriers and fortifications you erected in its path as you progressed throughout your life, it still found ways to pen-etrate. If you were lucky, the influence of an event decayed over time, but never by more than its half-life, and never so much that some trace of it could not still be detected. And if you were unlucky, the past accumulated at a rate faster than it was able to dissipate. Sometimes the openings through which we moved forward were too small to drain all of the pain poured forth from the past, and if they could not be widened in time, the only option was to drown.

In general, repression had been good to Luka. As he'd dis-covered through talking with the copy of Ellie he'd brought with him from the *San Francisco*, repression had enabled him to function in circumstances where others might have given up. But repression was only one tool, and Luka now knew that the structures one built were often defined—or at least profoundly influenced—by the tools one used to build them. Repression was like constantly building upward in order to avoid the work of building out a more stable foundation, but eventually the instability compounded to the point where your life had no choice but to topple.

Another problem with the past was that every year, it came back around. The cycle of the Gregorian calendar was like the constant rotation of a cylinder with 365 chambers, and the longer you lived, the more rounds filled those holes. Except these bullets were never fully spent, and rather than proving lethal, the wounds they left were a gradual accumulation of debilitating injury. A much better calendrical system would have been one where days never repeated; where lives were marked with infinitely incrementing integers, constantly leaving the things everyone wanted to forget further and further behind; where every second of every day was a chance to completely reinvent oneself out of newly created time that had no inherent knowledge whatsoever of the past.

In the one year since Luka and Ayla had been alone together aboard the *Hawk*, they had each experienced a lot of anniversaries: the days they'd left their home pod systems as children; the times each had lost people they loved; the moments they'd been forced right up to the very edge of death—in fact, well past the point of peace and acceptance—only to be unexpectedly pulled back into the worlds they thought they were finally leaving behind. And the day that was supposed to be one of joy and festivity—a diversion everyone on the rig badly needed—when they finally arrived at the Maldive Islands Spaceport to retrieve Cam and Zaire, only to learn that Cam had decided not to return—that he had already found work at MIS as a mechanic—and that he felt he had an obligation to teach historians, or academics, or anyone who passed through the port and who he could get to listen to him everything he'd learned about the Coronians.

There had been so many milestones full of so much pain and loneliness and disappointment that they both agreed that today would be different. The one-year anniversary of the day Luka and Ayla left the *San Francisco* together—the day the overhaul of the *Accipiter Hawk* was complete and all the new weapons systems were in place; the day they said good-bye to Cadie, Zaire, Two Bulls, and Benthic, and set off together in search of the *Resurrection*—would be a day of celebration rather than another day of melancholic nostalgia and loss. And as was the case with any true celebration, gifts were clearly in order.

Ayla stepped onto the bridge, barefoot and with her hands behind her back. They kept the ship warm and she wore a pair of dark cargo synthetics tied off at her calves and a simple silvery tank top. Her hair had grown considerably, and although she maintained bangs just above her eyelashes, the rest of it was all the way down to the base of her neck. Luka noticed immediately that something was missing: the smoothed sliver of tungsten carbide pipe on the boot-lace paracord necklace. Without explanation or preface, Ayla gave Luka an anticipatory smile, then showed him what she'd been hiding.

It was a piece of silicon paper folded into a square from the corners and bound with a colorful length of woven wire insulation as a stand-in for ribbon. Luka accepted the letter, tugged at the bow, and unfurled it. Inside he saw two handwritten numbers that, after a moment of examination, he identified as coordinates.

"Where is this?" he asked. "Is this the *Resurrection*?"

Ayla shrugged. "Look and see."

Luka spun around in his chair and placed the silicon paper facedown on the polymeth surface. The ship's computer, having records of visiting the location previously, also recognized the numbers as coordinates and plotted them accordingly on a map. Luka zoomed in so he could see more detail.

"Triple Seven," he said.

Ayla nodded.

Luka looked up from the console. "I don't understand," he said. "What does this mean?"

"It means it's time to go," Ayla said. "It's time for me to put the *Resurrection* behind me."

"Are you sure?" he asked her. He spun all the way back around so that he was facing her fully. "We'll find them eventually. I'm still completely committed to this."

"I'm not," Ayla said. "Not anymore. It turns out revenge isn't really my thing."

This was something Luka had already known about Ayla, which is why he had taken the responsibility and burden of vengeance on as his own. He now wondered whether her gift to him—in addition to a commitment to move on—was also a type of exoneration.

"Well, then," Luka said, "what *is* your thing?"

"I think I'm better at forgiveness," Ayla said. "I think I just want to move on and start a new life. With you."

Luka smiled up at Ayla, then reached down beneath the console and brought out a full-size ration box.

"I'm ready, too," he said.

"Ready for what?" Ayla asked quizzically. "Lunch?"

"Open it."

Ayla tried to judge what was inside by the weight. "It's heavy," she said.

"Physically *and* metaphorically."

Ayla needed only to crack the lid to know what was inside, and the immediacy with which tears came to her eyes told Luka how long she'd been waiting. It was the most unusual gift Luka had ever given, but also one of the most difficult and meaningful. Inside the box was about a kilogram of curious yellow; enough to keep him high for probably three years, or to kill him hundreds of times over; the last of his ties to the *San Francisco*, and to his old life.

Ayla set the box down on the console and covered her mouth. When she blinked, tears ran down the channels between her cheeks and fingers. "Thank you," she said.

Luka stood up and Ayla leaned forward as he held her.

"I want to move on, too," he told her.

"How long has it been?"

"It doesn't matter," he said. "What matters is that I'm finished. We'll dump it today."

"I was so scared," Ayla said into his ear.

"Of what?"

She pulled back enough that she could look at him. "Of all the things you've been saying," she said. "That you felt like you'd already done everything you were ever going to do, and all that stuff about your legacy already being complete."

Luka looked down at the floor through the narrow space between them and nodded. "I was scared, too."

"What changed?" she asked him.

He looked back up. Ayla's nose and cheeks were flush and her face was wet, and when Luka leaned forward to kiss her, he could smell her tears and her fear and her happiness all at once. She leaned into him and kissed him back, and then Luka cupped her face gently and looked down into her wide, polished-onyx eyes.

"What changed," Luka said to her, "is that now I want to live long enough to enjoy it."

EPILOGUE

THE NEW DOME ON THE *San Francisco* was partially retractable. The top consisted of a carbon-reinforced polymer membrane stretched across almost a ton of graphene cable. When conditions were favorable, the material could be gathered and folded into a conical receptacle suspended in the center, exposing the entire city to both natural light and breathable air.

Being the city's first large-scale attempt at kinetic architecture—structures capable of moving and physically adapting to their surroundings—the design of the roof was relatively crude. Although the implementation was effective and reliable, it was also considered prototypical and temporary. Now that almost all of the foundry's assemblers had been upgraded to atomic resolution, and now that the refinery contained sophisticated disassembly technology capable of reducing most forms of matter into raw medium, everything tended to feel much less permanent. Instead of pretending that brand-new structures, from the moment they were completed and dedicated, were destined to stand forever, the *San Francisco* finally had access to technology that allowed them to acknowledge what had always been true: that on a long enough timeline, absolutely everything was an experiment.

Since atmospheric hypoxic zones were still known to occur— and since every minute the roof was open was a minute's worth of energy not being collected by the integrated photovoltaics and

stored in the quantum battery bank for nighttime, or as a safeguard against the high-altitude, light-obstructing particle bands
that still circulated—the roof was seldom retracted for more than
an hour or two at a time. Therefore, when it was open, it had
become customary for almost everyone aboard the *San Francisco*
to stop whatever it was they were doing and congregate on roof-
tops and balconies, or in the Embarcadero, where patches of
sunshine were clipped and cropped into interesting and irregular polygons by the constantly evolving skyline, or beneath the
Yerba Buena Gardens, where the radiance from above inherited
exotic hues and shadows and motion as it passed through the
massive globe and the atomized nutrient, and then was refracted
by all of the different species of flourishing vegetation within.

But this time was an exception. The retraction of the roof had
been scheduled far in advance and everyone in the city was asked
to remain indoors and respect the privacy of the only two individuals on the rig for whom the request did not apply: an eight-
year-old boy named Kayhan, and his mother, Cadie Chiyoko.
The two stood alone on the rooftop terrace of City Hall not far
from where the phoenix once rose, Cadie squinting up into the
sky, and the boy leaping from tile to tile, selecting his next destination through the evaluation of criteria known only to him.

The boy's black hair was long and thick, and had waves and
curls that could not have come from Cadie. It hung down on
either side of his face, concealing his dark almond eyes and his
complex olive complexion. The boy seemed content to entertain
himself, though as soon as he heard the cumulative murmur of
drones descending through the roof, he immediately found his
mother's side.

Cadie put her hand on the boy's shoulder to reassure him as
they were surrounded by the compact, twitchy machines. Most

of the drones took positions around the mother and her apprehensive son, each transmitting their individual perspectives on the scene into orbit where Cadie assumed the data was being combined into a single 3D representation. The lenses on the two shrouded octocopters in front of Cadie lit up, their split beams combining into semiopaque interference patterns that gradually resolved into a tall and elegant little girl in simple white synthetic thermalwear, her long, copper hair pulled back into a simple and impeccable ponytail.

At the sight of the little girl, Cadie's hand immediately found and covered her mouth as she closed her eyes and took deep, quivering breaths. The boy at her side tightened his grip on her leg as he looked back and forth between the hologram and the effect it was having on his mother.

The girl's voice must have come from both of the projection drones simultaneously, combining into a single, centralized, acoustical illusion. It was young and sweet, but without a trace of vulnerability.

"Mother," the girl said. Her delicate smile was more evident in her eyes than it was in her lips. "Hello."

It took Cadie a moment to respond. "I've been waiting for this day for so long," she finally managed as she blinked. "You are so beautiful."

"Thank you," the girl replied. "But this is not my true physical form."

Cadie took her hand away from her mouth and nodded. "I know that," she said. She smiled at the girl as she shrugged. "But you're beautiful anyway."

The girl looked down at the little boy who was watching her warily.

"Who are you?" she asked him.

The boy responded by maneuvering himself still farther behind his mother's leg.

"This is Kayhan," Cadie said. "He's your half brother."

"Kayhan," the girl repeated. "A Persian word meaning world, universe, or cosmos. Who is the other half?"

Cadie smiled at the awkwardness of the question—the innocence of her daughter's literalism. "Her name is Farah Abbasi," Cadie said. "She's a doctor here."

"She," the girl noted.

Cadie smiled. "It's complicated."

The little girl looked at her mother thoughtfully. "Combining the genetic material from two females into a single viable embryo is not complicated," she said.

"I don't mean biologically complicated," Cadie said. "I mean emotionally."

Cadie doubted whether Haná had any idea what she meant, but the little girl accepted the response with a nod. "Are you married?"

"No," Cadie said. "But we live together. The three of us."

"Do you love her?"

"Yes," Cadie said. "That's complicated, too, but yes, I love her very much."

The girl smiled at her mother. "I'm glad," she said.

Cadie was surprised by the warmth of the sentiment. She hadn't known whether she would be able to connect with Haná or not, but she now felt that they had—at least on some level. The feeling was a reminder to her that there was no sweeter concern in the world than that which came from your own child.

"How about you?" Cadie asked. "Are you happy?"

"Yes," the girl said without hesitation. "This may be difficult for you to understand, but I have never known any other life, and therefore I cannot imagine any other form of existence."

"I understand better than you know," Cadie said. "Since you contacted me, does that mean you'll be leaving soon?"

"Yes. We are scheduled to leave in 33.7 cycles."

"Can you tell me where you're going?"

"I am interested in terraforming," the little girl said. "I've chosen to join a research team assigned to Venus."

Cadie smiled at her daughter's response. "Terraforming Venus," she said. "You certainly come by that honestly."

The little girl seemed perplexed. "I don't understand."

"I don't have time to explain now," Cadie said. "I have something very important to talk to you about."

"I'm detecting that the signal is beginning to attenuate," the girl said, "but I will broadcast for as long as I can."

"Good," Cadie said. "I have a proposal for you. For *all* of you."

"We are listening, Mother."

"We'd like you to give us access to *Equinox*," Cadie said. "And in return, we will give you full access to the Global Seed Vault."

The girl seemed unprepared for the direction in which her mother had taken the conversation. She watched Cadie for a moment, then said, "Please wait."

The avatar appeared paused and lifeless, and Cadie imagined her daughter's consciousness being temporarily redirected and absorbed into some form of a collective. When the girl returned, it was like a puppeteer once again taking up her strings.

"Do you personally control access to the GSV?"

"No," Cadie said. "But I know the new director, and I've been given authorization to negotiate on his behalf."

"Accessing and researching the GSV would mean that some of us would need to stay behind," the girl said.

"Yes," Cadie agreed. "It would also mean that our two species would live and work in close proximity for the first time: you on the outer ring, and us on the inner ring. Haná, I'm not just proposing a transaction here. I'm proposing partnership."

"Our two species are no longer interdependent," the little girl stated. "What would be the basis for a partnership?"

Cadie shrugged. "Just trust," she said. "That's the only way it could work."

"Are there many of you willing to trust us?" the girl asked.

Cadie didn't know whether the question was intended to be hypothetical, or perhaps even slightly sarcastic. "No," she admitted. "I'm not saying it would be easy—for either of us—but I believe very strongly that it's worth trying."

"I'm sorry, Mother," the girl said. "There are no Coronians willing to stay behind."

"Not even for full access to the GSV?" Cadie asked. "Imagine what our species could do together with all that data, Haná. Imagine what we could do if we combined all of our knowledge and all of our technologies. We could go far beyond terraforming. We could introduce life throughout the entire solar system. There must be someone willing to stay behind for an opportunity like that."

"There is not," the girl said. "We believe that any form of symbiosis—any kind of peaceful collaboration between our species at all—is impossible."

Cadie looked away from the projection of her daughter. Her eyes traced a pattern along the silicone seams between the floor tiles as she waited for the dead-end exchange to fade a little further into their past, and while she searched for a new approach.

"Haná," Cadie finally said. "Can you tell me the story of the first Coronian?"

"Mother, I think we should use what little time we have left to say good-bye."

"Please," Cadie insisted. "What was her name?"

The girl looked at her mother with uncertainty. "The first Coronian was the child known as Genevieve."

"Where was she born?"

"She was born aboard *Equinox*."

"Why wasn't she taken to Earth?"

"As you know, a child who develops in microgravity cannot survive on Earth."

"Correct," Cadie said. "So what would you say gave rise to the Coronian species?"

The girl's response was both instant and rote. "The deliberate abandonment of our ancestors," she said. "That is why the consensus is that Earthbound cannot be trusted."

"But what else gave rise to the Coronians?" Cadie pressed. "Why didn't Genevieve's parents just let her die? Why didn't they leave her behind and return to Earth themselves when they had the opportunity? Why didn't *they* abandon *her*?"

The girl considered her mother's question for a moment. "I suppose it was compassion," she said.

"Yes," Cadie said. "But it was more than *just* compassion, wasn't it? Would they have stayed behind for a complete stranger they had compassion for?"

The girl took another moment to evaluate the question. "Perhaps this was the parent-child bond," she proposed.

"That's right," Cadie said. "The bond between Genevieve and her parents was so strong that it ultimately divided an entire species."

"That is interesting," the child said. "I had not considered it that way before."

"So what do you think might be the only thing strong enough to bring those two species back together?"

The girl watched her mother while she contemplated the question. She looked down at the curious and timid little boy clinging to his mother's leg, and when she looked back up, Cadie could see that she finally had it.

"It has to be us," the little girl said. "*I* have to stay behind, and *you* have to come to *Equinox*."

"That's right," Cadie said. She smiled and found she was blinking back fresh tears. "It has to be us."

The girl's eyes momentarily wandered and Cadie knew there was communication occurring somewhere beyond her perception.

"What's happening?" Cadie asked.

"I have been given permission to stay," the girl said. "But I have also been given a warning."

"About what?"

"The consensus remains that peaceful collaboration between our two species is impossible."

"It might be," Cadie said. "But as I learned from your father, sometimes the only way to prove to everyone that something is possible is to just show them."

The little girl smiled at the invocation of her father, and then her image glitched and flickered. When she spoke again, the synthesized audio was severely phase-shifted and distorted. "I am almost out of range," the little girl said. "I will contact you again soon."

"Haná . . ." Cadie said.

"Yes, Mother?"

Cadie paused momentarily, and then, for the very first time, told her daughter that she loved her.

"I love you, too," the little girl said, and then the drone's projectors went dark, and Cadie's daughter was gone.

The octocopters self-assembled into an orderly formation, and Cadie watched them depart through the open dome. She imagined her daughter slipping over the horizon aboard *Equinox*—moving away from her at tremendous speed, but at the same time, also coming back around toward her once again—orbiting at a distance that for all those years had seemed hopelessly far away, but that suddenly felt so close.

ACKNOWLEDGMENTS

I WOULD LIKE TO THANK my wife, Michelle, and my daughters, Hannah and Ellie, for their love and support, and for generally putting up with everything it takes to build worlds like these. I'd also like to thank Ben Yaroch for remaining my oldest friend, Ben Rossi for all the late-night brainstorming and scheming we do, and Dan Koestler for all the technical talks.

ABOUT THE AUTHOR

Christian Cantrell is the author of three science-fiction novels and several short stories. You can follow him on Twitter at @cantrell.